Praise for Jewels of Kidron

Jewels of Kidron is a unique journey of self-discovery and friendship, interlocking the imaginative, the mystical, and the magical that adults will also love. Treasure, jewels, elves, villagers, characters you want to meet in person and crawl into the pages to help. An enchanting debut you don't want to miss.

—Pam Sparks, Covered Treasures Bookstore

Jewels of Kidron grabs the reader's curiosity from the first sentence and by the second sentence, the reader is helplessly pulled into this imaginative and action-packed tale of two girls in parallel worlds. It's rare to find a book so immediately captivating, and the author, Susan Miner, is strategic and masterful in weaving this nail-biter story from the get-go! Excellent storytelling, character development, and the complex storyline keep the reader ravenous for what lies on the page ahead. Love, love, love this book!

—Vivian Cobb, TEDx Talk speaker, founder and owner of Vivian Cobb Speaking.

Jewels of Kidron is a book that captures the imagination and the role dreams, perseverance, bravery, and wisdom all play in our lives. As we read the story of a wounded girl trying to find her way in the world, we watch the magic of it all unfold and weave a tapestry of healing.

The book is not a childish book although it has many elements that children (and the child inside of adults) will relate to. It is much deeper and more realistic. It honestly portrays hurt, abuse, and fear but driven by it. Perhaps you think you, too, are being brave by keeping secrets or running away from them. A girl doesn't have to be physically abused to experience those things. We can become targets of bullying on many levels, and all of them can lock us in prisons if we let them.

You are also about to read a story of hope. A story that will show you that although you will be tested, you are strong. That using your voice is the brave thing. That you do have the courage to face anyone who abuses you—call them out— bring them to justice. Like the unforgettable characters you will soon meet, you can say, for yourself, for someone you love, for your whole generation, "This is going to stop, and it's going to stop now."

As a long-time advocate for women eight to 88 and beyond, as writer, mentor, and friend, I can say this without pause: You will find friends in Angelina and Katie and their cohorts. You will be inspired by them. Long after you turn that last page, they will still whisper to you, "You have a voice. Let it be heard."

> —Nancy Rue is an American novelist, writing mentor, and prolific author of the Lily Series, Sophie Series, and a multitude of other titles for tweens and young adults. She has recently released the first two books in The Footnotes Collection, novels for women of all ages.

Jewels of Kidron

Jewels of Kidron

By Susan Miner

Dedication

To my husband, Bob, who always had a pen available when inspiration struck. He took over managing the household when the chapters needed polishing, and he was always there with encouragement and pride during the long nights when I needed to catch up on editing. But best of all was his bedtime affirmation of "Goodnight, Author."

Table of Contents

Running From Demons

THE DREAMS WERE ALWAYS THE SAME.

Katie felt his hot breath fill her ear.

"Don't you dare move."

She winced as zip ties tightened around her wrists. Kicking her feet, she found his arm and knocked the cigarette out of his hand.

"You little tramp!"

She could see his shadow as he scrambled to find the burning butt. Focusing on the hot glow as it came closer and closer to her thigh, she screamed and lurched, twisting and kicking.

Her thoughts grew foggy and disjointed as a soft hand shook her gently. The voice had changed from his raspy evil growl to a quiet calmness urging her to wake up.

"It's okay, Katie. Wake up, honey. It's just a nightmare. You're okay now. You're safe."

Katie instinctively flung her arms around Miss Brenda's neck, but as she regained her senses, she quickly withdrew and wrapped them around her ribs. Katie looked at the drowsy bed-headed faces around the dorm room and wondered how her world could have come to this. Her bronze skin, dark hair, and eyes made her odd from day one in this field of pre-teen girls with their light skin and dirty blonde hair. How did she end up living with this group of hand-me-down girls?

"Come on, ladies. Get it together. Breakfast will be cold if we don't get over to the dining hall."

Katie watched Miss Brenda with a mix of curiosity and suspicion. As the house mother, she was the one they were supposed to trust and go to with questions or problems. Still, Katie was pretty sure anything they told Brenda got shared with the social worker or, worse yet, the police. Her smile seemed steeled in place. She constantly shoved her mop of curls out of her face and rarely looked like she was in control of anything.

Katie watched Miss Brenda move in behind Char and knew it was a mistake. Katie bit the tip of her tongue as Miss Brenda reached out and put her hand on Char's shoulder. Char jerked out of reach.

"Oops, sorry," Miss Brenda whispered and grimaced, twisting her smile into an oddly jagged shape. "Chrissy, Mel. Stop bickering and get dressed, please."

From her perch on her bunk, Katie pulled her knees in tight and watched the rest of the morning routine unfold. It had been pretty much the same every morning of the three months she'd been here.

Every day after breakfast they went out to exercise: run, play basketball, or volleyball. It was the only time they were allowed to mingle with the boys. Katie, not much for anything athletic, didn't want to have much to do with the opposite sex. All they wanted to do was flirt or show her how superior they were at whatever game was being played. She usually made up some excuse—her legs hurt, she had cramps, her back was sore. Today she sat with her arms wrapped tightly around her knees, watching the others play volleyball. Spending her 'free time' doing something so lame was not her idea of freedom, especially on a day that was so cool and misty.

"Come on, Katie. We need help here."

"You're doing all right, Mel," Katie called back, tucking her hoodie tight around her ribs to lock out the cold. "You don't need me."

Mel made a hand gesture that Katie chose not to return.

"They do need me," she said under her breath as she watched Mel try to organize her gangly arms and legs that were flailing at the ball.

"Katie, help them out!" Char called. "I can't leave Annie. Come on. They are losing their shirts out there."

Katie ignored Char. "Chrissy, you go get in the game," she shouted back across the court. It wasn't really fair to think Chrissy would get involved with a game that included boys, especially if it meant they might come into physical contact. Katie returned Char's sneer and blew a kiss to Annie.

Darrell yelled out to the girls, "Way to go, team. Get in there and go, go, go." He jumped up and down, trying to perform some bizarre version of cheerleader moves. Katie gagged as he moved over to sit next to her. He was such a nerd. His slicked-down hair was parted way too low on the side of his head, making his horn-rimmed glasses stand out even more than they did sitting on the end of his nose. Why couldn't he wear jeans like everyone else? His wrinkled Dockers piled up on his wingtip shoes, whose thick soles made his thin legs look knobby. No wonder he was the teacher's pet to the staff. He showed no shame in kissing up to them, making it even harder for the other kids to like him.

"Shut up, Darrell," Katie snarled as she moved to the end of the bench.

"Come on, Katie. Team spirit. Take one for the team." He pressed without daring to move closer to her.

"Bite me," Katie replied.

"Yawow!" Mel shouted as she lunged for the ball, landing flat on her face. Everyone ran to see if she was okay—everyone but Katie.

She had spotted what she'd been hoping to see. Leaning against one of the light poles, Miss Brenda was engaged in a flirty conversation with Jerry, the house dad for one of the boys' cottages. Katie watched how Miss Brenda tossed her curls and how Jerry couldn't take his eyes off her. Reliving how she'd fallen for His flirtations, watching this display made Katie's skin crawl. But taking a deep breath, she regained her focus. This was her chance.

She stood up, pretended to stretch, then pulled down the tail of her oversized tee-shirt. When she was sure everyone was still focused on Mel and no one was looking her way, Katie pulled up the hood on her hoodie, stuffed her hands in the pockets, and slowly wandered off toward the north end of campus. She had to find a way out of this place. Maybe it would be at that end of the property.

Walking slowly so she didn't draw attention to her movements, she wove between the cottages that had once been tiny little neighborhood homes. She tried to imagine what it had looked like before the streets had been removed and replaced with grass. It was hard to tell where one yard stopped and the next one started since the fences were gone—all except the eight-foot chain link perimeter fence that kept her and all the others inside. Trees and hedges had been left in place making it feel more like a park than an institution but knowing what was really inside the houses made Katie feel sad. She shuffled her feet in the grass as she struggled to comprehend how all these children could be abused. How could all these cottages be filled with so many damaged souls?

Wandering towards the grove of tall pine trees, she found two old storage sheds and a maintenance building at this end of the Aspen Meadows campus. As steam rose from a building that must house the boilers, a blanket of fog enveloped everything in front of her.

"What I need is a hole in the fence," she mumbled as she walked around the end of the boiler house.

The mist rose and swirled. She blinked twice, not sure what she saw rising up out of the ground. The wind shifted the fog, and she realized it was a massive glass structure. A greenhouse. Surely there would be a delivery entrance somewhere near, one she could pry open. Her steps quickened with excitement as she dashed to the wide double doors.

"Come on, open," she said as she rattled the old warped wooden doors. "You have to open."

The locks didn't budge.

She was not about to give up. She slid around the long side of the green-house, pulling at every window until finally one gave way. She wriggled inside. Dropping down on the soft, powdery dirt, she looked up at the panes of glass crusted with dirt and moss. The musty smell was like the root cellar at her grandparent's farm. She wasn't sure if this place was cool or creepy.

Like long-reaching fingers, vines hanging from the ceiling brushed her cheeks and toyed with her hair. Weeds and the brave remnants of flowers once grown here now lived in the cracks of the dirt floor. She wandered down the long aisle past rows of waist-high planting beds filled with moss-covered dirt, weeds, and the occasional abandoned gardening tool. Her lungs filled with the musty smell of dampness. It was so quiet, yet there was a sort of peace in the silence. It felt safe and still.

Suddenly, the spell was broken by the sound of keys rattling at the double doors. Katie dropped to the floor.

"Hey! Who's in here? I know you're in here!"

Shit!

If she got caught, she'd get detention for sure. She crouched down low enough to get under the planting trays. Holding her breath, she watched a pair of heavy work boots covered with mud and bits of mulch walk slowly down the center aisle toward her. The light of a flashlight waved from side to side. Whoever it was limped so his steps tapped out an irregular rhythm on the hard dirt floor.

"Come out, now. You can't be in here."

Being trapped made Katie's lungs tighten. She was beginning to feel light-headed as panic flowed throughout her body. She scanned the perimeter of the greenhouse.

Damn. Nothing.

She knew she'd never be able to get back out the window she'd come in through. He'd see her for sure. Her frenzied search didn't produce any means of escape until she looked back at the double doors. He hadn't closed one of them. She had to get to that door. She watched him limp past her again. She took her chance when he was at the far end of an aisle of planting beds. Dirt and gravel shot out from under her feet as she darted down the aisle. Lame as he was, he was right behind her, but spotting another chance to slow him down, she grabbed the handle of the wheelbarrow sitting in the middle of the path and dumped its entire load of clay pots.

He swore as he stumbled over the broken shards of clay. "Stop!" he growled. "Get back here!" Katie hit the door with a bang, grateful for the fog of the boilers.

"You don't belong in here! You stay out, you hear. Stay out!"

As she ran, Katie heard the bell ringing for everyone to get back to the school. Free time was over. She still might get detention if she couldn't get there in time for roll call.

"Katie? Is Katie here?" Katie heard Miss Brenda call just as she slid breathlessly through the door. Their eyes locked, and Katie knew she'd been had.

"Katie, you'll stay after class today. Apparently, we need to review some of the house rules."

Katie took her seat, fully aware of the stares from the other students and the glare from Miss Brenda. They all just needed to mind their own business. At the end of the day everyone grabbed their books and made their escape to free time. Mel, Chrissy, and Brittany giggled as they passed Katie, who sat tall in her seat, which doesn't mean much when you're only 5'2" to begin with.

She was sure detention was her next stop.

"Shut up," she hissed at the giggling trio. She watched Char ignore them all and wished she could master that knack.

"Katie, you've been pushing the limits lately."

Katie hated Miss Brenda's whiney voice. She stared at the floor and squelched a smirk.

"What's going on?"

"Nothing." Katie knew that the less she said, the less there would be to talk about, and this meeting would be over fast, but she struggled not to make eye contact.

"All right, since you weren't officially late, I'll let you off with a warning, but you have to understand that we have rules here for a reason. Rules that are designed to keep you safe. You have to abide by them. Every. One. Of. Them. Every. Time. Do you understand?"

"Yes, ma'am." Katie continued to stare at the floor.

"Next time, it will be detention."

There was no way Katie was willing to acknowledge the bullet she had just dodged, especially by giving Miss Brenda a glimpse of gratitude.

"Okay, you can go."

Katie stuck her tongue out at the back of Miss Brenda's head as she turned to wipe off the board and grabbed her books. She ran, eager to see if there was a way to get to that greenhouse from here without being seen.

Secrets

AS THE WEEKS WENT BY, KATIE managed to cover her tracks to the greenhouse during free time. She'd told the field athletic teams that she was working out in the gym and then told the gym squad trainers that she was doing track, yoga, or some other solo activity. That way, she could get to the greenhouse at least a couple of times a week. And thankfully, no one had found her open window and locked it.

She pried that window back and slid inside, sighing as she smelled the wonderful aroma of moist, mossy soil. She had created a cozy nest out of sacks of mulch draped in burlap bags in the far back corner. The chips of bark in the mulch molded to her body just like a bean bag chair so she could flop down and gaze up at the sky through the smudged glass panes of the ceiling.

She liked to pretend that she lived in a beautiful place surrounded by flowers and trees. She imagined that there were birds nesting in the rafters above her. They'd peck at the dirt for worms and sing to their babies. She'd have a garden filled with roses and daisies and tulips. Grass and moss would cover every surface so everything would be soft and cool when she touched it. And there'd be a pond with gold fish. Hearing the water dripping through a hole in the ceiling, she changed her mind. No, there'd be a waterfall filling the pond and fish performing a ballet in the eddies. The steam from the nearby boiler condensed on the greenhouse roof and dripped in tiny rivulets down the glass so it always looked like a storm had just passed.

Once, she'd actually seen a rainbow inside the greenhouse as the sun sliced through the humidity. Her spirits sank when she thought about the sad part of this imaginary world: she would eventually have to leave it.

Her gut had gotten really good at telling her when it was time to get back to the others, and it was beginning to pester her. Reluctantly, she left her little nest and headed for her secret entrance. Part way out the window, Katie looked back at her private hideaway. This part of her day was good. And she had just enough time to sprint around the cottages to get back to class.

Katie dashed through the door in time to hear Miss Brenda announce the lessons for the day.

"Girls, girls, settle down now. I have a great new project I want to tell you about. Mel, leave Chrissy's hair alone. Brittany, sit!"

She paused until everyone had settled into their seats. "Okay, everyone. We're going to start a new craft project that will incorporate English and math, and some biology. We are going to create a miniature village!"

Miss Brenda's enthusiastic 'ta-da' moment was met with groans from every last girl. Except for Brittany who squealed an enthusiastic, "Yes!"

Katie couldn't hold her tongue on this one. "You have to be kidding, right? We're going to play doll house?" Throwing her arm over the back of her chair and slumping, she rolled her eyes. "I don't think so."

She could tolerate the stupid team-building games they were made to play. She could even tolerate pretending like they were a "family," but this crafty stuff was just too much.

"But that's why this is going to be fun—you get to decide who you are building for, what they need, what kind of stuff they'd have."

Katie was well aware that the undertone of desperation meant that Miss Brenda had to win Katie over, or she risked losing the entire group.

"Your character doesn't even have to be human. It can be anyone you can imagine. "

Mel and Chrissy looked at Katie but she withheld any facial responses until she'd thought this one over. The ice under this project was thin. After some hasty consideration, Katie decided she was willing to do something that didn't involve sitting behind a desk all day.

"The character can be anything—an alien?" Mel was beginning to hop up and down slightly.

"Absolutely, Mel. An alien or an undiscovered creature or anything living."

"Can I have a dragon?" Chrissy asked

"Sure! Katie, what do you think you'd want to have as your character?"

"I'll get back to you on that." Katie's response was surly. But Miss Brenda looked relieved.

"Okay, let's get started. Take out some paper and start working on a profile of your character. I want you to write down everything you know about it, him or her. What kind of a creature is it, how tall, what color, does it have long hair on its head or all over its body? There are no rules. It's all up to your imagination. But you do have to use complete sentences and watch your spelling."

"Can we draw a picture?" Brittany loved to draw so Katie wasn't surprised.

"Yes, Brittany, you can draw. Char, what about you? Any ideas?"

"Yeah, I want to think about it, though." She snuggled Annie, who was sitting on her lap sucking her thumb.

Slowly there were some signs of life for this project. Miss Brenda had turned on the background music—to inspire creativity, she said—and sat back to watch. "I think changing how we do things in the classroom will be fun," she said. "Like having learning tables instead of sitting in straight rows. This way you can all move and create and be in control while you learn."

Miss Brenda sucked in her lower lip. Katie twisted up the left side of her mouth and sniffed. She had to give the woman some credit for trying.

But Katie stared at her paper. This was stupid. Make up a character. Why not work on something useful? Like how about they figure out a way for her to go home?

She picked up her pencil and flipped it up and down on the page, making little bird track marks across the whiteness. That was as far as she got.

Fear of Nightmares

KATIE WAS ALWAYS UNSETTLED AT the end of the day when everyone was getting ready for bed. She dreaded when they turned out the lights and the world went dark. Her demons, held bottled up all day long, fought their way out in the darkness, and she couldn't stop them other than to drown them in tears. If she could just get to sleep without having to face them when peace came as sleep took over.

"Katie, what is your character?" Brittany said.

She knew Katie hadn't written anything down. Katie had caught her looking at her paper with the bird tracks all over it. She needled Katie, and Katie hated that she always fell for it.

"Shut up."

Katie stumbled over the twisted legs of her pj's. They were all looking at her and laughing.

"You don't have one, do you? Nothing, nada, zip," Brittany said, voice taunting.

"Leave her alone." Char's tone of authority brought everyone to attention. The oldest at 15, she commanded a respect that none of the others could. "Get off her back, and mind your own business."

Brittany mechanically pulled the sleeves of her nightgown down over her fingers. She faced her bunk without another word while the others went about their routine of brushing teeth, washing faces, and climbing into bed. Katie made sure she was on her top bunk and under the covers before Miss Brenda came in for final bed check.

Compulsively she began her bedtime ritual of arranging her bedding. She pressed her back against the wall and pulled the covers tight over her left shoulder, tucking them tightly between her knees. Then she wrapped her right arm around her pillow and pulled it tight into her chest. The fingertips of her left hand found the small round scars on her thigh. She held her breath and waited, hoping that tonight would be the night nothing happened when it got dark. But it wasn't meant to be.

As the lights clicked off, it was as if that switch also unleashed her fears. Darkness settled in. Her eyes filled with hot, salty tears that ran down her cheeks and filled the crease between her lips. The ache started in her shoulders, wrapping around her collar bone, and her lungs lurched, sucking for air. She sobbed.

"Please, please, let me go home," she pleaded into her pillow just as she did night after night. "I didn't do anything wrong. I didn't tell. Nobody'll get killed. I just want to go home."

Mel kicked her foot deep into the bunk above her. "Katie, shut up. I can't sleep with you crying all the time. Outbursts'll get you locked in the closet. Grandma always put me in the closet. Shut up!"

"Leave her alone. We're all doing the best we can so just let her be." Char's voice was firm, and no one dared argue with her.

Katie buried her head under the covers and pressed her face into her pillow, crying herself past the point of exhaustion.

Later, she smelled Annie coming before she heard her trying to get into Char's bed.

"Awe, Sweetie. You wet the bed again. Come on, let's get you out of those wet things."

In the dark, Katie could hear Char stripping urine-soaked clothes off the little two year old, reaching into her dresser drawer and pulling out a clean diaper and one of Char's own tee shirts. Katie knew the routine. The tee-shirt dropped over the curly head of hair, enveloping Annie in a tent of fabric. Annie pitched herself backward onto the mattress, causing the bunk next to her to sway. Katie knew Annie was ready for the dry diaper now. Once swaddled in clean, dry clothes, she would reach up, wrap her arms around Char's neck, and almost instantly fall asleep as the two snuggled under the covers again. This, too, was a nightly ritual. They all had something.

What Lurks in the Shadows

"KATIE, WHATCHA MAKING? DO YOU have a character figured out?"

Brittany tried to peek over Katie's shoulder to see what the blob of clay they'd each been given was becoming. Katie pulled the clay in closer and hovered over it to block Brittany's view.

"None of your business."

Katie pinched off a bit and rolled it between her fingers. She had decided on her character but wasn't going to tell the others until she had to. It wasn't any of their business.

"Girls, today's assignment is to write a three-page description of your character. You have to describe what they look like, where they are from, why they live in the village, anything you can think of. Here's a list of vocabulary words you need to use in your story."

Miss Brenda handed out the lists outlined by age and spelling ability, so, in reality, none of them had the same list.

Shit. No way to cheat on this one. Katie shoved the list inside her hoodie and zipped it up.

"Miss Brenda, what if we don't know what they look like?"

Katie huffed and shoved her chair away from the table. "Geez, Chrissy, make it up. This is all make-believe." Katie tossed her pencil at the crayon box. "You never get anything."

Chrissy's lip shot out, and she began to cry. Mel leaped to her feet. "Don't cry. Don't cry. They'll put you in the closet. You'll hate the closet. No crying."

Mel was trying to put her hand over Chrissy's mouth to hush her when Miss Brenda raced over.

"Mel, you know we don't have any closets here." Her soothing tone turned cold and harsh. "Katie, you apologize to Chrissy right now. She didn't deserve that."

Miss Brenda glared at Katie. Katie glared back. "Now!"

Katie turned her chair around to face the table, grabbed her clay, and as it squeezed out between her fingers, she muttered, "Sorry."

Katie and Miss Brenda both looked at the clock, but Katie snapped her head back down as she pretended to concentrate on her work. When Miss Brenda cleared her throat, Katie knew she wouldn't get out of this one.

"Time to head over for your appointment with Miss Johnson."

Katie replied with a heavy drop of her hand to the desk, adding a sneer to her glare she hoped would help change Miss Brenda's mind.

"Don't give me that look. Scoot! You can work on your project tomorrow. I want you to pick out some books that you've read for your character to read. Book reports on two of your favorite choices and why. Due next Friday."

Katie put her supplies back in her locker. The warped door of the classroom made a whining sound as she swung it open. She let it slam behind her as she reluctantly set out towards the house that held the staff offices.

She hated walking the path around the commons alone. The entire route was lined with bushes and pine trees. Branches bowed to the ground making perfect little caves below where anyone could hide. Her eyes scanned the perimeter of the circular park, digging deep into the shadows.

"Hurry, hurry," she chanted with each step.

Being near the bushes was the worst. The shadows might be hiding Him. He might leap out at any moment. Breathing heavily from her sprint, Katie bent over at the waist, catching her breath before facing her next demon. She set her jaw, squared her shoulders, and grabbed the door knob firmly, ready to face Miss Johnson and the conversation that always led to a place Katie had no intention of going.

"Hi, Katie. Come on in." Miss Johnson gestured to the overstuffed chair by the window in her office. "How are you today?"

"Okay, Miss Johnson." Katie rolled her eyes at how lame that question was for kids in a group home for abused children. She shrugged, caught the sneer escaping her lips just in time to make it a half smile, and replied with an obvious effort to be polite. Obediently, she took her place in the chair as expected.

"Katie, you can call me Karen."

"That's okay, Miss Johnson." Katie knew this disappointed her, but she didn't really care. There was no way they'd ever be friends. Katie knew she had to control the information in this room. If she told Miss Johnson anything, she would endanger Angel's life, and she couldn't do that to her best friend, no matter what.

"Katie, tell me why you decided to go to Mrs. Carson's house instead of going home when you were hurt."

"I don't know. I just did."

"You know, unfortunately, when Mrs. Carson took you in and had you take a shower while you waited for the police to arrive, all physical evidence that might have helped in the prosecution of whoever hurt you washed away. I'm hoping you'll tell me what happened."

Katie sat stone-faced and did not reply.

Miss Johnson pressed further. "Were you afraid of what your parents would do if they found out you'd been hurt? Are you afraid of your father? Has he ever hurt you?"

"No, he's okay."

Katie picked at her fingernails and twisted one foot around the leg of the chair. Her other knee bounced up and down and up and down. Katie saw the look on Miss Johnson's face as she stared at Katie for a moment. Then she wrote all kinds of notes on the page in the file. Katie had to do something. She'd never get to go home if they thought her dad was the one who hurt her.

"Really, he's okay. He's a good dad. He comes on field trips and takes me fishing and used to let me stay with my grandparents for two weeks in the summer." Katie realized that she still didn't explain why she didn't go home, so she added, "Mrs. Carson's house was the first one I came to. She's nice. She lets me help in her garden. I just went there."

Miss Johnson continued to ask questions and Katie continued to evade them by using short, terse replies.

"Katie, you know we can't let you go home until we know you're safe there. Social Services brought you here for that reason. We know your parents fight a lot. So much so that the neighbors have called the police more than once. And your mother has had several DUIs. We have to know you are safe at home. It would be good if you'd tell me what happened, who hurt you."

Katie watched her, staring at the file. There wasn't anything more she could say.

She hated that the clock was hidden from her view, but she could tell by how many times Miss Johnson glanced down that they were getting close to about 30 minutes of this old worn-out banter.

"I hear you're working on a miniature village."

Katie frowned and shifted her eyes from side to side, trying to grasp how the conversation had just taken such a sharp turn.

"You've created a character? Tell me about it. Who is it? Does it have a family?"

Katie's face went blank. This crossed a line. Her lip started to quiver, and tears welled up in her eyes. Katie wanted so badly to be home with her family and having Miss Johnson imply that an imaginary creature could have one, but Katie couldn't was just mean. Katie sat motionless except for her bouncing knee. She stared at Miss Johnson who was apparently making every effort to salvage the session. But it was no good. Katie had shut down.

"I got to go now."

Katie stood up and stared out the window as if searching for escape routes. She needed to get to the greenhouse. She slowly edged her way to the door, tuning out Miss Johnson's pleas for her to stay just a bit longer.

Katie could see Miss Johnson standing at the window and watching her run across the commons. Katie ran like she was being pursued by the unseen monster. She held back the tears until she slid through her secret window, sobbing as she hit the ground.

"I didn't do anything; I didn't tell. I won't tell. I just want to go home."

Katie snorted back her running nose. Wiping her nose on her sleeve, she stared up at the ceiling, watching the clouds shift from one shape to another. Her sobs had turned into staggering gasps and sighs as her body sagged into the hollows of the mulch bags. Soon sleep took over and she was at peace. For now.

Angelina—Elf or Gen Z

THE FRONT DOOR SLAMMED AND everyone in the house held their breath. Angelina didn't dare move until she knew if this had been a good day or a bad one. It was only when she heard her father's chair creak and his groan of satisfaction that she allowed herself to breathe. No one was going to get beaten today. At least, not yet.

She cringed when she heard her mother's voice calling up the stairs. What could she want now?

"Angelina, come down now. It's time for your voice lesson."

"I'm busy, Mom. Later. Maybe," she hissed through clenched teeth.

"Angelina?!"

"Mom, I said I'm busy!"

She reached for her brush. Her thick mane of chestnut brown curls cascaded over her slender shoulders and midway down her back. She smiled as she caught sight of herself in the mirror. The other elves envied her luxuriant hair. She was pretty, and she knew it. She wondered if the human girls would think she was too.

She tried a variety of poses to see which did the most to show off her green eyes, long lashes, and strong cheekbones, yet also hid the bruises her father's fingers had left on her neck. Spitting on her middle finger, she smoothed her eyebrows into graceful arches.

"Now!" Her mother's tone was hushed.

Angelina knew she was trying not to disturb her husband. She rolled her eyes and made a sneering face at the beauty in the mirror.

Mocking the hushed tone, she replied, "I'm busy," emphasizing the 'busy' as if her mother was too stupid to get the meaning without the added color.

Which top should she wear this afternoon? It had to be perfect. Today she planned to head over to the edge of the Woods and watch the human girls coming home from school. They might invite her to join them if she could catch their eye. She'd been dying to hang out with them.

"He's wrong. I'm not worthless. Or stupid," Angelina whispered, desperate to convince the image looking back at her that it was true.

Another truth: she was lonesome. The only time she got to be with friends was the rare occasion when she was allowed to go to her friend Yasmine's house for a slumber party. She and Yasmine's friends would stay up late talking about what fascinating creatures humans were, telling stories about someone whose cousin had talked to one once and imagining what was in the shopping bags—clothes, makeup, and shoes! Oh, the shoes!

"Hey, Angelina! What are you doing?"

The sound of Yasmine's voice whispering from outside her window made Angelina smile. Yasmine always whispered out of fear of Angelina's father. He frightened everyone.

Angelina leaned out her window and smiled broadly at her friend hanging in the branches below.

"Hi. Don't come up. Mom's on a rampage about voice lessons again. She's liable to come in here."

"Why don't you just study your voice lessons and get it over with, you twit? You're going to have to master it one of these days anyway."

"Not me. Besides, there won't be any need for it when I move to the city."

"Angelina, you're such a dreamer. Those human girls are never going to let an elf be in their group—if their mothers won't let them. Give it up!"

"Hey, I'll talk to you later." Angelina waved at Yasmine as her friend sprinted off into the woods.

Angelina was startled by a knock on her door.

"Angelina, I'm not going to ask again. You have to practice," her mother said in guarded tones as she pleaded from the other side of the closed door. "Please, dear. Do as I ask. Let your father hear you. You know how he gets when you don't obey."

Angelina tossed her hairbrush at the wall. Her mom stepped out "No! Not now. Later!"

She could hear her mother still pleading as she quietly slipped out her open window. Angelina wrapped her long fingers around the first branch she could reach and swung out into space, high above the floor of the Woods, and glided from branch to branch until she was well out of earshot of the house.

"I can't hear you." She sneered and dropped down onto the path that led to her favorite spot where she was sure to see the human girls.

She knew she was going to be in so much trouble when she got home. She knew her father would get out his belt and beat her. He beat her for no reason, so at least this time, she'd have gotten something out of it first.

Her mom was too afraid of him to try to stop him. Besides, as tiny as her mom was, he could probably kill her with one firm backhand across the face. Angelina was tired of tiptoeing around, trying to please him. She hated being pressured to sing. She hated living in fear of his next fit of rage. She wanted what the human girls had—to be safe, carefree, and happy.

She wondered if they'd mind that she wasn't very tall. At five feet two, she was tall for an elf, but these girls must all be over five feet seven for sure. Stretching her spine as straight as she could, she thought about maybe getting some high heels. And some of those white things they put in their ears with little cords that went into their pockets. Smoothing her hair around her ears, she wanted them too even though she had no idea what they were for.

She began to trot. They'd be passing by soon, and she didn't want to miss them. Not today. She looked good, and they were going to see her at her best.

She was getting close now. The undergrowth was thinning. The trees were skinnier with fewer branches. As she reached the edge of the Woods, she could hear the human girls and their giggles amid the sounds of traffic and music. The quiet of her Woods was too quiet for Angelina now that she'd heard the sounds of the city. From atop the fence that had become her lookout post, she could smell the musty aroma of hot concrete and fast food. Her eyes widened and her smile spread from ear to ear. She loved humans! A thrilling rush of envy swept over her.

Excited, she leaped for the chain link fence to climb to her hideout. Realizing she'd get a better look if she moved farther down the fence towards the corner, she climbed quickly hand over hand, taking care not to mess up her hair. It wasn't until she felt the wall of fencing give way and pull towards her that she realized something was wrong. Terribly wrong.

She hit the ground hard. Dirt and gravel ground into the palms of her hands and her knees.

"What the—?" Angelina's brain could not put the last few moments in order. Now she was on the ground, covered with dirt and scrapes. She had been on the top of the fence, about to see her future. The two didn't fit together.

Frantically her eyes widened, and a wave of hot panic overwhelmed her when she realized she was in a cage of chain link fence. Scrambling to her feet, she turned and was shocked to find her only means of escape, the door, was blocked by a dirty-faced little boy with thick curly red hair.

"I caught one! I caught an elf in the dog run! Sissy, I caught one!"

He slammed the gate and locked it with a padlock with a loud snap.

"You miserable little creep!" Angelina shouted. "Open this gate!"

He picked up a rake handle from the pile of yard tools. The rake head was missing, leaving a nail sticking out of the end. He poked Angelina with it as she charged the gate. Pain stabbed deep into her thigh.

Over his shoulder, Angelina could see a bouncing bob of fuzzy blonde plaits as a little girl ran up to join him. Her legs were thick, full of rolls of baby fat, and the dimples on her elbows were deep enough to hide all kinds of mischief.

"Make her sing, Tom. I want to hear her sing. Mom said they have beautiful voices, like in the fairy tale. Make her sing." The little girl twisted her pudgy fingers around her braids in rhythm with her sing-song whining.

"Sing!" he shouted. "Sing, darn you!"

"Sissy? Tom? Get in the house now! It's almost dark. Now! Get in here!"

Angelina realized the voice was their mother's and was grateful to hear her call to them across the yard. She yelled like her own mother. When her father wasn't home, at least.

The kids disappeared through the hedge that separated the back lot from the rest of the yard. She'd been lucky. For one, their mother hadn't found her. She'd heard that human mothers were frighteningly defensive when it came to their kids. For another, the dog was gone. Elf children were raised on stories of dogs eating elf fingers if they were caught on the ground. As her stomach twisted with panic, she knew that regardless of her luck, she was still trapped.

"Dang!" The gate rattled, but the lock didn't budge. "Think! Think…"

She paced the perimeter of her cage twice but found nothing that looked like a way out. Grabbing the mesh of the chain link above her head, she swung up fast, hitting the lid with her feet.

"Come on! Move!"

But the lid was tightly fastened. It wasn't going to come loose.

Angelina dropped to the floor and sank into a heap. If there was a way out of this cage, she hadn't found it.

Lost and Found

EVERY DAY THE CHILDREN CAME. THEY poked her with the rake handle, pelted her with crab apples, or sprayed her with the hose. Today, she gripped the chain link walls of the dog run and swung up to the farthest corner. Her slender fingers had long since gone numb. Anger took over every muscle in her body. Sorrow permeated her soul as her eyes filled with tears.

"Stop it, you little jerk! Stop it!" she hissed as she swung from the roof and slammed her feet into the side of the rake he used to poke at her.

She guessed the miserable redheaded boy must be about nine. His sister looked like she was maybe seven and had never combed her hair, just braided her bedhead to keep it out of her face.

"She swings like a monkey. I told you elves are like monkeys! I told you! Make her sing, Tom. I want to hear her sing!"

Her brother poked at Angelina again. After that jab to her thigh on her first day of capture, she'd been able to avoid the nail head sticking out of the end of the handle. But now, after days of this battle, her tunic was torn, and the sleeve of her blouse was ripped. She was just glad she was wearing her knee boots. The heavy soles had literally been a lifesaver.

"Sing, darn you. We know you can sing; all elves can sing. Do it!" He jabbed at her again.

"Sissy? Tom?" Their mother. Thank goodness she still hadn't bothered to come looking for them.

Angelina's father might have been right after all. She just might be stupid. After all, she did end up locked in a dog run. Angelina dropped down on her hands and knees on the dirt floor of her prison, tears dripping off her nose. She had to find a way to escape.

She yanked at the chain link repeating a futile ritual she'd done every day for what seemed like weeks. Nothing was any looser now than it was before. There wasn't a thing in this cage that she could use as a tool to pry up the jammed lid or dig under the wall. She was trapped.

Near defeat, she slid back down on the ground, thinking about her fight with her mother just before she decided to run off. "Sing, sing," she sneered as she mimicked the little brats. That's what had started all this in the first place.

Angelina rolled her eyes at the thought of her pathetic mother cowering in the presence of her father. She knew he'd be furious that she was gone, and, of course, he'd blame her mother. He was such a brute. Angelina had thought she couldn't wait for the day when she could leave home and be like the human girls she saw when she first climbed this chain link fence months ago. She'd often snuck out of the house to climb it so she could see the girls coming home from school. She had loved to hear their voices, so clever as they chattered about clothes and boys. She smiled, remembering how they'd dropped a fashion magazine and how proud she was that she'd managed to slip out onto the sidewalk and grab it without being seen. She had hidden it under her bed. At night, she would pour over the pages learning all she could about the girls she idolized.

Picking at a scab forming over a gash on her arm, she sighed. Now she was sorry that she'd refused to practice and had snuck out of the house instead. Resting her head on her knees, she had to admit that she'd purposely come to a forbidden place as revenge for her parent's strictness. She'd only planned to be gone a few hours, long enough to see the girls and to make her parents worry. She'd always timed it just right, knowing that if her father was worried, he wouldn't hit her. He'd just ground her forever. Realizing how ridiculous this plan sounded now, she rolled her eyes again.

If she'd just been more careful, she wouldn't have slipped off the top of the fence, and the roof of the dog run wouldn't have slammed down on top of her, jamming shut so tightly it couldn't be opened. She'd never seen any children here when she'd come before. That creepy little boy standing in the doorway of the run was quick. He'd locked that door faster than she could get up off her butt. Now, here she sat, trapped, hungry, and exhausted.

As it grew dark, she started to cry. "I want to go home. I don't even care if Dad beats me." He'd done it before and she'd survived. She'd even stomach her mother's quivering pleas to behave.

She picked up one of the crabapples the children had thrown at her. It was bitter and tasted nasty, but it was all she had.

"Oh, gag." She rolled up in a rug that had been the dog's bed from the disgusting smell of it. "I'm so sick of sleeping on this stinking rug." It was better than nothing to stave off the cold, but she wanted her own bed.

Now the rain began to fall harder than her tears. Wet and worn out, she needed rest. If tomorrow was to be like any of the other days she'd spent here, the kids would be back with that blasted rake handle.

"Gawd, I have to get out of here!"

Eventually, Angelina stopped crying and drifted off to sleep, no longer dreaming of the human girls, their fine clothes, and the pretty bands in their hair. She didn't dream at all. Her dreams were gone.

Sometime late in the night, Angelina awakened to voices, faint and drifting in and out on the wind. She crawled out from under the rug to listen. She caught only a few words at a time.

"Serves her right…. runaway…. tired of her…… deserves what…. happened."

"Please…. Angelina…. it's Mother…. where are….?"

Her parents! They were looking for her! She leaped to her feet and frantically gripped the chain links.

"Mom, Dad! I'm over here! Help! Help!"

Her heart pounded. The wind shifted. She couldn't hear them.

"Mom!" she screamed.

Still nothing. Then the wind shifted again, and she heard her father clearly.

"She's worthless. We're all better off without her. I'm sick of the drama. She wanted to run away. Let her go!"

Stunned, Angelina couldn't believe what she was hearing.

"Daddy, Daddy! I'm here!" she sobbed, trying to be heard over the wind.

Now she heard her mother pleading. "Please, Father. Please, let's look a little while longer?"

Then she heard what she had heard too many times before. Angelina's body sagged toward the ground, but her hands refused to let go of the fence. She winced when she heard the sound of her mother's muffled cry as her father hit her. Angelina crumbled to the ground as the hope drained out of her heart.

"Shut up, woman. We're done with this. We're going home."

Katie woke with a start. It was dark. Really dark. Her stomach was lurching with panic. She was in so much trouble.

"Shit, what am I going to do? They're going to kill me," she told herself hoping that saying it out loud made it stupid. It didn't.

Then she heard it. Voices. Calling her name. It sounded like everyone was out looking for her. Swinging her head from one side to the other, she frantically searched for a place to hide or a way to get back to the cottage before they found her.

"They can't find me, not here." She scrambled to her feet. A wave of desperation flowed over her. "This is mine."

Katie began feeling her way along the planting beds. It was so dark, and she bit her lower lip trying to hold back the terrifying image of Him reaching out of the darkness and grabbing her.

A flash of light swung in wide arches from one side of the front of the greenhouse to the other. Katie froze. The door creaked as the rust on the hinges gave way and the light burst down the center aisle, stopping inches from her shoes. All she could see was his silhouette, and she knew she was trapped. He'd seen her.

"So, there you are." He limped in and closed the door. "Do you have any idea how much trouble you've caused?"

Tears ran down her cheeks and dripped off the edge of her jaw. "I'm sorry. I didn't mean to." Her eyes searched his face, desperate to determine what he was planning to do next. "Are you going to tell?"

"Oh, I don't think there is any way out of this one. You're the one I saw in here before, aren't you?"

He moved towards her, and she stepped back far enough to stay out of reach, lurching to the side as he stretched his arm out to pull the long cord of the ceiling light. As the room lit up, she realized it was the grounds keeper, Mr. Stanley.

Katie panicked. She could feel her eyes widen and her face grow stony. At the same time, his eyes grew softer, and he let a tiny smile creep across his mouth.

"I come in here myself sometimes. I like the quiet." He held her gaze firmly with his. "I found your nest back yonder. Not bad for havin' just the junk in here to work with."

Katie's eyes narrowed as she took it all in.

"Oh, I didn't touch nothin'," he assured her.

"I figured I'd meet the creator of that enchanting lil hideaway one of these days. Tell you what, I'll keep your secret, but we have to get you back to the cottage. And we're going to have to make up one whopper of a story for where you've been."

He pointed the way out with his flash light, and Katie mechanically moved out into the cold night air. Turning to watch Mr. Stanley pull the cord, she saw the darkness wrap around her secret hiding place once again. He closed the greenhouse doors but didn't lock them.

They walked out into the commons, Katie keeping enough distance between them that she could flee if she needed to but close enough to keep the demons in the bushes at bay.

"Look who I found," Mr. Stanley called out to a crowd gathered at the steps to the office building.

"Oh, my heavens!" Miss Brenda ran up and wrapped her fleshy arms around Katie, pulling her in so tight Katie thought she might break some ribs. "Where have you been?"

Katie was shocked to hear Mr. Stanley say, "I had a hunch about that big old pine tree in that far north corner." Mr. Stanley stepped to the front of the group to explain. "There she was, sleeping under the branches, draped down to the ground like a tent they were. Hard to see her with the pine needles and all, but I did, yep, found her sound asleep."

Katie turned and looked at him, her eyes wide and her mouth gaping open. He wasn't going to tell. Why would he do that? Why would he cover for her like that?

When he nodded at her, she groped for a lie of her own. "I was looking for pine cones for my project and must have fallen asleep," she said. "That's all."

One half of her lip curled into a weak smile as she searched their faces to see if they bought it or not.

"I don't know if we should have a party or put you in detention for the rest of the year. My lord, you scared us all," Miss Brenda gushed.

"I'd say it's time we all went home and got into warm beds. Too cold to stand out here any longer."

Mr. Stanley slipped a wink Katie's way, limping off as she was led back to her cottage, still wondering why, why her, why didn't he tell?

Except for the sound of the wind rustling the leaves and the tree branches creaking as they swayed, there was silence. No more voices. Angelina sobbed as her heart shattered like glass.

With the sun coming up, she lay curled up on the ground in the corner of the dog run. She ached all over—but mostly in her heart. Her father didn't want her. Her mother was too afraid to search. She was all alone and too tired to fight anymore. Before long, those kids would be back. Staring into the dawn, she didn't move. What was the point? Maybe if they thought she was injured or, even better, dead.

Suddenly, the dawn's silence was broken by a rattling at the gate of the dog run. Angelina squinted, trying to see clearly in the pre-dawn light. Now what?

"Hey, girl, you." The shadowy figure jiggled the lock, poking a wire into the keyhole. "Come on, you gotta get out of here. Those kids are talking about throwing rocks at you." More jiggling and then clink. The lock broke free and the gate swung open. "Come on, get moving!"

Unsure of what to do, Angelina stood up with her back against the chain link. Then she heard Tom's voice. "Hurry, Sissy, come on."

Whoever this guy was, he had to be better than those kids.

"Run!" he shouted and ran.

Angelina bolted for the open gate running faster than she'd ever run, straight into the early morning light. Behind her she could hear Sissy wail, "She's gone, she got out! Find her!"

Angelina grabbed the first low branch she came to and swung up in the tree, climbing until she was beyond reach and hidden in the safety of the thick canopy of leaves. A hollow emptiness replaced the panic that had propelled her. In the distance, she could hear the children searching for her.

"Go after her!" Sissy screeched.

"You go after her. Those woods are full of wolves and bears. I'm not going to be eaten alive!" Tom's cowardly streak was expanding by the minute.

"Stupid brats," Angelina murmured.

There hadn't been wolves in these woods for generations, and bears could care less about boney little human kids. Angelina held back a snicker as she dropped to the ground and listened. Relieved, she picked up her pace to a trot. No sign of the mystery boy. No matter. She was safe from the rake handle. Smiling, she began to run, this time because she wanted to get home, not because she was being chased.

She ran until she couldn't breathe anymore. As she hung over at the waist, massaging the ache in her ribs, she caught sight of her reflection in a small pool left behind by the rains. Her expression fell when she saw the pitiful face looking back at her. Her beautiful mane of hair was matted and frizzed; her cheeks were drawn and dirty. There were dark circles under her eyes. Then she came to her cracked and broken nails.

"I hate those kids," she said to the face.

She frowned at her reflection. Running her fingers through her matted hair, she gathered her waist-length mane into a ponytail and reached for the scrunchy that was always on her wrist. She was amazed that it was still there.

"Gawd, I have to wash my hair!" she exclaimed in disgust.

Angelina would never, ever be caught looking like this: matted, greasy hair, no lip gloss, torn and dirty clothes. Fingering the tears in her tunic and blouse, she pressed her thumb into the hole in her leggings.

"These are my favorites. I hate those kids!"

Her mind wandered to the human girls and what they'd think if they saw her now. Those pretty girls she'd admired had no idea what lay beyond the fences. She'd dreamed of how she would reveal her secret to her new human BFFs. They'd be amazed to find out that she was a real elf. They'd all want to go to the mall with her. She'd be the most popular girl in school. Now, she was sure they wouldn't even look at her.

"I have to get out of these woods!" she shouted.

She got up, and a wave of nausea filled her gut. She realized she had nowhere to go. She couldn't go home. Not after last night. Her mood swung rapidly from anger to rage.

She shrieked at the god she'd heard of but never felt. "This is why I never believed in you! You are never there when I need you. Never! This is not fair!"

She was no longer able to control her tears and sank to the ground where she cried and cried and cried. Finally, there were no more tears. Exhausted, she sat up, wiped her face with the back of her least dirty hand, and stared into space, hoping for someone to just come and get her.

"Maybe Yasmine's folks will let me stay with them for a while."

Her chin dropped to her chest under the weight of how pathetic that thought really was. But it was the best she could come up with. It was all she had.

She reached up into the nearest tree and began swinging from branch to branch toward home. When the trees got far enough apart that she had to depend on flips and curls to span the distance, she dropped to the ground and walked for a while. Soon she came to a clearing she recognized. The tall grass waved gently in the spring breeze, unable to decide what color it wanted to be and instead choosing to be all shades of greens, yellows, and gold.

She started to bound through the grass, lifting each knee up to her waist to clear the tops of the grass. There should be a brook on the other side. She'd played in it once when she was little. She and her mom had packed a picnic and gone for a long walk. She remembered how she tried to drink the cold water but couldn't get the hang of keeping her fingers together to make a cup. Every time she lifted her hand filled with water, it ran out between her fingers just as she got it to her mouth. They'd laughed and laughed.

It had been a long time since they'd laughed.

She sighed. "Mom and I should have done that more."

Angelina felt the shadow engulf her and heard the swooping sound of wings, deeply disturbing the air. It wasn't until she felt the sharp grip of the talons clench her arms and she was hoisted up with a jolt that the heat of panic invaded her body, and a scream caught in her throat.

Looking up over her head, she watched as her nightmare began. Kicking and screaming indignantly, she twisted in the grip of an eagle's talons.

"Put me down! Drop me!"

Realizing that might not be the best idea since she was now soaring high above the treetops, she changed her tactics to try to hurt the bird to get it to land. Swinging her feet above her head, she kicked at the eagle's beak.

"Let me go!"

Twisting around to look behind her for anything that might get her out of this mess, she gasped at what she saw. The darned beast was just that, a beast. It had the hind legs and the tail of a lion.

Making Connections

KATIE REACHED INTO THE BIN of plastic animals and rummaged until her fingers felt a shape that seemed interesting. She pulled out what she thought was an eagle, but when she saw what it really was, she dropped it as if it were a burning coal, staring at it intensely. How in the world had she picked that creature—a griffin? Why not a chicken or a deer or a lion?

Mel thrust her hand into the bin and started to stir. Katie snatched the griffin and sat down hard, her fingers tracing the form of the eagle/lion. As she studied the creature, she felt bits and pieces of a dream she'd had the night before drift into her consciousness, but she couldn't get them to fit together. She brushed it off as nonsense. She never could remember her dreams anyway. But now, she had a creepy feeling that her fantasy world and this one were starting to morph. She had a beast in her hand.

Cradling it as if it were made of spun glass, Katie moved to the table with the craft supplies. The thing had plastic feathers. The slick skin bothered her. Katie fought to get her thoughts in order. Yeah, some paint might help. She pushed aside the glitter and tissue paper. Frowning, she stood right in front of the table and stared at all the options.

"Shoot. Nothing."

Then under the tablet of construction paper, she saw a packet of small brown feathers. Yes. She snatched it up and headed for a table in the back of the room where no one else was working. On the way, she plucked up a tube of glue. This was what she needed.

She slowly covered the griffin's wings, one feather at a time, top and bottom. The only things missing were some features for his head.

"I need smaller scissors," she said, aware that Mel and Brittany had turned to see who she was talking to. Katie moved past them on a mission.

She headed back to her workspace with sharp embroidery scissors, a fine paint brush and a jar of tan paint in hand. Mel and Brittany followed.

"Wow, Katie, this is cool. What is it? Where did you find the feathers?"

Mel reached out to touch and looked stunned when Katie swatted at her hand.

"Don't touch. Over there, there's lots of cool stuff."

Brittany pulled her hand back so quickly that Katie laughed. "Got the message?"

She watched Brittany slink back to her project. Mel, always slower to read the cues, took a bit longer but soon got the chill and moved away, too. Katie shook her head as she heard Mel growl, "Bitch."

Katie ignored the slur. Returning to the tiniest feather, she turned it around and around in her hand until she figured out how to make it fit on the eagle's head and not look like a hat. Snipping the hairs one at a time, she shaped a perfect crown for the head. One more drop of glue and her eagle was done. The downside to how great the eagle part looked was how bad the lion end looked.

"Paint," she said, and single-mindedly, she returned to work.

"It's time to clean up so finish what you are working on and turn it in at my desk."

"Miss Brenda, I'm not done yet," whined Chrissy.

Katie scoffed. Chrissy was never done on time with anything.

"Turn in what you have. No more stalling."

Katie watched Miss Brenda avoid eye contact with Chrissy, which always triggered a long, drowning plea for more time.

Seeing Miss Brenda coming, Katie wrapped her arm around the griffin. She continued to intently fill out the assignment form that she had to hand in with it. She wanted to be last to put her work on the desk, so she wrote slowly. Character's name—Unknown; character's role in the story—not sure; what happens to the character in the story—don't know yet.

"So, how's it going?" Miss Brenda leaned in. "Katie, that's amazing. May I see it closer?" Katie opened her arm a bit so Miss Brenda could see more of the feathered wings. "Oh, my, what is it?"

"A griffin."

"What made you think of this?"

Katie had to admit she was pleased to hear the hint of amazement in Miss Brenda's voice.

"It just came to me. Can I just turn in the paper since you've seen it? I don't want the others to mess with it."

"Sure, show me the rest, and then turn in your paper. I will grade it from that."

Katie carefully turned the creature over in her hand so Miss Brenda could see all sides, proud that she hadn't missed any detail.

"Off you go. It's free time. Enjoy it."

Relieved that the craft paints dried so quickly, Katie tucked the griffin inside her hoodie and dashed out the door, zig-zagging her way across the campus so no one could follow.

She was amazed that Mr. Stanley hadn't locked the greenhouse doors. She appreciated being able to walk in instead of crawling through the window. Stepping inside, she took a deep breath of the dank, musty air and loved the feel of the humidity as it clung to her skin. She brushed the vines clinging to the metal ribs of the ceiling and made her way down the long dirt path. She was aware that it was no longer brown, having turned a deep green from the moss and lichens growing in the pores of the damp earth. She listened to the soft sounds her tennis shoes made on the dirt floor as she tried to walk without sounding like the American Indians used to.

She slowed her gait. She sensed that something wasn't right. She should be able to see her nest from here. Caution and fear mixed as she crept slowly toward her secret place.

"What the... what's all of this?"

There were at least a half dozen pots filled with all kinds of bushes and small trees, and there was a worn old needlepoint pillow on her bedding.

"Where did all this come from?" she said.

And then she saw the note taped to a watering can: Water regularly, and they will thrive. There was no name signed. Mr. Stanley must have written it. Shaking her head and smiling, she picked up the watering can and soaked each of the plants.

"I think I'd like you over here and, ah, you over here, and you, you stand by this one," Katie directed as she moved the trees to the back and the bushes nestled around each one until she had created a rich forest of greenery.

"Now, we have a place to live." She reached into her hoodie, releasing the griffin to its new home in the Woods. "You have to leave everyone alone, though. No more of this stalking and attacking business. None of the diving and snatching, either." She scolded as she flew the griffin up and down and around the trees. Her aggression grew with each swoop.

Katie flew the griffin right through the trees and crashed it into the ground. She stared at it, not moving, feeling like she had killed it for a moment. She stopped, wondering where in the world a thought like that came from. Shrugging off yet another thought, she reached between the branches, picked the fallen leaves off its feathers, and placed them softly in the dirt under one of the bushes.

Nestled back in her 'nest' as Mr. Stanley had called it, imagining it swaying in the breeze, she curled up, sighed wistfully, and drifted off to sleep.

"Geez, a griffin!"

Angelina kicked frantically. The griffin screeched a cry of triumph and seemed to take no notice of Angelina's efforts to escape. Banking into the wind, the giant winged beast made a wide turn heading deeper and deeper into the Woods. It shifted its excruciating grip as it flew, and the force of the talons let up for just a moment. Squirming madly, Angelina was able to free her right arm. Frantically she swung it out just as the griffin's tail twitched her way.

"Gotcha!" Angelina cried.

She tightened her grip and yanked hard. It was hard enough to throw the griffin off balance, and they began a free-fall spiral toward the trees. Branches cracked as they crashed downward. Leaves slapped at her face, bark scratched her arms, and she prayed that she'd land on something softer than a tree trunk when they finally came to a stop.

Angelina was buried in leaves and feathers with moss in her mouth. Now her scrunchy was gone, and moss and twigs were tangled in the hair that hung in her face. Spitting out the moss, she sat very still.

Where was that griffin? She knew she couldn't afford to stay on the ground with that thing. Legends said they could be as fast on foot as they were in the air. She had to get up into the thick of the trees where that beast wouldn't be able to get its wings spread to fly.

She listened intently. Nothing.

Wait. Something was moving above her.

Slowly looking up, it took everything she had to not burst out laughing. That dumb griffin, now screeching in frustration, was strung out upside down, tangled in the vines and branches.

"You deserve it, you jerk!" Angelina taunted as she picked herself up and brushed off the debris. "It'll take a week to get out of that mess!"

In a flash, Angelina disappeared in the thick growth of the Woods. Focusing on what to do next, she was unnerved by the feeling that she was being watched. She could have sworn she saw faces in the shadows of the trees, but when she turned to look, they disappeared. There were definitely voices, but she couldn't make out what they were saying.

The truth was that she was beyond being afraid with all that had happened today. All Angelina knew was that she had escaped but now was more lost than ever, and it was going to be dark soon. Breathless, she figured she'd put enough distance between her and the griffin, and now she could afford to rest. She ripped the torn sleeve off her blouse and used it to wipe the blood off the scrapes on her arms and legs.

"I loved this blouse. Gross!"

Upset by the condition of her favorite tunic, she pulled it off over her head and tied it around her waist. Ordinarily, she would rush to a mirror to be sure her hair was all back in its place after upending it by pulling clothes over her head. There was no reason to bother now.

Squatting to sit on the ground, she crossed her legs underneath her and dropped her head into her hands. She had no idea where she was. The lush green canopy was so thick above her that she couldn't tell one direction from another, and what sky she could see showed the promise of rain again.

"Mom," she cried.

Her head knew her mother was too far away to hear; her heart ached with the hope that someone, anyone, would. Her voice echoed off the rock walls around her: Mom, Mom, Mom.

With a start, her hand shot to her throat. The air rushed out of her lungs. Sighing in relief, she fingered her most precious possession, the necklace her mother had given her for her birthday.

"It's still there," escaped from her lips.

The pendant was half of the design. Her mother's sister had the other half. Angelina had refused to let her mother know how honored she really was to have been given such a special gift. Now she wished she had. She would tell her mom, "thanks." If she ever went home again.

Drip, plop, plip, drop. It began to rain again. This time, she didn't have the dog's rug. Angelina's fingers searched anxiously for something to cover her and keep her dry. Finally, on the edge of a large rock, she was able to pry up the lip of a blanket of moss and, pulling gently, a section large enough to cover her slipped loose. The black dirt below was warm and dry. She slid into the space, pressing her back hard up against the rock for safety.

The rain fell for hours, but she stayed dry, warm, and safe in her hiding place. As it stopped and the full moon came out, Angelina began to hear sounds. Voices, whispers, faint giggles, and gentle sighs. If she weren't so tired and hungry, she would have sworn it was the trees. They seemed to bend down with the wind as if to study her, curious about her.

"Great. This can't get worse. I'm all alone, starving, exhausted, and hearing voices. Gawd."

She pulled the moss tightly up around her chin. She could have sworn the wind whispered, "I'm here." Above her was the sound of something shifting in the branches. The wings of a great bird spread widely as it silently took flight, crossing the moon and gliding into the darkness.

An owl had been watching her.

Then she felt something brush her cheek gently. Creepy. She pulled the moss up with a firm tug. She jerked her shoulders in tight as she felt someone or something tuck her in. Her eyes scanned the darkness wildly to see what was out there. She couldn't see anything, but she sure felt its presence, whatever it was. In the wind, she heard faint voices crooning what sounded like a lullaby.

"I am not sleeping tonight," she said to them.

But she was too exhausted to stay awake, and strangely, she slept peacefully.

At dawn, she awakened to the sun's warmth as its rays slid between the leaves. Bright slashes cast tiny prisms as the light bounced off the rounded drops of rain left behind from the night before. She lay still, opening her eyes slowly.

Where was she? Not home. Not in her down-filled bed. The air smelled of roses, jasmine, mint, pine, oak, and so many other scents in an intoxicating blend. The aromas were individually familiar, yet together they were something she'd never experienced.

As the fog of sleep lifted, she began to remember where she was, or more accurately, that she had no idea where she was. A quickening flashed through her head. Panic, fear, and confusion swept over her, dissolving the peace from last night.

"I've got to find a way out of here," she said to no one.

She knew she should walk downhill and follow the water. Villages are always built very near water. She headed up the mountainside, hoping that if she got high enough, she could see a great distance.

She walked for miles while eating berries along the way. At the crest of every hill or turn in the trail, she was amazed at the brilliance of the colors and the intensity of the smells. She'd never seen anything like this in the woods around her house. The farther she walked, the bigger the flowers and trees got until the dandelions were the size of basketballs and the trunks of trees were so vast it would take three people holding hands to circle an aspen. The fragrance of wild roses was as strong as any perfume she'd ever smelled. The meadowlarks were singing with such joy. Hummingbirds darted all about her, seemingly curious about her ears. She laughed out loud as she gently brushed the insistent tiny birds back from her face.

"This isn't funny! I'm lost!" she scolded them.

Rounding a bend as the trail topped yet another hill, Angelina gasped. Before her were acres and acres of delicate yellow and orange flowers that seemed to go on forever. She couldn't resist reaching out her hands on each side to touch the blossoms and see the colors wave gently as she caressed them. She left the trail to wander waist-deep into them, wondering if they smelled as scrumptious as they looked.

"Whoa!"

Suddenly every blossom in the field rose and burst into flight. Thousands of brightly painted butterflies flew in circles like leaves as they were picked up by the whirling winds of fall. Round and round her they flew. She twirled until she was dizzy with delight and sank to the ground in wonder.

Then, they were gone.

"Wow." She could have sworn she heard a faraway sound of applause. She stood, still not sure what to think. "This place is so weird."

As lost as she was, Angelina knew she should be more discouraged, but it was almost impossible to feel fear and delight at the same time. This place was so wondrous. Nothing in this part of the Woods resembled anything in her woods. She was hearing things she'd never heard before. The smells were more intense. Colors were deeper and brighter.

But she couldn't tell which direction she was heading because the sun was hidden by the dense tree canopy. Finding east or any other direction was impossible. When she did get out in the open, where there were clear skies, the sun seemed to come from everywhere.

And she was sure the trees were moving.

Just when she was certain she'd identified a landmark, a cluster of trees, or one with a distinctive knot hole, she turned back to get a visual picture of where she'd been. It didn't look anything like what she remembered. The trail seemed to appear out of nowhere and disappear behind her as she traveled. She couldn't be sure if she was walking in circles.

Occasionally the clouds gathered like thick, billowing waves of sea foam, covering the sun. Dark shadows lurked as if woven in with the sun's rays.

Exhausted, she plopped to the ground to get her bearings. "Wow, what a mess."

Angelina pulled on the loose threads of the holes in her leggings, swearing with frustration. Behind her, she heard someone—or something—gasp. She grabbed a stick and spun around to confront whoever had snuck up on her, but no one was there. She was still very much alone.

In the following days, Katie tried every trick she could think of to avoid turning in the paper describing her character. She was really tired of Miss Brenda pestering her about it. Now she knew she had to come up with something, or she was going to flunk this semester. She stared at the paper again. Nothing.

Char poked her in the ribs. "Hey, are you still trying to create a character?"

Katie tapped her pencil on the paper, making little bird tracks in an arc, and shoved the paper across the table.

"Look, makeup something quick. " Char pushed the paper back towards Katie and leaned in close to her ear, whispering, "If you don't get something down soon, the rest of us are going to be in a holding pattern doing math problems until you pull it together—and I hate those math problems."

Katie reached for the paper and began to doodle. The mindless wandering of the pencil was interrupted by Miss Brenda calling all to attention.

"Girls, Katie is still struggling to find her character, so I want you all to come over and sit on the rug. We are going to brainstorm and see if we can't get her creative juices flowing."

Katie cringed as she watched Mel race to sit in her regular place at the end of the sofa. Brittany and Chrissy giggled over some childish secret as they walked the long way around the room to be sure they passed by the table where Katie sat.

"She doesn't have any creative juices. She's cried all her juices into her pillow," Chrissy said, and Brittany giggled even louder.

Katie pinned her glare on them as they plopped down on the rest of the sofa, crowding Mel, so she had to drape herself over the arm. It was a cheap shot to torment Mel, and Katie hated that they did it all the time.

Char had taken her favorite place, the rocker, so Katie took the last space available—the "old lady" overstuffed chair. Her butt dropped deeply into the sagging cushion.

"Okay, ideas? Anyone." Miss Brenda held the tip of the marker against the paper of the flip chart as if she were eager to capture all their anticipated brilliance. "Mel, Brittany?"

"Clarence." Katie's eyes rolled at how proud Mel was of this ridiculous idea. "What? It's my cousin's name."

"Rachael, no, Darla!"

Chrissy elbowed her way forward so she could be at center stage. Miss Brenda was trying to keep up, get it all spelled correctly, and make sure everyone's ideas were represented. Katie considered it all a waste.

"What about Angelina?" Char suggested.

Katie bit her lip as she tried to hide the shock she felt over this one. Angel was the name of her best friend. Did she tell Char that? Her thoughts were broken by the resounding agreement from the group that Angelina was it.

"Okay, good. Now is Angelina a mouse or a squirrel or a girl?"

Chrissy cleared her throat and whispered as if she were telling a secret. "She's an elf."

Katie wondered if she whispered for dramatic effect or was afraid the others would think it was a really dumb suggestion.

"Chrissy, you're as dumb as a box of rocks and so are your ideas," Katie tossed back at her. "I can't believe anyone could be so stupid."

The girls gasped, and Katie knew she'd crossed a line. There was a long silence. Katie decided she'd better end this before it got worse. She could feel the energy shifting. There was a good chance they were all about to gang up on her.

She muttered, "Okay. What?" The entire group was staring at her. "I get it. Angelina the elf. Are we done now?" Katie rolled forward to get herself out of the chair without falling on her face. "I'm going to go to the bathroom."

Closing the restroom door behind her, she put the lid down and sat on the toilet. She felt like a stranger had just been forced into her life. Angelina? Really? Who knew what an elf's house looked like, anyway? She sat there thinking for a long time.

"Katie, get it done." Chrissy banged insistently on the door. "I have to pee."

Katie flushed and ran the water in the sink for effect. As she opened the door she made a face at Chrissy who growled "bitch" as she nudged her way past.

Angelina haunted Katie for the rest of the week. Every night in bed, before the tears, which were now more seeping out of her than convulsing, Katie imagined how tall Angelina was or what clothes she wore. Katie imagined she had long hair like Angel, but it was brown, not blonde, and thick enough to hide her elf ears, which were her secret.

Most annoying was the way Angelina would just pop up at odd times, like when Katie was getting dressed and trying to decide whether to wear leggings or jeans. Apparently, Angelina wore leggings. One day, as Katie was walking to her counseling appointment, she even yelled at Angelina to "Get out of my head," making a group of boys hanging out at the basketball court turn around. This annoying elf was taking over Katie's brain.

That same day in counseling, Katie was lost in thought during most of their session. Then, without thinking, she started talking about Angelina. Her hair was long and golden brown, and her fingers with gorgeous nails. She grew up in the woods and could climb trees like a squirrel. Katie was just thinking out loud until she realized Miss Johnson was vigorously taking notes.

So for the next several sessions, Katie was careful about what she said. She was onto the fact that no matter what she talked about, Miss Johnson twisted the conversation to focus on Katie and wrote down every word. But it wasn't long before a perfect opportunity to see her file presented itself.

On that day, when Katie arrived, Miss Johnson was on the phone. It was obvious that it was a personal conversation because she turned her back on Katie and faced the windows, speaking quietly into the receiver so Katie couldn't hear what she was saying.

Katie reached over the desk and turned her file around so she didn't have to read upside down. She carefully flipped it open. From the notes, it was clear that Miss Johnson couldn't know whether Katie was describing herself or not. She had written things like "Katie has created an alternative fantasy world…Katie confuses the lines between herself and Angelina… Katie is deeply disturbed by her experience."

Katie was careful to close the file and sit quietly back down in her seat just in time for Miss Johnson to turn and face her as she hung up the phone.

"Well, how are we today?"

Katie pasted on a smile and vowed to never talk about Angelina to Miss Johnson again. It was none of her business—time to clam up and get out of here. And true to her vow, Katie stopped talking. Finally, after week after week of the silent treatment, Miss Johnson just closed her notebook and stared at her.

Katie stared back, and the two locked eyes in the final stare-down that ended most of their sessions.

"I gotta go now," Katie would say, defaulting to her mantra.

Miss Johnson would get up from her chair and walk Katie to the door. As she headed out, Katie hoped she had enough time to get to the greenhouse. This counseling shit was really taxing. She needed some alone time.

Zig-zagging her way across the commons, Katie slipped behind the dining hall. Once she was sure she was out of sight of Miss. Johnson's window, she sprinted to the greenhouse. Katie was still so grateful that Mr. Stanley had never come back to lock the door. As she closed it, waiting to hear it latch behind her, she was startled to see that there was a pile of things in the middle of the aisle, way down by her makeshift nest.

She approached cautiously. Chards of sunlight making way through the scum on the glass ceiling slashed across the pile. These were not like the plants Mr. Stanley had brought her. These were clearly chosen for Angelina's world, something Mr. Stanley knew nothing about. Somebody had been in here and was bringing Angelina stuff.

Wandering and Settling

ANGELINA WANDERED FOR DAYS, FOLLOWING a creek that seemed to know where it was going. But it never seemed to merely get from one place to another without having to fall over something along the way. Occasionally it cascaded into pools of liquid luxury, the water always the perfect temperature. It babbled between falls and was cold, clear, and delicious.

The banks of the creek and the frequent ponds were surrounded by a thick blanket of velvety moss with large flat stones just the right size for laying out in the sun. Some of the warm pools were perfect for bathing and had delicate little fish that would nibble at her toes. Others had blossoms of flowers large enough to be floating islands and so fragrant that bathing in those waters left her skin feeling soft and smelling sweet.

Sitting on the banks of one of her favorite bathing pools, she saw her reflection in the water. She was pleased to see that at least her tangled mess of hair that had begun to look like dreadlocks was now replaced by soft, natural, cascading curls. She had started to chew her nails which had been badly broken by the battles in the dog run.

But she was no closer to finding a home than when she arrived here. She still had no plan. Sleeping on the ground had been novel, but the night sounds were still unnerving, so she rarely slept all night. She missed her room. She missed dinner at a table. She missed having a door to open when she called, "I'm home." It was spring, but the nights were cold. Angelina couldn't deny that she had some decisions to make.

"Gawd, what am I going to do?" Talking to herself made her thoughts seem so much more adult than just thinking them in her head. "What am I going to do?"

Her anger mixed with desperation. She stared into the water and waited as if the answer would float to the top at any moment. Yet nothing. Not even the ripples of fish swimming below.

She watched the reflection of an owl drifting silently in the sky above her, and a fitful wind began to blow, giving her the creeps. Leaves rustled, sending some floating down to the surface of the water. She rolled over to lie on her back, watching the owl's flight, when she saw it land on the top of a broken tree trunk above her.

"It must have snapped off during a storm or something." Angelina was very aware that she was talking to herself again. There was something odd about the top of that tree, though. It didn't look like any broken tree trunk she'd ever seen. There were small holes where branches had once been that now looked more like windows. They glowed with sunlight.

When the owl disappeared inside the trunk and reappeared, Angelina realized it was hollow. She frowned and looked back down to the ground, trying to decide if she had finally caught a break or if this was an idiotic idea. She looked again at the top of the tree, shading her eyes from the sun this time.

"That could work," she said as she got up and wiped her hands on her shirttail. Besides, optimism felt better than despair. The owl flew away. "Yep, that might work!"

It didn't take much to swing up into the lower branches of the tree and make her way to the jagged edges of the top of the trunk. Hopping down over the edge, Angelina was pleased to find that the still intact bark was just high enough to give shelter. The floor was surprisingly flat, and the leaves of neighboring trees created just enough cover to be a roof.

"Yep! This can work!"

Angelina finally felt her fortune was changing. She'd make this her base camp while she searched for her way out of these seemingly infinite woods. Intent on finding something soft enough to sleep on, Angelina climbed down the tree and leaped the last five feet to the ground. The force of her landing disturbed the quiet. Small birds hopped from branch to branch. Somewhere above her, a flock of magpies spontaneously burst into the air in unison.

Angelina kicked at a slab of moss growing on the rocks at the base of her tree and stuck out her lower lip, blowing out a sigh that made her bangs flutter. She wanted something easy, and she wanted it now! She was tired and desperately wanted sleep.

Gathering grass for a bed, she discovered that if she pulled it from the bottom she not only got long soft blades but the thick thatch of undergrowth too. She gathered enough to make a very plush mound and piled it at the base of the tree. She flopped down in the middle of it to test it.

"Nice!" she exclaimed proudly. "Very nice!"

Now. How would she get all this up to the top of that hollowed-out tree? Another exasperated sigh fluttered her bangs. After some serious thought, she decided she'd have to make bundles and haul them up backpack-style.

Over and over, she struggled to get the bundles up the tree before they disintegrated. Twice every blade of grass slid from her grip as she climbed. Frustrated, she threw the whole lot up in the air, kicked the trunk, and cursed. When she'd calmed down, and her need for sleep outweighed her anger, she started over and soon had created six thick bundles using vines as a cord. Climbing into the trees with a bundle of grass longer than she was tall took some effort, but as long as she kept her temper in check, she could haul all the grass up into the hollow.

Now she needed something for a mattress top, and her bed would be just about right. Angelina peered over the edge of the bark wall to see if she could spot some of the plants she'd played with when she was little. It had soft velvety leaves.

"Oh, my gosh!" She gasped when she realized she could see deep into the canyon. "There's that waterfall and that bottomless swimming hole! And the orchard with the peaches." The distant mountains were still covered with snow but shone purple in the sunlight. "This is amazing," she said softly.

She stared in wonder. How could a place this beautiful exist and no one know about it? Indeed, this was a real place.

As the shadows grew long and the light grew dim, Angelina slowly climbed down. Partway down, she spotted the owl perched on a branch of a tree near hers. Their eyes met for just a moment. The owl winked one of his great round eyes. Angelina shuddered at the thought that he, too, was stalking her.

She found the fuzzy-leafed plant; one leaf was big as the quilt on her bed at home. She had to carry it on her back like a cape. How some things grew so large in this part of the woods was bewildering.

But when she returned to her treehouse, she was puzzled by what she found. Somehow a huge bird's nest had appeared in the branches that dipped into her hollow. Baffled, she climbed up the wall to peer inside, cautiously looking over her shoulder. This might be a cruel trick meant to lure her into a trap.

She studied the nest. It was made of tiny twigs woven together and lined with soft downy feathers, and it was large enough for her to curl up inside. Looking around guardedly, she saw the owl watching her. Again their eyes met. She stood very still, wanting him to be the one to make the first move. With another wink, he spread his great wings and silently flew away.

"What in the world?"

She was perplexed. How did the nest get here? Who…?

She looked around suspiciously. This place was so strange, and she wasn't sure what to think. The thought that someone was watching her was frightening. But there was no sign or sound of anyone anywhere.

Angelina tested the branch the nest balanced on to be sure it would hold her weight. It bobbed a bit but was certainly sturdy. She crawled in and wrapped her arms around her knees. A smile crept over her face. It felt good. Soft, warm, cozy, and much better than her mound of grass.

"Thank you," she whispered, a bit begrudgingly, not sure who she was thanking.

The leaves around her danced in the breeze. She heard the same tiny little giggle she'd heard before.

Darkness slid over the woods, wrapping Angelina's home in stillness. She lay back in her nest. Gazing at all the stars, she felt small and lonely. Below her she could hear the night prowlers out searching for food, but with the nest wrapped around her, she realized she felt safe for the first time in a long while. She closed her eyes and listened.

She longed to hear familiar sounds, the sounds of her own home the way it used to be. Mom would be puttering in the kitchen with the final clean-up of the day. Her father would be closing his book and, with a thump, dropping it heavily on the table as he fell asleep in his chair. Their tree house would be creaking in the night.

Warm tears filled her eyes and rolled into her ears. She sighed, and just as she was about to drift off, she could have sworn she heard something in the wind. It sounded like someone was whispering, "It's okay." Too tired to be concerned, she slid quietly into a deep sleep. She still felt like the woods were watching her, but now it felt good. That night Angelina slept soundly in a bed that swayed in the night air, gently rocking her.

Katie approached the pile of who-knows-what with great caution. Using only her index finger and thumb, she discovered a large circular section of tree bark, pine cones, seeds, and bits of fabric. And a note. "Hope you enjoy using some of this in your project." No signature.

Katie sank to the floor and pulled her knees close to her chest. The thought that someone was watching her was creepy. It must be like how an animal feels when being stalked by a predator. Panic set in. What if it was Him? What if He'd found her? Leaping to her feet, she scanned every corner of the greenhouse. Her safe place had been violated. She wasn't safe anymore.

Suddenly she had a fierce headache. Stars glittered in front of her eyes, and pictures flashed across her mind like she was scanning through to find a specific one. But these were not of her life. They were of Angelina and the griffin and a bunch of strange people.

Frightened and in pain, she grabbed her head and ran to her nest, burrowing her face in a soft quilt that wasn't there yesterday.

"Please, no, please stop. Please, I want to go home."

As suddenly as it all began, the ache was over. The pictures disappeared. Outside, a twig snapped.

"Holy shit, what was that? I gotta get out of here and lock that door." Katie hurried to the door and found that it couldn't be locked from the inside. She'd have to jam it somehow. Searching under the planting beds, she found what she needed—a wooden fence post just long enough to wedge under the handle.

She dug it deep enough into the dirt to keep the door from opening. Once she was sure everything was in place, she slid out her broken window, tested that the door jamb was going to hold, and ran until she was in sight of the cottage.

As she approached, she heard giggling and laughter. She knew she had to shed her sense of panic and invasion before she went in. These girls may be a pain to live with, but their abuse had earned them all a sixth sense about people, and they'd know something was up. Straightening her back, she brushed the hair out of her face and manufactured a smile that should pass the test. Firmly grabbing the door, she made her entrance.

"'Bout time you showed up. You almost missed getting one of these!" Chrissy held up a huge homemade cookie. "Mrs. Kovacs made them just for us."

Katie watched as Brittany reached for one. "They're called kolickky." Everyone laughed.

"No, dear, they are kolachy cookies," Mrs. K gently corrected. "My mama taught me to make them when I was a child, and I will teach you."

Katie liked Mrs. Kovacs. Her words were always kind. She treated them all like real people, not as damaged goods. She was like everyone's grandmother like her grandmother had been.

"Come, come now into the kitchen, and let's get started. We will need flour, butter, milk, and sugar."

Katie smiled. The first step would be cutting through that very thick Hungarian accent. All her v's were w's, and some of the letters came from deep in her throat like she needed to clear something out of it.

Katie was aware that Mrs. Kovacs was making eye contact with her. Did it really show on her face that she'd been scared? Pain struck again, and pictures flashed. An old couple, cookies, lots of trees. And then it stopped.

Miss Brenda nudged her. "Katie, Mrs. Kovacs asked you a question." Startled, Katie shook off her mind mess and turned first to Miss Brenda and then to Mrs. Kovacs.

"Sorry, what?"

"Please reach over there to get me that rolling pin, dear."

Katie turned in the direction of Mrs. K's gesture, fetched the rolling pin, and as she passed it into the chubby little fingers, she caught Mrs. K's cheery little wink.

Three batches of cookies later, Katie offered to help Mrs. K clean up, not because she was so thoughtful but because she wasn't ready to face the drama of the other girls. Now, she was beginning to feel quite comfortable in the presence of this kindly old lady. When they were done, it was time for dinner, another place Katie had learned to be anonymous. Keep food in your mouth, and you don't have to talk to anyone. Just watch. She had to find out who was watching her.

For the next few days, Katie scanned everything around her, hoping to spot someone who might be showing a little bit too much interest in her. She made sure she had her back to the wall or that she walked in the middle of the sidewalk away from the bushes. She even took to looking up into the trees in case someone had climbed up in the branches to watch her. Nothing. No one was paying any attention to her. Not being watched was almost as unnerving as being watched.

Finally, when she felt like the threat had passed, at least enough to go back to the greenhouse, she chose a sunny day. Shadows still made her jumpy.

"Ugh," escaped her lips with a hiss. It was a long way down from that window, and she usually landed on her hands and knees. "I gotta fix that."

Ducking under the planting beds and rummaging in the corners, she found a pile of apple crates that would be perfect. Stacking three of them, she made a nice set of steps from the ground to the window. She slapped the dirt off her hands and surveyed her work.

"Nice." She laughed. "You're talking to yourself, Stupid. And you're answering, Fool!"

Cautiously, she moved to the back where her home away from home was waiting. She almost felt safe in here again. The pile of "things" was where she'd left it, which was good news, but she still approached it with great caution. What if it was a trap and some creepy handcuff thing grabbed her if she touched anything?

She found an old fence picket and used it to poke at the fabric that lay on the top. It was a pretty paisley and would make a cute blouse, actually. Then she moved the bits of bark and branches. When she got to the bird's nest near the bottom, she was pretty sure there was no trap, at least not this time. She put the picket down and picked up the nest. It filled the palm of her hand. Picking at the tiny feathers, she tried to figure out what kind of a bird would have made such an exquisite bed for its babies.

Not being the Martha Stewart type, creativity was new to Katie. Creative thoughts flooded her brain, making her feel slightly out of control. But she made a sink out of a walnut shell, a broom from the fibers she pulled off a coconut shell and a twig handle, chairs out of branches, balls of yarn from salvaged threads, and knitting needles out of pine needles.

"This nest would be a perfect bed. I'll line it with the paisley fabric." She would put in on the floor—no, wait—the bark—it could make a tree-house, and she'd put the branches up the outside, and the nest would be in the branches.

Exhilarated by her results, she dashed across the greenhouse and, scrounging in the cupboard above the potting table, Katie found floral wire and a ball of twine and started to work. By the time the sun began to slide down behind the evergreens outside, she had crafted a perfect home for Angelina.

"I like it," she declared with her hands on her hips, shoulders back, and chest puffed out ever so slightly. She had to admit she was kind of impressed with herself. Who knew she could make something out of practically nothing?

That's when it hit her.

"I can't take this back to the classroom. Everyone'll want to know where I got the stuff to make it." She paused as the real issue overcame her thoughts. "AND where I made it."

Now what? As she stared at her perfectly fabulous creation, her mind raced to figure out what to do. In one of those "duh" moments, she realized she would make just the minimum necessary to get by in class, then she could leave this creation here and make her own version of an enchanted village right here in her own secret place. It would be all hers; nobody else would know her secret. Except whoever put the things here for her in the first place.

She'd held the thoughts of a stalker at bay as long as she could, but now they were back. She quietly put down the ball of twine and moved cautiously down the path. She climbed the crate stairs and slid out the window into the dusk. Her feet moved as if she was race walking. She had to get to dinner and away from... whoever.

"I think we all have angels," Brittany announced later that night as she pulled her sweater over her head and tossed it on the floor. When Char pointed at the sweater, Katie smirked and cleared her throat, forcing Brittany to pick it up, fold it, and put it in her drawer.

"You're full of it. If we had angels, I would have seen one in the closet, and I can tell you there wasn't no angel in that closet."

Mel's point was well taken. Katie had to agree that surely angels would have stepped in to save her or any of them from the creeps that hurt them.

Brittany stopped buttoning her 'jama top." But wait, if there aren't angels then why are they painted all over the ceiling at the church? My aunt told me we all have guardian angels. So those are lies?"

Katie watched Brittany's face fall. She knew fantasies like angels gave Brittany hope.

"Of course, there are angels, Brit. They just have lots of people to watch over, and sometimes bad stuff happens while they're taking care of someone else," Char said.

Even though Katie didn't agree with the angels' part, she was glad Brittany had some hope to hang onto.

"Come here, Annie," Char said. "Let's get your jammies on."

"I saw my guardian angel once," Chrissy said. Her voice was hesitant. Katie knew she was probably remembering the last time she said something Katie thought was stupid. "She's really pretty and was standing at the foot of the bed when I was in the hospital. She told me I'd be okay and kissed me."

Katie had heard this story before, but the last time Chrissy told it, it was a pretty lady who kissed her. Time before that, it was a ghost. She flashed Chrissy a skeptical smirk. "Really!"

Katie got up and took her turn in the bathroom.

She was pretty sure she didn't have a guardian angel, but if she did, who'd it be? Some beautiful young woman or a wise old one? Did guardian angels get married? As she brushed her teeth, she imagined a mate for the young woman and one for the wise old one. She liked the idea of an older couple. You could have two Guardian Angels, couldn't you? More experience, more creative ideas for how to get out of here. She stopped brushing and stared into the mirror, toothpaste foam all over her mouth. Angelina would have 'old people guardian angels.'

As she crawled into bed, pulled the covers up to her neck, and tucked them between her knees with her back pressed to the wall, tears leaked from under her lashes. Still, she was calmed by the thought of that little old lady and her cute 'old man' husband. Tonight, for the first time, she slid into dreams of Angelina's life in the woods with her guardian angels. They were puttering around their yard in front of their tiny cottage, hidden under some ferns at the base of a large old tree.

The Magic of Milk and Chocolate Cake

ANGELINA WOKE UP AND STRETCHED, pleased that the nest turned out to be such a good bed. Like so many things in the woods that amazed her, it was just her size. Nothing here seemed to be the size she'd expected. Things she expected to be small were huge. Things that were big back home were often miniature here. And some things came in all sizes.

Acorns, for instance; yesterday, she'd found some tiny acorns and used the cap from one to make a cup for water. Some were normal-sized but too bitter for eating; some were the size of pumpkins and came from oak trees so huge you could play hide and seek around the trunk alone. The caps from those acorns made great baskets for gathering berries and now the spinach she'd found.

"Funny how that path to the spinach patch was not here one day and clearly appeared the next."

She was still talking out loud to herself. It made her feel like someone was there, especially when she answered. Having 'someone' to talk to made it less lonely, being all on her own. 'They' discussed the weather, what to do first in the day, and how to do things like pick the peaches in the top of the tree. Angelina's shoulders sagged when she realized how lonely she really was. Maybe running away wasn't the best idea she'd had.

"Well, we'd better get a move on. We've got things to do."

Leaping out of bed and down to the floor, she stretched again. This was the first of two times a day when she missed her mom the most. She missed having her mom tickle her nose to wake her up quietly. Her father liked to sleep in, so it was important that Angelina not disturb him in the morning. She also missed finding breakfast on the table. Now she had to go out and find her breakfast.

She missed her mother at night as well. Here, except for that weird breeze that seemed to bid her goodnight each night, there wasn't anyone to tuck her in and talk about her day. But she didn't miss hearing her father stumble in drunk or having to pretend to be sleeping so he'd go away if he stumbled into her room, suddenly wanting to be a devoted father.

For all the bad things that were now gone from her life, she still missed the predictability of home. A tear threatened to escape her lashes. Soon, hunger overtook sadness, and she shook off the tears, wiped her nose on her arm, and thought about food. Not that there was much to choose from. So far, she'd found raspberries, currants, spinach, pine nuts, and bitter acorns. Since she'd had currants for dinner, she decided on raspberries for breakfast.

Angelina slipped on her boots, and, reaching up for the branch above her head, she swung herself through the trees until she landed gracefully on the trail. The sun was warm on her face. Squirrels raced from tree to tree while the dragonflies glided in and out of sharp rays of sunlight. The birds were up and chattering about their plans for the day.

Out of habit, Angelina scanned the sky in search of the griffin. Who knew what provoked that beast?

"Good, clear skies. That stupid beast can pester someone else today."

She hadn't actually seen it since their first encounter, but she'd seen its shadow as it circled overhead. She'd had to be quick to escape its eagle vision by ducking under the ferns for cover.

"Phew." She wrinkled her nose as she smelled her hair. "Time to wash."

She decided on a bath before breakfast, following the path created by her many trips down to the creek. The same giant plant with soft, fuzzy, pale green leaves grew near the pool, so she picked a 'towel' each time she went to wash up. She hadn't figured out why, but this path was one of the few that didn't disappear.

"Mmmmmm," she sighed as she slid into the bath she'd fashioned using rocks to divert the water into a shallow pool warmed by the sun. "Nice job."

She was proud of how she'd created the tub with large slick rocks. She floated her hands across the water's surface, letting the ripples slide between her fingers.

After she'd washed her hair, scrubbed her toes, and soaked a bit longer in the deliciousness of the warm water, she stepped out onto the matt of moss. Watching the beads of water on her skin turn into tiny little diamonds, she wiped the sparkles off in a cascade, giggling as they bounced off the moss and disappeared between the blades of grass.

Now she was all clean and fresh smelling,

Angelina trotted down the trail anticipating the berries' juicy tartness. As she came up the hill overlooking the raspberry patch, she was so startled to see an old couple that her feet slid on the gravel path. Holding her breath, she ducked behind an oak tree, pressing her back into the thick folds of the bark.

She hadn't seen anyone since she left home. She was both excited and alarmed. Who were they, and where did they come from? And they were gathering berries—her berries! She flipped around and clutched the bark tightly as she watched them.

As the shock of seeing someone else in the woods wore off, she realized that these old people had to come from somewhere, meaning they had to know how to go back. Frantic that they might leave before she could reach them, she crashed through the bushes and clamored down the trail, kicking pebbles and stones every which way.

Once she was close enough for them to hear her, she began to shout. "Hello! Hello! Please help me! I'm lost. Please help!" Her feet slid out from under her, and she landed on her bottom right at the old woman's feet.

The old woman pushed her hat back into place. "My goodness, you do make an entrance!"

"Yeah, right, hmm," Angelina gasped, out of breath. "I'm lost and need to get out of here. Can you show me how you got here and how to get out?"

She leaned over, trying to catch her breath. That's when she noticed the old lady's shoes. Her shoelaces were made of vines with little flowers. How in the world did she lace them without knocking off the blossoms?

The old man's voice brought her back to the problem at hand.

"Good morning. I'm Joseph. This is my wife, Mauve. And you would be…?"

Angelina stood up. At first, she was startled at how old these two appeared as she got closer to them. The old man's legs were so bent and crooked that he couldn't straighten them when he stood. His pants piled up on his worn work boots, which had odd little bits of string hanging out of every lace and fold. The hand he extended was as gnarled as a twisted piece of driftwood, so Angelina wasn't exactly sure how to best take hold and return his shake. But his fuzzy whiskered face was kind, and his eyes sparkled, so she reached out in return.

He brushed a wild hedge of coarse white hair back from his forehead as if he was preparing to tug on his cap when he realized his cap was on the ground at their feet. His wife giggled. Angelina followed his animated gaze to her round and rosy face. Her eyes sparkled as well. She patted the ground beside her, encouraging Angelina to sit. As she did, she bumped her nose on the long-stemmed sunflower arcing fantastically from where it sprouted out of the brim of her hat. Angelina waited as she moved her flower-printed skirt and crisp white apron out of the way, making a place for Angelina to join their picnic.

"Angelina. I got lost. Actually, I got snatched by this beast, a griffin. He dropped me over there, and I haven't been able to find a trail out of here." She knew she was rambling, but she had to make them understand.

"Goodness, child, sit down, rest for a moment. Catch your breath. A griffin, really? What a terrifying experience! Joseph, dear, get this child a sandwich."

Angelina didn't have the time or the patience for small talk. She wanted to get back to her life. But she was hungry, especially when she spotted the large wicker basket filled with sandwiches and cakes. She'd have to be polite until she got all the food and information she needed, so she was careful not to snatch the sandwich Joseph offered.

"Mmmm, well, it's kind of a long stwory, and I hate to take up your time," Angelina mumbled through the gooey peanut butter stuck to the roof of her mouth. She leaned over to look into the basket. "Do you have any lemonade in there?"

"Of course, dear." The old lady reached for a pitcher that Angelina could have sworn was not there a minute ago. When she filled a glass that also seemed to come out of nowhere, Angelina began to wonder if she was safe with these two. Gulping down the cold drink, she gave them the short version of the dog run and the griffin.

"Now I just need you to show me the path out of here," she said, her patience running thin.

Joseph was the first to speak. "Well, Angelina, … may I call you Angelina? You are a very long way from where any elves live, and it will be a long and dangerous journey to get you home if you aren't prepared. You're going to need food and some basic tools, at the very least. Do you have any survival skills other than those that have served you up until now?"

Perplexed, Angelina wasn't sure how to respond. "Like what dangers?" surviving danger was all she'd thought about for weeks.

"Well, river crossings, scaling canyon walls, and basic woodlands first aid. Those boots you have look like they were good for city walking but not for mountain trails."

Angelina's spirits sagged. She broke the silence, "So, what do I do?"

Joseph sat beside her and handed her a slice of chocolate cake and a glass of milk. "You need to put together a plan. That's what you need to do. Figure out where to begin."

Mystified by where the milk came from, Angelina took a gulp to wash down the cake. "But I don't know what to do. I've never been here before. I'm just an elf…."

Her voice trailed off as she absorbed the hopelessness of the situation. She was trying really hard not to cry again. She clutched her necklace and bit her lip. Now she wasn't so sure she'd ever get back to her forest or the city, and her heart sank.

Mauve patted Angelina on the knee. "Now, now, dear. You are going to be fine. And you will get to where you are supposed to be in good time. Have faith. You will have all you need if you can just have faith." She filled Angelina's milk and lemonade glasses.

Angelina twisted the corner of her mouth up in an insincere smile. Anyone who depended on faith was going to be in for trouble. Faith had never gotten her anywhere before, and she wasn't going to count on it now. These two old people were definitely peculiar.

Since she didn't have many other choices for help, though, she'd have to take what she got. She took another slice of cake, closing her eyes to savor the rich sweetness of the thick dark frosting. When she opened her eyes, they were gone—Mauve, Joseph, the picnic basket, everything but one glass of milk.

Angelina screamed, slamming her hands to the ground as her chin dropped to her chest. How could they just leave her? Where did they go?

"This is so not fair! I just need a little help here, and do you think anyone will give it? NO!"

Her anguish echoed throughout the hills. She snatched up the glass and drank every last drop of the cold milk. She was too confused by this place to even worry about where the milk came from. Beds showed up out of nowhere, and people appeared and disappeared silently. The night was filled with whispers.

As she turned to drag herself back the way she came, a path that wasn't there materialized from nothing. She blindly followed.

Finding herself back at her hollowed-out tree, she leaped up, grabbed a branch, and swung herself onto the bare floor of her new 'home.' She slowly looked around the room at all the bits and pieces that she had gathered. She weighed the longing to go home and the comfort of a place of her own, bit her lower lip, and sighed.

Going Home—A Good Thing or Not

KATIE WOKE UP IN THE DARKNESS with her sheets twisted around her legs. She needed a plan. Just wanting to get out of Aspen Meadows wasn't enough, but she had no idea where to begin. Restlessly she tossed and turned the rest of the night as she tried to figure out what to do next.

The nights Katie did look forward to were the ones when the girls would lie in the dark and share their fantasies about life beyond Aspen Meadows. Char was going to get a job and an apartment so she could have all her brothers and sisters with her as a family again. Mel was going to get an RV, probably because they didn't have closets. Chrissy was sure she'd been kidnapped at birth, and her real mother was out there looking for her right now. No one had the heart to tell her that she looked just like the woman in the family photo by her bed.

Katie longed for the days when she would spend weekends at her grandparent's farm just outside of town. Her grandmother smelled like cookies. Her grandpa smelled like pipe tobacco. No one yelled. She could ride her bike up and down the long dirt driveway. That was her fantasy place. But she was going to need more than a fantasy to get back home.

Spring was finally arriving, and everyone got to spend more time outside, which was a good thing. Katie was sick of playing board games with Mel and

Chrissy, who cheated or reading stories aloud with Brittany, who was way behind in her reading skills and, in Katie's opinion, was not trying to learn. She'd even agreed to participate in the volleyball games now and then.

She still found time to sneak off to the greenhouse. Angelina's world had grown from just a tree house to a school house surrounded by vegetable gardens, wading pools, and a tree swing. She'd made Aspen Meadows more bearable for now. But she wasn't staying here forever.

As the weeks blended into each other, the one thing that didn't change was Tuesdays when Katie had her counseling appointment. And the only good thing about that was the little sack that waited for her in the dining hall when she was done. When she missed dinner because of her counseling sessions, Mrs. Kovacs always left her a tasty meal in a bag on the end of the serving counter.

Today's session with Miss Johnson had been a pretty good one. Miss Johnson had learned not to ask about Katie's assault anymore, so Katie didn't have to dodge her questions anymore. Now she skipped down the dining hall steps with her brown bag filled with thick sandwiches, veggie sticks, and cookies swinging in her left hand.

Walking across the commons gave Katie time to think about her sessions. Now she and Miss Johnson mostly talked about what Katie liked to do and what things she did with her friends before she came to Aspen Meadows. So Katie told her all about snowboarding, how she was getting pretty good at skateboard tricks, and how much she missed her dog, who died last year just after her grandmother had also died. Miss Johnson said she'd look into what she might be able to do about some of that. Katie smiled. She was sure she'd heard Miss Johnson all but tell her that she was going to get to have a dog here.

"Hey, everybody!" Katie called out as she entered the Cottage, tossing her jacket on the chair, eager to tell them all about the possibility of having a dog living in the Cottage. She'd share, of course, but the dog would be hers mostly. The wall of silence that hit her was a shock.

"What?"

Mrs. K was there—she must have brought cookies again. But the sadness on Miss Brenda's face didn't look like a cookie face. She searched everyone's face for a reply.

"What!?" Katie demanded.

Chrissy snuffled back her tears. "Annie's gone."

"Where? We have to find her! Why aren't you out looking?" Katie reached for her jacket, pulling it on both sleeves at one time.

Char blew her nose. "She's not lost. They took her."

"Who?!" Katie's voice grew increasingly shrill every time she opened her mouth.

"Her parents took her. They came and took her home." The grief seemed to make it hard for Char to even speak.

"But they didn't take her blankie or Miss Mousie. She can't sleep without Miss Mousie." Chrissy dissolved into a heap at the end of her bed and sobbed.

Mel wailed, "And she'll cry, and they'll put her in a closet. They always put you in a closet when you cry."

Katie could see the panic growing on Mel's face. She reached over and, putting her arm around Mel, slowly sat down on the bed.

"They won't put her in a closet," Katie said. "She couldn't go home if they thought anyone would do that." Katie searched Mrs. K's and Miss Brenda's faces for some sign that Annie was going to be safe. " Would they?" Their expressions offered nothing in the way of comfort. Panic gripped Katie's gut.

The women began to tell them all the reasons this was a good thing for Annie—how everyone at Aspen Meadows hoped they would all get to go home someday; that's why they had all the counseling. But what came out of their mouths sounded like the voices used for adults in cartoons—'waa waaa wa wawa wa waaa". The girls migrated towards each other until they had formed one tight, tear-soaked hug.

Katie couldn't understand how Annie could go home with the very people who had done something that led to her coming to a group home for abused children. How could she be safe without all of them to protect her? Katie's heart spun as she tried to pull the pieces into order. Her parents hadn't abused her, so why couldn't she go home if Annie could go home to the parents who hurt her? None of this made any sense.

Finally, Miss Brenda convinced them all to get into bed. Things would look much better in the morning, she said. Katie knew none of them believed her. Watching Char gather up the blankie and Miss Mousie and tuck them into the bed where Annie had lain so many nights broke Katie's heart. She'd never really thought of Char or any of them as friends, but tonight, they were sisters, and the littlest of them all was missing.

Katie could tell she wasn't the only one lying still while watching dawn creep into the bedroom. There were more sniffles than the sound of the snores of young girls. Soon the need to pee overcame their blanket of sadness, and one by one, they stirred.

Char was the first to get dressed, and when she took off, Katie wondered if she should show her the greenhouse. It was a place where badness was not allowed. She'd have to think about that. Sharing a dog was one thing, but her safe place was altogether another.

A couple of days later, Miss Brenda proudly announced that they would be getting a pet for the Cottage. Katie's heart leaped immediately as she searched around the classroom to see where the dog had been hidden. It sank when Miss Brenda unveiled the hamster in the cage on her desk.

"I know how much you all miss Annie. We thought this would take your mind off her, give you something new to love."

"You're kidding me!" Char exploded. "You really think a hamster could replace Annie?"

Katie followed her, and they both bolted out the door, staggering onto the courtyard grass.

"I miss Annie," Char said. "I miss my baby sisters. I have no idea where they are. I may never see them again. I'll never see Annie again."

"You might. And they must have to tell you where your sisters are." Katie realized she was making all this up, but she had to tell Char something, anything that might help.

Char spun around and spoke sharply, cutting Katie to her soul. "You just don't get it. They either send you home to the same mess they took you out of, or they send you to foster care!" Char's face grew still, her jaw set. "I've got to go find my brothers."

Katie stood on the porch of the cottage and watched Char take off for the boys' side of the campus. She almost called out to warn Char that she was dangerously close to the imaginary line that separated the girls from the boys. Knowing how much pain Char suffered, she decided it wouldn't do any good.

Seeing her brothers across the dining hall on the rare occasions when they ate at the same time had never been enough. Katie knew nothing was going to stop Char now that foster care threatened to rip them from her life. She needed to touch them, breathe in the smell of little boys' heads. Being alone was too much to bear now. Katie understood what it felt like to need to be with your family.

Katie watched Char disappear between the buildings in search of Mark and Nathan and wondered what it was like having siblings. She didn't even have cousins.

"I will not go to foster care," she whispered. "And if they won't let me go home, I will have to find a way to get out of here. I just need that plan." As she declared her strength, Katie's lower lip quivered. Tears filled her eyes, blurring her vision, but she knew she had no choice but to be brave.

The screen door screeched as she opened it to go back inside. Darrell stood in the middle of the room with a look that clearly said, "I didn't do anything."

"Don't you have someplace to be?" Katie snarled.

Darrell didn't dare open his mouth and try to say anything. He slithered out the door. After that, Katie heard the sound of his badly polished wingtips smacking the sidewalk as he ran.

Tears, Sap, and Friends

S ITTING ALONE, ANGELINA STARTED TO CRY. At first, she fought the tears, wanting to be braver than she really felt. After a while, she gave up the battle and just let them flow. It took a while but finally, her tears dried, and anger replaced her pity. Her thoughts were filled with lots of 'why me? And 'this sucks' and 'it's all their fault—it's all his fault.'

Taking a deep breath, she declared, "Okay. If I'm going to get out of here, I'm going to have to figure it out on my own. Until then, this stump is going to have to be home. I'll just have to make something out of it."

Furniture would be a good start. She set out to see what she could find.

Brushing past the low evergreen branches that reached out their soft arms to touch her legs, she backtracked down the path that followed the brook, surprised to find that it had not vanished since the last time she'd passed this way. She couldn't figure out what made one path vanish while another didn't. She put her hand out to lean on a tree to gather her bearings. Cold, sticky goo squished between her fingers and ran down her hand.

"Oh, gross!" she said, pulling her hand out of the sticky mess. She couldn't wipe it on her clothes. It would never come out. Finally, she rubbed her hand in the dirt and coated the sap with enough dust to keep it from sticking to everything.

Following the path, she wandered around the hillside and down into the valley. Once again, she had the strange sensation that she was being watched, but when she stopped short and spun around to catch who or whatever it was, there was no one there. Whoever it was had better make themselves known pretty quick. Angelina was losing patience with this game of cat and mouse. Lifting her face, she bathed herself in the warmth of the sun and let her heart feel lighter. For the first time in her life, she was actually in control. Having power, even if it was the power to pick out something with which to make a table, made her feel good.

Off the path below a beaver dam, she spotted a small pile of logs and smiled at the thought of finding a beaver scrap heap. Picking through the pile, she found four that were about the same length. Mostly aspen, the logs were long and even.

"This'll work for legs." She set them aside. Now, for a top. This was going to be tricky. She did find a slab of bark that looked promising. Annoyed by the wad of gunk on the palm of her hand, she hoisted her supplies over her shoulder and headed home. Funny, she thought. Calling her hollowed-out tree stump "home" had been surprisingly easy.

Back at the hollow, Angelina tried to figure out which leg to put where to make a level table, but being unsure of where to start was frustrating.

"Geez, nothing around here is easy."

She lined the legs up, first this way, then that, hoping she'd find a combination that would work. Three of the four legs worked out, but the fourth one was too long. Realizing that she was going to need more tools than she had in her little house, she climbed back down the tree and tossed the legs down to the base of the tree. She tried putting the long one across a rock and stomping on the end to break it but only succeeded in hurting her foot. Next, she tried hitting the end with a rock to break it off, but the rock just bounced.

Looking around for anything that might help her shorten the branch, Angelina was shocked to see a young man sitting on a boulder up the hill from her tree. Startled, she jumped. He laughed, took off a well-worn cap, and ran his fingers through his straw-like hair.

Angelina struck a defensive pose, ready for a confrontation. She wasn't sure whether to be afraid of this stranger or glad to finally see another creature that walked on two legs, especially one with such big brown eyes.

"What are you looking at?" she said.

"Sorry, I'm not spying. I was in the neighborhood and happened to catch sight of you struggling. You need help?"

"No, I'm fine," she shot back indignantly.

"No, you're not." He slid off the rock and started towards her. "You know, you'd be dangerous if you had the right tools. Looks like you are trying to cut one of those branches off, right?"

Angelina was wary as she watched him swagger in her direction. She needed help but wasn't sure she was willing to trust this guy. He wiped his hands down the length of his thighs, rubbing the dirt into his jeans.

"What a slob," she whispered. When she realized he had probably heard her, she took control of the conversation again. "Yeah, but I'm fine, so you can just move on."

Angelina held her ground. She didn't want to reveal the location of her hollow to this stranger. He might be the one who had been stalking her. She backed up, keeping a measured distance between them in case she had to run.

"Trek, here." He shoved a hand toward her with such force that she stepped back to avoid being stabbed by his fingers. "What's your name?"

She stepped back again, never letting her eyes leave his. Her lips tightened into a hard straight line.

"Okay, we can do the formal introductions later."

She didn't respond. His words were safe enough, but his tone was cocky and spun with arrogance.

She thought he looked familiar, but she was sure if they'd met, she'd have remembered him. She bet most girls did. But she gave him a blank stare. They couldn't have met. Besides, she bet she was the first elf he'd ever been this close to based on the way his gaze kept darting back to her ears.

"A table, maybe?" he said, and reaching into his pocket, he took out a length of chain. Angelina shifted her weight to her right leg and made a fist.

"Don't worry," he laughed, "it's a pocket saw."

Embarrassed by her overreaction, she relaxed her fist but didn't move any closer. He proceeded to measure and cut and, using his pocket knife, he carved out a hole here, a notch there until he had parts and pieces all coming together as a table. Carefully, he tested each piece one at a time to be sure he was satisfied with the results. Then, without a word, he disappeared into the Woods with a piece of one of the branches in his hand.

Angelina stood there, watching the place where he had disappeared. She thought how odd he was, showing up out of nowhere, building her a table, and then disappearing as quietly as he had arrived. Her caution was being replaced by fascination. She watched him make his way back through the brush with a huge blob of something dripping from the branch in his left hand.

"This here is the stickiest sap we've got in these parts. When it dries, it's a permanent bond."

Angelina held out her hand, and he burst out laughing. She hid it behind her back as her emotions spiked between embarrassment and anger. She felt her ears begin to burn and knew they were turning bright red. She swung her hair around, so they were covered, hoping he hadn't noticed.

"Guess you've already met this stuff! Don't worry. Magda will have something to get that off. She has potions for everything. We'll finish this, and then I'll take you back to see what she can do."

Angelina frowned. Magda? Who was Magda? And who was this conveniently handy guy who showed up just when she was struggling to make something on her own? She cocked her head to one side and tried to study him without him noticing.

He continued to smear one end of each table leg with the sap and twist it into one of the holes on the underside of the table. With all four in place, he flipped it over, tested it for level, and stepped back to admire his work.

"Reckon that will work for you. Now come on, let's get you to the village and see what we can do to get that crud off your hand."

He started off into the Woods. The path appeared the minute his foot hit the ground.

"Wait?" she called after him. "Village? There's a village near here? How come I never found it?" Angelina didn't move. Part of her thought he seemed nice enough, but something told her to be cautious. Maybe this was a con of some sort. She knew just enough about these woods to be suspicious. Was this boy one of the dangers the old man had warned her about?

She watched him start down the path that had just appeared. He turned to see if she was following.

"Well?" He shrugged and motioned for her to follow. "Look, it's up to you. You can come with me, or you can live with that stuff on your hand for weeks. But when it wears off it will take part of your skin with it, so you'd better prepare some sort of bandage to cover it until it heals, or you'll have quite the infection to tend. Up to you."

She looked at her hand. She'd have a sore the size of her entire palm if he was right.

"Don't try anything funny, then," she said. "I know how to defend myself, you know." Trek snorted. "Whatever," he tossed over his shoulder.

Her steps quickened as she trotted to catch up with him. The path he took began to fade behind him.

As they traveled deeper into the woods, Angelina reached out and quietly broke the ends of branches along the way making sure she could see one from the last. She wanted to be sure she left enough clues so she could find her way back by herself.

They traveled over a ridge into the next valley. The path was narrow, almost invisible below the curls of the ferns that stood over four feet tall. There were places where the trail disappeared completely. Sometimes it was because of a boulder field they had to cross or because of a cascading stream that came tumbling off the hillside and took over the trail until it found a spillway wide enough to let it splash its way on down.

Since he was in front of her she couldn't help but study how he walked. He had a funny man/boy swagger, part confidence, part not sure of his stride. She thought it was kind of cute. She also liked how the breeze played with the curls on the back of his head. He definitely had potential—but not enough for her to trust him.

Topping a wall of boulders, Angelina saw delicate swirls of smoke rising from a clearing below. As they got closer, she could make out small huts and people gathered in groups chatting, working at cutting wood, cooking in big black pots, and children playing games. She stopped in her tracks, confounded. How, after wandering around for weeks, had she not come across this place?

Trek motioned her forward. "Come on."

She was unnerved by the commotion as the villagers murmured something about a stranger coming into their village. Angelina was concerned because they didn't look all that pleased. She made sure to stay in step behind him.

With that annoying air of arrogance, Trek walked coolly into the clearing in the center of the village. He approached a small hut on the far side, bounding up the stone steps as if he were a frequent visitor. Like all the huts, this structure was made of long, flat slabs of bark, making it almost impossible to see from a distance. The windows were large with flower box planters filled with ivy that climbed this way and that, much like it would grow on the branches of the trees. The roof was covered with moss, vines, and small flowering plants. It was no wonder she hadn't realized they were approaching a small village when they came over the hill.

"Magda, I've got someone here who needs your magic touch," he called out.

An old woman stepped into the doorway of the hut wiping her hands on an odd little apron made of many scraps of fabric sewn together without much thought to patterns or colors. She wore a hat, a knit hat, also of many colors, with a ruffled brim pulled down low on her head. Her hair, streaked with grays of all shades, was pulled back into a braided bun at the nape of her neck.

"Why, what have you found now?"

Her voice was soft and gentle; Angelina felt Magda's gaze take in every detail of her unkempt appearance, seemingly taking note of every scrape and bruise covering Angelina's legs and arms.

"My, my. You've got yourself an elf."

Angelina held out her hand.

"And one that's gotten herself into a mess of sap. Let's see what we can do for you, dear. Trek, now you wait outside. You know I don't like too many folk in my house." Taking Angelina's elbow, she guided her inside.

The hut was small but cozy and filled with odds and ends of everything. The walls were covered with shelves stacked with books, boxes, and jars. There was a rocking chair in one corner with several throws and blankets folded over it. A small table by a large open window held bits and pieces of pine needle baskets in all stages of creation. A crate on the floor was filled with needles. Angelina guessed that they, too, would soon be woven into one of the delicate vessels. The room was lit by an oil lantern. Angelina was struck by how shadows danced about as Magda shifted bottles and jars, looking for something as if she knew she had it somewhere.

"Sit down, dear." Magda motioned to a straight-back chair in front of the stone fireplace. She shifted bottles in and out of their places on the shelves, never turning to face Angelina. "What's your name, and what brings you to the Enchanted Woods, dear? You're a long way from somewhere."

Angelina ran her clean hand over her hair making sure that her ears were covered. Her fingers grazed the last remnants of the scrapes the griffin's talons had left on her shoulders. She knew Magda had seen her ears and the wounds, but she was still self-conscious around those who were not elves.

"Angelina. Ah, I was attacked by a griffin."

Magda paused for a moment, still facing the shelves. "That must have been a frightening experience." She set a jar on the table and resumed her search.

"Yeah, but I grabbed its tail, and we crashed. I got away, but now I'm pretty lost." Angelina didn't really care to tell this old woman the details of her life, but she needed help. "Maybe you can show me how to get out of here?"

"Well, first, we have to get that sap off your hand before it does any more damage." Moving a huge brown jar out of the way to see what was behind it, she said with satisfaction, "Ah, here it is." She wrapped her gnarly fingers around a small purple bottle with a stubby brown cork in the top. Angelina watched anxiously as this strange woman reached for a bowl and a rag. "We'll get this stuff off."

She added a bottle of some green liquid, a chipped ceramic bowl, and a torn piece of an old tee shirt to the jar on the table. She measured as if she'd done it a thousand times and mixed it with a wooden spoon. The smell of the concoction stung Angelina's nose as it joined the earthy musk of this mystifying hut.

"Set your hand in the bowl, dear. Let the potion soak into the sap. That's it."

"It stings." Angelina slowly slid her hand under the cool green film that floated on the purple liquid. Seconds later she jerked it back out splashing the concoction all over the table and floor.

Magda patted her hand, guiding it back into the bowl. "No, leave it. You must be patient and let it do its work."

They sat in silence for what felt like a very long time. Finally, Magda lifted Angelina's hand out of the bowl and tested the thick swell of sap with her nail. The sap was soaking up the potion and was forming a thick rubbery layer on the palm of her hand.

"A few minutes more."

Again, the silence made Angelina nervous, so she cleared her throat several times. Finally, Magda removed the bowl from the table, wiped the dripping green goo from Angelina's hand, and, using the back of the spoon, rolled the entire slab of sap from her palm.

"Wow!" Angelina was amazed. The palm of her hand was smooth and soft and very clean. "Geez."

"You're very welcome, dear. Now let's go find Trek, and he can take you back to where he found you."

Deep in wonder about how the potion has worked its magic, Angelina was jolted back into the moment she heard the words "take you back."

"Oh, but wait! Can you help me? Can you or anyone show me how to get out of here?"

"Getting into the Woods is not something that just happens, my dear." Magda turned to face the shelves, putting each bottle and jar back in its designated space. Over her shoulder, she continued, "You have to be chosen to be here. And someone has chosen you. Getting out of the Woods isn't an easy task either. You'll want to consider your choices carefully."

Wiping her hands on her apron, Magda turned and looked Angelina straight in the eye. This intimate contact made Angelina very uncomfortable. What did the old woman mean she'd been chosen?

"Come." Magda held open the door and Angelina, confused by the old woman's meaning, stepped out into the sunshine.

There was a small group of people arguing about something, and Trek was right in the middle of it. As Magda and Angelina approached, Angelina realized they had all turned to look at her. She felt a sick feeling in the pit of her stomach. This didn't look like the village welcoming committee. "Who are you, how did you get here, and what do you want?" they were all shouting at once.

"Leave her alone!" Trek said. "She can't do any harm. She's clueless and has no idea where she is or how to even take care of herself. She can't hurt anyone.

Besides, I'll take her back, and she won't be able to find her way back here."

The crowd was obviously not buying it. "We can't afford to risk it. She can't leave here now. We'll have to keep her here." This came from a short, fat man with more hair in his ears than on his head, and he spit when he shouted.

"Now, wait, let's all calm down. We need to talk this over. Figure out what is best here and not make rash decisions."

Angelina searched the crowd to find out who was standing up for her. It was a pretty young woman standing in front of a man who had his hands on her shoulders, her husband by the matching rings on their fingers. He nodded in agreement.

"I don't want anything except to find out how to get out of here," Angelina said. "If that stupid griffin hadn't grabbed me, this wouldn't be happening!" Her frustration was starting to show as her body shook.

The group gasped in unison. "A griffin? Not only does she know where we are, but she brings a griffin down on us!" The fat man was spitting again.

Angelina began to panic. This was not a friendly group of neighbors but a mob about to do something horrible to her. Her thoughts racing, she scanned the perimeter of the clearing, searching for the way they'd come in. She couldn't see any break in the trees or bushes. Where was it?

Remembering that they'd walked almost straight to the old woman's place, she turned, faced away from that hut, and ran. Bursting through the branches, scratching and scraping her way, hoping to find the trail, Angelina could hardly see through her tears.

"Someone, please help me!" Desperately she covered her eyes with her hands. "I just want a place to belong."

She sobbed as she ran until she tripped over a small rock and landed on her knees on smooth ground. She wiped her tear-streaked cheeks with her hands, smearing dirt and mud all over her face. As she blinked the tears from her eyes, she had to blink twice to be sure she saw what she thought she saw.

The path. She'd found the path!

Scrambling to her feet, she ran until she couldn't run anymore, always keeping an eye out for the broken branches she'd left to guide her back home. She never stopped long enough to look back.

By dusk, she'd made it over the mountain back into her valley and could see her tree up ahead. She knew her face was streaked with a muddy mixture of tears and dirt, and the scrapes on her legs stung, but she was home.

She swung herself up into her hollow, hitting the floor hard as she landed on her hands and knees. She listened for the sound of running and angry shouts. Nothing. It was quiet except for the sound of crickets. As she staggered to her feet, she banged her head on something and swore.

"Dang table!"

Rubbing her head, she pulled herself up and sat down on the chair.

"What?"

She sprang to her feet. She hadn't made a chair.

"How in the world?"

Her table was not on the ground but here in her house, and where had the chair come from? As she pondered all this, she also realized that the table was set with a wonderful plate of bread, fruit, and cheese. Real cheese. Sniffing and wiping her nose on her arm, she sank down on the chair, exhausted and bewildered.

"Oh, good, you're home!" Mauve appeared from the air, startling Angelina so much that she almost fell off the chair. "Love your new furniture. Joseph brought it up for you. We stopped by to see how you are doing and bring you a bite to eat. My, looks like you have had quite the day! Well, I'll leave you to your supper. You'll want to go to bed early tonight—you look like you could use some sleep. And you might want to wash your face."

Angelina rubbed her face with both hands, releasing chunks of mud and sand onto the floor. Mauve reached out and, licking her thumb, rubbed some of the mud off Angelina's cheek. Mauve kissed her on the clean spot. "Night, dear."

Angelina stared down at the furniture and the food, and when she looked back up, the old woman had vanished. Angelina was too tired to try to make sense of anything now. She felt a shadowy sadness come over her.

"Nobody ever stays with me around here."

She ate her dinner alone. Then, hand over hand, she climbed into her bed and pulled her quilt tight up around her chin. As she was dropping off to sleep, she heard faint voices faintly floating on the night breeze. As the pain in Angelina's heart gave way, she slid into sleep on the melody of a lullaby whispered by the winds.

Plans and Deception

K ATIE'S PLAN WAS FALLING INTO PLACE. She had come up with a bunch of schemes for where to go and how to get there. Going home wasn't an option. That's the first place they'd look, and then she'd end up right back at Aspen Meadows. Living on the street wasn't an option. She knew she wasn't smart enough for that kind of life. She thought about getting a job like Char so she'd have money to rent an apartment. But she didn't have any skills. And where would she live until she saved enough for a place?

Finally, she had a plan that she was sure would work. If she could find a way to get off the Aspen Meadows campus and get to her grandparent's farm, she could live there until she could figure out how to get home where she belonged. It was just close enough that she could almost ride her bike to it—if she had a bike. It had been abandoned when they died, but her mom had never sold it. The last time she was there was about a year ago, and she remembered being surprised to find everything was the same as it always had been, even the food in the pantry. She still had to figure out a way to get there. From that moment, how and when to escape was never far from her thoughts.

Today, she realized, the opportunity had just presented itself right here in the classroom. Miss Brenda's purse was open, her wallet right on top, and she'd just left the room.

Katie turned and looked at Brittany, her thoughts still focused on that purse.

"Katie, can I have it or not?"

"Sorry. Have what?"

Looking down at Brittany's hand and seeing the bits of paisley scraps clutched between her little fingers, Katie mumbled, "Ah, sure. I don't need it anymore."

"Geez, what a pain—all you had to do was answer me."

Brittany tugged her sleeves down over her wrists and huffed off. Katie blinked a couple of times when out of the corner of her eye she realized blood was on Brittany's wrist. She grabbed Brittany's arm but wasn't fast enough to get a hold of it.

"Brittany, what have you done? Give me your arm—show me!"

Brittany jerked her arm away and moved out of reach. Katie stood up, grabbed Brittany's other arm, and marched her into the bathroom. She locked the door.

"Brittany, show me. Now!"

Reluctantly, Brittany slid her right sleeve up to reveal slice marks all up her arm.

"Don't tell, please, Katie, don't tell. I promise I won't do it again. Please, Katie. They'll never let me go home."

Brittany's pleading made Katie's stomach lurch. If she didn't tell someone she knew Brittany wouldn't stop. If she did tell, Brittany might be right—they might never let her go home, and Katie would be responsible for her going to foster care.

"How in the world did you do this? We can't have anything with a blade."

"I rubbed the edge of the cardboard until it got sharp." Brittany started to cry.

"Get the blood cleaned up. Now," Katie barked, grabbing a paper towel and blotting Brittany's wrist. It was hard to do without opening the cuts and making them bleed again. "What possessed you to do this to yourself? Are you crazy?"

Katie didn't actually expect an answer. Everyone had been so upset by the loss of Annie that she was amazed someone hadn't done something more drastic. Knowing all that didn't make the ache in her gut go away, though.

"Now get back out there and do something with that fabric."

But just as they stepped back into the classroom, Miss Brenda appeared.

"There you two are. Oh, Brittany, you've gotten your sleeves all wet. Let's roll them up so you don't spoil your project."

She reached out, but Brittany jerked her arm back. The button of her cuff gave up in the tug of war and flew off. Brittany's secret was exposed.

Miss Brenda's expression was a mix of shock and disappointment. Disappointment hurt all of them the most. Katie felt the weight of trust doubling as Miss Brenda soaked in the depth of the betrayal, not only of Brittany's relapse but Katie's part in trying to hide it.

All business, obviously following the rules in the book, Miss Brenda led the sobbing girl out of the room and across the lawn to the infirmary. Katie knew that would be the last she would see of Brittany.

They all gathered at the window to watch as Brittany and Miss Brenda made the long walk.

"How did they not know she does that to herself?" Chrissy was lecturing. "We all know she does it. Really, I think most of the adults around here are just plain stupid."

Mel chimed in. "They're going to beat her. They told her not to do it again… and she did. They'll beat her for sure."

Seeing a clear shot at Miss Brenda's money, Katie moved slowly to position herself between the group and that purse.

"Mel, no one is getting beaten." So tired of Mel's obsession with closets and beatings, Katie barked at her with a sharpness that cut the conversation into pieces. She put her hand on Mel's back and maneuvered Mel so that they had changed places, putting Katie closer to the purse.

"They'll probably send her to lockdown so they can watch her. She's not coming back for a while, that's for sure," Char said. "But it also means we're probably going to get some new roommates soon. They won't let beds go empty for very long."

The thought of new personalities in the cottage made Katie cringe. New girls meant new emotional baggage and everyone getting used to each other all over again. At least this family had found balance in its own personal version of weird.

As Mel continued to fret over Brittany being locked in a closet, everyone piled on that there were no closets. Katie, who hadn't taken her eyes off the purse, took her chance to reach down and extract $20 from Brenda's wallet. Her fingers brushed along the side of the cell phone. Katie almost took it, too but realized the loss of a cell phone would launch an immediate search and serious restrictions. She would need a phone at some point but now was not the time to obtain one.

Slipping away from the purse, Katie tucked the $20 in her jeans pocket and sat back down in her seat, pretending to work on some clay fruit for Angelina. She felt power in having the first deposit to her escape fund. Stealing turned out to be pretty easy.

For the next few days, no one slept, and no one was hungry. They moved through their days like zombies. Even Katie felt terrible for Mel who was the most out of sorts. With the housemates disappearing one by one, Mel seemed sure she'd be next. She clung to Chrissy and Char like she was about to drown, and they were the only lifejackets. And everyone stayed away from Katie. After all, she was the last one to be with Brittany.

Katie sat on the edge of her nest in the greenhouse, her head in her hands. She really felt like she was going to be sick. How did all this happen to her? Everything that was happening was doing nothing to move her closer to home. All she was doing was walking home from Angel's. He grabbed her, beat her, and left her bleeding on the ground. And now she was stuck here, surrounded by craziness and pain. She didn't belong here. And she certainly didn't deserve foster care. That "I have to get out of here" feeling, the fear that she might be the next to disappear into the land of the lost—foster care.

Brittany had been gone for about a week. There were rumors though no real information about how or where she was. Katie knew they'd all feel much better if they just learned something. Slowly the daily routine replaced the fear and sorrow. The classroom became a safe place for almost everyone except Mel. Even though Miss Brenda had taken the doors off all the closets, Katie sensed Mel's panic if she had to go near them. To cope, Mel had created routes to get where she needed to go without passing one.

Life was slowly moving on. But Katie was more intent on her escape plan than ever.

Free time came the day she began to get ready in earnest, and everyone scattered. Katie took her long, twisting route to the greenhouse, making sure she wasn't being followed. She had found a good hiding place for her stash and started a list of things she'd need. Katie had to be sure she had everything before she fled. She couldn't afford to be out on the streets without all the necessary items for survival.

Things were still showing up in the greenhouse, but since they didn't seem to be attached to any type of threat, Katie had gotten used to them and didn't respond with her panic at first. This time there were some pretty rocks, some tiny china dishes, and some bits of broken ceramic tiles with flowers painted on them. Tempted to work on adding them to Angelina's tree house, Katie checked herself. The most important thing right now was to make sure her hiding place was secure and that she had a place to stash her escape items. Then she'd work on her plan.

Katie searched every inch of the greenhouse until she finally found the perfect place. On the back wall, high enough that she needed a ladder to reach it, she discovered an old swamp cooler used to cool the greenhouse during the peak of summer heat. It had a grate on the front that had been held on by screens, but they had rusted off, so she could pry it open enough to reach in and out to put things into the well that once held water.

She took out her list and tucked her $20 bill into a jar, tightening the lid to keep it dry just in case, and put it into this vault. "There. This is going to work out great. Now, the list."

She hopped off the ladder and moved it back into the corner. She couldn't afford for Mr. Stanley to suspect her plan.

Katie's thoughts were racing, imagining where she could get the things she was going to need. She cleared off the top of her apple crate desk, paper and pencil in hand. Checking off the items on her list—money—check, cell phone—hold off, food—get from kitchen, warm clothes, something to use for a sleeping bag, rain cover, something to carry it all in—sneak those out at the last minute.... the list grew. No time to lose, she stuffed the list into a gap in the frame of the planting bed and set off to find the things to complete her list.

In the next few days, she collected a couple of trash bags, one to use as a rain cover and one to use as a carry-all. She had a stash of cookies, chips, half a sandwich, and a fried chicken leg that she had salvaged from mealtime leftovers. She was scrounging around the trash behind the cafeteria building when she was startled by a male voice.

"Looking for something special? You're Katie, right?"

Katie recognized Kevin when she looked up from her position hanging over the trash dumpster rummaging in the garbage at the bottom. They had played 'glance tag,' eyeing each other in the dining room. She knew he worked in the kitchen because he always wore an apron smeared with gravy, peanut butter, or some other ingredient of the day ingredient. He was cute, and she was mortified to be caught hanging over the edge of the dumpster.

"Yeah," she managed to say, hoping that the red in her face looked like a healthy glow and not the hideous embarrassment she was feeling. She rubbed the mashed potato slime off her hand onto her jeans and offered to shake. He declined, and she felt the red heat in her face rise to a glowing level.

"Look, if you're still hungry, I can get you something from the kitchen," he said. "Come on in. You'll have to stay in the dining room. No one is allowed in the kitchen but staff. Sorry."

Kevin tossed another bag of trash into Katie's dumpster. He started to walk around the building to go in the front door, but he stopped and turned back to face her. He reached out for the screen door handle and held it open for her. She mumbled a weak 'thanks' and slid past him. She was risking detention, but the thrill of breaking the rules had always been her downfall.

"Won't you get in trouble if we get caught"? Katie whispered as they passed through the kitchen, her imagination spinning at a dizzying speed.

She saw scissors, knives, food, dishes, stacks of soda cans, and huge bags of chips, not to mention the rows of refrigerators filled with all the food she was going to need to start her new life. And Kevin was going to be her access.

She was going to get to know him well, really well.

"We just have to be quiet," he said. "I'm not supposed to let anyone else hang around while I work, but it gets lonesome in the afternoons after everyone leaves. I've seen you around. You sure don't stay long after lunch. Hope it's not the food."

Katie could tell by his smile that she had his attention. Getting access to the kitchen wasn't going to be as hard as she thought.

Over the next two weeks, Katie split her free time between the greenhouse and the cafeteria. Mrs. Kovacs didn't seem to mind the two of them hanging out in the dining room and talking after meals while Kevin cleaned up. In fact, occasionally, she would slip a wink at Kevin when she found them together. Kevin always blushed, and Katie had to turn her head to hide her giggle.

Flirting with Kevin turned out to be more fun than she expected. She learned how to flip her hair and lean in when he told her things like how he got the job as a cook. He cleverly showed the interviewing panel how to make a perfectly healthy pizza and the art of loading the commercial dishwasher and on and on. She couldn't believe anyone could be so passionate about food.

They talked about the restaurant he planned to own someday. "This job is just so I can get the experience of serving large groups. And you guys are a hard crowd to please. And Mrs. K, she's great. She's teaching me about baking."

He was so busy being proud that he never appeared to notice that a fork or a spoon disappeared now and then. Katie really wanted one of his large butcher knives or the scissors he used to cut up the chickens. She needed one of those to cut through the fencing behind the greenhouse.

As the weeks went by, Katie managed to hang back when everyone went out for free time after lunch so she could help Kevin clean up the dining hall. She could tell he looked forward to their time together. He'd changed his routine too. He'd made sure he got his kitchen chores done first so they could be together picking up dishes and napkins and trash.

And as she often did, Katie pretended to search her backpack for something.

"Come on, Katie. We're going to run laps to get ready for the 5K Challenge," Mel called out across the hall.

"Maybe later. I can't find my math homework. I have to do it over." Katie was now lying with ease. Kevin shoved a chair to let her know he was on to her. Katie ducked her head into her collar to stifle a laugh.

Mrs. Kovacs came out of the kitchen with her purse over her arm. Her little pillbox hat was perched on top of her head. Katie thought it was cute how Mrs. K held on to so many of her old-world ways.

"Kevin, I'm off now." Mrs. K turned towards the door as she pulled on her gloves. "Oh, hello, Katie." Turning back to Kevin, she adjusted her tone, adding a touch of firmness. "Be sure you sort out the trash carefully. We're missing some utensils." With a wink, she said, "You two behave." And she slipped out the side door.

Katie wadded up one of the paper tablecloths, and as Kevin locked the door behind Mrs. K, Katie tossed it and hit Kevin squarely on the back of his head.

Soon things were flying, turning a paper toss into a food fight when he planted a leftover piece of cherry pie on her right cheek. He spun around defensively, but when he saw the grin on her face, he called out, "Game on!" It was all over but the mess.

Amid giggles and taunts, he pulled her into the kitchen. He guided her until she leaned back on the counter by the sink. He reached over her to get a dishcloth. Katie felt the heat in the room rise as their eyes met, and he leaned in closer to turn on the water to wet the cloth.

His cheek brushed up against hers. He gently wiped the cherry filling off her face. His lips were dangerously close to their target when he stopped abruptly.

"Wait, stay right there. Don't move. I'll be right back. I need to be sure the doors into the kitchen are locked."

Once he was out of sight, Katie leaped up on the opposite counter, grabbing a knife and the scissors off the magnetic rack on the wall. Shoving both into the outside pocket of her cargo pants, she had just enough time to get back into her position by the sink when he came around the corner.

"Now, where were we..." He smelled good, a mixture of cologne and French fries. His soft lips touched hers, and she forgot all about how she was never going to let this happen. Not with him or anyone.

"Ah, I've got to go. They'll notice if I'm too late. See ya later."

Katie couldn't think of any more graceful way to get out of that kitchen. When Kevin kissed her, her mind filled with dark, smoky memories of how gross it was that the guy, the one who was the reason she's living in a group home, slobbered all over her face. She'd wiped his spit off her face with her shirt. It grossed her out so much that she later threw that shirt away but not until she'd shredded it with a knife, cursing him the whole while. Kevin's kiss was nothing like that, but she couldn't shake the old memory out of the way to make room for what should have been her first real kiss.

She left by the kitchen's back door, coming around to the front of the building so people would think she'd just finished eating late. She saw Darrell stash something under the front steps and then run towards the athletic field. When he was far enough away not to see her, she reached under the steps to retrieve the paper bag he'd hidden. As the campus kiss-ass nerd, he got to work in the office a few days a week, which meant a lot of running off to find people mostly.

She scanned the contents slowly. "Gross." She shoved the girly magazines back into the bag using as few fingers as possible. She didn't want the filth to get under her nails. She pushed the bag and its contents back under the stairs. "Ick, I need to wash my hands," she said as she tried to wipe what she'd seen off her hand by rubbing up and down the legs of her jeans. She sat down on the steps trying to un-see what she'd seen and figure out what she was going to do with the information she now owned.

She realized he was on his way back from the athletic field and hadn't seen her until they both hit the path from the dining hall across the commons. Katie kept a distance between them as if she was afraid his interest in porn might jump from him to her like fleas.

"Oh, there you are. I've been looking for you. Miss Johnson wants you in her office pronto. Some woman is here to see you. I think it's your mom. At least she looks a lot like you."

Broken Hearts and Vision

KATIE DIDN'T WAIT TO HEAR the rest of what he had to say. She was going home! She bolted for the counselor's office, counting the steps as she always did but this time it was not because of dread.

"Mom!" she exploded as she fell into her mother's arms for the best hug ever.

"Katie, dear, goodness." Katie soaked up the smell of her mother's hair and clothes and everything. Katie realized that for the first time in a long time, she smelled her mom's perfume first, not the booze. In fact, her mom didn't smell like a drunk at all.

"I'll just go get my stuff. No, I don't need any of that anymore. Where's Dad? Are we going in his car or yours?"

"Katie, sit down. Listen to what your mom has to say." It was never good when Miss Johnson spoke. Katie's heart began to pound, and her stomach lurched again. She sat next to her mom, and her right leg started to bounce wildly.

Her mom cleared her throat, smoothed her skirt, and then raised her head to look Katie in the eye. With all the sweetness she could muster, she began gently, "Katie, honey. You know I have always tried. I tried so hard not to drink. And your father tried to be patient with me, but it was too much. Too much for me to overcome."

Sweetness and gentleness weren't working for Katie.

Katie was confused. She thought her mom sounded tired, almost pathetic.

Her mom continued with a more confident tone this time. "But when they brought you here, I knew I had to do something, so I checked into rehab. I'm doing great! I have been sober for months now."

"Great, Mom. But when do we go home?" Katie gripped the arm of the chair so tightly that her knuckles were turning white.

"That's just it, dear. Not now. I have to be sure I'm all good, and your dad and I have to get counseling to be sure we can focus on you and not fight. I don't want to relapse and start drinking again. It won't be good for anyone of us."

Katie was confused by how her mother was searching her face for some sort of response, but Katie didn't understand what she wanted. She was trying to pull all this together when her mother spoke again.

"Don't you see, dear?" Her mom leaned in and put her forehead on Katie's, "And you can get the help you need here. Miss Johnson is the best one to help you heal from your ordeal." She leaned back and put both hands on Katie's face. "But I had to see you." She reached out and stroked Katie's hair and around to her chin. Katie pulled back and turned her head away, her lower lip trembling. She pressed her lips together hard so her mom and Ms. Johnson wouldn't see that she was about to crumble.

Suddenly the voices in the room had turned into that adult "waa wa waaa" and all she could think about was that they were going to leave her here. Her parents didn't want her home.

Katie screamed, "Mom, you don't heal from this 'ordeal.'" She leaped to her feet, pressing her fists to her chest. "You just learn to cope with it. You bury it deep where it can't get out, and you move on. What are you thinking?!" She started for the door and turned sharply to face her mother again.

"No, Mom. I'll do great at home. Better than here. You have to take me home. I want to go home." Katie wasn't asking. She was demanding.

Katie watched as her mother's face grew wooden and sad. Tears filled her eyes as she rose, gathering herself and her purse.

"This is best, Katie. I'll be back in a few weeks." Katie watched her mother grip the doorknob and hesitate. She looked down at the floor and slowly reached to pick up her purse. Without looking up again, she said, "Your father sends his love." She kissed Katie on the top of her head and didn't look back.

Katie's heart was working so hard to rewrite this scene. She's going to change her mind. She's going to grab me. And we're going to run out of this place was the only thought in her head. It had to have a better ending than this. But her mother just squared her shoulders and quietly walked out, closing the door behind her.

Stunned, Katie just stood there. What had just happened? She thought she was going home. Was this just step one to giving her up and sending her to live with a strange foster family where she'd be the maid and do all the chores for all the other children? How could they do this to her?

Miss Johnson came around her desk and sat in the chair next to Katie. "Let's talk about how you feel, Katie."

Katie's head flung upright, her back stiff, her jaw rigid.

"I'm not talking to you about anything. This is all your fault. You just want to keep me here so you have a job. Well, that's not going to happen. I'm out of here."

Katie firmly walked out, slamming the door. This was going to end here, and it was going to end now. She was leaving Aspen Meadows. Somehow, she was going home.

Katie was growing more and more exhausted. Every night from that day forward, she fought the nightmares. She called out, cried, tossed and turned, and, sometimes, woke with such a fright that she woke the others.

She knew they were growing annoyed with her. Not wanting to be a problem and put herself on any list for removal to foster care, she knew she had to do something. She needed something to help her sleep. But she couldn't go to the infirmary. Those visits went on your official record, and Katie wasn't going to give Miss Johnson any more reasons to get rid of her. Maybe Mrs. K. would have an answer. Her kitchen was full of all kinds of herbs and stuff.

Katie waited after dinner one night, making sure Kevin was tied up in the kitchen cleaning up. Shyly she approached Mrs. K while she set out the muffins for tomorrow's breakfast. "Mrs. K., Can I talk to you?"

"Why, certainly. What can I do for you?" Mrs. K wiped her hands on the dish towel she always had tucked into whatever was around her waist. "Now, what is it, dear?"

"Can you tell me what I can take to help me sleep? I don't want to go to the nurse. She'll write me up, and I don't want it on my record that I have a problem."

"Of course, dear. You do look tired lately. Come sit down. I want to ask you something." They found a table in the corner that had already been cleaned and set for the next day. This meant they wouldn't be overheard by the rest of the staff still working.

Mrs. K patted the back of Katie's hand. "So, what is interfering with your sleep?"

Katie lowered her head and her voice. "Nightmares."

"Ah, I see. Well, I can certainly give you some teas to drink before bed, but I'm not sure this will get to the source of the problem."

Katie waited. Her eyebrows rose, and her eyes widened. Mrs. K leaned forward and, in a whisper, asked, "You can see it can't you?"

"See what?" Katie wrinkled her brow and squinted her eyes as if that would bring this conversation into focus.

"See into the World of Fantasy." Mrs. K never broke eye contact with Katie, who was sure this was what it felt like to be hypnotized. "Very few can, but I sensed it in you the first time we met over cookies. Concentrate. It will come to you."

As much as she liked Mrs. K, Katie didn't like where this conversation was going. She had hoped for herbs or something, not Ouija board-mystic-voodoo-woo-woo stuff.

"I don't know what you are talking about." But no sooner had she uttered these words than her head began to ache, and pictures began to flash. Angelina was being blown by winds and rain. Lots of rain. Her tree house was rocking back and forth violently. And then it all stopped as suddenly as it had started. Katie's hands involuntarily shot to her head. She blinked hard.

As her focus returned, she heard Mrs. K say, "You see, don't you? You are one of the ones who sees." Mrs. K's smile indicated pride. She took Katie by the hand, and they went into the kitchen to Mrs. K's locked cupboard. Looking around to make sure Kevin hadn't come into the kitchen, she began rattling around through boxes and tins of who knows what. She finally handed Katie a bundle of homemade bags of herbs.

"Just mix a teaspoon of these into a glass of water and drink it after you brush your teeth at night." Katie stared at the gauze pouches in her hands. She looked up at Mrs. K, blinking back the tears that hung off her lashes. "What is it? Why does it happen? And why me?"

"No one really knows, dear, but some of us can see beyond this world to one where amazing and magical things happen." Katie's eyes widened as she struggled to soak in what Mrs. K was telling her. "You will learn to live with it, even enjoy it. My ability lasted for many years; one day, it was gone. I envy you. I loved my adventures to so many exotic places, meeting so many unusual creatures."

Katie wondered if she should tell Mrs. K what she'd seen in her dreams. It's not every day that you tell someone that you see elves. But she had to…

"Angelina and a griffin are in my head. I thought I was going crazy with some mysterious mental illness. So, this is okay?"

"Oh, yes, dear. It's okay. These dreams of fantasy can't harm you. In fact, they could be a source of great comfort. You must learn to go there when you need to rest from this world." She tweaked Katie on the cheek. "But never stay too long. It is not a place where you should live. Just visit and enjoy. Now, you must get back to your cottage, or there will be talk of detention again. Scoot. And tonight, open your mind to Angelina and then follow her."

As Katie turned to leave, she saw Kevin slowly push open the door to the kitchen. She could tell he must have heard them talking from the perplexed look on his face. She shot him a look that clearly said, "Mind your own business." The kitchen door slowly closed in agreement. Katie thanked Mrs. K for the herbs and pushed past Kevin as she walked in a very straight line to the front door of the dining hall. She walked slowly back to the cottage. Tonight she dressed for bed slowly, thoughtfully, ignoring Mel's nightly closet check and Chrissy's lecture on the topic of the day. She watched as Char struggled, as she did every night, with how empty Annie's bed was except for Miss Mousie tucked in under the blankie. Finally, tucked in herself, with the blankets snug between her knees and her back pressed firmly against the wall, she took a deep breath. As the lights went out, she imagined Angelina snuggling down in her nest under the stars. They both fell asleep.

Longing to Belong

DAYS TURNED INTO WEEKS AND more. As the months went by, Angelina grew more comfortable with her place in the Woods. The pain of her experience with Trek's people had numbed, and she was resigned to making a home for herself. She was going to prove that she was not clueless. She could take care of herself.

She'd even made friends. The squirrels were generous in sharing some of their hiding places, so she had nuts as the days drew colder. The birds had led her to little-known patches of berries. Mauve and Joseph called on her often and taught her how to preserve fruits and vegetables for the winter. She was learning to knit and was doing well enough to make herself a sweater and some slippers.

Joseph had added some shelves to her hollow where she kept bits of fabric and the crafting supplies she had picked up here and there. She suspected that Mauve was leaving the bits of fabric in places where Angelina would find them. Really, how else would a folded yard of fabric just happen to get lost in the Woods? Angelina appreciated that Mauve and Joseph were quite clever scavengers. They brought her lots of useful things, like a thimble to use as a bucket for the sap so she could glue things together. She was proud of the paint brushes she'd made out of sticks and animal hair she'd found caught in a bush.

Joseph had also brought her a gift. Somehow, he'd found an old clock and fixed it up for her. He was so proud when he presented it. Angelina was pleased that he thought she was special enough to go to all that trouble.

"Joseph, it's lovely, really it is, and I really like it. But." She paused and smiled at him, hoping to gauge his temperament before continuing.

"Yes, dear, but what?" He didn't seem to have a clue.

She pondered this for a moment, and she chose her words carefully, not wanting to hurt his feelings. "There aren't any hands. How can I tell the time without hands?"

"My dear, you're in the Enchanted Woods. You only need to know it is Now. There is no need to worry about the past or the future. Hands would be useless!" He winked at her and gave her a bit of a pinch on the cheek. Angelina giggled. She had never known her grandparents, but she liked to think that they would be just like Mauve and Joseph.

Trek also came by to visit now and then. She suspected he just wanted to see what mess she'd made of things since his last visit but liked that he came to see her. She liked having company. She still found his arrogance and familiarity really annoying, though. He acted like God's gift, and she owed him somehow. He talked a lot about his family and friends. And she envied how lucky he was.

"So, why are you all living in the Woods? Are you really bandits? I've heard people living in the woods are all bandits and thieves."

Trek laughed. "No, not at all. My ancestors decided to stop traveling and settled in the Woods. They believed in living in harmony with nature: you know, leaving no mark of their existence. Like the native people."

"Like the American Indians? We read about them back home." She could say "back home" now without crying, even though she still missed her mother so much.

"Come on, I'll show you." Trek showed her how they farmed in odd patches all over the Woods, not in rows. He explained that by using this method, they could hide their existence from anyone who might venture this deep into the wilderness and still not disturb the natural plan of the Woods. After all, God doesn't plant vegetables in straight rows, so why should they?

He showed her how they made syrup from the tree sap, gathered honey from the bees, and made jellies from fruit. They built their homes like the animals do. Since trees in this part of the Woods could grow to over eight feet in diameter, it was easy to hide a house by building it out of bark and digging deep into the hillside for more space and shelter. Roofs were covered with duff and moss and their fires were always kept small, so the smoke was rarely detected. Most of the warmth radiated from rocks kept hot by glowing coals, not burning wood.

They paused their tour when Angelina got the courage to talk about that first night in the village. "I'm glad your friends trust me," she said. She was fishing for information but hoped it wasn't too obvious.

"Oh, they don't trust you." Trek let out a short laugh at Angelina's mistake. "Not yet at least. Magda and I convinced them that you aren't a threat to our secret life. They're willing to accept you as an occasional visitor to the village but not without reservation." He turned to face her. "There are still many in the village that are suspicious. They're not shy about making it known." He picked up a twig and picked at it nervously.

Angelina avoided eye contact with Trek. She didn't want him to see how much it hurt to hear.

"But Magda said to bring a basket of berries or nuts to share when I visit. That helps, doesn't it?"

"Oh, yeah, that's a nice idea."

"Conda lets me go the schoolhouse. I really like being able to go to the schoolhouse." Again, Angelina was fishing. She thought being allowed in the school meant she was welcome. Now, she wasn't so sure.

"Being home-schooled, I'd never seen so many books in one place!"

She'd been most excited to find out they had a library of books. Conda was very secretive about where they came from but generous in letting her borrow them as long as she brought them back promptly, as promised.

"It was nice of Conda to convince everyone to let me borrow the books." Angelina had learned that Conda, the pretty young wife who'd spoken up for Angelina when she first arrived in the village that day with Trek, was the teacher. She had invited Angelina to visit the school. She searched Trek's face hoping to find that he thought these were all good signs, too. But he just stared at the twig, picking off the bark.

Thinking back to those early days of visiting the village, Angelina remembered how, at first, she couldn't figure out why they needed a school.

This group only had two children. But when she was invited to the schoolhouse, she was amazed to see at least a dozen of all ages.

Angelina had asked Conda, "Where they'd all come from?"

Conda was amused at Angelina's lack of awareness and had explained, "The Woods are full of people. They live in groups of about a dozen families to keep their secret and to make sure there is enough food and shelter for everyone. The children from all the surrounding villages attended my school to meet others and make new friends."

"Angelina? Hello? Earth to Angelina?" Trek teased her out of her daydream.

"I was just thinking about Conda. She's really nice. And so's your dad. I appreciated him speaking up for me when they were all so angry that you brought me to see Magda about the gunk on my hand."

Angelina was painfully aware of how awkward this conversation was, but it was so nice to have someone to talk to that she didn't want it to end.

"Yeah, Dad's great. His name, Gastor, means great thoughts. He's really a caring man and one everyone looked to for guidance. He gets that from his dad and his grandfather. My grandfather was great. I really loved spending time with him. He loved to carve things. His dad, my great-grandfather, was a carver too. He carved an amazing box that we use for the collections at church. They all were Elders."

Trek proudly continued explaining to Angelina about the Elders and how each village had one Elder representing their group when the leaders gathered several times a year to discuss life in the Woods.

"My dad was selected by their group because he's fair and willing to listen to everyone regardless of age or occupation. See, everyone in the group has a job to do, one that we love and that allows us to contribute. Each family is expected to provide for themselves but not at the expense of others."

He turned to look at her like he wanted to be sure she was listening. Angelina realized this was important stuff that he was sharing. She watched his face light up with pride at telling her about his friends and family, making her smile. He smiled back, obviously glad to see that she was watching his every move. He continued.

"Stealing, lying, or greed are not tolerated. And everyone's success is acknowledged equally. Like when Thork, the young guy who tends the goats, made himself new milk buckets, everyone gathered to celebrate his workmanship. Dad gave a grand speech. We all congratulated Thork, and he got the first serving at dinner. That's a sign of great honor when you've done something to make something better."

"So, how do you buy things? You know, things like your tools and stuff?"

"We go into town several times a month and sell stuff at the flea market."

Flea market! This was the first Angelina had heard of a flea market. That had to mean going into town. This could be her way out.

Angelina's heart raced. "Oh! When do we go?!"

"Whoa. Back up, missy. Nobody's going to trust you that far. That path must be kept secret so outsiders don't find a way to get into the Enchanted Woods."

Angelina felt a sinking sensation in her stomach. How could he just point blank tell her no like that?

He must have realized how shocking that seemed to Angelina, so he continued. "Look, most humans have no respect for the Woods. Look at the damage they do where they camp and fish and hunt. The only way to keep this part of the Woods safe was to keep it secret."

Her unspoken disappointment hung in the air like a dense fog. "Come on. I've got lots of cool stuff to show you." He held out his hand to help her, and she took it.

As the months went by, her frustrations grew. She'd tried to trick Trek into letting her go to the flea markets. Each attempt failed. Every time she had a chance to drop by the village, she'd begged Magda and Conda to let her go with them, but no one would give in. By now, Angelina had given up yet hoped to earn the trust so they'd let her go along one day.

Angelina envied this life, so different from hers with her family and the other elves. Here, everyone cared for everyone else. They weren't competitive or greedy. Elves were constantly working to have something better, bigger, and more than their neighbors. These villagers had a sense of contentment she'd never known before.

Most importantly, no one hit anyone else. She was still trying to get used to not living in fear. She wondered if she'd ever really trust someone.

They also talked a lot about God. And they made a point to ask her to join them for church every week. Angelina was very uncomfortable with this. She couldn't decide if they were ignorant fools believing in something that didn't exist or if they really knew something she didn't. How could she believe that there was someone who loved and cared for His children when He'd let her be beaten and ignored most of her life by the very people who were supposed to protect her? And if He did exist, why hadn't He loved and cared for her all those years? Why was she stuck here, and why couldn't she go home and find parents who would treat her like these people treated their children? None of this made sense to her, so when they prayed to God, she looked at the ground and counted pebbles. She was starting to be accepted and couldn't risk them throwing her out because she didn't believe.

One Sunday after church, Angelina overheard a small group of women talking.

"She never prays. During prayer time, I've seen her looking at the ceiling or braiding her hair."

"I know, and she never puts anything in the offering box. You'd think she could come up with a little something."

"How is she supposed to get money, Alana? She can't go to town to sell anything?"

"Well, she could make something and have Trek sell it for her. They spend enough time together."

Each woman's comment was wrapped in disappointment, more intense than the last. Angelina slipped past unnoticed. She dropped her head so her hair fell in sheets on either side of her face, hiding her tears.

"They can be so nice to each other. Why not to me?" Angelina sniffled under her breath. "How can I ever be good enough?"

But tonight, happy to be at home in her hollow making herself dinner, she looked at her salad and declared it wonderful. Bright greens, ripe, juicy currents, and crisp pine nuts tossed together in the acorn cap bowl made her mouth water. All that was left was to slice the puffy round mushroom, and dinner would be served.

"I should invite Mauve and Joseph for dinner one of these days. Mmmmm, a glass of raspberry juice would be perfect."

Angelina reached for the juice jug, pleased with the jug she'd made out of a gourd. Careful not to glue her fingers together again, she used the sap to glue a twig for a handle and berry juice to paint flowers on the sides. She stopped and looked around her little house. Its cozy warmth made her happy.

Her home was full of gifts. Conda had found a postcard of a mountain scene and framed it for Angelina as a thank you for watching the schoolchildren one afternoon when she was sick. Angelina liked being with the children and hoped she could help out again. She was still very cautious about getting too close to any of the older people, but now and then, it was nice to be with them. It wasn't often that she let herself get lonesome, but when she really missed her mother, spending time with the children helped her forget.

Once, on a trip to the flea market, Gastor, Trek's dad, had given him $15 to buy some things for her. He'd brought her the rug and the bell on the front gate she and Joseph had built. On the way home, Trek found a beautiful plate in a trash heap, but it was broken on the trip back. She'd used the pieces to make a perfect tile floor for the entry to her hollow. She'd almost given up hope of going to the flea market and found she enjoyed finding things in the Woods anyway.

She walked across the room to get her utensils from the basket on one of the shelves Joseph had put up. She loved the feel of the rug under her bare feet. Absentmindedly she reached up to her necklace and sighed as she thought of how proud her mother would be. She pushed away the thought of how her father would have made fun of everything she had done.

No, bad memories were not going to ruin this moment. Her little home was just about perfect, complete with treasures that made her happy. What could be better than living in a place where you're surrounded by the sounds of birds and the sweet smells of the forest, and gifts from friends?

Dinner was good. Now that her tummy was full, she had a few nighttime chores to do before dark. Even though the stars were bright, it was still very dark on nights like this when there was no moon. While she tidied up, putting her dishes away, she realized the breeze was picking up.

"Looks like tonight might be windy." Then, listening intently, she realized there were no bird sounds. She had learned that birds always find shelter before a storm. This silence warned Angelina that tonight it might rain, too.

She stowed all her loose items in her acorn baskets to keep them from blowing or getting wet.

"That should do it," she assured herself and climbed the vine ladder into her nest. The canopy of leaves above her bed had always kept her warm and dry. She snuggled down under her quilt. She thought this was a good home. She smiled as she heard the voices of the fairies singing the lullaby she'd heard every night since she came here. As she drifted off the sleep, she heard, "Your Father loves you," and felt the lightest brush of a kiss on her cheek.

Sleeping was difficult. The winds continued to blow harder and harder. Her nest bobbed and swayed with every gust. It wasn't long before lightning split the skies. Thunder crashed in response. Angelina instinctively grabbed the sides of her nest like the sides of a small boat being tossed in the rolling seas. She bit her lower lip as her mind raced, trying to decide what to do. She needed to get out of her nest. Where was the closest shelter?

Another flash, crash, and sheets of rain flattened the leaf canopy above her, drenching her to the bone. Sweeping her dripping hair out of her eyes, she gripped the vine ladder and began her descent; being on the ground had to be better than where she was now. The winds blew her ladder wildly in circles, and she hung on tightly to keep from falling. The last thing she heard was a deafening clap of thunder. In the blinding flash of the lightning, she saw her beautiful home swept away in the winds. The last thing she felt was falling.

Fear and Escape

KATIE FELT A WAVE OF dread flow over her, like something awful had just happened. She looked around her trying to pinpoint the source, but all she saw was Kevin up to his elbows in suds and a mound of dirty dishes. "That was weird."

"What?" Kevin wiped his hands on his apron, took her hand, and pulled her in for a bear hug.

"I just felt like something terrible was about to happen."

"Everything's fine. Come on, let me show you how to make world-class mashed potatoes."

Katie followed him around the island to the far side of the kitchen, giggling at how anyone could be so passionate about mashed potatoes. She avoided his grasp as he reached out for her.

"No, I have to get back to the cottage. The girls are starting to talk about where I go at free time. We don't want to get caught."

She gave him a peck on the cheek and headed out the back door, past the dumpster, and across the commons. She was aware that she was leading him on, but he was cute and she really liked him. She knew he'd be upset with her. She also knew that the only way she could get what she wanted was to keep some distance. It was getting harder to steal from such a nice guy.

Bounding up the steps to the cottage, she heard the evening conversation begin as it did almost every night lately, "Anyone talked to Brittany? I bet they won't let her out of the closet to talk to anyone."

"Mel, enough with the closet!" Chrissy threw her pillow at Mel and hit her square in the back of her head.

Mel responded by throwing her pillow, but it bounced off the frame of Chrissy's bunk and hit Char. That did it. It was a free for all, and Katie had to join in. Feathers, stuffing, and the collateral damage of stuffed animals were all over the cottage when they were interrupted by a knock on the door.

Mel was the closest, so she opened the door to find Darrell standing there. His overfriendly, kiss-up manner annoyed everyone. Katie didn't like Darrell even more now that she'd found his stash. Actually, no one really liked him.

"May I speak to Miss Char, please?" he said.

Mel stepped aside, and he sauntered past her, shuffling through the pillow debris. "Char, Miss Johnson wants you in her office now. Told me to get your brothers, too."

The entire group froze. This couldn't be good. They all stood silent as if they had been playing Spin the Statue.

"Why?" Char pushed the torn pillow and Miss Mousie off her lap as she stood to face him.

"I don't know. There's some lady there. Looks like a social worker to me." He picked at a zit on his face. "I did hear them say something about her taking your brothers. I'd suggest you hurry. It seemed important."

Katie watched as the entire group refused to move. 'Foster care' hung in the air like a stench, making her feel sick. She reached out to touch Char as she began to pace the room and rant a long string of expletives.

"I have to get them out of here." Char turned to face the group, planting her feet firmly. "I will not let them take my boys. They have my baby sisters. That should be enough. No! They can't have them." She was choking the words out between sobs. "What am I going to do?" She sank down on her bed.

Katie bit her lip and thought about her plan. She'd stolen almost enough to get herself out of here. Adding two little boys to her plan would jeopardize her getting away. She looked at the panic on Char's face. But how could she let their family be split up into little pieces? Katie didn't stop to think about whether it was enough for three or not. In the flash of that moment, she stepped towards Darrell and took charge.

"Darrell, go get the boys but tell them to get to the kitchen dumpster. And don't you dare tell anyone, and I mean anyone, or I'll make sure you never get any privileges again."

He started to speak, but she interrupted him. "Don't even think about it. I know what you keep under the steps to the gym, and I won't hesitate to tell. And if you find a new hiding place, I will find it. Now get."

Darrell backed out the door and staggered as he turned to run down the front steps.

"Char, come with me," Katie said.

Katie and Char stepped out onto the front porch. Darrell was halfway across the commons, probably going to report back to Miss Johnson like a good little weasel.

"Look, I can get them out. Don't ask how but I've been working on it for a while. I'll take them with me." She paused for a minute, reading the look of panic on Char's face. "I'll send you a letter in a pink envelope and tell you where we are. It will have to be in code, but I'll make sure you can figure it out. Don't worry. I'll make sure they're safe, and no one finds them. You go stall Miss Johnson and whoever's in her office."

Char was frozen as she faced Katie. "No, there is no way I'm going to be separated from my brothers. This is crazy, Katie. You'd never get away with it. I can't risk it."

"You don't have a choice. If we all run they'll know right away and have the cops out after us before we could get a few blocks from here. If you go and stall them, your brothers and I will have a chance to escape. Look, Char. What you can't risk is going to foster care. You have to trust me on this one." Katie's voice was calm and confident. Her gaze never left Char's. "Go. Makeup something about where your brothers are and send them on a wild goose chase trying to find them on campus. I'll get them out of here, and they'll never find us."

Katie could see Char weighing the options, and her face clearly reflected that there were none. "Okay. Tell the boys we're going to play the lizard and the fly. It'll keep them from being afraid." In response to Katie's confused look, she added, "It's our version of Hide & Seek. And have them pinky swear to follow the rules and no cheating."

Char started down the steps of the porch but stopped. She turned on her heels and charged back to Katie, who was sure Char had just lost her nerve. "Thank you. Take good care of them. They're all I've got." Char kissed Katie on the cheek and disappeared across the commons.

Katie dashed back into the cottage, grabbed her jacket and a few other pieces of clothes, stuffing them into her book bag. As she ran back out onto the porch, she stopped long enough to see if she could see Char. And then Katie was gone.

She heard Mel whine, "Where is she going?" as Katie ran dangerously close to the bushes that had frightened her for so long.

Breathless, she found the boys waiting for her at the dumpster, out of sight of most of the campus. Mark had his hand pressed tight to his lips. Nathan's brow was deeply furrowed. Katie dismissed the confused looks on the boy's faces. "Come on, boys. We're the lizards. Stay close to me."

"What is going on? Where's Char?" Neither of them budged except to back up closer to the dumpster.

"Never mind for now. I'll fill you in later. Right now, you have to keep up and keep quiet."

Kevin must have heard her because he stepped out of the kitchen, wiping his hands on a dish towel. "Hey, what's up?"

Katie reached for the boys' shoulders and gently pushed them behind her. "Hey, these little guys have an appointment in the office, and they are late. I offered to fetch them to get it all back on track."

Kevin's expression was confused. Katie had to think fast. "Yep, they're late, all right."

"But I thought Darrel did all the fetching around here. In fact, looks like he's headed across the commons now. Let him take them, and you can stay and hang out for a bit." He tossed the towel and leaned back on the door frame. She knew that seductive move and had to think fast to dodge it without suspicion.

"Ah, Darrell had something else to do, so I took this one. Come on, guys. Let's get moving." She began herding the boys towards the side door, the shortest route to the greenhouse and the only way to avoid running into Darrell. With as much cheer as she could muster, she tossed over her shoulder, "Rain check." And they were gone.

They clamored to fall into step with Katie as if they were being manipulated by the same puppet strings. Both boys stopped and turned to look back over the commons. Char had just stepped down from the porch of the office when she spotted them. Seeing the boys lean forward as if they were about to run to her, she held up her hand, warning them to step back. Then she gave them a reverse wave that told them not to come to her. Once she saw they understood, Katie watched Char clasp her little fingers to one another in a pinky swear. She knew the boys had understood the code and led them slowly around the corner of the dining hall.

"We're going to play the Lizard and the Fly game, and Char said you have to pinky swear not to cheat." Katie led them past the steam plant and to the back side of the green house where her broken window was jutting out as always. She pressed upwards until the window was open enough for each of them to shinny through. Once they were all inside, Katie looked them both in the eyes.

"Look, guys, I lied. We're running away. They want to put you all in foster care, and you're not going if I can do anything about it. Look, guys, we can do this."

Mark's lip started to quiver and Katie's heart began to ache for the little guy. Five was too young to have to be running away.

"Nathan, you're a big boy. Seven is almost grown up. Now help your brother. We need to look for anything we might need to take care of ourselves." Katie tried to sound perky like this was an adventure. She didn't think they bought it—she didn't. "We're out of here."

Nathan stopped short and dug in his heels. "What about Char? We can't go without Char."

"She's stalling them in the office so we can get away. As soon as we get settled, we'll let her know where we are so she can find us. Get a couple of those burlap bags and some string. We can always use string." Neither of the boys moved. "Git! We don't have much time."

Katie dragged an apple crate into place so she could reach into her hiding place to get the things she'd squirreled away. She was glad she'd gotten Kevin's watch and class ring. They just might be worth enough to get three bus tickets.

"Come on, guys, time to go." She took the few things they had gathered and stuffed it all in a burlap bag with her clothes but kept the knife, and the shears tucked in her jacket pocket. She herded the boys back out the window and around the corner towards the fence, dropped her bag on the ground, and started to climb up the chain link. About two-thirds up, the fence began to wave and flex, causing her to lose her balance. She fell and knocked Mark to the ground underneath her.

"You broke my arm!"

"Shush. Let me see." She ran her hand up and down his arm, squeezing gently. "It's not broken. Get up and hang onto this bag for me." Reluctantly he rolled over and rubbed his arm again.

Katie dug the shears out of her pocket and started cutting the chain link behind an evergreen bush. She turned to see how confused the boys looked. "Look, we don't want anyone to find out how we get out. This will be hard to find, and it'll buy us time. Come on, out."

Katie knew the minute they were found missing, Darrell would lose his courage and squeal, and Miss Johnson would call in an Amber Alert. They were running out of time. They'd already wasted too much time getting this far.

Clear Coast Filled With Cops

THE THREE OF THEM SCRAPED their way out onto the alley, looking to see if anyone had seen them. "The coast is clear," little Mark declared bravely. Nathan shot him a glare that made Katie smirk.

"This way," she said and led them down the alley, then across the street, then down the next alley, zig-zagging their way toward downtown. She told them to pretend they were playing that game of hide and seek in case they were spotted. "Act natural, not too fast. Don't draw attention."

It was blocks until they got to Union Street, and Katie knew right where she was. Just another few more blocks, and she'd be where she wanted to be. She pointed to a bus stop bench, and the boys sat down obediently.

As Katie rummaged in her bag, gathering the things she intended to pawn, Mark's quivering voice broke her concentration. "Katie, why are we running?"

She looked at his sad little face. She reached out and stroked his cheek.

"Darrell said some lady had come to take you boys away, and Char freaked out. I promised her I'd get you someplace safe so she could come and get you. You know, she's almost old enough to be able to take care of you by herself. Foster care won't be an option. I just have to hide you until then."

Katie's heart sank when she saw Nathan's concern was still reflected in his face.

"But where are we going? Where are we going to sleep?" And why should we trust you? How do we know you're not going to sell us to some creepy people?" Nathan's voice was adamant.

"I get it. You're scared. I am too. But how would I know that you and Char always pinky swear on things that are important? Why would I include you in my escape plans, let you slow me down? Why? Because Char's my friend, and this is important to her."

Nathan looked at her intensely. She stared at them both hoping to see some signs of acceptance if not agreement. Mark tugged at Nathan's sleeve, pulling him over so they could talk in confidence. His little whisper was loud enough that she heard him say, "She did know about pinky swear. Char would never tell anyone unless they were a friend."

"We're going to a place where we'll be safe. The house is empty. We can stay there, and nobody'll know we're there. I just have to pawn this stuff to get us some bus tickets, that's all." She pointed to the bus bench. "Wait here." Mark looked up at Nathan clearly not sure if they were doing the right thing. "We're going to be fine," she said as she patted his cheek again. "Pinky swear."

She shoved her burlap bag towards Nathan and, giving Mark the evil eye of "don't you move," she headed across the street to the store with the big "Pawn here for big bucks" sign.

The alert bell rang as she pushed the door open. The wall of cool air hit her in the face, and it felt really good after all that running.

"Hello, little lady. What can I do for you?" The clerk rubbed his hands down his pants legs and then slicked back his greasy hair.

Katie dropped her pile on the counter—the knife, Kevin's class ring and his watch, a compact she'd slipped off Miss Johnson's desk, and a silver spoon she'd found in the pile left by her secret Santa in the greenhouse. Last, she added Mel's hand mirror and Chrissy's jeweled lipstick case.

"I'd like to pawn these, please."

The guy behind the counter looked her over. His hair was oily, refusing to stay put and hanging in his face. Every time he pushed it back out of his way, his dirty fingernails made her avoid touching anything he had just touched. He fingered everything she laid out until he came to the watch. "Nice watch. Where'd you get this one?"

"My brother just joined the army and gave it to me before he left. With that ring too. He said I should have fun while he was gone, so he won't care that

I've hocked 'em. Are they worth much?" She was working very hard not to sound eager or greedy.

"You know, I'm going to have to look this one up. You just wait here, and I'll be right back." He hitched up his worn blue jeans, cleared his throat, and stepped into the back room.

Katie wandered the store looking at all the things people had once treasured and had now put out there for the first buyer. How sad, she thought when she saw all the wedding rings. As she wandered along the back wall thinking all she needed was enough for three bus tickets, she heard him on the phone.

"Yeah. I don't buy the 'brother gave it to me' story. She might be the one the Amber Alert is about. No, she's alone. No boys. Yeah, I'll stall her till you get here."

He hung up. Katie darted back to the counter. As he came back into the store, she brushed all her offerings into her hands and raced for the door.

"Hey, wait! Come back. Let's talk about money."

But she was gone. Katie hit the door hard, making the bell intended to welcome customers scream. She grabbed the bag, grabbed Mark by the hand, and shouted, "Now!" In the panic, Mark's hand slipped from hers, and the boys ran across the street without stopping to look either way for traffic.

"Boys, quick, run."

A police car was just coming around the corner, and she waved at Mark and Nathan to follow her. "Now!" but in their panic, the boys ran across the street, turning right up an alley. To avoid the police car, she had no choice but to run left.

Katie ran down every alley and street, praying she'd cross their path. Exhausted, she would have given anything for a chair and a soda right now, everything except those boys. She'd promised to keep them safe, and now she'd lost them all in the first two hours. What was she thinking? How did she think she could get them all to the farm? She'd never forgive herself if anything happened to them.

Just as she started to cry, still running and searching, she saw Nathan about a block away at the end of the alley. He just stood there, rigid.

"Nathan!" He didn't seem to hear her. "Nathan! Where's Mark?" Still, he didn't acknowledge her, so she ran faster in his direction.

She crossed the street, dodging cars and shouting at him over the traffic. She saw what had his attention: a police officer backing him up to the wall of an office building.

She ducked behind a dumpster and dropped her head as she realized another officer had Mark grasped by the back of the neck of his shirt.

"Shit."

That was all there was to be said. She'd not only lost them, but she had also handed them over to the very people they were running from. She sank to the ground and put her hands over her eyes. They'd go to the worst foster home now. Some military guy who'd whip them into shape, make men out of them before they ever got to middle school. They would be miserable, and it was all her fault.

And Char! Char would never forgive her. She'd hunt her down and make Katie miserable. Just as her pity party was about to go full swing, Katie heard someone at the end of the alley. She froze. Footsteps seemed to be coming this way. She slid on the garbage until she was behind the dumpster, pressed up against the brick wall.

"I don't see her. She must have gone the other way. I'll get the squad car, head back to Union, and see if anyone's seen her. You take those two back to the station."

The sound of footsteps grew faint and finally disappeared.

Katie waited for about an hour more, shooing a very mangy cat away from her to preserve her hiding place. As dusk set in, she crept out, covered in stench, and terrified. She had no choice but to keep close to the shadows she feared the most. Lugging her burlap bag, she made her way toward the railroad tracks. She was glad she hadn't told the boys exactly where she was taking them. There was no way they could tell. Nobody knew where she was or where she was heading. She was on her own. Alone.

She walked, her shoulders sagging, barely able to pick up her feet, not because she was tired but because her future was nothing more than a long straight road to—who knows where. She could hear Mrs. K telling her to let go, let the fantasy world fill her mind with possibilities.

"I can sure use some possibilities about now," was all she could manage. Finally, at the edge of town, she came to the tracks and, best of all, the culvert that ran under them. The ground was mostly dry. All except the rivulet of stormwater that ran down the middle. Under the light of a streetlamp, Katie could see one puddle of water in the gutter.

It looked clear enough to wash her face and hands and maybe get some of the garbage off her jeans. As she leaned over, she was so startled that she fell back on her heels. That was not her reflection.

She didn't have pointed ears.

Overcome by curiosity, she slowly leaned forward and looked again. This time it was her face that she saw.

"I must need sleep."

In the middle of the culvert, Katie arranged her clothes into a pillow. She drank half of the water bottles she'd hoarded from a field trip they'd taken to the zoo and ate one of her protein bars, another stashed.

She was exhausted by the thought of what was happening to the boys. Her mind spun as she tried to imagine how to break them out again. But she couldn't risk getting caught with all this stolen stuff. She'd go to jail for sure.

"How did I get from hanging out at Angel's house to being a thief running from the cops?"

Then the rain started. "Great."

The sarcasm and irony were not lost on her as she climbed up as high as she could on the walls—and slid down the culvert, drenching her feet in the cold rising water.

"The only place for miles to get out of the rain, and I get soaked from falling in." She looked out into the rain and yelled, "I could use some help now."

Near the top of the culvert was a ledge, but as she climbed up the walls, she kept losing her footing, and more than once, she slid down, soaking her feet in the icy water again. She finally made it to the ledge. It was small and cold. Katie didn't sleep much until near dawn.

The sunlight slashed deep into the culvert when she slid into a dreamless sleep. Katie was awakened abruptly.

"That's so rude," she echoed as she rubbed her eyes, stood up carefully, and slid down the side of the rounded tunnel, avoiding the slimy mud that ran in a tiny river at her feet. After scrounging another protein bar and more water, she gathered her things back into her burlap bag and crawled up onto the railroad tracks. An early start meant she'd avoid the heat.

She looked over her shoulder to make sure the town was behind her. "This is the right direction." She chuckled, well aware that she was talking to herself again.

"I wish I knew what time it is. Duh. I guess when you steal something to pawn and forget you have it—is it really yours?"

She dug into the bag to find Kevin's watch.

"Ok, 10:38. I've been walking forever. When we drove to the farm, it took about two hours, so I won't get there until tomorrow." A heavy sigh rushed out of her, causing her shoulders to slope in despair. "No going back now."

She trudged on. Several times during the day, she had to jump off the tracks and hide in the bushes that lined most of the way, trading one fear for another. Still afraid to be near bushes where someone waiting to grab her might hide, she knew she couldn't let an engineer see her. They'd report a young girl walking on the tracks with a burlap bag bulging with whatever, and she'd be headed to juvenile hall before the day was over.

By dusk, she'd found a small grove of trees surrounded by alfalfa fields. It was a great place to spend the night. At least better than her lodgings last night.

"Okay, now for a bed." She tore off a bunch of alfalfa, made a pile just about as long as she was tall, dumped the contents of her bag on the ground, and spread the burlap over the pile. "Nice. But this burlap is scratchy. Ah, this shirt will do."

Spreading the extra shirt she'd brought over the burlap was good. She pulled off her shoes and socks and gently rolled herself down onto her bed. Eating another protein bar and opening the last water bottle, she watched the sun slide down behind the green, waving mass of alfalfa.

Sometime during the night, Katie was awakened by the frightening feeling that she was being watched. Something or someone was rustling the leaves around her.

"Shit, why didn't I get a flashlight while I was stealing things?" she whispered, still hoping that whatever it was wouldn't know she was there.

A "hoot!" made Katie jump. Then, suddenly, something large and black descended on her from the top of one of the trees. Screaming, she leaped up and took a defensive stance that she imagined a Ninja would be ready to attack.

The owl landed in front of her, talons wrapped tightly around a mouse that was in the process of snacking on one of her protein bars. Within a blink, they both were gone.

Katie sank to the ground in the middle of what was left of her bed.

"Okay, so that was scary. Big brave Ninja saved by a mouse-eating owl. This place is making me crazy."

She rolled her blouse into a ball and tucked it under her ear. The alfalfa smelled sweet as she breathed deeply, hoping her heart would stop racing soon. Finally, she fell back asleep again, under the burlap bag this time.

The next day, scratching the rash left by the burlap sleeping bag, Katie was no longer walking on the railroad tracks. She'd learned that walking in the ditch formed by the raised bed of the tracks and the fields below was much easier than walking on the stone rubble that filled the gaps between the railroad ties. She was also harder to see down that low; if she came across a farmer out on a tractor in his fields, she could duck down until he passed.

Stopping to mop the sweat from her forehead and neck, she dug into her bag for the water, glad she hadn't finished it all last night. "I'd better get there soon, or I'll have to start stealing water too."

So far, nothing had looked familiar, but one field of alfalfa or hay looked pretty much like any other, so that wasn't a surprise.

Tipping the bottle and draining far more than she should, Katie spotted something far off to the left that she thought she knew. A large rusty red barn with a tall silo. She strained to look at it closer. She was sure she'd seen it before.

"Yes!" It was the barn of the farm just before her grandparent's. She'd made it! A few more miles and she'd reach home. Or at least what was going to be home for now.

The next mile seemed like ten. How was it that the closer you got to where you were going, the longer it seemed to take to get there? Finally, she saw things she really did recognize. A grove of trees, a cluster of bushes, a curve in the road, and finally, she could see it. She stood still and soaked it all in. The white farmhouse with green shutters with a porch that wrapped around it like her grandpa's strong arms. The lilac bushes were in full bloom. The only thing missing was Nana in the garden.

Her steps quickened as she walked down the long road to the house. Katie's heart was all a jumble with feelings of hope and joy, and sadness. The last time she came to see her grandmother Nana was so thin and pale. Katie remembered how she smelled of old people and nutmeg. Katie would never forget holding her Nana's hand that last time. It was boney but so soft, and Katie had said she should paint her nails because they were a funny yellow color. A rosy pink would have looked nice on her. Katie was glad her mom had done it. Nana's hands looked pretty in the casket.

The front steps still creaked. The key was still under the corner of the worn-out old rug in front of the wicker loveseat and two rockers. It was eerie how everything was as if Grandpa had gone down to the barn and Nana was in the root cellar getting a jar of beans. The screen door squeaked a welcoming hello, and Katie opened the door.

Her eyes filled with tears. She wanted to shout, "Nana, we're here." She wanted to run and hug her Nana and hear her mother and father's heavy footsteps coming up the front stairs. She always packed everything she knew she couldn't live without for two weeks on the farm.

Instead, she pushed dangling cobwebs out of her way and soaked in the view of the living room through the haze of dust motes playing in the sunlight. "I'm home..." she whispered, wiping tears from her face. "I'm home, Nana."

Nobody's Home but the Memories

KATIE WANDERED FROM ROOM TO room, greeting memories in each one, making sure all her favorite things were right where they should be. Once she was quite sure the first floor was in order, she climbed the staircase to the second floor. She was alone, and the house was secured from critters and vandals. Grandpa and Nana each had their own rooms. Grandpa's smelled like a mixture of alfalfa and pipe tobacco. His nightshirt was hanging on the hook behind the door, and his work boots were placed neatly by the bed as if he had taken them off for the day.

Nana's room smelled like lavender and nutmeg. Katie walked up to the dresser as if it were an altar. Nana's jewelry box was one of Katie's favorite things in the world. Nana used to let her play dress up with her costume jewelry. Katie smiled as she pulled out the strands of pearls and the clip-on rhinestone earrings she used to don to pretend she was a queen.

She lifted the tray to reveal the hidden bottom section of the jewelry box where Nana kept her best pieces. Her fingers traced the shape of each one until they landed on the locket. It was Nana's favorite because it held pictures of her and Grandpa on their wedding day. Katie lifted it out and carefully put it around her neck, gently touching it as it came to rest on her chest. She kissed her fingertips and touched the locket. With a sigh, she closed the box and walked into the hall.

Next, she had to check out the linen closet. It held the secret entrance to her most favorite place to play, the attic. Grandpa had replaced the drop-down ladder to the attic with a hidden staircase behind a funny little door that looked like a linen closet at the end of the upstairs hall. With this staircase, made just for her, she could go up and play for hours in her secret hiding place.

There were two doors, the one from the hall to the "closet" and the one made by the shelves he'd left attached to her secret door to the stairs. It was magical, and Katie made many imaginary friends to play with in this special place.

She skipped the third step as she always had. It groaned in protest when stepped on, so she just never stepped on it, not then and not now. The window in the eave that overlooked the driveway was smudged over with dirt and grime. It reminded her of the glass on the roof of the greenhouse, which, right now, seemed a lifetime away.

Katie's mom had always talked about spending more time at the farm, so she wasn't surprised when she pulled the string of the ceiling light, and the bulb came to life. She gasped, then squealed. She whispered a thank you to her mom for not turning the power off.

"It's all still here! My dolls, my puppets, my daybed, my books, my art table, and everything! Oh, Nana, thank you for keeping it all. Thank you."

Not knowing where to start, she roamed from one corner of the attic to another, touching everything, blowing the dust off her dolls' faces, fluffing the pillows on her bed, and straightening the stacks of books on the floor.

"This is my new home. Or my old home. Whatever. I'm here now, and this is where I'll be safe."

Katie dashed back downstairs to close the front door and lock it, the key no longer under the porch rug but safely tucked into her pocket. She grabbed her bag and took it upstairs to get settled. Later, she'd reclaim the attic as hers, but for now, she'd see if she couldn't find some food.

The kitchen still smelled like Nana, nutmeg, and cinnamon. The pantry hadn't been touched since Nana died. Actually, nothing had.. Everything was just as she'd left it. There was mac n cheese, spaghetti noodles, dried beans, and staples like flour, salt, and sugar. Even her favorite coffee mug was on the peg by the window over the sink. She'd helped her grandmother bake a lot, so she knew she'd be able to make something to eat from all this—though she wasn't sure what.

"Nana, where's your cookbook?"

Of course, it was under her apron on the kitchen table. "Thanks, Nana." Pulling out a chair, Katie began to read. She finally got to the section on pies and decided that was just what she wanted—a pie. But what was she going to put in it?

"Wait, the orchard. Of course! There's peaches and apples and plums out there."

As she pushed open the back door, she thought she saw her grandpa down in the barn but knew it was just her mind being wishful. He died years before Nana. Katie walked down to the orchard, using the footbridge to cross over the stream that ran through the farm. She remembered how she used to ride on her grandpa's shoulders into the trees so she'd be tall enough to pick the fruit and drop it into the pouch he wore over his shoulder.

The memories and smells, and sounds all made her smile. She could hear his voice telling her stories of the woods on the far edge of the fields of his farm.

"Don't want to go into those woods, little lady. No, sir. All kinds of strange things live in those woods, that's for sure."

Katie was certain he made all those things up to keep her from wandering too far from the house. Still, she'd never set foot in those shadowy groves of trees. You never knew which of Grandpa's stories were true and which were tall tales.

The apples were still too small to harvest. The plums were getting ready, but the peaches were perfect for a pie, so she filled her shirt tail with a dozen or so with one extra that she began eating right off the tree.

Feeling very self-sufficient and grown up, she headed back for the house when she stopped short. She was sure she saw someone down in the barn. An older man. She crouched down and waited. Nothing. No one came out, and there were no sounds except the birds and the breeze in the trees.

"I'm going nuts," she whispered and continued making herself a pie.

A couple of hours later, Katie sat before a plate with a slice of peach pie square in the middle. "Here goes," and she dug in with her fork. "Tasty, a bit too much sugar. Nana, the crust isn't like yours. I guess you can't substitute Crisco for butter. This is more like pizza crust than pie crust." But not so bad that she didn't eat half of the pie in a heartbeat. She was hungry enough to eat almost anything.

Lighting the oven hadn't been hard. Nana had taught her how to many times. Thank goodness someone had cleaned out the refrigerator and turned it off. Katie remembered how awful the refrigerator smelled after Nan left it full and Grandpa unplugged it before they left for a month to visit relatives down south. She found the plug and plugged it in to get it up and running, removing the rock that kept the door from closing and growing science experiments inside. The pie looked sad sitting on the shelf all alone. "There will be more to keep you company, little pie. Don't you worry. That or I will eat you all, and it won't matter if you are alone."

Alone. This was a concept that Katie was now getting used to. She was pretty sure she was alone and would be for some time. Maybe forever. She'd have to get used to it, too.

Later in the day, her first day, Katie found herself surrounded by an earlier life. She loved that the attic hadn't changed but, having decided that she would live up here and leave the rest of the house undisturbed, changes needed to be made. First, she needed some sort of window covering so she could have light that couldn't be seen from the road at night. An old wool blanket was draped over a rocking chair, but holding it up to the window, she could see it was full of moth holes that would leak light.

Finding nothing, she decided to try the barn. Katie took a deep breath. She needed to stay in the shadows to be sure she couldn't be seen by passersby, but even here, she didn't feel totally safe near bushes and shadows.

Before she slid into the barn where her grandfather had kept old wood and a bit of everything else, she paused to listen. She had to be sure there really wasn't someone in there. Digging through the pile of scraps, she found a partial sheet of bead board.

"This'll do."

Dragging it across the yard to the house and maneuvering it up the narrow stairs was not as easy as she'd hoped. Partway up the stairs, the panel got wedged and wasn't moving.

"Great. Now what."

Puzzled, Katie studied the board and the angle of the stairs and finally figured out that she needed to turn it with the short side top to bottom to clear the stairwell's angled ceiling. Struggling to make that turn, she heard bits of something click off the wall.

"Darn! I can't believe it." She chewed on the broken nails to remove the jagged edges. "What a hassle."

Finally making it up the stairs and into the attic, she was pleased to find that sure enough, it was just the right size to cover the window completely. She had to prop it up and slide the old trunk in front of it to hold it in place.

"No one can see any light from here at night. Tomorrow, I'll clean that window. Now, let's see. Books."

She sat on the dusty wooden floor and started to go through the books. "This is like meeting old friends again," she exclaimed, stacking them in a pile of children's books, a pile she'd like to read and a pile of ones that she didn't know if she wanted to read. Reverently, she moved the stacks to the bookshelves tucked under the eves.

Next, she tackled the trunks. The three in the attic had always been a mystery to her. She was not allowed to play with whatever was in them. One was still locked. She remembered that the key was on a pink ribbon hanging on the corner of the mirror that went with the dressing table in the back corner of the attic.

Katie carefully opened trunk number one, feeling guilty that she was violating the "don't touch" rule. Dust cascaded off the top and poofed a generous cloud off the back side as the lid opened. She thumbed through the stacks of wool.

"What's the big deal here? This is nothing but old suits."

She was disappointed that there were no secret maps or a treasure.

But as she pulled them out of the trunk, Katie realized she did find a family treasure. There were military uniforms that belonged to someone named Larry, but the last name was her mother's maiden name. She'd never heard of anyone named Larry, but they must have meant something to someone to be in the category of "don't touch."

She dropped the lid. Trunk number two was filled with papers, mostly newspaper articles, and documents.

"Nothing here," she ruled, slamming the lid on that one too.

Trunk number three was locked. Katie knew the key on the ribbon opened this one because she'd tried it once when she was about six. Still, Nana had come up the stairs, and she was lucky to hang the ribbon back in its place just in time to avoid being caught.

She sat on the floor, key in hand, and looked at the trunk. This was one more violation of trust that had become her way of life. She knew there was something in here she wasn't supposed to see. But Nana and Grandpa were dead. What difference would it make now? Her parents had never forbidden her. And she wasn't going home to them anyway, so disappointing them wasn't a factor.

She put the key in the lock. Staring at it, she couldn't bring herself to turn it. Not yet. Not now.

The rest of the day was consumed with getting something to eat for dinner. The root cellar was full of canned vegetables and fruits from the summer before last, so Katie decided they'd still be good enough to eat. The final menu was completed with noodles, stewed tomatoes, green beans, and peaches. Katie clattered in the drawer for the right pots and pans and found all the right utensils.

"Yuck" was all she could muster the first time she filled the pot with water to boil up the noodles. She wasn't surprised to find the discolored water in the toilet. Still, somehow she thought the kitchen water would be clear, so she let the water run for a long time to get the rust out of the pipes before filling the big sauce pot again to cook the noodles.

She opened the china cabinet drawer where her grandmother kept the placemats and napkins, setting the dining table as she had always done. Carrying her plate in from the kitchen, she paused in the doorway and looked at the table. Absentmindedly, she had set three places, not one. The sun was ducking down behind the barn, the shadows grew long, and she sat alone at the table with the first meal she'd ever cooked for herself.

As night fell, Katie made sure all the doors and windows were locked on the first and second floors. She stopped at her bedroom. It was across the hall from Nana's. All this time, she'd not made an effort to return to the days she spent playing music, reading books, and playing with her dolls.

She opened the door slowly. Like the rest of the house, nothing had changed. Her four-poster bed was dressed with the quilted bedspread Nana had made for her. Her dolls were lined up with their heads resting on the pillows as if they were just going down for their nap. But the attic beckoned, and Katie quietly closed the door. She made her way up and closed the closet door and the fake shelving door behind her. No one would ever know she was up there.

Window covered, Nana's nightgown borrowed, pillow and blankets laid out. Ready for bed, Katie turned off the light. A few minutes later, the light was on, and Katie was sitting on the floor in front of the trunk staring at the key. The little voice in her head told her to do it. The little voice in her soul told her not to do it. After several rounds of this battle, Katie gave the key a twist, and the lock clicked open. The trunk was open.

In the bottom of the trunk, wrapped in an oilcloth bag tied with string, was a book, a very large book. Carefully, Katie removed the string and pulled the book into her lap.

"The Enchanted Woods."

She ran her fingers over the magical illustration on the cover. The colors were bright, blending many layers, making it almost a three dimentional image of the Woods. She began turning the pages, gently rubbing her fingers together, feeling the thickness of the paper. She ran her fingertips over the beautiful scenes of trees, deep grasses, and many animals. Furrowing her brow, she glanced towards the art table with her childhood art supplies.

"It's almost like watercolor paper."

But the real curiosity came when she read the list of chapters. There were ones about being captured by kids, chased by a griffin, and finding fields of huge flowers...

"NO way! I know this story." She sat back in astonishment. "This is Angelina's story."

Hurriedly she flipped through the pages until she came to the illustration of Angelina. Her flowing brown curls, her long fingernails, how she could leap through the tree's branches.

"That's her. I saw her in the puddle of water two days ago. That's my Angelina."

She put the book down in her lap. "Nana must have read this to me when I was little. Sure, that's it. How else would I know all this?"

Further in the book was an illustration of Angelina's tree house, remarkably like the one Katie had made for her in the greenhouse. There was a tree house with a table and two chairs. Angelina slept in a bird's nest like the one

Katie made. The pictures had baskets of nuts and yarns, just like in Katie's. How could this happen? Not sure whether to be freaked out or amazed, Katie returned to the beginning and started reading.

She found she already knew most of the story. It had come to her in those flashes and dreams. How could she have seen in her head what was written in this book? How had she become connected to Angelina? Was this what Mrs. K had been trying to tell her when she told her to let the fantasy world in? Had Mrs. K known all along that Katie and Angelina were connected?

Katie moved the book to her bed and read late into the night, long past the point where her eyes struggled to focus. But she stopped when she got to the rainstorm.

"I felt this," Katie told the dolls at the foot of her bed. "Really. When I felt like something awful was going to happen, it must have been happening to Angelina, not me." She looked at the dolls, waiting for someone to confirm her suspicions. Shocked at how real it all felt, she clutched her chest and gasped, "Oh my gosh." And she read on.

What Was Is Gone

THE WIND RIPPED ANGELINA'S HOME apart, hurling her belongings in every direction. She felt her body being thrown into the air, tumbling in slow motion as everything around her flew at a frenzied speed. Her body was being slashed by flying debris. Her arms and legs flailed frantically, searching for something solid to grasp as her world spun out of control.

She screamed, but the sound was sucked into the wind. Tears mixed with rain and dirt streaked her face. Finally, as she hit the ground, she heard her skin tear. Stones and pine needles ground into her face as they slid along the ground, and her left shoulder caught on a tree root curling out of the mud. Pain shot in hot streaks down her arm and across her shoulder.

The flood waters rose, and darkness set in rapidly. Confusion swept over her as Angelina crawled along the ground in search of a safe place.

"God, please, help me," she cried, crushed by desperation. She had vowed never to ask for God's help since the day that her father had beaten her senseless and broken her arm. She'd cursed Him for not saving her and her mother. Now, desperately alone, she hoped He'd forgotten her outburst. She needed help, and He was all she had.

"Please, God, please." She looked up to the heavens, but she saw nothing except darkness.

Exhausted, she drifted into unconsciousness for what seemed like an eternity.

Pale streaks of sunlight and the sweet smell of lavender and lemon tugged gently at Angelina's nostrils. Her eyelashes fluttered as she wrestled with her desire to wake up and her need to sleep. Her tongue traced the outline of her lips, which were dry and pasty.

"Welcome back." Someone touched Angelina's cheek gently and offered her a sip of water from a tiny glass. She knew right away it was Magda.

Struggling to clear the fog from her head and the mist from her eyes, Angelina began to make out jars and bottles on the shelves that lined the walls. She recognized Magda's hut, but how had she gotten here? She had to go home. She was sure to have a mess to clean up after the storm.

A sharp pain shot through her shoulder as she tried to sit up. With a wince, she laid back against the down pillow.

"Oh, no, you don't. You are in no shape to get up yet." Magda repositioned the pillow as Angelina settled back.

"I need to go home! I need to clean everything up. I can't stay here."

Angelina spoke more sharply than she meant to. The old woman was only trying to help. She knew, but …

Then she saw her quilt laid out by the fire—her baskets and bowls. "Why are my things here? Why aren't they in my house?" Her voice was shrill, and she struggled to understand what was happening.

Before Magda could speak, Trek opened the door, peered in, and whispered, "Can I come in?" Angelina watched his face brighten. "Oh, you're awake! Welcome back, Pixie!"

"Why do you keep saying 'welcome back'? Why am I here?"

A hot wave of fear began to overcome Angelina. Thoughts of how to flee again tugged at her.

Magda sat down beside her, taking her hand. Angelina started to pull it away but hesitated.

"Angelina, dear, last night's storm was one of the worst we've ever seen." Magda bowed her head slightly. "So much of the Woods was destroyed."

Magda's voice was soothing but not reassuring. Angelina didn't like where this was going.

"Trek risked his life to find you."

Trek stepped up behind Magda. "You wouldn't believe how bad it was out there. Dad and I were lucky to find you when we did."

"What are you trying to tell me?" she whispered, her stomach twisting with dread. Trek sat on the edge of the bed and looked down at his hands. Nervously, he twisted the hem of the quilt into a knot. "It was awful. I had to do something." He looked up and pinned his eyes on hers. "You were out there alone." Angelina's eyes followed his as he looked down at his hands again. She knew then that he was trying to gather the courage to look at her before he told her what was next. Her face grew hot with dread.

"We've never had a storm like this, ever. Everyone in the village was frightened. Dad said it was too dangerous. We'd have to stay put until the storm let up." He wiped the tear that had slipped onto her cheek.

He turned to look out the window. "The clearing in the village began to flood. But I had to be sure you were safe, so when my dad turned to look out the window, I took my chance and ran out the door and across the clearing. What I didn't know was that dad followed." He wrapped her long fingers in his hands. "You'd gotten under our skin." He winked.

Angelina slid her fingers out of his hand and wrapped them around his. "How? "

He lifted his sleeves and showed her the scrapes and cuts on his arms and hands. Angelina gently ran her fingers over the newly forming scabs, wincing at how raw and red they looked.

"The rocks were slick, and I fell more than once. Thank God for the lightning. Without it, I couldn't tell where I was going in the blackness. The ferns had lain down, too exhausted to stand against the rains and winds. They'd even covered the path completely in some places. But with every flash, I could see I was getting closer."

His voice rose. Angelina could feel his exhilaration, and with every word, she grew more aware of the danger she'd been in.

"By the time I found the boulders that marked the entrance to the valley, I was frantically shouting your name. Dad kept calling my name, and when he came over the hill, he struggled against the wind."

He turned to Magda, who added, "You should have seen him shiver. He was really limping badly. The rain had completely soaked his clothes, and he kept falling, clamoring to his feet only to fall again. He'd twisted his ankle, and his fingers bled from grasping at the rocks trying to stay on his feet."

Angelina gasped. Trek turned back to her.

"This is awful." Angelina pulled her hand back from Trek's and covered her mouth, stifling a cry.

"We hollered 'Angelina! Angelina!' but my voice kept coming back at me on the wind. I finally made it to where your tree should have been." His voice dropped to just above a whisper. "I couldn't find your tree. I was alone in the dark with my dad. We were pelted with rain and shoved by the wind, and then the reality slowly soaked in. Your tree is gone. All that's left is a broken stump barely a few feet tall."

He paused. Now she just stared at him as if this was a tall tale, and soon he'd say something like "fooled you!" and he'd tell her what really happened. She cringed and leaned forward just a bit, urging him to get on with it.

"We searched everywhere. I found baskets, acorn bowls, and your quilt. I kept calling out your name, but you didn't answer." He paused again. Angelina was struggling to absorb all this. He scooted over closer to her, putting his arm around her shoulder. "It's all right. You're safe now."

"How did you find me?" Angelina's voice trembled.

"There was this huge flash of lightning, and in the glare, I saw it. Your nest was upside down, lying in a pool of muddy water. I called my dad to help. He had to scramble over broken branches and debris, but we each got on a side and flipped the nest over." His voice cracked when he got to this part, and Magda put her hand on his shoulder as if encouraging him to move on. Angelina could see how hard this was for him.

"You were limp and all folded up. You didn't move. I took your hand. It was warm. I shouted to Dad, 'She's alive!' He flashed his cheesy grin. We couldn't waste more time, so I gathered you in my arms, fought the winds and rain, and began the long journey back to the village."

Magda added, "He was very worried about you. He won't admit it to you, but I will tell. We all were."

Trek smirked and waved her away. "Magda had seen Dad and me race out into the storm and knew something was very wrong, so she stayed at her window. Conda, Tanner, and Rabea were all watching the storm from their huts and saw us coming. They thought I was going to drop you the way I was stumbling." He chuckled. "Once I got you inside, I took over, telling everyone to get dry clothes and blankets. You were dangerously cold and getting colder by the minute.

Magda reached over and tucked a loose strand of Angelina's hair behind her ear.

Despite Magda's efforts, Angelina could still see the concern in her eyes. "Thank you," she whispered, looking around the room at everyone who'd gathered at the news that she was awake. "Thank you, all of you."

Trek cleared his throat. "You know what was amazing? When the night lifted, and the sun came up, the raindrops rested on the leaves and flower petals and sparkled like diamonds. The air was so crisp and clean. You could smell the rich black dirt mixed with pine and wet grass. Rabea and I left before dawn and watched the sunrise from the trail. It was so cool."

Angelina could see it in his face as he pondered the contrast between the night's fury and the morning's awesome calm. She knew he was searching for a silver lining to give her. It wasn't working.

"Trek, tell me the truth," Angelina pressed.

"When I came up the rise to the boulders at the edge of your valley, trees were ripped up by their roots and tossed aside at random, crushing bushes where they landed. The creek water ran thick with mud smothering everything in its path." His voice trailed off. "Your quilt was tangled up in one of the bushes where I'd seen it during the storm, muddy but intact. Rabea remembered how proud you were of it. She said your face lit up when you told us about each scrap and where it was found.

"Rabea stepped closer, holding up one edge of the quilt for Angelina to see. "We washed it, and it's going to be okay."

Angelina sighed at the sight of her prized accomplishment, now stained and torn, lying limp over the back of a chair.

Trek continued. "The pack rats have already gathered their pick of the items in the debris field."

Angelina cringed at hearing her home described as a 'debris field.' She saw Rabea kick Trek gently on the shin before she took over the conversation. "They skedaddled into the shadows, though. After a few hours of searching, we found many of your things. Most of it can be salvaged with a good scrub and drying out."

Trek quietly added, "We couldn't find the clock Joseph made you, though. At least not yet."

Rabea had settled into a chair by Angelina's bedside. Sadness filled her face. "Angelina, I'm so sorry. Your tree is gone. Your house is gone."

Angelina clenched her fists tight, pulled her knees up to her chest, and rolled over to face the wall. She began to cry now. "It wasn't just a house. It was my home. Nothing in my life ever lasts. The minute I reached 'happy,' something happens to ruin it all."

She wanted to scream at God and ask Him why, just when she felt safe, why had He ripped it all away from her? But she knew that anger at God would offend everyone else in the room, and she needed these people now more than ever. She just let the anger fill her heart.

Angelina heard Magda whispering to Trek and Rabea. "Let her grieve, son. She's lost so much. She has to feel the full depth of her loss before understanding the bounty she's gained. Leave her alone for now. Come back for supper."

Angelina rolled over and watched Trek as he reluctantly turned and walked away. She knew she should say something grateful but right now, her despair overwhelmed all other feelings. He had saved her life, but for what? How could she thank him when she had nothing left but a dirty quilt and some broken dishes? She rolled back to face the wall.

It was hours before Angelina stirred again. She was hungry and needed to go to the bathroom. The house was quiet. She was glad Magda was out; somehow, being alone gave her comfort.

She found the bathroom, and then, wandering around the hut's few small rooms, she grabbed an apple from a bowl in the kitchen. The apple gave way to her bite with a crisp crack, and juice ran down her chin. She walked back into the living room using her sleeve as a napkin. Her quilt was spread out on the backs of the chairs with mud stains all over the lighter patches of fabric. The feathers were wilted. Shadows danced over what was left of her home laid out on the table.

"It's all ruined." Her voice filled with despair. She heard the sound of the screen door, aware now that Magda had come in and was right behind her. "Why is it that every time I get something I want, it's taken away?"

Magda finished folding the towel she had brought in off the line. Sitting down in one of the straight-backed chairs, she studied Angelina.

"And what is it that you want, dear, that was taken from you?"

Fingering the rim of one of her acorn bowls, Angelina whispered, "I wanted a home where I 'd be safe. I deserve that, don't I?"

Angelina's sorrow was so complete that it filled the room. Magda reached out for her hand and led Angelina to sit on the sofa in front of the fire. Angelina was still chilled to the bone, so the warmth radiating from the burning logs felt good.

"Tell me about your home, your things. Did you make the bowls, the quilt?"

Angelina pulled the quilt off the chair back and wrapped it and her arms tightly around herself, mud stains, wilted feathers, and all. She meant to just answer Magda's question about the bowls, but somehow she couldn't stop herself. Once she started it all just poured out: the running away, the dog run, the griffin, Mauve and Joseph, the things they taught her and helped her make, the gifts she had been given. Her clock.

As she talked, her arms relaxed, and she let a slight smile escape. Mauve's memories appeared and disappeared randomly, and her hiccups even brought a chuckle.

"How does Joseph get all those tools in one pocket?" she asked Magda, who just shrugged. Angelina sighed.

"Mauve was teaching me how to knit. I've got the knit part down, but I'm not too good with the purl thing yet. I was almost done with my first sweater—for the winter." She shook her head. "I had this great little mirror shaped like a flower. A Pack Rat left it for me. And a squirrel, a big fat one, kept bringing me seeds. One of them was large enough that I carved a flower vase out of it." As she described her little house and its treasures, she felt her heart sink as she took stock of what was lost forever. "Now, it's all gone."

"Are you sure?" Magda asked.

"Duh?!" Angelina all but sneered as she waved her hand at the table where her last few belongings lay.

"You know, Angelina, God gives gifts of all kinds. The most precious are the ones you keep in your heart, the ones no one can take away."

"Yeah, right." Angelina scoffed.

"Did you have fun decorating your house, making these things for yourself?"

Angelina nodded cautiously.

"Did you make new friends in the process?"

She nodded again.

"Did all that make you happy?"

She nodded once more. She could see where Magda was going with this, but it didn't help her feel the hurt any less.

"And none of that is gone. It's all still right here, in your heart, where you can enjoy it no matter where you are. You see, you have so much more than you thought. Now come with me. This little hut is too small for both of us, but Rabea has offered to have you stay with her."

Magda stood. Apparently, Angelina's pity party was over.

Magda moved towards the door. "Let's go see the next place you will call 'home.'"

Reluctantly Angelina stood, but her feet were not ready to move. The thought of having to make someplace else her home was not something she was looking forward to.

Coming Back but Not Alone

KATIE CLOSED THE BOOK, EXHAUSTED not only from lack of sleep but also from experiencing Angelina's horrific event. Which was really puzzling. How can reading about something make it seem so real? Her heart alternated between racing in fear to breaking at the sadness for Angelina. She hugged the book to her chest and rolled down, nestling her head deep into her pillow. Sleep came quickly.

When she woke up the following day, Katie was still consumed by Angelina's circumstances. At the breakfast table, Katie mindlessly stirred her spoon in her oatmeal. The bland monotony of her menu brought her back to her own circumstances.

"Ok, today we go to town. Although, what's this 'we' business? Anyway, I have got to get something to eat besides oatmeal, canned tuna, and Nana's canned peaches."

Katie sighed as she soaked in how pathetic she had become, talking to herself all the time and arguing back at herself. The reality of having no money made her pause. She'd probably have to try and pawn some stuff, but after the disaster of the last time, she decided she'd have to think of something else. That's when her gaze settled on the orchard out back.

"Peaches. Lots of peaches. I can sell those at the flea market." Rolling her eyes, she added, "Hopefully, this is Saturday." She smiled as she remembered walking the two miles into town with Nana to sell her jellies at the market—on Saturday.

Her next thought: "I wonder if my bike is still in the garage."

The garage doors swung open heavily, and the air was filled with dust that choked her throat as she let sunlight into a place that had been dark for years. Sure enough, there was her bike. It was coated in dust and cobwebs laced from the handlebars to the seat and through the spokes of each wheel.

"Right where I left it." Her voice seemed to rattle as it bounced off the old car and metal yard tools that hung on the walls. "Wonder if the tires still have air?" They didn't. But it didn't take long to find the pump. Grandpa was meticulous about what went where in his workshop. Once she filled the tires with air, hosed off the bike, and filled the basket on the handlebars with bags of fresh peaches, Katie started cautiously down the old highway. Making sure no one saw her come out of the driveway, she pedaled quickly, constantly checking over her shoulder to be sure she wasn't being followed. The sound of the gravel crunching under her tires, the two-mile trip was shorter than she expected.

"Now, to figure out what day it is."

The electronic sign on the bank had the time and date but no day. Katie stopped at the curb and thought hard, scanning her eyes back and forth as if that would help her think of something. Then she spotted the newspaper box in front of the coffee shop.

"Yes!" She got off the bike and slowly walked down the sidewalk toward it.

But they were all sold out. The only thing she could do now was to ride on out to the old churchyard and see if anyone was there. Shoving off with her left foot, she began weaving her way through side streets and alleys toward the church. The people she passed nodded or said a polite hello, but no one seemed to recognize her. She was glad she'd changed so much since she'd spent time at the farm in the last few years.

As she got closer to the church, she heard vendors calling, "Watermelons, cantaloupes, cucumbers!" But the smell of popcorn and funnel cakes drew her into the crowd in the churchyard. The sign read 'Flea Market Today.' Rivers of people were flowing in all directions at once. She had to get off the bike and walk to avoid hitting or being hit or, worse yet, spilling the peaches.

Rows of tents, tables, carts, and bins of everything you could imagine teased her to buy. But she had to sell first.

It didn't take long before she came to an old-fashioned covered wagon surrounded by baskets of fruits and vegetables, jars of jellies and jams, and a bit of everything pickled.

But no peaches.

She stood and watched an older woman with wild hair tucked under a woven sun hat greet her customers. She seemed to know most of them by name. Slowly, Katie moved closer. She was so excited to see that they had milk and eggs too. Taking a deep breath, Katie pressed forward until the old woman spoke to her.

"Well, what wonderful peaches. Did you buy all of those?"

"No, I brought 'em to sell." Katie opened one of the bags to show her how beautifully juicy they were.

"Oh, so tempting. Our crop has been late this year. We don't typically buy produce at the market, but …" The old woman paused as if to think. "I would be willing to make a trade." She tilted her head towards the milk and basket of eggs. Katie's stomach was beginning to growl at the thought of a real breakfast for a change.

"Okay, a gallon of milk, two dozen eggs, and a chunk of that ham for these peaches?" Katie surprised herself with how boldly she'd named her price for the trade. She held her breath, not sure what she'd do if her offer was turned down.

"Oh, that's not really a fair trade."

Katie felt her stomach sink.

"Your peaches are worth more than that. I'll add a couple of loaves of bread and a tub of butter. Will that do for you?"

Katie let all the air in her lungs escape in an embarrassing whoosh and sputtered, "Yes." She added a weak smile and hoped it looked polite.

She swapped out the bags of peaches in her basket for all her bartered groceries as she and the old woman exchanged pleasantries about the weather.

She turned her bike around to leave, her basket full and bags securely tied to the back, and realized she'd failed to see past the produce to all the other things they sold. Clocks were hanging all over the canvas of the covered wagon.

"Nice clocks," Katie said.

"Thanks."

They waved to one another as if they'd been friends for a long time. It felt odd since they'd just met. Katie began weaving through the market, making her way home while soaking up all the wonderful things for sale.

There were purses, shawls, hats, and belts. Signs for kitchens and bathrooms. Dreamcatchers and bits of glass to catch the light in the garden. There was even a booth with boots made by an American Indian. They were beaded and fringed and gorgeous. Especially a pair of white boots. He had them on display in the center of a table in the front of his booth.

She stood and admired them for a long time. They were gorgeous. Her fingers ran over the beads. She slipped her hand inside the left boot and felt the soft silkiness of the leather, imagining what it would feel like on her feet. Her sensory daydream was suddenly interrupted by a guy who bumped into her as he raced up to the booth.

"I'm sorry," she apologized out of habit. She turned to look at him and came face to face with the most amazing brown eyes she'd ever seen. She couldn't believe how cute he was. She felt the stammer rising in her throat.

"No problem. I wasn't looking, either. Have a good day."

He reached out for those boots as if she didn't exist, but her hand was still inside one of them, and he dragged her off balance. As she stumbled to catch herself, she considered, for a split second, the benefits of falling into his arms.

"Oh, sorry. Let me help you." He took her hand and gently removed it from the boot. She did nothing to take it back.

"I'm buying these for a friend. She's going to flip when she sees them. Don't you think?" He held the boots tight, stroking them with care.

"She must be special to deserve a gift like this." Katie tried to hide the disappointment that he had a girlfriend.

"Yeah, she's something, all right. Hey, sorry I knocked you over. You have a good day." He maneuvered his way to the guy in the back of the booth and started fishing in his pocket for the money. "Will this be enough for you to hold these until I can get the rest of the money?" As she turned to look at the rest of the items in the booth, Katie heard him bartering with the American Indian about the deposit and deadline for payment.

Disappointed for many reasons, Katie moved back into the current of people until she flowed out onto Main Street. "Somebody else always gets the cute guys," she muttered.

It was nearly noon when she got back to the farm. She slipped the key back under the rug on the front porch and put all the groceries away. Nothing had tasted better than the slab of fresh bread plastered with a thick layer of butter and a chunk of ham. Licking her fingers, Katie felt so satisfied. Her stomach was full. She hadn't had a nightmare in weeks. And even though she was sometimes lonely, she felt safe for the first time in months.

The sound of gravel cracking under tires broke the spell, and she sat up alert. Someone was coming up the drive. Rushing to the front room, she peered out the gap between the lace curtains on the kitchen window to see a car headed for the house.

She couldn't be found here. Time stopped. She didn't breathe.

Someone was on the porch. What if they found the key? Katie panicked. She had to get to the safety of her attic. She shoved her chair back from the kitchen table, knocking it on the floor. Dashing for the stairs, she leaped up every other one—forgetting about the third stair. When it creaked, she froze, still not daring to breathe.

Whoever was coming in didn't seem to hear it or the sound of the chair falling, so she quietly made it up the stairs. She jerked the door to the linen closet open and grabbed the shelves to access the hidden stairs. As she closed the door behind her and slid past the shelves, she heard the key rattle in the front door. Someone was coming in the house.

Quietly she closed it all up and tiptoed across the floor to sit on the edge of the bed, where she could see into the room below through the floor grate. Taking in shallow gulps of air, she waited.

She was familiar with that room. It was her bedroom. She stared into the grate, straining to hear every little sound coming up from the house below.

"So this is where you guys used to hang out," said the male voice. "I'm glad you decided to share this with me."

Katie's head shot up. She knew that voice. It was Him.

But who was He talking to?

"I feel so much closer to you knowing about the special places in your life."

Katie's brow furrowed as she wracked her brain for who it could be. Who would know about the farm?

"You know that's important for people who care about each other. Don't you think? Someday, I'll share my special places with you. Come on, don't be afraid. You can trust me, right? Right!"

Why wasn't the other person talking? Katie had to know who was down there with this awful man.

The man's voice dominated the room as he moved from one to the next. Finally, Katie heard something she thought she recognized. A girl had cleared her throat. Finally, she spoke.

"Ah, yeah, sure," was the young girl's reply.

"Yeah, sure, what?" he pressed.

"Yeah, sure...., baby." She hesitated but seemed to add what he was waiting to hear.

"We will have to come back here again," he said. "We'll make our own memories here. Won't we, Angel?"

They'd entered the room right below Katie. Paralyzed, her whole body flushed with heat, and sweat dripped from her hairline down her cheeks.

Angel. Her best friend, Angel, was with that awful man. That's how they got in. She knew where the key was! But why? Why would Angel bring someone here to her grandparent's house?

All the pieces started to fall into place. The realization of what he was planning struck her like a punch in the stomach. She recognized the color of his hair and the stench of his cologne. She knew what he was planning next.

It really was Him.

He had Angel and now he was in her house. It took everything she could do to keep from throwing up.

"Come on, baby," he said, "let's go back to your house and watch a movie. I am so glad I finally got you to tell me about this place, and we will come back. Yes. We will. Come on, now. Come on."

He glanced up at the grate. Katie ducked back out of view, and for one horrific minute, she thought he was actually talking to her.

She saw him put his hand on Angel's back and firmly guide her out of the room. Angel moved as if she was in a trance. Had he done to her what he'd done to Katie? Had he drugged her, too?

When she heard them on the front porch, she guessed putting the key back under the rug. Katie realized she had to get out. What if he'd seen the plate on the table or the chair on the floor in the kitchen? Were her shoes still by the back door? Her mind went blank. She couldn't remember.

"Shit!"

She grabbed everything she could get her hands on—her grandpa's pocketknife, the matches she used to light the scented candles, a handkerchief, and tissues. Still, she stopped short when she pulled her hoodie off the bed, revealing the open pages of the Enchanted Woods book.

There was an illustration of a covered wagon filled with produce, covered with clocks, and an old woman.

There was no time to try to sort that out now. Katie hadn't heard the car doors close or the car start. She was running out of time.

She slipped down the stairs into the kitchen. Her shoes were by the back door, adding to her panic. He had to know someone was here in the house.

She wedged her feet into them and slipped out the back door, hoping to get to the barn. She knew there were lots of places in there that she could hide. She just hoped she remembered some of them.

As she approached the fruit trees, she turned to look back just in time to see Him walking around the driveway side of the house. He'd seen her. Their eyes locked for what seemed like an eternity. Her heart leaped into her throat threatening to choke her.

Suddenly he lurched towards her. Adrenaline surged through her as she ran, chased by the sound of his shoes crushing the gravel on the drive. There wasn't time to open the barn doors and then shut them again behind her. She'd have to go somewhere else.

Her throat burned as she ran under the clothesline and leaped over the picket fence around Nana's garden. She slipped on the dried-up remains of the lettuce and fell. Hard. The next thing she felt was his hands grabbing her shirt's back.

A fierce will to survive grabbed her soul.

She rolled over on her back and, growling like a wild animal, kicked wildly, catching him squarely on the chin. She could hear his teeth crack together as his jaw was shoved shut. He screamed, and she knew he had bitten his tongue from the gush of blood.

Over his shoulder, Katie could see Angel just standing there.

"Run, you fool, run!" she shouted to Angel but didn't take the time to see if she actually moved or not.

While he mopped up the blood from his mouth with his sleeve, Katie was able to get back on her feet, leap the picket fence on the back side of the garden, and head across the field.

They had not been planted for two years, so there was no corn or wheat crop to hide her path. Her only option was the Woods. The one her grandpa had warned her to never enter. Katie could still hear Him running at her, screaming her name. But she was far enough ahead that she reached the edge of the field in time to turn and see that now he'd fallen in a cloud of dust.

"God damn it! When I catch you, I'm going to kill you. Do you hear me? You're dead."

She didn't stop to look back again.

Facing the darkness of the woods, she looked frantically for a way past the tangle of brush and branches. She found a path leading into the woods at the north end of the barbed wire fence surrounding the farm. Not stopping to question why she hadn't seen it before, she ran, knowing her life depended on it. The next time she turned around, the path behind her was gone. There was no sign or sound of Him coming after her. Nothing. Nothing but a deep, frightening silence until she dared breathe again.

Every muscle in her body gave in to exhaustion simultaneously, and she fell heavily to the ground. Her hands burned as her palms dug deep into the gravel. Her cheekbone hit the ground hard enough to make her teeth rattle, and her legs flew in opposite directions, making catching herself impossible.

For a long time, Katie lay sprawled across the ground. When she finally raised her head, she was shocked to see that there was no path. Nothing anywhere. She had no idea which direction led into the forest or which led back to the fields. Her face hurt, her head ached, her knees burned, and her heart was broken. She couldn't stop the tears, and the salt burned the cut on her lip.

"Why? Why God? Where can I be safe?"

Desperation drained all the strength out of her. Her thoughts began to blur, so much so that just lying here forever seemed like a reasonable option. She was getting cold. She just wanted to sleep. She wanted to sleep forever. Maybe …

Starting Over Again

RABEA'S HUT WAS MUCH LARGER than Magda's, but all the huts were almost invisible in the Woods. The outside walls, all clad in bark, blended into the trunks of trees. The pinecone roofs mixed with twigs, vines, and moss made the huts disappear. Angelina was surprised to see that this hut was bigger and two stories bigger.

The first floor was a lot like Magda's: quaint and comfortable. Above, a loft and an attic room gave the hut plenty of space for two.

Rabea looked almost apologetic. "I know, it's a lot for one person. My folks built it when I was a teenager but decided to move deeper into the Woods. They love to gather mushrooms to sell in town. I decided to stay here and study herbs with Magda." She winked at Magda and turned back to Angelina. "You can have the loft. It's private, and the bed's pretty comfortable. I sleep down here on the daybed most of the time anyway."

Angelina wandered around the room, running her long elfin fingers over each object. There were not many things in the home she grew up in. Her father had broken almost everything in his drunken rages. She'd never realized how much you could learn about someone from their things. According to the books on the shelves, Rabea loved romance novels and horticulture. She collected shiny colored rocks. Nothing matched, but the quality was top-notch for sure. Angelina fingered the fabric on the pillows and guessed Rabea didn't have much fashion sense. She turned and looked at Rabea and Magda blankly. It wasn't home, but it would do for now.

"Come on, I'll show you your room."

As Rabea and Angelina climbed the stairs, Magda slipped out the front door leaving the girls to settle in.

Katie woke to the warmth of the sun on her face. Lying on her back, she looked at the sky through the tall trees surrounding her. It was all so disorienting. The light was everywhere, but she couldn't find the sun. She rolled over, sat up, and realized she was being stared at by a couple of furry-tailed squirrels. She cleared her throat to speak, but they dropped the nuts they'd carried and dashed off into the brush and up one of the trees, chattering as they went. Her stomach made encouraging sounds at the sight of the nuts.

Looking around to see if anyone or anything else was watching, she crept over and gathered up the nuts. A few sharp snaps of a rock and the shells offered her first meal in the Woods. Katie hadn't tasted anything so good in a long time.

Then she spotted a cluster of lusciously red strawberries peeking out from under a preposterously large leafy lettuce plant.

"What in the world?"

She crawled under the lettuce leaves and plucked the strawberries, each the size of a cantaloupe, one at a time. The sweet juice ran down her arms as she gnawed her way into them until she was too full to move. But she didn't really care why—she was hungry and grateful for whatever she could find, no matter how illogical it looked.

Katie sighed as she leaned back on a small boulder, swearing that she also heard it sigh.

"I'm sorry, Grandpa. I had nowhere else to go," she whispered.

The breeze picked up, and the ferns and ground covers parted. A path slowly emerged. Katie stared at it for a long time, unsure whether it was a trick. When the squirrels came down from their tree and scampered down the path, disappearing around a bend, she decided it must be safe enough.

"Things can't get much worse than being lost in here," she muttered, dusting off the seat of her pants as she stood. She filled her cheeks with air, blew it all out at once, and said, "Here goes."

As she marched into the depths of the Woods, the path behind her disappeared. She was too confused to worry about it now.

"Well, there's no going back."

The path led her up and down hills, through fields of multi-colored wildflowers, and across streams of glistening cold water. Birds came and went, singing and chattering as they flew from tree to tree—all except an owl that seemed to be there no matter where she was. Everything was brighter and smelled more intensely than anything she'd ever known. So many plants and flowers often were not the size you'd think they should be. She ate berries, nuts, and leafy greens for lunch, washed down by the sweetest water she'd ever tasted. Finally, when she realized she was walking in circles, she sat down on a log and began to think about what she would do next.

"I can't stay here forever. Somehow, I have to find a way to get out of these Woods."

Sap and Syrup

A S THE WEEKS WENT BY, Angelina realized how much she liked laughing and working with Rabea. Angelina had never met anyone as smart and as hard-working as Rabea. Angelina even began to enjoy gardening, especially learning the fine art of harvesting and drying herbs.

"You know," Rabea told her one day, "soon I'll complete my training in herbal medicine. I think I'm ready to move to one of the other villages to care for them. Maybe you'll be Magda's next student. Someone needs to be trained to take her place someday."

Rabea winked and glanced over her shoulder at Magda. Angelina was beginning to understand what it might feel like to have a sister, someone to talk to at night about things you can't tell your mother, things like dreams and boys. She still wasn't ready to tell Rabea about her life at home. Her past made her feel dirty. She'd been able to keep that part of her life a secret since Rabea hadn't asked.

They did talk about the girls Angelina had watched over the fence. Rabea called them 'one-dimensional,' whatever that meant. She didn't have much respect for that type of girl, so Angelina was careful not to reveal her longing to be one of them. Rabea said girls who were selfish cared too much about looks and clothes and being popular and that they were cruel, especially to the shy girls or those who were different.

Angelina was confused. From her perch in the tree, she saw the fun they had laughing on the way home from the mall with bags full of clothes.

It made her wonder how they would have treated her once they saw her ears. Rabea didn't seem to mind that Angelina's ears were pointed and said she loved Angelina's long, slender fingers. Rabea had said they were friends, but Angelina was perplexed about how you can tell when someone was really your friend. She hadn't had many friends, so she had no idea if Rabea liked her or was just being nice.

No matter! She was having fun for now. She could always move on if things didn't work out.

Trek caught up with the girls one afternoon as they were gathering mint by the creek. "Hey ladies!" he called out.

"Hey, Trek. What are you up to?" Rabea seemed friendly to everyone, which added to Angelina's confusion.

"I'm headed up to check on the sap buckets." He held up two large empty buckets. "They should be getting full, and I bet I need to change 'em out."

"Sap buckets?" Angelina had no idea why anyone would want to capture sap, especially since her experience with the gunk on her hand.

Trek laughed, set the buckets down, and turned one upside down to make a stool.

"We make syrup out of it. It's how we make a living. Sell it at the flea market or trade at the swap meets. Want to see how it's done?"

Angelina looked to Rabea for permission since they had chores to do.

"Sure, go ahead," Rabea said. "I'll finish up here."

Trek handed Angelina a bucket, and they took off on a path that appeared as they walked. Trek explained that since fall was not far off, there wouldn't be too many more weeks where they would be able to get sap. It would freeze soon, and the sap would drop deep into the roots.

"So, what do you do all winter?" "Don't you get bored?" Angelina said.

"Oh, we aren't ever bored! We'll have enough sap left to make syrup for several months. We've also canned lots of fruit so we can make pies and pastries to sell at the markets."

Trek reached down to get Angelina's hand to help her over a large trunk of a downed tree. As he pulled her up and over, they startled a flock of birds so brightly colored that their wings looked like stained glass as they took flight, and the air filled with the sound of harps. He seemed to take little notice, but Angelina was amazed at the beauty. Suddenly aware that he hadn't let go of her hand, she jerked it back and shoved it into her pocket.

"We try to practice the same kind of habits as nature. Snow is like a blanket that keeps the earth warm during cold times. You know. Plants use the winter to develop deep and sturdy roots, so when spring comes, they're ready to display the fruits of that growth in grand foliage, flowers, and fruits. We use the winter time to read and study, so in spring, we can be more productive than in the year before. We also use the time to fix our tools and equipment and make things like furniture. Come on." Trek didn't offer his hand this time, forcing Angelina to scramble over the next set of boulders on her own.

The afternoon rain clouds were gathering, so Trek found a perfect shelter hidden in the oaks, and they settled down on the moss-covered floor to wait out the rains. They were surrounded by vine-covered scrub oak. The smell of wet oak mixed with the sweetness of rotting leaves filled Angelina's nostrils. She sighed contentedly and watched a tiny worm inch across the ceiling.

Angelina felt her body relax, which, she realized, was odd because she was usually wrapped in confusion or apprehension. She was beginning to like the serene feeling that was flowing over her. She caught sight of Trek staring at her with a cheesy smile on his face.

"What?" she snapped, her body tensing up from head to toe.

"Nothing. You just looked so, ah, I don't know, happy. You haven't looked like that since you got here." He changed the subject. "So, tell me about yourself," he said as he pulled up a stalk of grass and began to chew on it lazily.

"There's not much to tell. I'm just a 13-year-old, no, 14 now. I had a birthday. Never been anywhere. I was homeschooled; studied mostly music, some science, and math. That's about it."

Trek shook his head. "Oh, there's more to you than that. You've been hoisted by a griffin, for goodness sake!" He fixed his eyes on her until she acknowledged his point.

"You're right. There's that. That stupid creature will not leave me alone. When I go out in the Woods alone, he always swoops down on me, snatching at me. I have no idea why he's so fascinated with me."

"Because you are fascinating."

He reached over and moved a lock of her hair caught in a twist of the vines. It made Angelina nervous about having him so close. It made her nervous about having anyone this close to her. Her eyes searched his face. When they first met, he was so annoying, always telling her he could do things better than she could. Now, she could see that he was kind. And he was cute. But when he began to lean in to kiss her, her stomach leaped, her heart fluttered, and she panicked.

"Ah, looks like the rain's stopped. We'd better get that sap before it gets too late."

She smoothed her hands over her clothes to be sure everything was in its place. Self-consciously, she smoothed her hair, too.

Trek chuckled. "You've never been kissed, have you? It's okay. Your time'll come."

He gathered the buckets and stepped into the crisp, clean afternoon air. Angelina stared at the back of him. How dare he presume to know if she'd been kissed or not? Curling her lip up, she wondered if it was really that obvious. Before she could work this one out, she realized he had disappeared into the woods, and she'd better catch up if she didn't want to spend the night out here alone.

They reached the stand of maple trees, and Trek teased her about her fear of grasshoppers, admitting that fourteen-inch-long grasshoppers can be a shock the first time they land on your arm. Angelina couldn't hide her sense of wonder at the magic of the Enchanted Woods or her confusion at things not being the size she expected. She was still afraid of the sounds she heard for the first time. And she was not sure how to react when he talked about how the hand of God worked in this extraordinary place Trek and his family called home.

Angelina suddenly ducked and was embarrassed to find it was only a massive dragonfly on a branch near where they sat. Its wings stretched at least six feet across, and they glowed so iridescently that they sparkled in the crispness of the afternoon sunlight.

"What was that all about?" Trek smirked.

"Oh, nothing. I thought it was him again. That griffin." Not wanting to go into it anymore, she changed the subject. "Have you ever thought about riding one of those?" Angelina asked, half serious. She realized that when she was in the clutches of the griffin, she hadn't thought much about any other flying creatures.

"Yea, one of my buddies and I tried it once a few summers ago. They're hard to catch since their wings are so delicate. Their bodies are so slender that there's not much for your legs to grip. And they're hard to stay on. Not like riding a unicorn, you know!"

She wasn't sure whether to believe him about the unicorn or not and was too embarrassed to ask. "So, did you do it? Ride a dragonfly?"

"Well, technically, I did, but I fell off before it had all its legs off the ground, so, to be truthful, no." They were close to the maple grove now. "Come on. I'll show you how to swap the buckets without pouring sap on your head."

Angelina flipped from bliss to confusion again. Was she really at risk for pouring sap on her head?

Angelina learned quickly, and soon she had mastered the bucket swap and had moved on to clearing the taps of dried sap. No sap in her hair, either. She was proud of her new skills. She had felt helpless since her house was destroyed. Now, she'd be able to earn her keep and be a productive part of the community.

"You know, something's strange going on out here, though," Trek said with a tone of puzzlement in his voice. "Some taps have been tampered with. Someone is trying to get the sap but doesn't know what they're doing. And there's sap spilled on the ground under some of them." Trek fingered the tap when they stopped at the next tree. He kicked at the sap in the dust with the toe of his boot. "I don't know. Might be raccoons. They're pretty resourceful when they put their minds to it."

As they started for home, Angelina looked back at the tree, trying to figure out how a raccoon could reach a tap four to five feet off the ground. Seeing the look on Angelina's face, Trek chuckled, "they're really resourceful, and they can climb almost anything."

Each carrying two buckets, they made their way back to the village, stopping off at the still to put the day's harvest in the root cellar so Tanner could process it tomorrow. They wanted to have as much syrup bottled as possible for this weekend's market. Angelina saw Conda waving broadly at them as they approached the village green.

As she wandered, Katie was surprised that some of the trees had strange faucet-like things drilled into the bark. Curious, she twisted one, and a stream of goo flowed out all over the place. She stepped back to keep it from getting on her shoes. She reached up and turned the knob in the other direction, and it stopped gushing, but now she had it all over her hands. She sniffed her fingers.

"Hum, this stuff smells sweet. What the heck," she said, touching the tip of her tongue to her little finger. "Cool. This is syrup."

She sat down on a stump to finish licking the nectar off all of her fingers, feeling pleased with herself that she'd found such a wonderful treat. She was so engrossed in getting every drop off her hands that she didn't see the clouds gathering. At least not until she felt the first raindrop land like a small bucket of water.

"Oh, shoot."

Katie grabbed a huge oak leaf to use as an umbrella and ran for a pile of huge boulders. By the time she reached them, the raindrops were leaving puddles with each plop. Fortunately, there was an opening in the rocks just big enough for her to squeeze into for shelter. Flipping her hair off to one side, she wrung the water out. When she stood, she realized she was inside a remarkably warm and very sizable cave.

Light came in from gaps near the top like little skylights. The air smelled fresh and clean.

"This'll do for the night. Maybe longer."

When the rain stopped, Katie went in search of something to make into a bed. Fortunately, the ferns were so thick under the trees that the thick mounds of dried grasses hadn't gotten wet. Pulling out armloads of long strands of grass at a time, Katie had a pile built up in almost no time.

Lying down on her back, gazing up at the sky, she declared, "This is not half bad."

Before she knew it, she had fallen asleep and slept soundly. Later in the day, Katie woke up from her nap thinking she'd heard voices nearby, but by the time she shook the sleep out of her head and scrambled out of her cave, there was nothing but silence and a few birds.

"You are going crazy, you know. And you're still talking to yourself." She shook her head and went back to bed for just a bit more sleep before she had to think about dinner.

Waking up to Music

"ANGELINA," CONDA CALLED. "DO YOU have a minute?" She was coming down the path from the schoolhouse carrying a stack of papers and her book bag. Angelina was amused at this reference to time, remembering Joseph's chiding about having nothing but time in the Enchanted Woods. She was so glad their house needed only minor repairs after the storm.

"Sure. What's up?"

"I have to go help Rabea and her parents tomorrow. There has been so much rain lately that the mushrooms are coming up everywhere, but it seems something is digging them up, so we want to get as many as we can. This weekend should be one of the best mushroom sales ever." She shifted her book bag from one shoulder to the other. "What I need is some help at the school." She handed Angelina the papers so she could button her sweater. Taking them back, she continued, "The students will all be out working on their earth science project—gathering rocks, you know—but the classroom is a mess. If you could just tidy it up for me, you know, put the books back on the shelves, arrange the desks back in a circle, dust and sweep the floor. It's not hard but really important. Can you do it?"

"Sure, I'd be glad to." Disappointed that she wasn't asked to join her and Rabea, Angelina was glad to at least be asked to tend to the schoolhouse. Whenever she got a chance to help Conda, she was willing to do whatever she asked. She loved seeing so many books in one place. She was thinking she might be able to help teach someday.

"No problem," she said.

"Thanks, you're the best!" Conda dashed off to find Rabea. Angelina couldn't help but smile. She was sure she was making points with Conda, and as well-liked as Conda was with the others, it wouldn't be long before she'd convince them that Angelina should be allowed to go to town with them.

The next morning Rabea and Conda were up and gone way before dawn. Angelina was startled and slightly annoyed when Magda's twisted fingers touched her shoulder gently.

"Wake up, child."

Angelina could barely make out Magda's face in the early morning darkness. "What? What's wrong?" she whispered as she worked to rub the sleep from her eyes.

"Get your shoes and come with me." Magda slipped out into the dawn.

"Where are we going?" Angelina said, hopping on one foot, trying to get her shoes on the right feet.

"You'll see soon enough! Come, come!"

Magda led the way down the path toward the great meadow. She climbed up on the east rocks when they reached the edge and settled down to wait.

Confused, Angelina didn't dare move. The air was motionless. The sky was just beginning to glow with the warmth of the sun. The Woods was absolutely silent.

And then it began. Angelina heard the faint sound of music, violins mostly, and then cellos and flutes as if they were in the balcony of a great concert hall. The volume of the music rose with the sun. Before long, the air was filled with the glorious sounds of a great orchestra. Angelina's jaw dropped. She looked over at Magda to find her mouth wide open with delight too.

When the sun crested the horizon, the music reached its crescendo and ceased. Birds sang, frogs joined the chorus, and the Woods awoke.

"Wow! Where did it come from? How did that happen?! Magda, how did you know where to be?" Angelina was having a hard time controlling her excitement.

"Calm down, child!" Magda laughed. "When everything is just right—the winds still, the sun rising gently, and the earth warm and content—the grasses can be heard to play. We were fortunate enough to share it this morning."

"I recognized that music! It was Vivaldi! I studied music! How did the grasses know?" Magda held Angelina's gaze. "You assume, my dear." Intently she watched for Angelina to understand.

"But who taught the grasses to play Vivaldi?" And then, as if she had been splashed by icy water, Angelina gasped as she understood the reality of what Magda was saying. "You mean? Really?"

Magda giggled. "Yes, dear, Vivaldi learned it from them! You see, there is nothing ever created by the creatures of the earth that God and Mother Nature didn't first enjoy. God thought of everything, and if you're very lucky, He will share something special with you. But you must learn to open your mind and your heart so His gift can be received."

"Is that what you do every morning when I see you meditating under the willow tree? Ask God for something special?"

Angelina had shifted on the rocks so she could see every inch of Magda's face. She studied each movement of the wise woman's eyes to ensure no flicker of truth escaped notice.

"Every morning, I clear my mind of all the clutter from my dreams and worries for the day to come, and I tell God that I am grateful for His gifts and am willing to fulfill any wish He has for my day. Then I listen. Most of the time, I am not the one chosen, and I end my meditation with a prayer of thanks and set out to live my day as best I can. But sometimes, I am chosen! And I start my day knowing that I have been asked to share something extraordinary, something just from God."

"Hmm," Angelina replied, struggling to take all this in. "What if you don't get the message? Then what?"

"It happens sometimes. Sometimes my head and heart are so full of my concerns that I am sure I miss an opportunity. Accepting is a choice. You can choose to ignore or turn God down. I'm sure many have. But what if Vivaldi had been too busy that day to hear the music? Think of what a loss that would have been for the world."

"Hmm." Angelina squinted her eyes and thought hard. She wondered if she had missed a gift from God. She wondered if the clutter in her head had ever cost the universe something important. With her imagination in full gear, she left Magda sitting on the rock and headed home.

Belonging Means Longing

ANGELINA HURRIED BACK TO RABEA'S, eager to get into the schoolhouse. She grabbed an apple for breakfast and some bread and ham for her lunch. She dashed out the door and across the clearing to the head of the path. Nothing happened. No path appeared.

"What's going on?"

This had never happened before. She stepped back and tried again, slowly approaching the edge of the green. Still nothing. Her brow furrowed as she tried to figure out what she was doing wrong. Why wouldn't the path appear?

Probably on his way to the root cellar, Trek found his path opening immediately. Gastor's path to the wood piles was waiting for him. Confused and very disappointed, Angelina returned to Rabea's hut and sat on the front steps. Retracing her steps in her head, she remembered getting out of bed and getting dressed. She had an apple for her breakfast and made her lunch. Shoes—yep. Jacket—yep. What was she missing?

Then she remembered. Even though she wasn't entirely sold on trusting God, Rabea had convinced her to start each day by giving thanks and asking for blessings. Just a simple prayer, not more than two sentences, that's all. Angelina closed her eyes and whispered her thanks, and requested blessings. When she opened her eyes, there, across the green, was the path. She shook her head. This all seemed like so much fuss over trying to find a path, but it seemed to work …

She went along with it.

The path to the schoolhouse was lit by a shaft of sunlight slashing through the trees, causing everything to glow. Today it was a luscious deep purple. She chuckled as she thought back on the colors of the last week; yellow, lime green, then blue, and now purple. She skipped her way down the path, across the creek, and up to the door of the school.

Inside, the desks were clustered in small groups where the children had been working on their team project. Books and maps were scattered everywhere. Straightening the room took much longer than it should have because Angelina stopped to read almost every book she picked up. Her mother had been a good teacher, but they hadn't spent much time on places like India and China, and Tibet.

And she'd never seen pictures of creatures under the sea. Mesmerized, she studied the color pictures of living things that looked like sheer iridescent butterflies and giant underwater plants like exotic trees dancing gracefully in the ocean currents. And fish that blinked on and off like fireflies.

Angelina read book after book until she realized hunger was taking over her thoughts. She set aside a stack of books about Josephine and the court life in France to pull out her sandwich and a juicy peach. As she sucked out the sweet juice, she scanned the bookcases for other adventures she could take after she swept the floors. That's when she noticed that one of the bookcases was not pushed into place with the others. She pinched off a piece of her sandwich and pushed it back against the wall. She gave it a good shove, but it barely moved. She tried again and again with no better results. Finally, she pulled it completely out to see what was back there to keep it from moving. That's when she found it.

Angelina pulled the tall oak bookcase away from the wall and peered behind it. The cobwebs were furry with thick dust. A mouse scurried to hide again under the other cases. Curiosity overcame her fear of spiders, and she reached into the darkness until she felt a thick leatherbound book almost as big as the top of one of the desks.

Using both hands to get it under control, she laid it down on the big library table. It landed with such a thud that a cloud of dust enveloped her, causing her to choke for several minutes until the air cleared.

With a swipe of her hand, Angelina brushed away the dirt from the title: The Legends of The Valley of Kidron. The leather was hand tooled with every scroll and flourish rubbed with gold leaf. Angelina had never seen such a book. It was gorgeous, and the etchings were incredible. She could tell from the age of the book that most were hand-colored and lettered by quill pen.

For hours Angelina pored over the pages, reading about the legends of great and evil beasts and the harsh perils of the valley. Just when she thought she'd read all she could bear, she came to the Legend of the Red and Blue Diamonds.

The storyteller told of a long-lost cave filled with jewels. Thumbing through, eager to learn more, she turned page after page until she came to the center of the book. Deep in the crease was a map, yellow with age and brittle at the creases.

Carefully, she peeled the map from the binding where it had been wedged for all these years, and, taking care not to tear it, she opened it wide on the table. The author had identified all the landmarks of the Enchanted Woods down to the clearing where the villagers now lived. Beautiful hand lettering noted the woods with the giant trees, the maple grove, the waterfalls, and the butterfly fields.

Turning the map over, Angelina saw a deep canyon at the end of a long valley and an arrow pointing to a cave at the top of a steep and rocky mountain. Someone had hand-painted an image of a large seashell filled with pearls, emeralds, and hands full of red and blue diamonds, the rarest of all jewels.

"This is really cool."

Just as she was getting her bearings, she heard Trek calling her name. Realizing this map might be able to show her how to get out of these Woods, to the city, in a split second, she decided not to mention it to Trek. She had just enough time to fold up the map, tuck it back between the pages and close the book, creating another cloud of dust. Trek opened the door to the schoolhouse to find Angelina sweeping with great enthusiasm.

"Goodness, girl, leave some dust to fill the holes in the floor; otherwise, the mice'll be comin' in and eatin' everyone's lunch!" He laughed at her. "Your face is so dirty."

Reaching out to take the dustpan, he helped her finish her chores. Then they walked back home together. He told her all about what he'd learned about India in school. Angelina tried to seem interested, but her thoughts were lost in the mysteries of Kidron and the lost jewels. What an adventure it would be to travel somewhere and find something that no one remembered was lost. Trek nudged her back to reality by asking her opinion on whatever he was discussing. She bluffed her way through the conversation until she had figured out what he was talking about.

"Well, I'd better get home. Tomorrow will be a really big day. Dad wants to leave extra early, so we get the best booth locations at the Flea Market. We have gallons of syrup, jars of jelly, and lots of mushrooms from Conda's family. If we can sell it all, we'll be set for the winter! Night!" He waved goodbye.

Angelina headed for Rabea's, her head swimming with thoughts of the jewels of Kidron.

The more Katie wandered around the Woods, the more discouraged she became. Loneliness followed her like a shadow. It was everywhere. The only companion she had was that owl. It was a constant presence, and she had begun to talk to it in addition to talking to herself. During the day, she was able to keep herself busy looking for food, making things like a toothbrush out of a funky bit of bark that shredded into bristles without shedding them. She'd made a hat out of a nutshell and some cups and bowls out of acorns. But nights were hard. She could feel depression settle over her as the sun went down.

"I really need to find a way out of here, you know." She looked at the owl perched on a branch above her cave entrance. "You could help me. You have to know how." He just blinked. Dusk muffled the rest of the sounds of the Woods. It really was just the two of them now.

"Look, Chuck. That's your name now. You act like I deserve to be stuck here. I don't, you know." Her voice cracked a bit as she began to choke up. She wiped her nose on her sleeve. "I don't deserve any of this." She bit her lip and picked at her fingernails, whispering under her breath, "I thought he really liked me."

There was a long silence. Katie didn't think Chuck would really answer, but the vacuum that followed her confession was deafening. She looked up at the owl as the tears filled her eyes. Blinking didn't help to contain the pools that threatened to spill over.

"He told me he loved me, that I was special. Different than other girls." More silence. "I believed him," she whispered. "I really thought I was special."

Katie stared at her feet and began picking at the scars on her thigh. She could feel them through her jeans. Even if she couldn't feel them, she knew right where they were. The owl silently flew off into the night. Katie crawled into her bed, pressed her back up against the cave wall, tucked her hands tight between her knees, and wept.

The Village Quiet

F LEA MARKET SATURDAY CAME QUICKLY, as it did every week. Unlike the others, Angelina dreaded Saturdays. The village was really quiet on those days. Almost everyone had gone to town and those who didn't used the time to visit family and friends in other villages. Magda had explained (more than once) why Angelina couldn't go along. Secrecy was essential to protecting their lifestyle. Suppose average humans, the ones the villagers call Takers, knew that this beautiful place existed. In that case, they'd be swarming all over with camping gear, guns, and off-road vehicles, bringing noise, trash, and destruction. It wouldn't be long before the Enchanted Woods would be ruined.

"You have to earn trust, Angelina. Everyone here has to believe that you love our home as much as we do. You will have to show all of us that you'd never do anything that would jeopardize our lifestyle. When you've done that, and we trust you not to show others the way into the Woods, you can come with us."

"But, Magda, I won't tell! I promise! Not a word! It's so boring here all by myself when you all leave. There is nothing to do here! Please, please let me go."

Angelina put on her best wide-eyed, pleading expression. It usually worked with her father and always worked with her mother. Magda wasn't moved an inch.

"Angelina, look at me. This is not about you and what you want. It's about trust. Spend today thinking about that, and we'll talk about it when I get back."

With that, Magda picked up a large sack filled with the baskets she'd made during the past month and gently lowered it into the wagon Trek had pulled up in front of her hut. He reached out his hand to help her onto the buckboard, winking at Angelina. She sneered back.

"Think about what I said, dear, and enjoy the Woods! There are lots to do."

Angelina watched as the wagons pulled out of sight. Everyone, even the children, was holding hands, laughing, and talking about what they would buy with their part of the proceeds of the day's sale. The wagon, loaded with bottles of syrup and jars of jam, was always last in the train. It was very full this time, and she watched as Gastor took great care not to jostle the load and risk breaking any of the precious cargo. They were expecting to make enough money today to buy everyone new shoes, so he needed to guide the mules slowly around the rocks and roots along the way.

Angelina twisted her lips to one side to keep from crying. She wanted to go, not so much now, to get away but because she wanted them to want to take her with them. She wanted to matter. She wanted to be one of them. She bit her lip. The tears rolled down her cheeks.

She wondered what the Takers thought of this funny band of people when they rolled into town with mule-drawn wagons instead of cars or vans. Elves had no need for vehicles since they ran fast and were very skilled at swinging from tree to tree. Peering over the chain-link fence, she'd seen the schoolgirls arrive at school in cars. Still, they usually walked home in the after-noon giggling and flirting with boys who rode bikes or skateboards. She had been so close to getting up the nerve to just fall into step with them, hoping to be accepted as one of the group. Instead, here she was, again, an outsider. All she wanted was to belong.

"Trust! You can't trust anyone. Sooner or later, they'll all betray you, that's for sure." Kicking at the dust, she turned to go see what she could find to do before she died of boredom.

As she turned to wander back into the village, she wondered if any of the them had left their doors unlocked. She was curious to see inside their houses. She'd seen Magda's, and living with Rabea, she knew all about her stuff, but the others were a mystery. Surely, it was fair game to snoop if they didn't lock their doors.

She'd always been curious about Conda and Tanner. They weren't that much older than she was but were married and disgustingly happy. They are always so polite to each other, holding hands and helping each other. Angelina had never seen any married couple act that lovey-dovey before. She wondered if it was all an act or if they really liked each other that much.

She looked over her shoulders to be sure she was the only one left in the village and then tried their front door. It swung open immediately. Cautiously, she stepped inside, pulling the door to but not latching it in case she was discovered and had to escape.

The living room and kitchen were all one room, round since it was made out of a hollowed-out tree stump, much like her little hollow. There weren't many books, but the walls were filled with gorgeous paintings of flowers and birds all signed by Conda. Angelina had no idea that she could paint like this. She paused, remembering how much she missed her little house.

Hearing Magda's words echo in her ears, she murmured, "But then I never asked."

The shelves were filled with bits of this and that, things they must have bought at the Flea Markets. But what caught Angelina's eye was a magnificent carved sculpture on the fireplace mantle. It was of two hands, fingers laced together to make a bowl. Nestled in the cradle of the fingers was a perfect tiny bird. Behind the pair of hands was one large hand that held the two. The inscription said, "In our hands together, held in the hand of God; T to C."

Angelina drew in a breath as she realized Tanner had made this for Conda. She ran her fingers over the delicate details of the smaller hand and then the rugged fingers of the other. The large, single one had big gentle fingers, strong and powerful but without any indication of harm. Fascinated, she studied the piece from every angle without picking it up because she was afraid she might drop it. She may be a snoop, but she had no intention of destroying anything.

"It's something, isn't it?"

A deep male voice startled Angelina, and she spun around, clenching her fists as she always did when she was taken off guard. It was Daiken standing in the doorway.

"What are you doing here?" Angelina demanded.

"What are you doing here?" he replied, raising one eyebrow.

Her mind raced to create a plausible lie to cover her crime.

"Ah, I was looking for something Conda said I could borrow. Why aren't you in town with the others?"

"I get tired of the heat and being nice to strangers. I decided to hang around today and spend some time with you."

Chewing on a stalk of wheat, he leaned on the doorframe, blocking her escape route so that she was forced to play along.

"Come on, gorgeous, let's get out of here, go somewhere where we can get to know each other. I know a great place where we can be alone and talk."

He offered his hand, and she took it, afraid not to; afraid also because she wanted to.

Katie woke early after a fitful night. She was hopeful that today would be the day she found a path back into the real world. She rubbed her eyes to remove the dregs of tears from the night before. The owl flew down, the grey and tan feathers of his massive wings making him almost invisible against the bark of the trees. He settled on a rock near the entrance of her cave.

"Nice of you to show up. Some friend you are. Get me to spill my guts to you, and what do you do? You just take off and leave me all alone." She pulled her hair back out of her face so Chuck could see her glare. "You're no better than my dad. He didn't listen either. Just yelled at me. Told me no self-respecting 19-year-old guy would want a 13-year-old girl like me." She pulled on her shoes and tied the laces tight. "Come on. We're going to find a way out of here." She followed the only path that appeared without thinking about which way to go. The owl flew on ahead.

"You know, it's not hard to imagine me with an older guy. I'm mature for my age." Her defiance grew with every turn. "And I'm not so bad to look at." Her pace slowed with that one. It was a stretch. She had a bunch of freckles, and her teeth were still trying to decide how straight they were going to be. "And I'm smart." Katie decided to give it up for the time being. She was too hungry to deal with her past right now.

"Chuck, go see if you can find us some blueberries, would ya?"

Chuck circled Katie and flew off. Katie was startled by what she thought at first was his shadow. This one had a long tail trailing behind two massive wings. She stood as still as a statue as she watched it glide past her and disappear into the canopy above.

Closing Doors and Opening Hearts

ANGELINA AND DAIKEN CLOSED CONDA and Tanner's door behind them. They walked off into the woods, Daiken asking her question after question about herself.

"You're beautiful, you know. And smart. I've been watching you. You aren't like the other girls here. You're something special. Tell me about yourself." And he listened intently to her as she answered all his questions. What did she like, what did she dream about, where would she go if she could travel anywhere? No one had ever really listened to her before, not like this.

"I want you to see something. These are secret, so you'll have to promise not to tell anyone I showed you. Promise? Swear?"

"I promise!" she said.

She took his hand, and he led her through dense undergrowth.

He showed her hidden caves where they explored, laughing at each other as they crawled in and out of secret hiding places. They ate berries and pine nuts. He took her to a secluded waterfall.

"Hey, it's a great day for a swim. Come on, no one will see us," he said as he pulled her towards the water. Angelina wasn't sure, but he was insistent. She grew more and more uncomfortable with how their wet clothes clung to their bodies. She had been taught to be modest and to wear clothes that weren't revealing.

"Come on, silly! It's just us. Nobody can see you but me, and I like what I see." And with that, he dunked her under the water, tickling her until she burst through the surface, laughing and clinging to his neck. Laughing felt good. Being with him felt good.

"Let's go dry off. I've got more to show you."

Lying on the soft grass, Daiken spread her long hair out over her head so it would dry. He arranged each curl just so, reaching across her body to make sure there were no twigs or grass caught in the strands. Angelina looked up at his strong face just above hers and felt the warmth of his breath. Their eyes met, and slowly, he lowered his face to hers and kissed her.

Angelina had never been kissed before. She'd always worried that she'd do it wrong, but this was nice, really nice. When he stopped, Angelina reached up with both hands and drew his mouth back to hers. They kissed again and again.

"Whoa, Missy! Let's rest a bit here."

He laughed. She was confused. He seemed to like it. Did she do something wrong?

"Come on. I know some more really cool places you'll like."

He reached out his hand and pulled her to her feet, wrapping his arms around her. The warmth of his hug reassured her. Slipping her hand in his, like the hand sculpture on Conda and Tanner's mantle, she followed him off for another adventure.

"Tell me about the hand carving on Conda's mantle. Did Tanner really do that?"

"Yeah, he gave it to her when they found out they were going to have a baby. Carved it out of one piece of wood, too." He reached down to get her hand as they climbed over a boulder to get up to an overlook he wanted to show her.

"Where's the baby?"

"They lost it—died right after it was born. Everyone was devastated. It's impressive how they pulled it together and just kept trying. Look!" He pointed to a pair of eagles circling out over the canyon. They watched them dive and play in the air currents.

"I'm going to be free like that someday," he said. It was more of a declaration than a statement. His gaze never left the birds in flight.

"What do you mean? You're leaving the Woods?" Angelina was surprised. None of the villagers seemed discontented. She didn't think any of them wanted to leave. "Where would you go? What would you do?" He might be her ticket out of here, too. "I could go with you!"

"Not where I'm going, Missy. I'm going to see the world. I'm going to hitchhike around the world, drinking with sailors, dancing with pretty women, and working just long enough to get money to move on. I'm tired of this place. Too quiet, no excitement." He grabbed her hand again and pulled her back to reality and the trail down the mountain. "Where do you want to go? I can tell that you've been itching to get out of here too."

Struggling to keep up with him as he raced down the trail as if he was on his way to catch the next wagon out of the Enchanted Woods, Angelina was surprised that he knew she was eager to get out of the woods. She thought she'd hidden her intentions better than that.

"Well, I thought I wanted to go home, but now I'm not so sure. I'm not sure where I belong."

"Right now, missy, you belong with me!" He grabbed her hand, pulled her up tight to him, and kissed her. Gently, he brushed a strand of hair out of her face and gave her a quick peck on her nose. They laughed and ran off to play some more. This was the best day Angelina could remember, ever.

Stolen Time

ANGELINA AND DAIKEN SPENT ALL their free time together for the next few weeks. They talked for hours about their dreams, making plans to get out of the Woods. When he wasn't working as a woodsman gathering firewood or tending crops or when she wasn't doing chores for Magda, mostly gathering herbs, they sneaked off into the woods.

"Tell me about your family. You never talk about them," she asked gently one day when they were on a picnic. Angelina reached over and twirled her fingers around the thick dark curls that had drifted into his eyes.

She had stolen bread and cheese from Rabea's cupboard, and they'd snuck off into the woods to make out. She decided kissing was one of her favorite things. She loved it when he was in the mood to kiss.

"There's not much to tell. We came here when my dad couldn't find work. He had met Gastor at one of the Flea Markets, and they got to talking about how hard times were. Gastor convinced him to bring me, my mom, and two sisters to the Woods. Things were okay for a while, but one Saturday, my dad went into town with everyone and never came home. No one knows what happened to him." Angelina reached for his hand and squeezed it. He squeezed back. She was puzzled by his refusal to hold her hand in front of the others. He said it was more special when their relationship was secret. Since she'd never had a boyfriend before, she assumed this was the way it was done, but she wanted the others to know how much they liked each other.

"That's awful," Angelina offered, hoping to comfort him.

"Not really. Mom says I'm the man of the house now, so I get to pretty much come and go as I please. He wasn't much of a dad anyway." He turned to look at her. "Besides, I got all I want right here, missy."

And he kissed her. As she closed her eyes, giving in to his embrace, she wondered if she should tell him about her father, about the beatings. He might respond like the heroes in the books she'd been reading. He might even offer to beat her dad up or something romantic like that. Then again, he might think she was damaged goods if she told. She decided not to. Not yet, anyway. As the afternoon wore on, they talked and talked about everything. She studied his face as if she was going to paint his portrait; his thick, almost black hair, the long eyelashes that framed his dark eyes, and the short rough whiskers that lined his jaw. He was very handsome.

One day, they had slipped off early to spend the whole day swimming by the waterfall. As they were lying lazily in the cool grass, she asked him if he'd ever heard the legend of the red and blue diamonds. Skeptically, he asked her what made her think there was such a treasure.

"I found an old book behind one of the bookcases in the schoolhouse. Remember when I helped out in the school when Conda was sick that day? The kids had all left for the day, so I sat down and read it. The story was believable enough, but I've never heard anyone talk about it, so I wondered."

"Well, if there is such a treasure, it would be enough to live on for years. I'm sure it's just a fairy tale, that's all. You say the book's in the school library? What's it called?" Angelina was pleased with his intense interest in the subject. She liked having someone pay attention to her when she talked, especially when it was something so mysterious—and she knew things he didn't know.

"Oh, I don't remember. I just put it back on the shelf with the other books. It had some cool maps in it, though. Hey, want to swim or kiss me?" she teased. He opted to kiss her before he picked her up and tossed her in the water.

"Hey, would you do something for me? I'd like to see that book, but I can't go into the schoolhouse. Could you get it for me?" He tweaked her nose and winked at her.

"Why can't you go in the schoolhouse?" She tweaked his nose back.

"I got kicked out of class in the 8th grade for cheating, which I swear was a lie. I never went back and finished school. Conda would be suspicious if I showed up now, you know, suddenly wanting to learn or something. But you could get it for me. I'd really like to see those maps you talked about."

They continued to meet secretly, sneaking out anytime, day or night, that they could arrange to be alone. Occasionally he brought up the book about the legend of the diamonds.

"Have you found that book yet?"

"No, one of the kids must have dropped it behind the bookcase again."

Angelina was more interested in kissing him than in some old legend. Still, he seemed more interested in getting the book. All he talked about was the maps and the diamonds. Frankly, she worried he was getting bored with her. She kept promising him she'd find the book but didn't try very hard. Once she handed the book over, he might not want her anymore, and she wasn't willing to let that happen.

One Hurt on Top of Another

"ALL THE VILLAGES ARE GOING to get together tonight to celebrate the harvests. We're going to have a huge dance right here in the clearing! Everyone will be there!" Rabea was more excited than Angelina had ever seen her.

"What's the big deal? It's just a dance," Angelina said.

"It's a big deal because my folks will be there AND because Markin is coming!" Rabea's eyes lit up when she said his name.

"You have a boyfriend? How did I not know this? Tell me! Tell me!" Angelina put down the laundry they were sorting and pulled Rabea to the floor, where they folded their legs, sitting face to face.

Rabea told Angelina all about how they'd met. "He's from another village, so we didn't know each other before. His family are farmers, and my parents knew his parents. He comes from good people, so my parents approved very much!"

"So, how'd you meet him? I've never seen you with him."

"We met during harvest. Markin and I sat together at meals. Pretty soon, we started going for long walks instead of joining the group for dinner. I think everyone knew we liked each other. They kept giving us chores so we'd have to work together."

Rabea giggled and then sighed as she continued. The harvest had been over for a few weeks, and she'd been busy helping the other women canning the food for the winter pantries. They hadn't seen each other for weeks. Rabea was giddy at the thought of seeing him again and eager to introduce him to her friends in this village.

Angelina was glad for her friend. She was desperate to share the secret of her boyfriend, too. But Daiken had been adamant that no one know that they were together. He threatened her if she told anyone. Once, when she suggested that they ask some of the others to join them on a hike, he'd grabbed her wrist, twisting it, and made her swear not to tell anyone about them. No one. The grip of his fingers left bruises on her wrist. Rabea had asked what happened, and she'd made up some stupid story that made sense at the time. It made sense enough that Rabea bought it anyway.

But now that they were sharing girl talk, Angelina couldn't stand it and decided to risk sharing her secret. She fidgeted in her chair as if she had sat on something uncomfortable.

"What's wrong with you?" Rabea said.

"I have a boyfriend, too," she whispered, testing the waters of secrecy.

Angelina smiled sheepishly as she watched the shock register on her friend's face. She was even more pleased when Rabea burst out, "Who?!" The idea of the two of them having someone special at the same time was such fun. More and more, they were becoming like sisters. Having a girlfriend-sister to share the excitement of a new romance made the whole thing even better.

"Daiken."

Angelina whispered his name and giggled. But Rabea didn't giggle back. Instead, Angelina watched as Rabea's face hardened. It confused her that Rabea seemed alarmed, not thrilled like she'd expected.

"Daiken? Angelina, you don't know what you're doing. You don't want anything to do with him." Rabea reached out to take her friend's hand. "He's trouble. You need to stay away from him."

Angelina snatched her hand back. "He told me not to tell. He said you'd be jealous and say bad things about him. He was right. I thought you'd be happy for me."

Tears welled up in her eyes, and she fought to control the quiver in her voice. Her heart ached with disappointment.

"Angelina darling, come here. I'm sorry, but he's no good. He uses girls. I know he talks pretty and makes you feel special, but he only wants what he wants.

You need to wait for someone who'll appreciate you for your special gifts and love you forever."

Rabea tried to reach for her again, but Angelina was up on her feet and headed out the door, angry and hurt.

The village center was filled with people. Everyone was arriving for the celebration. There was lots of bustle of tables being set up, musical instruments arranged and tuned, and lanterns were being hung in the trees since they all planned to dance well into the night. Angelina heard people talking about looking forward to seeing friends they hadn't seen in a while. Moms were filling each other in on the accomplishments of their children. A group of men was hashing over their concerns about damage to some of their crops. Something was pulling up the vegetables by the roots, eating the tops, and tossing the stems and the roots feet away from the planted site.

"Never seen anything like it, nope. Never seen it before," Gastor was telling Tanner.

"Trek, come help me with the food." Magda waved him over. Angelina ducked her head and skirted around past them. "Oh, Angelina, you can help too."

Angelina wiped her face with the back of her hand, erasing the tears and pretending not to hear Magda's invitation. She smiled and greeted people blankly as she pushed her way across the clearing, searching for Daiken. She needed him to hug her, reassure her, and make the hurt go away.

She was relieved when she saw the back of his jacket through the crowd and headed in his direction. She was rounding Conda and Tanner's hut, hoping to catch him, when she realized there was someone with him. She was pretty with long curly red hair. They were laughing and holding hands in public, in front of people walking by to get to the village green. Angelina slipped behind a tree, unsure of what she was seeing but sure she needed to see more.

"Oh, Daiken, you're so silly!" The redhead giggled, tossing her hair back with one hand, the other wrapped up in his. He whispered something in her ear, and they both laughed. Then he kissed her. Just like he had kissed Angelina.

Stunned, Angelina felt her heartbreak. Hurt and anger flared in her eyes, making everything look distorted and peculiar. Her gaze met Daiken's, but he didn't seem to care that she'd caught him. She heard him say, "You are something really special, Stacia," the exact words he'd said to her. She realized he purposely spoke loudly enough for Angelina to hear. He kissed Stacia again, this time wrapping both arms around her and pushing her back until she leaned against a tree, and he leaned heavily against her. She saw him smile slightly at her just before Angelina turned to run, the breeze muffling her sobs.

Buckets and Lock Picks

I**N THE DAYS THAT FOLLOWED,** Angelina kept to herself, more withdrawn than ever. She overheard Rabea and Magda talking while hanging the wash on the clothesline that hung like a spider's web between their two huts. She heard Magda first.

"Rabea, I am concerned about Angelina."

Angelina crept in closer so she could hear exactly what they said about her.

"I'm worried about her, too, Magda. I mean, she used to ask if she could help, find things to do, but now, when she finishes her work, she disappears to her room in the loft and reads or sleeps or just stares at the ceiling."

Angelina stood at the corner of their hut and watched as Rabea stopped hanging the clothes on the line to study Magda's face. She almost snarfed an audible 'duh' when she heard Magda say, "Something has injured her soul, and she is grieving." She wondered if Magda had figured out what had happened.

Angelina watched as Magda continued to pin the clothes on the line, not making eye contact with Rabea. She winced when she heard Rabea say, "Even those who don't particularly like her are worried."

What did she mean by 'even those who don't like her'—who didn't like her? It was when she heard Magda try to justify Angelina's behavior with, "I know. When anyone asks me, I tell them it's just the moodiness of a young girl. You know how girls that age can be". I don't really believe it, though. Angelina had enough of eavesdropping, slid back into the shadows of the trees, and made her way to the back of Magda's hut. She hated the thought that people were talking about her. Twisted between hurt and anger, she swore out loud.

"This was none of their business. They must all think I'm a fool."

Kicking at everything in her path, Angelina headed around the hut and crossed over to Rabea's front door. Her feet hit each step up to the loft with a vengeance. She couldn't believe she'd trusted Rabea with the secret of what had happened that night.

She relived the events of that evening, coming home from the dance, and sobbing uncontrollably. She regretted that when she finally calmed down, the story of Daiken and Stacia came pouring out. Now, on top of the hurt of being dumped for a giggling redhead, Angelina was heartbroken. Rabea had promised not to tell anyone. Angelina wondered now if she'd told everyone what she knew. Ashamed of being so trusting, Angelina slipped under the quilt on her bed and vowed never to share secrets with Rabea, Magda, or anyone else.

Her hopes for solitude failed when Trek came bounding into the hut calling her name. Trek had been doing his best to cheer her up and wasn't showing any signs of giving up. She knew what he was up to.

"Angelina!" he called up the stairs. "Come on. I saw you come in here. Come with me and help me. I have to collect the sap buckets and get them cleaned and stored for next year. If you don't come, I'll have to make four trips, and it's a long way back into the maple groves. Please?"

She tossed off the quilt and looked over the railing. He was making puppy dog faces, drooping his head and eyes until Angelina couldn't keep a straight face a minute longer.

"You're an idiot, you know, a real idiot. All right, but I'm not carrying the ones you slopped the sap all over the outside. Those are yours!"

"Deal," he said.

His efforts were to get her out of her funk. She was annoyed with how proud of himself he seemed. But she did have to admit, if only to herself, it was nice of him to care enough to try.

"Let's go the back way and see if the bears are in their dens yet."

"You know that most people go the other direction when bears are involved, not poking their heads in to say hello at bedtime." Her characteristic sarcastic tone was back, and it made him smile.

They headed west from the village with the warm morning sun at their backs. They laughed as they played a ridiculous game of tag. Angelina shrieked every time he tagged her, and he groaned every time she caught him. Fall had begun to settle in, and some of the trees had started to change colors. Indian Summer, that glorious season that combined the sun of summer and the cool winds of fall, had arrived early and seemed intent on staying late this year. There were hints of frost on the rocks, and mushrooms along the trail sparkled like glitter. Shades of orange and gold lay crisply against the deeper tones of greens and browns on every surface in the Woods. As hard as she'd tried not to, Angelina felt better.

Katie stopped abruptly. She was sure she'd heard voices in the distance. She scrambled up the hill in front of her, her feet sliding on the frost-tipped grass, losing at least two steps for everyone she gained. She was facing her worst fear. The ridge of the hill was a spine of outcroppings too vertical for her to scale. Discouraged, she searched frantically for a way to get around this wall of sharp rocks.

"Don't leave. Please don't leave. I need help." She called out over and over, hoping that her voice would carry on the wind and help would arrive.

But the voices faded as the sun's rays were lost in the thick density of the trees. Everything was so wet and slippery that it was difficult for her to search for a way to follow whoever it was she heard. Just as she was ready to give up, she spotted a gap in the face of the cliff where the rocks almost formed a set of stairs. Now she had a way to try to get to whoever was on the other side of this wall of stone. At least she knew now that she wasn't alone in these ghastly Woods.

She ran ahead in a desperate effort to avoid Trek's reach. Angelina stopped at the crest of a hill, looked down the valley at the creek, and smiled, hearing the water giggle with delight as it slipped over stones in its path.

"I just can't get used to the sounds of the Woods. I could have sworn I heard someone calling out to us."

"I know. It took me a long time, too. Now, when I get close to town, I miss two things—the silence of the Woods and the laughter in the Village.

Ever notice how little laughter there is in town?" He looked up just as she shot him a look. "Oops, sorry."

Leaves in the trees hummed to a tune in the breeze that only they could hear. Every Woodland creature seemed to be out today doing its last-minute fall shopping for food or winter bedding. So many sounds sailed up on the crisp air and drifted across the valley that they both laughed. Snow would be coming soon, and everyone wanted to be ready.

"We'd better get going." Angelina moved slowly. Trek stopped. "Now what?" Angelina didn't answer right away. She stopped right in the middle of the trail.

"Nothing. I was just looking, that's all. Hey, do you ever want to leave here? Go out and see the world?"

"No, not really. I mean, I might like to travel a bit. I'd like to see Tibet. You know, Conda's always buying old copies of National Geographic at the market. Those mountains look really cool in the photos. But other than that, I think I'm good here. There're parts of the Woods that I haven't seen yet. Mountains I haven't climbed, streams and rivers I haven't followed to wherever they go. Why?"

He reached down and pulled a long blade of grass as he leaned up against a tree.

"I don't know. I guess I've never been content with where I was, so I always wanted to be somewhere else."

She leaned up against a tree, too but didn't sit down. These thoughts were ones that she felt she needed to work through standing up.

"Aren't you happy here?" Trek said.

"That's just it. I think I do like it here. You all are so nice to me, and the Woods are so amazing. I can't tell if I think about leaving because somewhere in me, there's something more I'm supposed to do or see or if it's just a habit— never being content. There was nothing about my life before to be contented with, so I naturally always dreamed about all the other places I wanted to be. Now I'm just confused."

She sighed and picked at the moss with the toe of her boot.

"Well, the way I see it, God picks out the best place for us to be, and it's our job to make the most of it. Not just tolerate it, you know, but meet the people and find out what He sees in them that's special; find the gift of skill He gave me and make it an art, be the very best 'whatever' there ever was. Other people get to live in those faraway places. But, don't you know, somewhere in China, there's a guy wishing he could be me!"

He laughed at his joke and looked up at her, raising his eyebrows, expecting her to join in. When she didn't, he got up and stood next to her.

"You know, Angelina, I guessed that your life at home wasn't good, and you don't have to tell me any of the details if you don't want to, but you're here now, and we like you and want you to be part of our group, our family. That bad stuff is in the past, and you're safe now. Really."

She watched him stare at the ground instead of making eye contact with her. She was glad he made that choice. She took a deep breath and headed on up the trail.

Coming or Going

"YOU COMING? THOSE BEARS WILL be telling bedtime stories by the time we get there if you don't hurry."

Trek double-stepped to catch up to her, and just as he got there, Angelina leaped up, grabbed a branch overhead, and swung from tree to tree.

"No fair!" he called out, laughing as he ran to try to catch her. "Cheater!"

They found the bear dens, but no one was home, which was a good thing for bears. They walked down to the beaver pond, found the den well-built and large enough for a good-sized family, and watched the herds of elk moving to lower meadows for the winter. At the same time, the geese flew south in perfect formation. As they walked, Angelina began to feel comfortable with Trek-like they'd been friends for years. He was comfortable, kind of like a pair of slippers. Almost without thinking, she started to tell him things she never thought she would share. First, she told him more about being homeschooled and how elves live in very small family groups, not having contact with others except at life event celebrations.

"My folks didn't take much to celebrating so we rarely saw family and only had a few friends. I had Aunt and Uncle, but my Aunt disappeared when I was little."

"What happened to her?"

"No one ever talked about it, so I'm not sure what happened, and then my uncle moved away." The more she talked, the more truth there was to her stories.

"My dad was nice when I was little, but something changed, and he got mean." "Especially when he drank. He'd hit first and then yell." She paused, wondering if all this was too much.

Trek was silent. Angelina had expected some response. Finding none, she continued.

"I tried to stay out of his way."

"Hey, there's no need to explain. I'm sure you did what you had to do. The important thing is that you're here now."

Angelina told him about the thicket that lined a nasty marsh and separated the big houses on wide streets from the part of the woods where her family lived. She told him about the girls she had so admired.

"I figured if I could be one of them, have what they had, I'd be happy." Then she turned to look at him. He didn't look like he believed she was a freak or anything. She decided to go on without taking her eyes off his. She told him about the dog run, how her father had said it was good riddance to have her gone, and how her mother had given up looking for her and left with the man that beat her and called her names. Angelina had no idea why she was telling him all this, but she couldn't stop. It just kept coming. It felt odd how little all those stories hurt her anymore—they just were.

He was silent. The look on his face was almost blank. She decided this wasn't a good idea until his expression changed dramatically.

"Wait!" Trek stopped and stared at her. "Did you say you were in a dog run? With the door locked? Was it a padlock, like the ones that need a key?"

"Yeah, why?" She watched him reach for his hip pocket. He pulled out a small case from his hip pocket. Opening it, he revealed a set of small sharp tools.

"What are those?" she asked, trying to figure out if Joseph had shown her some of these before since he had every tool ever made in his vest pocket.

"These are lock picks, the ones I used to open a dog run gate to let a wet, dirty girl escape from two nasty little kids!"

"No way!" she shrieked.

"Way!" he shrieked back.

"But how? Why?" Angelina found this incredulous. How could it be? That dog run was nowhere near the Enchanted Woods. And that he had rescued her twice was bewildering.

"Dad had sent me to check out a new farmer's market to see if we should get a space there to sell stuff. I'd left before dawn, sure that I knew the way, but it was way on the other side of town. I took what I thought was a shortcut." He flashed her his signature cheesy grin. "Got lost." She punched his arm. "That's when I ran across you in that run. I heard the kids shouting about getting outside early so they could go make the elf sing. Their mom thought they were making up some game and was about to let them out, but they had to get their shoes first. I whipped out my lock pick tools and the rest, as they say, is history. Boy, you sure shot out of there like a rabbit. Not even a thank you, as I recall." He smiled a toothy grin at her.

Angelina had to sit down. This was way too weird. "I'm sorry." She twisted the hem of her tunic between her fingers. "I should have thanked you. I just wanted to be as far away as I could from those little brats. They were horrid! They had a rake handle with a nail sticking out of the end. They poked that thing at me 'til I bled, and then they laughed."

"What were they talking about making you sing? I heard the boy whining about not getting to hear you sing."

Angelina thought for a moment. There wasn't any reason to hold back the details of her life now. She'd already told him more than she ever intended to, so there was nothing left to lose. "Let's get those sap buckets, and I'll explain while we walk. It's a long story." They both fell silent.

When they'd found the sap buckets stacked up by the maple trees and sorted them, so he had to carry the sloppy ones, and she got the cleaner ones, they headed home. It was getting dark as they crossed the clearing. Everyone must have been inside getting supper because the entire village was quiet. Lights inside were coming on in the windows. The only light outside was the glow of the setting sun.

"Thanks for coming."

"Thanks for asking me. I had fun. Really."

"See you tomorrow?"

"Yeah." She just stood there, hands in her hip pockets, hair tucked behind her ears. She had forgotten that she was ashamed of her elf ears.

He turned to walk to his hut. She called, and he turned quickly. "Yah?" he said.

"Thanks for opening that gate on the dog run."

"No problem, anytime."

He mumbled something under his breath and Angelina knew he knew how lame that last remark had sounded. It made her smile.

Katie scrambled up the stacks of stones, almost able to take them two at a time like she did on the steps to the dining hall. So anxious to make it to the top, she didn't concentrate on her footing, and with only one more stone to scale, she slipped and fell, smashing her knees and elbows all the way to the bottom of the cliff. Covered in dirt and blood, she lay on the ground in a daze as her brain took inventory of her body to see what was broken. Finally, she slowly rolled over onto her back and stared into the blur of the trees. As things began to come into focus, she realized that Chuck had landed in the branches above her. The irony of his ability to always show up after she needed him struck her as funny at first. But before she could gather the strength to laugh, she began to cry instead. For the longest time, she lay there motionless except for the cascade of tears that flowed across her cheeks.

"Why couldn't I listen to my mother? Why? None of this would be happening if I'd just done what she told me."

Katie struggled to sit up and, with the back of her hand, smeared her muddy tears instead of wiping them away. Her words were garbled by the thick tears that ran down the back of her throat. She snorted the snot that ran out of her nose but continued her rant.

"She said any 19-year-old guy that was interested in a 13-year-old girl was just looking for trouble, but I wouldn't believe her. NO. I thought he loved me, that someone like him could actually love me." She cocked her head to one side so she could see Chuck beyond the tangle of hair that hung down in her face.

"He said he did. He actually said he loved me, and I actually believed him." Her voice trailed off. "Then he beat me." Her head dropped to her bent knees, and she sobbed, shoulders heaving with each breath. "What a fool," she whispered. "What a fool." Katie sat in the middle of the trail alternating between sobs and snortles until exhaustion won. "I'm so sorry, Mom. I'm so sorry," she whispered. She twisted herself onto her side and tried to stand up without grinding more sand and dirt into the wounds on her hands and knees.

Chuck cocked his head from one side to the other. Katie wished she could suck the words 'he beat me' back into her mouth. If she'd never said it, she could still hope it wasn't real. That it never happened. But it did, and she had said it out loud. At least Chuck wouldn't tell anyone. She'd gotten that part right.

"Come on, Chuck. I've got to get back to the cave and get cleaned up."

Secrets to keep

TANNER STEPPED ONTO THE porch holding the door for Conda, who was carrying their picnic basket. Angelina, who had also just stepped outside, watched them enviously. She secretly crossed her fingers, hoping someone would love her like that someday. She had to admit she didn't feel as bad about Daiken as she thought she would. In fact, she didn't feel bad about much of anything.

"Good morning!" Conda called. "It was a perfect day for hunting raspberries. The sky was so blue."

"True, hardly a cloud."

Angelina looked up at the few clouds that dared to drift overhead. They were just enough to cool her off but not enough to darken her spirits. Angelina could almost see herself bursting into song. Still afraid of her voice, she suppressed the urge and focused on her search instead.

"Have fun on your picnic!" she called over her shoulder as she skipped down the steps. By the time she reached the far side of the village green, a path appeared.

She climbed up the hillside above the creek hoping to find a luscious patch of juicy ripe berries. When she turned to scan the hillside, she saw Magda making her way to the pool below the waterfall, most likely to take a bath.

"Magda, Magda!" she called out, waving her hat, a lavish thing Mauve had made for her. Magda didn't respond.

"She can't hear me over the water."

Angelina leaped for a low branch and swung wide over the grass and brambles, landing on her bottom just at the top of the draw. The downed leaves were still wet with dew, a perfect sled as she cascaded down the hill and into the pool with a splash.

"Oh, my dear! You gave me such a start!" Magda exclaimed, wiping the splashed water from her tunic. "But it is nice to see you as always. Will you join me while I wash up a bit? My feet could use a good soak after such a dusty morning walk." She slid her feet into the pool's cool water and sighed with great satisfaction. "So, what have you been up to today, dear?"

Dripping from head-to-toe, Angelina settled on the grass next to Magda, thankful that Indian Summer had decided to stay. The warm sun felt good on her skin. "I was looking for raspberries but haven't found any yet. I thought I'd go up to the high meadow and see if there are any there if the bears haven't eaten them all!"

They both smiled knowingly. Bears somehow always get there first; it was a game of trying to outsmart them and beat them there. Angelina picked several long stems of clover and started to weave herself a crown. Few things smelled better than clover growing by a pond. As she reached across Magda for the next strand of clover, she bumped Magda's ever-present hat. Angelina had often wondered if Magda slept in the thing. It tumbled, and Angelina scrambled up to catch it before it went into the water.

"Just in time! I caught it."

As she turned to hand it back to Magda, she was startled by what she saw. Ears. Tall, pointed ears.

"Magda?!"

Magda slowly reached for her hat and carefully placed it tightly on her head. She didn't say anything. In fact, she showed no emotion at all. Her eyes stayed focused.

"Magda, you're an elf. Like me, you're an ELF!" Angelina was astonished. "Why didn't you tell me?"

"You never asked, my dear. And it is not something that I talk about."

Magda's remark, 'you never asked,' stung. She had never asked much of anything about Magda. She was, well, Magda. What was there to ask about? Still, Angelina was a bit ashamed.

"Why are you here living in the Woods with this group of villagers? Why aren't you with your family? Where is your family?"

Suddenly, there were so many questions to ask.

Magda was silent for a moment, looking thoughtfully into the deep waters of the pool.

"I have a sister, younger than me by twelve years. I had been married just a few years when she fell in love with a most unsuitable man. He was a brute and a bully and treated my sister with shameful disrespect."

Magda tossed a leaf in the water, and Angelina watched it swirl in a tiny eddy. "I told her he was a bad choice, that she would regret it later, but she was too much in love with the idea of a strong man to watch over her. She had an excuse for every bad thing he did. One day I caught him towering over her in the kitchen. He pressed his heavy chest against her so hard that she was bent backward against the edge of the table. He was yelling about the bread, something about the bread, and she was crying, trying to explain." Magda stopped again. "I told him to leave her alone and get out, but he just turned and looked at me. He shouted at me, 'Mind your own business. This has nothing to do with you.'" She wiped her face absently with the back of her hand. "He spit as the words growled from his throat. 'You'll get out and go home if you know what's good for you. Git!' I was so angry. My sister pleaded with me to leave. She was fine; it was fine. But I knew it never would be."

Angelina fixed her gaze on Magda, not sure where this was going.

"When I refused to move, he lunged at me. I grabbed the bread knife and swung it, catching his ear. The knife left a good-sized gash, and he bled like a stuck pig. I was stunned as I watched my sister rush to his side, using her tunic to try to stop the bleeding. I dropped the knife and ran home." Another leaf dropped into the pool and swirled around slowly. Magda's eyes never left the leaf. Angelina was shocked to learn that this gentle woman she had come to think of as a friend had the capacity for such violence. But she had to wonder if she wouldn't have done the same thing if she had been there.

"When I got home, I told my husband what had happened. I was horrified when he told me he must turn me over to the Council. You know, elf women are never supposed to show any signs of hostility or anger. I had shamed him and would most likely be shunned." Now she stood up and looked at Angelina.

"I left. I couldn't stay where I would be considered unfit for protecting my own flesh and blood from evil, where my own husband would sacrifice me to the others to be punished. And I ended up here with Gastor, Trek, Rabea, and the others."

Angelina was confused. "But they don't know you're an elf. They think you're one of them."

Magda turned and locked eyes with Angelina. "Yes, and it must stay that way. You can't tell. If they knew I'd hurt someone as badly as I did, they would turn me out, turn their backs on me, too." Riveting Angelina with her look, Magda said, "I am trusting you, child. Your honor holds my future." They sat in silence for a long time before Magda gathered her things and turned to go home.

"I'm going to stay for a while," Angelina said quietly. She wasn't sure exactly what had just happened and what, if anything, she was supposed to do with it.

Survival and Temptations

KATIE WAS RELIEVED THAT, SOME time ago, she had found a cave deep enough to provide shelter from the rain. Sensing that fall was coming, she had started foraging for pine nuts, fruits like apples and cherries, and vegetables like beans, cauliflower, and corn. At least she had no shortage of fresh water since there were ponds, streams, and waterfalls everywhere.

She had such a hard time keeping her footing on the edges of the water. More than once, she'd found herself with her arms waving madly in the air as her feet left the ground, resulting in some pretty spectacular dives into the water. She had been so frustrated that there were no trails, people, or game trails anywhere in this entire forest. She was sure she was wandering in circles since she'd seen the same rock formations and odd trees repeatedly.

She had learned which plants worked to disinfect the cuts and scraps she had all over her body from scrambling through the thick underbrush. She'd fallen before and suffered a crushing blow as her descent was stopped by a large aspen tree taking a bit of hide out of her arm. None of those falls had been as bad as this one. Now, she hoped the tales of the smell of blood drawing bears were nothing more than campfire ghost stories. Curling up in a ball and sobbing, she pleaded with God, "Why won't you help me? Why? Aren't I worth paying some attention to? Don't I count for anything to you?"

Just like at Aspen Meadows, curled up on her bunk, this was a one-sided conversation she had every night. There was never an answer, but she had to keep trying. There had to be someone out there somewhere that would be able to help her. In the morning, she'd find some berries and resume her hunt for the voices she heard and a way out of this awful, hateful place.

Excitement ran through the village. It was like this when the group was expected to return from a day at the flea market. They always brought back wonderful gifts for those who stayed behind. Angelina had always hung back and silently watched the children's faces as they unwrapped the treats and toys their fathers brought home, always sure to say "Thank you, Daddy" before running off to play under the scrub oak.

She envied them, the families, the children with parents that loved them, tousled their hair, and brought them sweets delivered with hugs. She fought back the tears as she adopted a pose of crossing her arms and resting her chin on her knuckles as if she was studying the gifts intently. In reality, she was holding her chin steady to hide the quivering.

Magda was always kind enough to bring Angelina a little something, scented soap, a hair comb, or some chocolates. She took care to thank Magda, especially now that they shared the bond of secrecy. As alone as she had felt these days, Angelina was increasingly at peace in the Enchanted Woods, missing her mother less and less. Lately, however, Angelina was actually caught up in delight.

"They're coming! They're coming!" the children shouted as they ran. Women came out of the huts and the clearing filled with greetings and joy. Angelina joined the children as they ran down the path toward the wagons. Trek was in the front wagon with a large box on his lap. He called out to her. "Angelina! Angelina! Meet me by the willow. I've got something for you!"

Angelina ran to catch up with him as he drove the wagon around the clearing, pulled up in front of his hut, tied off the horses before jumping down, and carefully set the box on the buckboard.

"I'll get this unloaded and be right there! Save me a place on the dry part of the grass."

"Ok, but don't take too long. I've got chores, you know." She laughed at her joke. She'd worked all day while he and the others were gone. There wasn't even a twig out of place in the clearing, much less any other chore left undone. She spread the branches of the willow and settled on the swing. Trek came bounding in with the box. He placed it right in the middle of the bench. "Open it," he declared and stepped back.

"What, is it going to explode? Why are you backing up like that?" Her suspicious nature was overcoming her curiosity.

"I want to see the look on your face, that's all. Go on, open it." He spread his feet and shoved his hands in his back pockets.

Angelina carefully untied the cord and lifted the lid off, fully expecting something to jump out at her. What she saw was a mound of tissue. Her long fingers gathered the crisp paper one fold at a time until she saw what was hidden underneath: suede, light tan, almost white, soft, and velvety. Using both hands, she cradled the most beautiful boots she'd ever seen.

"Trek, stop bouncing." Angelina shushed him so she could concentrate on what she was seeing. "These are unbelievable. They're gorgeous, but where did you find them?" She pulled off her heavy black knee boots as if they were filled with ants.

"There's this great American Indian who shows up at the flea market a couple times a year. He wanted a fortune, but I knew you'd love them. Feel that suede, soft as a bunny's butt. And the fringe and the beads are done by hand, just like the boots. He made them completely by hand. See the beadwork down the sides? Says, 'Chosen one.'"

Angelina's eyes met his as she slid her right foot into the warmth of the boot. "Chosen one? And you thought of me?"

"Do they fit? I hope they fit okay." He sat down on the swing and watched as she pulled on the left one and stood up.

"It feels like I'm barefoot. They're so light." She flexed her feet and spread her toes as she adjusted to the gentle fit compared to the stiff grip of her knee boots. "They must have cost you everything. How did you pay for this?"

Trek shifted on the plank. "Well, they were expensive. But I really wanted you to have them. I managed it."

Angelina sat down and stared at him. She knew he didn't have much money. The sap season wasn't that long this year, and they didn't make nearly as much syrup as they'd hoped. Everyone had to cut back, being careful what they bought in town since everyone's share of the sales was down.

"Trek. What did you do?" she insisted. Suddenly she pulled her feet up out of the wet grass.

"Hey, the suede sheds water, so you don't have to worry when they get wet. Well, you can't swim in them—at least not very far, without having to dry them out. Don't worry. I didn't steal them." She didn't take her eyes off his. She was going to hold out for an answer. "Look, I used money my dad gave me for parts to fix the sap boiler."

"You what?" she almost shrieked. "Your dad is going to kill you. That money was for parts. If you don't come up with the parts to fix that boiler, he will kill you!" She really was shrieking now.

"No, no. Relax. I've got it covered. I ran into a guy I used to know before my dad and I lived out here and joined the rest of the family. He loaned it to me. I just have to pay him back in the next month cuz he's going to get a new Harley. I'll make it easy out of the next batch of raspberry jelly and I'm good."

Angelina sat staring at him. This felt really wrong, all except for the part about how fabulously comfortable the boots felt on her feet. Looking down, she examined the stitches, so small they were almost invisible. The fringe was long but not too long. It swayed gently when she moved. And the beading, saying she was a 'chosen one,' was intricate with vines weaving around the letters so complex that the words were almost a secret puzzle. She loved these boots. But he shouldn't have risked the boiler repair money. Too many people depended on that boiler. He shouldn't have.

But she was glad he did.

"See how soft the bottoms are. You won't be tearing up the Woods when you walk around, and you'll be so silent that you'll be able to creep around and see so much more of life. Now, everything hears you coming from miles away. You sound like the Takers tramping around in those things." Trek had never made a secret of his distaste for her black leather boots with the thick rigid soles. He smiled, and those irresistible dimples formed in his cheeks.

"You're sure this is okay? The money and all? I do love them."

Trek beamed and slapped her on the thigh. "Enjoy," he said, returning to help the others finish unloading the rest of the wagons.

Angelina sat alone under the branches of the willow. The smell of the wet grass was sweet. Tiny little dripping sounds came from the ends of the branches as they draped down to the ground. She did love these boots. A giddy chill rose in her stomach as she comprehended that he had bought them for her. He'd made a sacrifice, risked getting in trouble, just to give her something beautiful. She was a chosen one. She giggled. Trek liked her! Someone nice really liked her! She snatched up her old boots and ran out to show off her new glam.

She smiled inwardly as she saw heads turn and people stop working to check out her feet as she strutted her way across the clearing and bounced silently up the steps to the hut. She startled Rabea, who was in the kitchen putting away some of the canned goods she brought back from town today.

"Oh, I didn't hear you come in," she said.

Angelina beamed as she pointed her toe, putting her right foot out into Rabea's view.

"Wow, where'd you get those! They must have cost a fortune."

"They did, and Trek got them for me. Aren't they to die for?! They are so soft you didn't hear me come up the steps." Angelina spun around in a circle giggling with delight. "Let me help you."

She grabbed a sack of sugar and hoisted it up onto the top shelf, standing on her tiptoes to show off the soft soles of her new boots.

"So, where'd he get them? At the Flea Market? He must have been saving a long time to get something like that." Rabea's tone had a tinge of disbelief, but Angelina wasn't going to let that take away from the cloud she was floating on right now. Trek liked her, liked her enough to buy her something special. That meant she was special, and she wasn't going to let anyone take that away today.

"Yep, bought them from a real American Indian who made them by hand. If you don't need me anymore, I want to go show Magda. Okay?"

Rabea leaned back on the counter and smiled, nodding her dismissal. Angelina silently darted for the door, smiling all the way.

All Abuzz About Boots

THE VILLAGE WAS BUZZING with talk about Angelina's new boots. Everyone was speculating. Angelina could hear the gossip as people whispered when they thought she couldn't hear, forgetting that elves hear better than humans.

"Did you see?"

"Where did he get that kind of money?"

"She acts like she's something special. They're just a pair of boots."

"That kind of vanity is a dangerous thing."

She didn't understand why they couldn't be happy for her. Still, every time she wiggled her toes inside the soft velvet of the suede, she forgot about them and thought about how lucky she was to have someone like her, really like her.

It wasn't until several weeks later that Angelina began to suspect that there was something really wrong with Trek's story about how he got them. Lately, when he'd come back from the Flea Market, he'd rush to get the wagons unloaded and then disappear into the Woods, telling her he had chores to do in the gardens. He was wearing long sleeves a lot, too. The air was growing cool with fall setting in, but there was something out of character with how he insisted on keeping the cuffs buttoned.

It wasn't until she followed him into Magda's hut one afternoon when Magda was at the creek doing wash that she caught him taking his shirt off. He was putting a compress of purple sage and cool mud on his ribs. That's when she saw the bruises. He was covered with them, ranging from purple to green and a sour looking yellow. She knew exactly what she was seeing. She'd worn those marks on her own body. Her father was always careful to hit her so her clothes would cover the evidence.

Trek didn't realize she was there until she was right behind him. A floorboard creaked under her foot, and Trek jerked around at the sound, groaning and wincing in pain.

"Angelina, you scared the life out of me. I was just…." Angelina watched as he wrestled to get his shirt on.

"Trek, who's doing this to you? Who's hitting you?!" She reached out and pulled his shirt open to examine the swelling on his ribs. "You've got to let Magda look at this." He pushed her hand out of the way and buttoned his shirt halfway, but he was off by one, and it was so crooked that he had to start over. "Don't worry about it. I'm fine."

"You are not fine. What is going on?"

She wasn't going to give up until she knew the truth. Pulling her into the shadows beside his hut, he leaned against the wall and winced again. She let out an involuntary cry.

"Okay, look. You've got to promise not to tell. I mean it, no one." She acknowledged his rules by nodding in agreement. "You remember I told you I'd borrowed some money from a guy I knew when I bought you the boots. He wants his money, and I don't have it." She started to talk, but he cut her off. "I thought I'd be able to get it from the jam sales, but it was so dry this summer that the berries were small. The bears got most of them before I got there. I paid him back some, but he keeps changing the deal and adding outrageous interest. He's cornering me every time I go to the Flea Market, and now he's threatening to hurt Magda if I don't follow him into the alley to 'talk'". He wrapped his arm around his ribs and hugged himself gently.

"Trek, you've got to tell. You've got to tell your dad or someone." She pleaded, knowing full well the helplessness of not having anyone you could tell. Somehow whoever he told would turn it around to be his fault. 'He made a foolish choice, made his bed, and should lie in it. Giving her the boots was foolish'—she'd heard that whispered by the others. And she knew how much honor meant to his father. If he knew what Trek had done, it would take years for Trek to regain his father's good opinion. Her heart sank as she realized how useless her advice was. She could never tell. How could she expect him to?

"I'll give the boots back. Get your money back and pay him off."

"Angie, that won't help." He'd never called her Angie before. "The American Indian's gone, and besides, the way you've been wearing them, he'd never take them back. I'll figure something out." He struggled to get his arm in the sleeve of his shirt. "Now that it's getting cold, I can tell Dad that I have to stay behind to cut wood and stay out of town for a while until I figure out how to get the money. I'll be okay, I promise." He was trying to sound reassuring, but they both knew how hopeless this situation had turned out to be.

Angelina left him to wrap his wounds. At first, she walked slowly, but as her anger grew, she began to run. She ran into the Woods as if she were being chased by something evil. In reality, she was. She was sure she had found a place where abuse didn't exist, where people didn't hit each other. All she wanted was a home where hugs were the way people came in contact with one another. Seeing the bruises on Trek's body, she knew that this place was no different than the life she ran away from. Trek had tried to hide the marks and made lame excuses for how he got hurt, just like she had. Rolling her eyes and scoffing, she realized how stupid the stories she'd made up to hide the fact that her father beat her must have sounded to those around her. What a fool she'd been to think that somehow, somewhere, she could find people who would love each other so much that they would never even think of hurting each other. Would she ever be free of abuse?

"Why can't I find a place where everyone can be safe? Why?" she pleaded with no one and anyone. The wind sighed.

Tears and Trust

TEARS BURNED ANGELINA'S EYES. HER nose ran. She wiped both off on her sleeve as she climbed up into the canopy of branches overhanging the bathing pool. Curling her long legs around the branch she balanced herself on, she stared at the sky turning bright, hot orange as the sun sank below the treetops. Stars were starting to come out. Her favorite, the one she wished on every night, was rising up through the leaves of her shelter.

Angelina felt safe here. She could go back to feeling safe being alone. She had learned how to survive without too many other people in her life. If she never let them get close to her, they couldn't hurt her. She drew a deep breath as if she had to save it for later and stared blankly at nothing.

Below her was the sound of something or someone coming down the path, gravel crunching under the weight of large feet. Even though she wasn't afraid, being so high up the branches, she lay still, listening. Whatever it was, it stopped at the base of her tree and settled below her.

"Angelina, I came to see if you are all right, girl."

It was Trek's dad. What was he doing here? What could he want with her?

"I know you're upset, girl, and I wanted to be sure you're okay. You ran off in such a state that we're all concerned." His voice was smooth and calm and reminded her of rich dark sap heated by the sun so that it slid off its log with ease. They were both silent for what seemed like a long time. Angelina watched the stars rise higher in the sky and burn brighter than she had seen them ever before.

"You know, I always seem to have to talk about what bothers me. Get it out in the open. Somehow even the things I have imagined to be the worst ever just don't seem that bad in the open, almost as if when I say it out loud, my troubles turn to smoke. Somehow sharing my fears with someone else, the power turns out to be mine." When he paused, she hoped he was going away. Then," Life's funny that way."

Again, they were silent. She heard him pick up a stick and knew he had started to whittle. She could hear the chips of wood clinking lightly as they bounced off the rocks at his feet. She wondered how he could do that in the dark without cutting himself.

"Trek's in trouble, I can tell. I can see it in his eyes. There's a look of guilt there. It's painful for a father to see that in his boy, you know. I always prayed he'd be spared the sufferin' of doin' wrong and having to make it right." He whittled some more. "Can't imagine how God feels carrying that kind of hope and suffering for all His children. How it pains Him to see His children suffer."

Angelina was sitting on the branch with her legs dangling like the Spanish moss that dripped from the trees by the ponds. Her stomach twisted as she looked at the boots on her feet. Darned boots! She should never have taken them. Now Gastor was talking about God, and she was really ashamed. She'd never thought much about God and how He felt about her. Nobody had ever cared much about her. But listening to Trek's father's gentle voice describing how much he cared for Trek, she wondered if it could be true—He did care about her.

"Angelina, I could use some company if you don't mind sittin' with a sad old man."

She wasn't sure she could trust Gastor not to take out after Trek and make things worse. But she needed to talk to someone about this mess. Angelina quietly shimmied down and landed lightly on the ground near Gastor. She'd liked him from the first time she saw him when he convinced the village that she deserved the chance to be a part of their family. She settled on the rock near his, wiping her nose on her sleeve again. They silently watched the moon rise, full and round. Its light was bright enough that she could see that Gastor was carving a small flute. The shadows softened the faces in the trees. Now that she had learned to find them, she found them a comfort, knowing that she did have friends in the Woods, even if she could only see them at night. Her throat tightened. She wanted to tell Gastor the truth so badly, but she'd promised Trek. He should be the one to tell. Her mind dashed between the vision of Trek's bruises and those she'd seen on her body for years. That was a secret she was so tired of carrying. Before she knew it, her story boiled to the surface.

"He sometimes beat me for no reason," she said quietly. "He'd beat me just because I was there." Tears started to pool in her eyes until her lids couldn't hold them any longer, and they splashed on the back of her hand. "For a long time, I begged for him to stop. Then I learned to hide, but it was worse when he found me. It was just easier to let him get it over with." She sniffed as she choked back the real pain that she felt welling up in her gut. "Why? Why?"

"I don't know, dear. But I do know that it was not about you. It was about him and his demons."

"Sure felt like it was about me when his hand hit my face. And nobody or God did anything about it."

Gastor put his big warm hand on her thin shoulder. "I can't imagine how alone you felt. The saddest thing about being human is not being able to see God when we're in pain. Somethin' in our hearts just closes up; no matter how hard He tries, we can't let him in. Pain's too great a shield."

The night critters had started to stir, and they were being surrounded by a chorus of crickets and frog calls. The wood nymphs and tree spirits, known to eavesdrop on forest dwellers, sighed sadly. She felt the breeze of their sighs and felt what she thought was dew settling as they let their tiny tears fall.

Angelina was deep in thought. Long ago, she had given up on figuring out why her father beat her and what she'd done to deserve it. Now, those thoughts were back but not as desperate as before. She was profoundly curious. The idea that God had been there all along wanting to help her, like Gastor wanted to help Trek but could not get past her pain, was confusing.

"Gastor, suppose God still wants me?"

Gastor hugged her tightly against his knee. "Of course He does. He always has. Why even your boots proclaim you to be a chosen one. He just needs you to let Him into your heart." Feeling safe in his embrace, Angelina held on tight, and for the first time in a very long time, maybe the first time, a feeling of peace came over her. They sat in silence, letting the bond they had created weave its way around their hearts. After a few minutes, he spoke.

"Trek will tell me what's wrong, you know. One day he will come to me and say, 'Dad, I have something to tell you.' And I'll forgive him, and we'll move on. I just hope it's soon. "

Angelina was suddenly struck by an understanding of what she had to do. She had to make it right. She had to save Trek from more beatings by those thugs and bullies.

"Gastor, thank you." She kissed him on the cheek. "But I have to get some sleep; I have something I have to do tomorrow." She got up and started back when she stopped and ran back to Gastor. She flung her arms around his neck. "Thanks." And with that, she swung herself through the trees and back to the village and the hut she shared with a friend.

She whispered to the Woods, "I've got to find that book and then find that griffin."

Partners

HOW WAS SHE GOING TO find the griffin? And when she found it, how was she going to convince it to stop grabbing her and instead help her? All night she tossed and turned as she played the scene over and over, each time with a different ending. Finally, she gave up, got dressed, and quietly slipped into the cool predawn darkness.

She took a few minutes to think about where to begin. The last time she saw the griffin it was just below the burn on Bald Mountain. She'd start there. She was glad she'd decided on wearing her old knee boots. Leather would protect her from cuts and scrapes if she had to cut through the thick brush down in the Glen, and she knew the thick soles would be necessary if that dumb creature did try to grab her again.

The sun was just rising, and Angelina heard music rising from the meadow below. It made her smile. At least the Woods were beginning to trust her and share its secrets. In moments like this, when she was alone and something magical happened, she felt the privilege of being a forest dweller. It was no wonder that everyone wanted to protect all this. Angelina hadn't gotten very far when she sensed something large looming over her. She began to shake all over. She had spent so much time and effort staying hidden when she was alone on the trails. The griffin had come so close to catching her more times than one. She knew better than to get out into the open like this. But what better way to capture a griffin than to set a trap? Sure enough, as she crested the hill overlooking the Glen, she felt the draft created by the swooping wings of that enormous beast. The skies split with the sound of its screech, and Angelina's spine tingled. Searching the sky, she spun in every direction, desperate to find it before it found her. There it was! Coming straight at her out of the glare of the sun.

Angelina ducked just in time. The griffin swatted at her with its tail, but she was able to roll under a thick downed log. The commotion rousted out a family of ferrets who scuttled out from under the log and disappeared into the shadows of the huge ferns.

The griffin circled back. When Angelina was alone in the schoolhouse, she'd researched this beast and knew it was searching for signs of her body heat. She realized it had spotted her because it started to dive! She knew what she had to do, and it took all the courage she could muster, but she rose up as tall as she could, standing boldly on the log that had been her sanctuary moments before. She had to show it that she wasn't afraid.

As the griffin loomed, Angelina screeched at it just as it had screeched at her. A shrill, piercing sound rose from the depths of her lungs. As the sound echoed down the valley of the Glen, Angelina realized that the griffin was falling. It was a slow glide more than anything, but falling nonetheless. With a gasp, Angelina covered her mouth. She realized she'd used her voice! Her voice! She'd used her gift to make that beast fall out of the sky.

In absolute wonder, she watched as it slipped out of flight and descended toward her. She jumped back just in time to avoid its somewhat awkward tumble to the ground, where it lay stunned. Angelina watched as the griffin struggled to get its legs back underneath its body while folding its wings deep against its sides. Its eyes never left hers. Its glare was intense. Somewhere behind its evil was the tiniest sign of something else. Still, Angelina wasn't sure exactly what and wasn't willing to find out. She picked up the biggest stick she could reach and waved it at the beast.

"You just stay put! Don't move!" Angelina shouted as she circled around the downed creature. "Look, I'm sick of you grabbing at me all the time. I didn't do anything to you, so you just leave me alone. Got it?!"

The griffin's right wing was awkwardly bent from its crash landing. It was very clearly painful. Angelina thought about hitting this brute as it lay helplessly on the ground. She could really do some damage with this stick.

Maybe a crushing blow would teach this stupid fiend to leave her alone! Raising the stick above her head, she shifted it so the sharpest remnants of a broken limb would be on the striking side. She made eye contact with her intended victim. It cocked its head left and then right, making no attempt to defend itself. It just stared blankly. She definitely had the upper hand now. She had the power.

Still, she hesitated. She knew that look. She'd used it on her father. It was her 'go ahead and see if I care' look, the one she used when she knew crying or pleading wouldn't stop him from hitting her. It was the look she used to tell him she didn't care, especially not for him. It never worked. He always hit her, anyway, carefully angling whatever weapon he used to be sure the bruises wouldn't show.

She couldn't do it. As visions of her father's raised hand flashed through her mind, she knew she couldn't bring herself to be like her father. She couldn't cross that line. Besides, she needed this jerk to get her where she needed to go. Cautiously she reached out and tucked some of its flight feathers back into place. Waving the stick, she shouted, "Now, I need you to listen to me. We're going to come to an understanding here. You're going to do what I tell you, and you're going to help me. But what's with grabbing me all the time? Huh? What's with that?" Now she held the stick in front of her, between them.

The griffin just stared at her. It tensed its legs as if ready to pounce. Neither it nor Angelina moved. Neither one trusted the other. Its tail twitched wildly. A low growl rumbled in its throat. Angelina stepped back a bit. She'd have a better chance of surviving an attack with a head start. It growled again. The hair on the back of her neck stood up.

"Your voice." "You sing." The griffin's voice was deep, strong, and every bit as frightening as its powerful body.

Angelina wasn't sure if a confession was in her best interest just now. That voice thing had caused her nothing but trouble so far. She wondered what admitting it now would do to change her situation. Before she could respond, the griffin growled again.

"Yes," she chirped. "Yes, I did, and I'll do it again if you don't stay where you are." Confidence made her feel bold even though she wasn't sure she could sing—it'd been a fluke.

"Now, what do you want?!"

"I want," the griffin roared loudly. "I want you to sing."

The tree nymphs and wood spirits shook with such fear that leaves fell from the trees around them. This standoff was clearly making all the forest creatures nervous.

"Put me back to one."

Angelina was puzzled. Put it back to one? One what? And how? She'd just now learned that her voice had power. She had no idea what it could do other than make griffins fall out of the sky. "What are you talking about? One what?"

"One me, one me." The griffin's tone had turned to pleading now. "Either eagle or lion but not both." Its voice dropped to a desperate whisper. "Not both."

"You mean you weren't born like this? You were born as something else?"

It never occurred to Angelina that griffins were anything but two beasts joined as one. One frightening beast. Come to think of it, she'd only heard the legend of this griffin. Now she was shocked by the thought that this might be the only one. "Are you really the only griffin?"

The giant beast swung its head from side to side. Up close, quivering as it pleaded, it wasn't really that scary at all. Its sadness was profound. All this time, Angelina had been angry and afraid of this poor creature.

"It's a long tale. You say you need my help. It's I that needs you." It let out a long deep sigh as it sank to the ground in defeat. "I was given the gift of living both on the earth and in the sky. On the forest floor, I silently prowled as a lion; in the skies above the canopy, I soared as an eagle. One day, partway through my transformation, I heard the most beautiful voice drifting in on the wind. I didn't know it was an elf, that it would change my life. I made the mistake of stopping to listen."

Angelina could see where this was going now. The song of an elf had created this half-eagle, half-lion beast who was now very frustrated at not being able to be what it was created to be.

"How can I help? I have no idea how to use my voice! Besides, I need you just as you are. Look, I've read that somewhere in these Woods is a treasure of red and blue diamonds. I've got to find them to get a friend out of trouble, and I need you to be able to run and fly."

Confused, frustrated, and desperate, Angelina released the stick and slumped down on the ground beside the griffin, dropping her head into her hands. They sat in silence.

"Are you the only elf?"

"No, there are lots of us. Why?"

"I think I know how we can help each other. I will help you find the diamonds, and you will help me find an elf who knows what they are doing with their voice."

This time the silence lasted a long time. Then, wrapping her arm around the neck of her new partner, she was pretty sure she never wanted to go home again. Now she just thought about how she was going to get what she wanted. She had to find those diamonds to help Trek. If she agreed to this, she'd have to go back home to find an elf who could sing well enough to keep her end of the bargain, and then she'd be in debt to someone else. She never wanted to owe anyone anything. She'd have to make the pact to get what she needed and back out later on the singing elf part. Maybe claim she couldn't find one. How would the griffin know if she'd really tried or not? Besides, he'd lived this long as a griffin. Someday he'd find another elf and get that one to sing.

"Deal!" she said firmly. She patted the beast on its twisted wing. "Can you fly with this wing like this? It looks broken."

A Name for Friend

THEY SPENT THE NEXT FEW hours straightening the griffin's wing. Angelina was amazed at what a big baby this thing was as it screeched every time she moved the wing while applying a makeshift splint. She made it out of a flat piece of bark, binding it with vines. She stripped the leaves so she could weave the vines in between the flight feathers while asking question after question about the legend of the diamonds. What did he know about the legend? Which direction did they have to travel? Was it dangerous? How long would it take?

Angelina wondered if she was talking too much since the griffin never replied and was beginning to fidget. Suddenly she stopped, and he was clearly startled by the abrupt shift to silence.

"What's your name?" Angelina quizzed. "I have to know what to call you."

"I don't have a name."

"What?! You have to have a name. How can you tell one griffin from another if you don't have names?!" Angelina's tone was mocking.

"I am the only griffin, so it's not hard to know it's me," he said, clipping his words so they landed like little porcupine quills. "Besides, in the Woods, we're known by our spirit and heart, not by a name. A name doesn't really tell you anything about someone."

Angelina had to think about that. She had to admit it was true. 'Angelina' didn't tell you anything about her as a person, just what she was called.

"Well, I need to have something to call you besides 'hey you,' so I'll call you—" She paused, thinking carefully, and then declared, "Leron."

He looked at her with anticipation. When that was all she said, he asked, "What does it mean? Leron?"

"What do ya mean? What does it mean? It means Leron." She brushed the bark chips off her lap and stood up. Aware that he was staring, she tossed her arms in the air. "What?!"

"You give me a name that has no meaning as if it's okay? Do you know what the others in the Woods will do when they find out I have a name? They will want to know what it means and how well I'm considered in your world where names are given. How am I supposed to tell them it means 'nothing'?" He hung his head, resting his beak on a rock. Angelina was stunned. What was he so upset about? Well, she couldn't afford to have this blow her chances at getting the red and blue diamonds.

"Okay, look, tell them it means friend. That's what you are—you're my friend, Leron."

For a few moments, he didn't move. "Leron. Your friend, Leron." He lifted his beak and looked her straight in the eye. "It's not going to be easy getting to the diamonds. You'll have to do everything I tell you. Crossing the valley of Kidron is dangerous. Very few survive, and even fewer return. Whoever you're doing this for must be very special."

"I'm doing it for me. I owe a debt and won't be beholden to anyone." Angelina stiffened her back and set her jaw. She knew that, in part, this was a lie. Trek and his family were important to her, but it wasn't anyone else's business. Her partner in this quest only needed to know enough to get her there and back. No more.

"We'd better get a move on. What's first?"

"You're going to need supplies, so you'd better get back to the village and pack up, nothing that won't fit in a pack on your back. I don't have a luggage compartment. We'll meet here in two days at sunset. We'll need the full moon to guide our travels at night."

"Why at night?"

This concerned Angelina. Leron's tone was harsh and business-like. She was beginning to question this whole idea.

"Most of the Valley's predators are nocturnal. They'll be hunting at night, but at least I'll be able to see where they are. During the day, while they're sleeping, we might not see them until we are right on top of them, and that's a battle I'm not interested in fighting. Now go, get ready."

Leron stood up slowly, working his feathers into place, ready to fly.

"Wait! What do I need?!"

"Friend, if you aren't prepared enough to know what to take to survive, you're not ready for this trip. What's it going to be? Are you going to be ready or not?"

Angelina shifted her weight from one foot to the other. No one was going to tell her she wasn't prepared. She'd come too far. She was a survivor. She'd made up her mind that she could do this.

"I'll be ready," she said. Turning on her heels, she ran, her head spinning, adding items to her list with every step.

"Angelina?"

She stopped and turned to see Leron in the shadow of the branches above her. "Yeah?"

"We will probably run into Paimon, and if we do, we'll need something to pay his ransom. Get something of value, something that means something to someone. It might be enough to convince him that we are traveling as thieves, and he'll let us pass."

With that, he spread his wings and slid into the dusk. Angelina could hear him groaning with every stroke of the night air as the splint on his wing pinched.

Angelina stood alone as the shadows wrapped around her ankles. What did Leron mean by 'might let us pass'? Who was Paimon? What had she gotten herself into? She bit her lip as she turned back towards the village. Her brain was trying to define the danger, but this was all far more than anything she'd ever encountered. Maybe Leron was just trying to scare her to see if she was serious about this journey. That would be like him. Why didn't anyone trust her?! Of course, she was serious! If she didn't get those diamonds, those bullies would never stop, and Trek—her thoughts halted abruptly. The thought of Trek caused her stomach to lurch, but she shook it off as quickly as it had come over her. Her pace quickened as her resolve became even stronger. She'd prove to Leron that she was serious and he couldn't scare her.

Katie had started to leave bits of bark and odd stones everywhere she went so she could figure out if she was traveling in circles or not. Finally, it occurred to her that whoever she heard would most likely build a fire at night. They probably cooked. They'd need to stay warm.

"Shit, why didn't I think of this earlier? I need to hunt for them at night. Not during the day." After a few palms to her forehead and a scolding for her stupidity, she began outlining her plan to Chuck.

Traveling Lies and Secrets

NGELINA HEARD RABEA COME IN the front door. She stopped tossing things when she heard Rabea calling out as she climbed the stairs to her loft.

"What's going on? My gosh! What are you doing?"

Angelina stepped over a pile of clothes on the floor, tossing a sweater over her shoulder to shield the view of the food and utensils all over the bed. She then dropped to the floor and squirmed half under the bed, her butt sticking up awkwardly and wiggling up and down as she strained to reach. Squirming out from under the bed, Angelina brushed her static-filled hair back into place. "Ah, I'm packing." She began rifling through the top drawer of her dresser.

"Where are you going? Angelina!" Rabea paused to catch her breath. "I thought you liked it here. I thought you were happy here."

Rabea was clearly confused by this change. Angelina didn't have time to explain. Even if she did, she couldn't.

"I'm not leaving, just taking a trip. I thought I'd get out and see more of the Woods. You know, take in the full beauty of the place."

Angelina pushed past Rabea and headed down the stairs. Two steps down, she stopped and turned around. "Ah, have you got a backpack I can borrow?"

Rabea sat down on the edge of Angelina's bed, rubbing her fingers along the stitches of the quilt Trek had rescued from the creek after the storm destroyed Angelina's hollow. "On the hook by the back door."

Angelina disappeared down the stairs and bounded back up, taking two at a time. "Thanks."

She began stuffing her clothes in the bag. She'd decided that the sweater she knitted last winter would be good to keep her warm, gloves—a gift from Magda—and the matching hat Mauve had made. She would need a change of shoes. Her heart sank as she reached for the boots that Trek had given her. If he hadn't bought her the boots, if he'd used the money to buy the machine parts like his father told him, he wouldn't have gotten mixed up with that loan shark and his gang.

A wave of guilt flowed over her as again she admitted this was all her fault. She should have made him take them back, but they were so beautiful, and she really wanted them. Well, now the soft soles would have to hide her tracks in Kidron so she could make all this right.

"Angelina, this doesn't feel right. What's your hurry? Are you going alone? I'd be glad to go with you. I know some absolutely gorgeous places I'd love to show you."

"NO!" Angelina's harsh response caught both of them off guard. "No, really, I'll be fine. I have a new friend, and we just decided to get away for a while. Look, you've got to promise not to tell anyone. I don't want anyone to worry about me. They've all been so nice, and you know what worriers Magda and Gastor are, and Trek's so—Trek. Promise—no one! okay?" Angelina stared coldly into Rabea's eyes. "No one."

"All right, I promise. But Angelina, I can't just let you go off with a stranger. So, tell me, who's your friend? Someone I know?"

"No, no one you know. Hey, look, I need to go borrow some things from Magda. Thanks for the backpack. I'll get it back to you—no dirt or anything. See you later." She stopped on the stairs, her eyes latching onto Rabea's. "Remember, you promised. No one." And she was gone, leaving Rabea stunned on the bed's edge.

What About Dragons?

ANGELINA DASHED NEXT DOOR TO Magda's and knocked loudly on the front door.

"Goodness, gracious! What's the hurry?" Magda opened the door widely, and Angelina pressed her way into the front room.

"Magda, I've been thinking. I should have a first aid kit. You know. I'm out in the Woods a lot, and all kinds of things could happen. Cuts, scrapes, bites, and such. Would you help me make one? Now?" She batted her eyelashes while she tilted her head gently to one side.

Angelina was pretty sure this old trick wasn't working as planned when she saw how Magda smiled. She had been counting on Magda having a hard time resisting the charms of a cute little Elf, no matter how self-serving her request was. Angelina was relieved when Magda laughed lightly and agreed.

"Sit down at the table, and let's see what we can find."

They chatted about which herbs, tinctures, and salves one should have in a well-equipped first aid kit. Angelina was full of questions. What about snake bites? And dragon burns or bear claw cuts?

"Your imagination is a wonder, to be sure! Dragon burns!" Magda laughed. "My dear, there aren't any dragons in the Woods! You are a silly one sometimes!"

"What about in Kidron? Are there dragons there?"

Angelina didn't take her eyes off Magda as she watched for her response. Leron's comments about Kidron's dangers worried her, and she needed to see what Magda knew. Magda didn't flinch, but she paused. "Where did you hear about

Kidron?" she asked quietly as she packed mint leaves into a small paper pouch. "These are good for settling your stomach."

"Ahhh, I read about it in one of the schoolbooks; sounds pretty scary, like dragons would live there."

"There are no dragons in Kidron. Now, where did I put that bee balm? It's perfect for burns, although I've never tried it on a dragon burn." The two continued the charade of making a first aid kit until all the essential ingredients were neatly packaged in a small tin box. "There you go. All set for adventure."

Angelina reached for the box slowly. Had Magda figured it out? Had she read Angelina's mind or something and figured out her plan? She was frighteningly wise about things.

"Thanks, Magda. You're a peach!" She kissed Magda's cheek and headed for the door.

"You take care, dear. Remember, knowing what you don't know is more important than knowing what you do know."

Kissing her dear young friend back, Magda closed the door behind her. Angelina stood on the porch for a few moments, unsure what to make of Magda's warning. Shaking it off as more than she could deal with now, Angelina smiled. Her skills at lies and manipulation had not been totally tamed by life in the Woods. She still had what it took to get what she wanted.

Now she was off in search of Joseph. She needed help with what tools to take on her quest.

A Lie for a Piece of Rope

ANGELINA CAME UP THE PATH at a very determined pace. She waved at Mauve as she opened the kitchen window.

"What a gorgeous day!" Mauve called out to her as the breeze stirred up her uncontrollable hair.

Joseph joined her at the window. Angelina hopped up on the porch and sighed at the sweet sight of him taking Mauve's hand and kissing her fingers.

"I think I might start on a new hat," Mauve commented to Angelina as she gestured for her to come on in the house. Angelina imagined that this was what it was like to have grandparents. Always having cookies in the cookie jar, someone to teach you how to do things like sew or whittle, someone to take you on adventures. But this adventure was one she would have to take alone, so she had to be clever in her story about why she needed what she was asking for. If they knew what she was planning, they'd put an end to it, and Angelina couldn't risk that.

"I just wanted to see you guys. So, what's up?"

"Oh, just doing some chores around the house," Joseph replied.

"Ah, Joseph, I've been thinking. I go out in the Woods a lot, and I liked the hike you took me on to the backcountry. The scenery was amazing!"

"We can go anytime, my dear, anytime."

"Well, I know, but someday, I'll be old enough to go on my own, and I thought I should start building a tool kit. You know, stuff I'd need for survival and all."

Angelina studied his eyes to see if he was buying her story. "So, what'd you think? Can you show me what kind of things I'd need?"

"Of course, dear, of course. In fact, I've been cleaning out my tools and have some to spare. A guy can never have too many tools, you know, and one of the joys of lots of tools is sharing them with your favorite people. Come with me."

As Joseph and Angelina started for the door to go out to the tool shed, Mauve cleared her throat. They both turned to see if she had something to say.

"Oh, nothing, just a little tickle, that's all. Joseph, give her some of your good ones. She should start off well, don't you think?"

His lips curved into a tiny smile.

The tool shed had always fascinated Angelina. It was a mess, an all-time, classic, in the records books mess, but Joseph seemed to know where everything was. There were hand tools and yard tools and woodworking tools, and construction tools. Angelina had given up trying to figure out how he got any of them in his vest pocket, let alone so many at once.

There was so much about the people of the Woods that mystified her. They all seemed to have found a peaceful place there. They liked themselves and each other, and everyone had something that they were good at. Angelina didn't have anything in particular that she was good at. Maybe someday she'd find something. The sound of Joseph rattling around in the tools on his bench broke her daze, and she bounced back to the problem at hand.

"So, what do you need to climb mountains?" She winced at how stupid that sounded.

"Just your feet, dear, just your feet. Now, cliffs are a different task altogether. For those, you're going to need a rope. Now, this isn't just any rope; this rope is special, made of really good stuff. Odd thing, though. I've never been able to determine just how long it is. No matter what, it always seems to be the length I need. You'll want this for sure. And gloves, a good pair of gloves is always important, especially with those long, nimble fingers you have. Want to keep those safe from scrapes and cuts. And let's see: you should have a small hammer; no, a hatchet would be better for being out in the woods." And he continued to add things to the pile he had created, rambling about this tool and that, showing her how many he had of each.

"Wow! Who knew it took so much!" Angelina mused, wondering how she would carry all this stuff and all the things she'd gotten from Magda too. "I'll have to make myself a pack or something to carry it all."

"Not to worry, dear. You can take this. I wore this pack on my back when I wasn't much older than you. My father took me on a trek across the great Himalayas. Oh, what an adventure that was. And the elephants, what fun they were!"

Angelina was puzzled. What was he talking about?

From behind them came the sound of Mauve's gentle voice. "Now, dear, don't bore the poor child with your old trekking stories. I thought you might like some cookies. Let's get all this stuff out of here and enjoy this beautiful afternoon under the trees." Mauve always seemed to know when to pop in with cookies. Angelina gave her a peck on the cheek as she took the biggest cookie off the top of the stack. With it held firmly between her lips to free both hands, Angelina gathered up her loot and shoved it into the pack.

"This is so great. I can't wait to go somewhere! Thanks, Joseph. I'll take good care of all this. You're the best! Wonder where I can go? Maybe Rabea would like to go see her parents, and we can take the long way around and camp on the way. Be real survivalists. Live off the land!"

Angelina winced again, thinking that was a bit over the top and hoping she hadn't blown her cover, but neither Joseph nor Mauve seemed to notice.

"Well, I guess I'd better get out of your hair. Thanks again for all the cool stuff." As she stood up and brushed the pine needles and tiny pinecone flakes off her leggings, Joseph reached into his pocket and pulled out his multi-tool pocketknife.

"Almost forgot! You're going to need one of these." And he put it in her hand, wrapping her fingers tightly around it. Angelina uncurled her fingers. The air around them was still, and she drew in a deep breath as she took in the true value of what he'd given her. "Joseph, this is your favorite. I can't take this."

"Not to worry. I have plenty more." He reached into his pocket and pulled out five, to be exact. "Can't ever have too many of these!"

They all laughed, exchanged goodbye hugs and kisses, and Angelina headed home, still trying to absorb all that had happened today. She hoisted the pack onto her back with a grunt. All this equipment was heavier than she'd anticipated, and she began questioning her decision to find the diamonds. Her mind was spinning. Her thoughts reeled between excitement, fear, and doubt. There must be an easier way to get the money Trek needed. Then it occurred to her—she could sell off some of this stuff. Joseph's tools must surely be worth something. She could hide in the wagon to sneak into town and set up her own booth to sell them.

She'd have to come up with a story to explain where all the tools went when Joseph asked to see what she had learned to do with them, and he would ask, she was sure. She tested one concocted tale after another. She looked back at the quaint little hut Joseph and Mauve called home and saw them standing on the porch, waving her on to her adventure. She tried to smile, but her lips twisted awkwardly.

Lying had become hard. She could imagine the disappointment on their faces if they ever learned that she had taken their things, their gifts, and sold them, even if it was for a good cause. Angelina wasn't used to the sour feeling guilt brought with it and realized that the trials of her quest couldn't possibly be worse than the way she felt right now. She grabbed the shoulder straps of the backpack and trudged onward toward home.

Packing Emotions

AS THE SUN BEGAN TO drop in the sky, Angelina hurried back to the hut. As she'd gone by the bathing pond, she'd heard Rabea and Trek talking about where she was going and guessing who she was going with. She had to get to the hut and reload her stuff into the pack Joseph gave her. It was leather and much sturdier than the one she'd borrowed from Rabea.

It wouldn't be long before everyone would start comparing notes on the stories she'd told each of them about her mysterious trip into the Woods. She knew Magda would give her the benefit of the doubt and trust her. Joseph's brow would furrow, and he'd agree as he fingered the tools in his pocket. Rabea would fret, and Trek would form a search party.

Angelina felt bad for Rabea. She was too trusting and gullible. It should have been harder to get her to buy into the story Angelina had dished out. Yet deceiving Rabea was uncomfortable. Angelina wasn't sure she liked living in a world where truth was the norm. Her old life, where she lied to hide the beatings, manipulated to get what she wanted, and punished her mom for being weak, didn't have emotions like guilt and didn't have attachments like friends. Numb was so much easier. But right now, she had to forget about all of that. She had to get the map to Kidron.

Angelina raced to the schoolhouse and was surprised to find the door ajar. Everyone was always so careful to shut the door, even though it was never locked. She had to shove the door open far enough to get into the room. Books and chairs and papers were strewn all over the floor. The worktable was tipped on its side. She reached down to upright the ant farm when she spotted the fishbowl tipped over and most of its water on the floor.

"Oh, Tinsy," she cried as she turned it upright, glad to see that the fish had survived the fall with just enough water. Speaking into the bowl, she reassured the poor little thing, "I don't have time to get you more water. Somebody will." The maps were mixed in among the books on the floor. Angelina picked through as many as she could, but the map to Kidron wasn't there.

Her face flushed with panic. "Where is it? I have to find it." Finally, she had to give in—it was gone. Whoever tore up the schoolhouse must have found it, but she had no idea who it could be, and there was no time now to solve that crime. "Damn." Angelina shook off her thoughts and focused on her next problem. She only had a few hours to get to the Crags to meet Leron, and there was still a lot to get done, not the least of which was to find something of value in case they ran into this Paimon guy. Angelina's mind searched the village, trying to remember what she'd seen that might work as a payoff for someone Leron seemed to think was evil. There was that wood carving that Tanner had made for Conda, but it was too big to carry. Magda had some rare herbs, but she doubted a bully would be interested in those. Books, tools, food. None of it seemed to rise to the value Leron had implied. If she just had some money.

Then it hit her—the offering box in the church. There must be a couple of hundred dollars in coins in that box, and she could fit in her pack if she left out some of the tools, her hat, and gloves. She made her way into the shadows. Once out of earshot of the clearing, she ran to the church.

Grab and Run

ANGELINA HADN'T HEARD TREK COME in the church and jumped with such a start that she almost dropped the collection box. Swiftly, she slid it into her pack.

"Wow! You scared me. What's up?" She gave her best shot at sounding casual and relaxed.

"You tell me. This is one of the last places I'd expect to find you." Angelina tried to match his casual air, but she knew neither one of them was being honest right now.

"Yeah, I guess so. But you know, it never hurts to explore new ideas. I saw the doors open and thought I'd check it out, that's all. What brings you here?"

"Well, to tell you the truth, Rabea and I were just coming to look for you. She found a travel book she thought you should see before you take this trip you're planning. We set out to find you and agreed to meet back at the schoolhouse. Let's go see where she is so she can show you."

Trek stepped forward, reaching out to take her hand.

Angelina smelled something fishy. Trek's tone was just a bit too thoughtful. The look on his face was a bit too pasted on to look sincere.

"Gosh, that's really thoughtful, but I'm in a bit of a rush right now. Maybe later."

With that, she pushed past him, walking slowly at first, breaking into a run as she got to the doors. As she ran, the coins in the box bounced, ringing against one another, and she was sure she'd given herself away. She had to run faster than ever now.

Stolen Treasures

THE SOUND OF THE COINS clattering in the box struck a blow in Angelina's heart like she'd never felt. She heard Trek shout "NO!" as she made a turn in the path.

"She couldn't! She wouldn't!"

But she did. She'd stolen the box and all the money in it.

"You thief!" was the last she heard of his voice before she disappeared into the dusk.

Angelina ran back to Rabea's hut to add the collection box to her backpack smashing it down on top of the clothes. She'd put her hat and gloves inside the box to muffle the sound of the coins and then stuffed the sweater around the tools. She shoved the herbs and first aid things into her white boots and jammed them on the top. Food went in last.

Locking it all in with the leather belt Joseph used for a strap, she slung it onto her back. Turning to take one last look to be sure she hadn't forgotten anything, she decided not to blow out the lantern in the loft so it would look like she was still home. She watched as her shadows preceded her down the stairs. She opened the door and peered out into the darkening night. The village green was quiet. Everyone must be having supper. She dashed across the green and back into the shadow, headed for the schoolhouse. She needed that map.

Angelina got close enough to see the shape of the Crags backlit by the dim glow of the sun setting. Focusing intently on where she was to meet Leron, she never saw the girl sitting with her legs stretched across the path, at least not until she tripped over her and rolled head over heels. Panic set in when she realized that the box had flown through the air spraying the coins in every direction.

"Noooo!" she wailed. The girl lifted her head as her legs curled towards her chest, an automatic reflex in response to her ribs being kicked so hard.

"What the..." Angelina rolled over to see what she'd hit. She was shocked to see a bloody, swollen face covered in mud and moss staring blankly back at her. "Who are you? Never mind. Help me get the coins. I have to have all the coins!"

Angelina reached down to help the poor girl up. When the girl looked up, she looked as if she'd never seen a real person's face. She was speechless at first. Frantically she grabbed Angelina by the leg and begged piteously, "You have to help me. I need to get out of these Woods. There's no path. I don't know which way to go." Angelina peeled the girl's fingers off her leg.

"Hey!" Angelina swallowed hard as she absorbed just how panicked this girl was for help. "Look, honey, the paths around here come and go as they please, not when you demand one, so you'll just have to go with what the Woods wants. And generally speaking, you're safe almost anywhere in the Woods. Now get up and help me. I'm running out of time."

The girl crawled over and picked up coin after coin until she and Angelina were sure they had everything to be found. "Thanks, got to go." Angelina got to her feet, brushing off the dirt that had ground into her knees as she fell. As she turned to leave, there was a tug at the hem of her tunic.

"Please, you've got to let me go with you."

Angelina looked at the pathetic face. She didn't have time for this. There was no way she was going to lug a pitiful passenger along on this trip. It was too important. And then she remembered how frantic she had been to find a way to go home not too long ago. She doubted that this hot mess of a girl could fend for herself alone in the Woods, enchanted or not.

"Ok, look, you can come, but you have to do what I tell you and stay out of the way. This is a dangerous trip, and I can't be worrying about you. Got it?"

"Thank you," was her flat reply.

"Let's go."

Angelina's throat burned as she ran. Her lungs begged her to stop. The silhouette of the Crags lay sharply against the black sky outlined by the moonlight.

Just a few more miles, and she'd be there. Leron had to wait. She'd explain the delay, but he had to wait. Then, he'd have to help her figure out what to do.

Angelina saw Leron's silhouette cross the moon as he took flight disappearing behind the streaks of clouds. She could see Leron standing in the moonlight as they came over the rise.

"Where have you been?" he said. "I was very clear about my instructions. We aren't making this trip if you can't do as I say."

Angelina reached up and held his beak, still trying to figure out how he could talk without opening it. Startled, he fell silent. "I couldn't find the map. I went to the schoolhouse and the place had been ransacked. Stuff was thrown everywhere, and the map was gone. I'm late 'cuz I was trying to find it."

"Come on. Get on my back and let's go." Leron's tone was firm. Angelina was confused. She hesitated.

"But the map?"

"We don't need a map. I know the way. Get on."

"Wait, there's something else." She watched Leron turn his gaze in search of her point until it rested on the girl standing behind her.

"Who is that? You can't be taking passengers. This isn't a cruise."

Angelina locked her eyes on his and held her gaze firm. Clearly annoyed, Leron flew down and grabbed Katie, bringing her up to drape over a branch near Angelina.

"This is—who are you?" Angelina realized she had been so intent on making it to their meeting place that she'd never asked this girl's name or any other vital details.

"Katie." That was all she offered.

"Leron, really, she can't be left alone. The Woods won't give her a path. She'll just get herself into more trouble. I'll look after her. You'll never know she's with us. Promise." Angelina turned and glared at Katie, hoping she was smart enough to get the message: behave, or we will leave you wherever.

"All right," Leron said. "I have no idea why I'm doing this, but I'm going to trust you on this one. I'm still in charge here. Got it?"

In unison, the girls replied, "Got it."

He turned around on the branch and crouched down so Angelina could crawl up and grip his feathers with a tug. Katie crawled on behind Angelina, holding tightly to her tiny waist.

"You on?"

She pressed her knees into his ribs with her legs. He spread his wings and she felt the three of them lift off into the night.

The View From Above

DIGGING HER FINGERS DEEP INTO the feathers between Leron's wings, Angelina held on tight as he began to soar upward in concentric circles. Katie was so overwhelmed by the very thought of flight she could do nothing more than gasp at the vastness of the ground below them. The view of the sunset was breathtaking. The full moon rose, looking huge against the blackening sky. Angelina was thrilled by how far she could see from this height. The sound of Leron's wings stroking the winds, the calls of small birds as they flew out of his way, and the smell of the crisp air was nothing like anything she'd ever smelled. She knew she was leaving everything she'd known for places she couldn't even imagine.

To the north, Angelina could see the silhouette of the tall trees that were so much a part of where she'd grown up. She was awestruck. For all the confidence she blustered, she was equally as fearful.

Angelina's lips curved slightly into a tiny smile. She wondered about her mother and sighed deeply as she considered what her mother would say about this quest. Her mother would never understand why she was willing to risk her life for someone else, especially someone who wasn't family. Courage wasn't a part of her mother's soul.

Leron circled over the village, and she saw Magda's hut, Gastor stacking wood. Then she saw Trek and Rabea race into the clearing. They must have been shouting from the way that everyone in the village came running. Arms waved. There was a great flurry of agitation. Angelina guessed Trek had discovered her crime and was telling the others. Her heart sank as she understood that all the work she had invested in gaining the trust of the villagers was now lost. They would never forgive her. They would never understand why.

Leron banked hard to the right, and she saw Rabea and Trek head towards Magda's. Looking at that scene below brought on an unexpected mixture of feelings of shame clouded with homesickness. As the little group of houses disappeared from sight, she felt her throat tighten, and as had happened more than once since she had cooked up this plan, she was having regrets. She was leaving the only place where she felt she truly belonged, a place where now she'd never be welcome again.

They flew for hours into the darkening night. Beneath her, the ground turned from lush, green rolling hills at the foot of towering blue peaks to dry, barren, jagged slopes at the base of steep crags. The thick canopy of branches that so playfully arced over the forest floor gave way to tree trunks with branches that clawed at the sky.

Her nose and eyes burned from a stench carried up by hot winds. Mile after mile, Leron's wings rhythmically pulled them forward. The moon was now hidden by dirty clouds racing across the sky. Shadows grew longer and more frightening. Katie's fingers dug into Angelina's stomach as she hung on tighter with each stroke of Leron's wings. Angelina felt his feathers get slippery as they soaked up the sweat from her palms. Concerned about where they were going, she was relieved as he dropped into a long, slow glide, landing on a ledge high on the south side of a steep cliff. She was relieved until she saw how high and isolated it was and realized a cave was set back into the wall. Katie didn't let up on her grip one teeny bit.

As they landed, a flock of crows swarmed around them, making horribly urgent cries.

"They're warning us to turn back," Leron commented casually as he groomed his feathers back into place.

Angelina stared at him blankly. "What?" She realized there was no reason to finish either of their thoughts.

"You two sleep here. I'm going to sleep in that forked tree there."

"Leron, please stay here. Not that I'm afraid or anything, but I'd feel better if we stuck together. You know, we have stuff to talk about."

Angelina tried to speak with confidence while struggling not to cry. She hoped Katie didn't see how afraid she was. She'd never imagined a place this awful. Everything was either dead or dying. The air was filled with a foul odor so strong that she could only breathe in small pants.

"Please?" she said.

He flew off into the darkness without responding to her plea.

The moonlight was dingy and the night grew black. Continuing her pretense of confidence and control, she defiantly settled down on the sandy ledge. She dug into her pouch for something to eat. She handed Katie half of what she had. The berries had mashed a bit, and the juice stained their fingers as they sucked up as much of the nectar as they could get. Angelina was struck by how the sweetness sharply contrasted all that she could see around her. She shifted, trying several positions, searching for one that didn't include something poking her in the backside. Angelina tucked the pouch that obviously contained food only meant for her back into her pack.

"Shoot. Now what?"

Angelina sighed in disgust as raindrops began to pelt her. She looked back at the opening of the cave. Clearly, she was going to have to make a choice. She hated small dark spaces. One of her father's favorite punishments for crimes undetermined was to lock her up in his tool shed. It was full of creatures that crawled on her in the dark. Afraid to touch them for fear that any effort to brush them off would result in painful bites, she would take a deep breath, grit her teeth and imagine herself someplace far, far away. She couldn't go in this cave. She couldn't go back to that fear. She'd rather be wet. Even if she didn't dry out for days. She drew her knees into her chest as tightly as possible, tucking her head between her knees. Her hair cascaded down over her legs, shaking from the fright she had hoped she could hide from Katie. Angelina felt a nudge, then a shove from her right. Clenching her fist, she pursed her lips and swung around, ready to fight whatever had invaded their space. In the light of the moon, she could see the huge outline of an eagle's head.

"Geez, Leron. You scared the life out of me. Where did you go?"

"Move over."

Leron stretched out his wing, making a warm and dry shelter for the girls. Angelina was grateful and snuggled in immediately. Katie shook her head, rejecting the offer, and tucked her hands between her knees.

"No thanks." She closed her eyes but only briefly.

Angelina wasn't sure what to make of this strange girl. "Whatever," she muttered and put her head down on Leron's wing.

Angelina, grateful for the warmth, snuggled in next to Leron's body and slipped into a restless sleep. Her mind was filled with flashes of her father's face, her mother's voice, and Trek's bruises mixed together in one person who lunged out of the smoky darkness at her at every turn. Through the fog of her dreams, she could feel Leron tighten his hold on her, and she hoped his energy would calm the demons that haunted her.

Sometime during the night, the rain stopped. The silence created a vacuum that seemed to suck the air out of the cave. Katie woke to a sense of dread so disorienting that she would have cried out had she not seen Angelina sitting on the edge of the ledge to their shelter.

"Angelina, where are we?" Katie's voice was just barely more than a whisper, all feeling having been drained out of her.

"They call it Kidron. The Valley of Death."

"Why?" A sick feeling settled into the pit of her stomach.

Over her shoulder, Angelina sighed and began, "It's a long story, but the short of it is that I made a mistake, and I have to make good on it. My friend Trek is being beaten up for a debt he can't repay. Since he went into that debt to buy me something I knew better than to accept." She glanced back at Katie, who locked her eyes on Angelina. Katie guessed Angelina had avoided this confession for a long time. Now it finally caught up with her.

"So now what?" Reality was soaking into Katie's gut the way the stench of the boiling mud below them was saturating her clothes and hair. She had no way to get out of here or get home on her own. Her only choice was to stick with Angelina and Leron and hope that they all got out of this alive and they'd get it together before it was too late.

"Angelina? Now what?"

Angelina sat up abruptly. Her tone was sharp. "Leron's missing. I have no idea where he went. Leron? Leron?!"

He was nowhere in sight. All Katie could hear was the echo of Angelina's voice bouncing off the canyon walls around them.

"He couldn't have gone far. He must have gone for food. I'm hungry."

Katie watched, fear gripping her stomach as she watched Angelina search the ledge for something. She finally found her pouch and dug into it for the last of her berries. This time she offered the first serving to Katie, who used her fingers to scoop up a portion of the mashed goo. Katie licked the juice off her fingertips,

Katie's fingertips looked eerie in the yellow-orange light of the sunrise. "This stuff really stains. It's not going to come off like it did yesterday."

"Leron?" Angelina called out in the canyon. No response. "Where are you!?" Demanding didn't bring any response either. Katie could see that Angelina was growing angrier by the minute.

"Where is that stupid lion bird! How dare he bring us here and leave? I'm going to get him an earful when he shows up. Leron?!"

This time her voice cracked as she pleaded for his return. Katie grew more and more nervous each time Angelina called his name.

Angelina and Katie sat alone on the ledge for hours. Angelina polished her scolding speech, but she began to cry by the end. This led to her and Katie composing their 'how could you scare us like that' speech instead.

Katie picked at the scars on her thighs. "Angelina, do you think he just left us?"

"NO. I don't know." Angelina bit her nails. "No, I don't think he left us." She reached out, slid her hand into Katie's, and held tight. "He'll be back."

Katie didn't let go either. Exhausted from this emotional roller coaster, she lay down and stared at the sky, listening for the sound of his wings. Nothing. She sat up suddenly, clutching her stomach, unsure if she would throw up or not. That sick feeling meant something.

"Something's happened to Leron." She gasped. "He's hurt? Something's wrong!" I have to get off this ledge and find him."

"Don't be stupid. There's no way down," Katie stated firmly.

Angelina turned to face her. Now she's going to be the voice of reason? "Geez."

"Angelina, this doesn't make sense." Katie's voice cracked.

"Nothing makes sense right now."

Angelina scanned the cliff below them. No roots or rocks, nothing she could get a grip on to lower herself down the steep face of the mud-coated rock face. This mountain was made of nothing but rotting rock. Going over the edge would mean a very long slide and a painful plunge into the rocky river below.

Going up was no better. There wasn't even a branch she could leap to. Pacing back and forth and begging her brain, Angelina was suddenly hit with a blast of wind coming from the mouth of the cave. She braced herself against the wall of the cliff. Katie rolled dangerously close to the edge of the ledge.

A second burst of wind exploded from the cave moments after the first. As abruptly as the wind had come up, it stopped. Angelina stood very still, listening, not sure if it was safe or not. She stepped carefully into the mouth of the cave. Her brow furrowed. Her mind spun with confusion.

"Wind doesn't just come out of nowhere. It had to get into the cave somehow. That means there must be another entrance to the cave." That meant she had to go into that cave. She was paralyzed.

"I can't do this." Saying it out loud made it sensible. "Leron!" she screamed. Her voice trembled as she whispered, "Leron."

"What do you mean you can't do this? This could be our way out of here. We've got to do this!" Katie shrieked as she grabbed Angelina by the shoulders and shook her hard.

"You don't understand. My father used to put me in his shed. To teach me to be a survivor, he said. I don't do dark places. I don't do wet places. I can't do bugs or bats. I can't!" She sank down on the sand and hugged her backpack to her chest. Katie slid down beside her and wrapped one arm around the pack on top of Angelina's.

As the day stretched on, the sun baked the walls of the cliffs and heated the sand on the ledge until Angelina couldn't move without burning her hands. As she shifted, trying to find comfort, she felt the tools in her pack shift.

Katie kept saying, "We've got to go into the cave. At least get closer to the shade."

Angelina cautiously slid back into the shade of the opening as her skin grew raw with sunburn. She slowly spread out the contents of her pack. Having packed so fast, she'd forgotten most of what she'd brought. There might be something in there that would change her mind, something she could use to defend herself from the lurking evil. But the thought of going in there was too overwhelming for Angelina.

Angelina pulled out the first aid kit and the sweater and laid out the tools Joseph had given her. Rope, string, hammer, the all-in-one pocket knife. Nothing shouted 'cave safe.' She raked her fingers through her hair and sighed.

Katie took a deep breath and sighed too. "This is taking way too long."

Angelina stared at the pile of stuff surrounding her. Out of the corner of her eye, she swore she saw the sweater move, and when she moved it aside, there was, buried below—the rope! She would have been terrified if a plan hadn't taken over her thoughts.

"So what are you going to do?" Katie asked.

Angelina didn't answer. She got to her feet, removed her gloves from the collection box, and put everything back into the pack except for the rope and the gloves. Hoisting the pack on her back and the rope over her arm, she put the gloves on. Turning to face the dark abyss of the cave with all the bravery she could muster, she resolved that if she was going to get out of here and go find Leron, she would have to find the courage to step into the darkness.

"Come on, Katie. We've got a griffin to go find."

Stepping into the Darkness

RELUCTANTLY, THEY INCHED THEIR WAY into the cave, looking for a way to anchor the rope. Katie was suddenly overcome by remorse for being so insistent that they go into the cave. She felt really bad when Angelina jumped. Katie was growing concerned that Angelina wasn't quite as invincible as she made out to be.

"Something touched me. Something touched my cheek," Angelina shrieked.

As she turned in to see what it was, Katie could see that Angelina's face and hair were instantly tangled in a web that clung to her skin. As Angelina flailed her arms wildly in an attempt to free herself, Katie heard something drop to the ground with a decided thud, followed by the sound of tiny feet skittering across the coarse sand of the cave floor. Katie froze, trying to catch her breath, when she saw something slither across Angelina's right shoe. That was it! Katie screamed and ran for the ledge. Breathless, she dropped to her knees. Angelina was right behind her.

"I can't do this!" Angelina shouted to no one and anyone. "Leron, you jerk! Where are you?!" and she pounded her fists on the ground in anger. "I can't do this."

"We have to." Katie's voice was becoming calm now. "You have to." This time Katie's voice was firm.

"Katie, you don't understand. I can't. I can't see in the dark. That cave is filled with who knows what, and I have no idea how to deal with that, much less knowing how to get out of there once I get in." Angelina continued to wail pitifully. "I've been afraid of the dark since my father started 'teaching me'. My gut told me I wasn't safe in the dark."

Katie did understand, but her panic was punctuated by a calm realization that in the Enchanted Woods, the nights never bothered her. The moon and the stars were always there to light her way. Here, there were no stars, no moon. She wondered if Angelina had ever noticed that too.

Slowly, the cavernous darkness around them faded. A light somewhere deep in the cave had begun to glow, just enough that they could see to the end of the passage. The pathway was narrow, but whatever creatures had been there before were gone. Slowly, Angelina took the hand Katie offered and picked herself up off the dirt, rope in hand, and turned to face the darkness again. Taking a deep breath and baby steps, she reluctantly re-entered the cave. The gravel crunched under their feet. Anything already in the cave could hear them coming and would have plenty of time to get out of the way. Or prepare to grab them.

Angelina felt curiosity overcome her fear. She was compelled to follow the path around one bend after another until they reached a place where the path widened. She ran her hands along the walls. Every ten feet or so, the walls were lined with clusters of crystals that glowed in the dark. Individually the light was too dim to see. Yet, together, they gave enough light to make the way in either direction clear.

Angelina paused to consider returning to see if Leron had shown up yet. "What if Leron has come back for us and can't find us?"

"And what if he hasn't? Don't you need to get those diamonds?"

Cautiously, Angelina murmured, "Ok then, let's get out of here."

She raised her eyebrows in amazement as Katie pushed ahead of her like she had any idea of where to go next.

They followed the winds in the cave at every fork in the path, ducking under the large crystals protruding from the cave walls. Finding one at just the right height, Angelina used the knots Joseph had taught her and firmly tied the rope to it. She hadn't really believed Joseph when he said the rope had no fixed length, yet now, it seemed to have no end. The rope uncoiled as she walked, giving her confidence to find her way back if she needed to.

Exhausted after walking for hours, Angelina found a large rock to sit on and took out the pouch that held her last few pine nuts. When these were gone, they'd have to go hungry. But before she had time to despair over food, the rock below her moved. Not only did it move, but it made growling sounds. Angelina leaped to her feet, grabbed her pack and Katie's arm, and ran. The light in the tunnel was fading, and she wasn't sure which way to go except to follow the wind and pray for the best.

Pray.

"God, help me!" she shouted—just as her feet slid out from under her, and she careened downward, rolling over and over as she fell.

With one hand, she held on tightly to the straps of her pack, while with the other, she desperately grasped the rope. She'd have no way to survive in this awful place if she lost either! Her eyes and mouth were so filled with dirt that she could barely see. She knew she was headed for trouble.

Suddenly light! She could see the palest of light! The rope burned into the palms of her hands until she was forced to let go. But Angelina's relief quickly turned to panic as she realized she was free-falling into thin air! Screaming for Katie was all she could do at this point. Scream and pray. Angelina heard a familiar voice exclaim, "There you are!"

Leron swooped down. With exacting precision, he snatched her up just before she would have entered a narrow crevasse. She felt Katie bounce off his back and saw her land hard on the edge of the abyss, where she was able to clutch at branches that overhung the opening to a bottomless pit.

"Eeoww!" was Angelina's exclamation. Recognizing the feel of his talons around her arms, she yelled, "It's about time you showed up! Where have you been? I can't believe you left me there! I trusted you." Her voice trailed off as tears streaked her face. "You jerk," she whispered.

Leron glided into a large dead tree above the river and landed Angelina on a wide thick branch. When she had a firm hold on the trunk, he let her go and settled beside her. Impulsively, she threw her arms around his neck.

"Don't ever leave me alone like that! Please don't ever." She sniffled so he wouldn't know how afraid she'd really been.

"Look here, little one. I left you safe on that ledge while I went to investigate something. Now, where is your friend?" Leron scanned the terrain.

"Oh, God, no!" Angelina shouted over the sound of her racing heart as she spotted Katie dangling over the edge of nothing but darkness. "Leron, hurry! Go get her!"

Leron followed Angelina's gaze and took flight immediately. Angelina sucked in all the air around her as she realized how close Katie was to being lost forever.

"Help me!"

Katie's panicked cries were swallowed by the depth of the darkness below her. Her grip was slipping because of the layers of dust and the bloody rope burns in her palms. Gritting her teeth hard, she pulled herself, hand over hand, her feet scraping at the overhanging dirt and thatch until she could crawl onto solid ground. It was only when she tasted the all-too-familiar salty tears that she realized how hard she was crying. Now she was too relieved to care.

Leron landed beside her and asked if she was all right to fly. She realized that she no longer found it incredulous that a mythical creature could speak, much less care about her wellbeing. Grandpa had been right about the Woods. Very strange things did lurk in its depths.

"Sure, let's go," Katie said.

She climbed on Leron's back, clinging tightly to his feathers as he lifted her into the air towards Angelina and her perch. With that, he flew off to fetch Angelina from the tree and gently landed both girls on a patch of high ground where they could tend to the cuts they had careening out of the cave.

Katie didn't like the look on Angelina's face. "What's wrong?"

"Where's the pack? I lost the pack with the first aid kit and everything else."

"It's okay," Katie said, only because she desperately needed it to be okay.

Angelina gasped as she wailed. "It's not about the survival supplies. The collection box was in it. We need it to pay off Paimon. I must have dropped it when I was hanging on to that tree."

Katie shot a sharp look at Leron, who lost no time in disappearing. He returned in what must have been only a few minutes but felt like hours and dropped Angelina's pack on the ground between their feet.

But before there could be any display of gratitude or elation, Katie could see that he was still unsettled.

"Now what?"

"I have had this feeling that we're being followed, so I went to see what I could find. I'm sure someone is after you, one person, maybe two.

"Leron, who do you think is following us?" Katie asked.

"Is it Paimon?" Angelina added cautiously. She felt bad that she'd yelled at him when he had been looking out for them and had rescued her—again.

"No, it's human. Look."

He nodded towards the valley behind them. There, in the growing darkness, was a tiny bright spot, signs of a fire.

"Animals don't build fires, and Paimon's heart is as hard as a stone, so he doesn't need the warmth. This is someone looking for you. I'll fly down in the morning and see who it is."

Again, he disappeared into the dusk, returning with pinecones before disappearing into the darkness again. Angelina and Katie dug into them eagerly, peeling down to the creamy, rich pine nuts hidden within.

Katie winced as she watched the night swallow him. Why did he keep taking off like that? She settled into thinking of nothing, but her blank thoughts were rattled when Angelina asked her, "Who were you trying to get away from when you ran into the Woods?"

Katie looked away. Peeking out of the corner of her eye, she'd hoped that her silence had sent Angelina the clear message to leave it alone. Angelina's stare was unwavering.

"Katie, is that who's following us?"

"NO. No. I don't think so. When I got into the forest, the path just disappeared. I think the brush was too thick for him to get through. I just kept running."

She stared at the ground, wondering if it were really possible He could have followed her this far.

"Why was he after you?"

Katie didn't like when Angelina kept pressing her. "Just leave it, Angelina. This is none of your business." Katie stood up and turned her back on Angelina. But she couldn't walk away. Everything was so very dark.

"Look, this could very well be my business. Leron and I could be in danger if there is some bad guy after you."

Whipping around and planting her feet firmly, Katie glared. "Like hauling me into The Valley of Death without telling me anything about it was fair." Katie knew she had Angelina on that one. But Angelina sat on the ground and put her hand out to Katie.

"Look, a wise man told me once that things always look better when you tell someone. Come on. Tell me what happened."

Knowing that Angelina wouldn't give this one up until she had heard all the gory details, Katie slid down to the ground. "He beat me."

Angelina rolled back on her hips as if knocked over by a punch, "Holy shit, Katie. I wasn't expecting that. Did you know him?"

"Yes. He lives in our neighborhood, and I thought he really loved me. He flirted with me for weeks. Then one day, out of the blue, he jumped me from a bunch of bushes and dragged me into an abandoned house and…."

"Geez, what did your parents do with you told them?"

Katie didn't respond. She just stared at the ground, twisting a twig over and over until it finally shredded.

"Katie? What did they do?"

"Nothing."

"Nothing!?" Angelina's outrage echoed in Katie's head.

"I didn't tell." Once she said it, her face flamed. What if she had told? Would none of this other stuff have happened? Would all this be over? Or would he have made good on his promise?

"Why the hell not! Katie, you have got to tell someone."

"Angelina, I can't. He said if I told anyone he'd kill my best friend. I know he means it. I saw them together, and she's terrified of him. I could see it in her eyes. I can't risk it. He will kill her."

"But you can risk him hurting her." Angelina slapped her hands on her thighs, "Unbelievable. I'm glad you're not my friend."

Neither of them said anything more. Katie felt the silence solidify until a wall that seemed impenetrable had formed between them.

Leron drifted to the ground. "We're okay for tonight. You get some sleep now. Tomorrow things get hard, and you'll need your strength."

"Who is Paimon?" Katie whispered with hesitation.

"None of your concern," Angelina said. "You heard him. Tomorrow things get hard."

Angelina's stomach churned. "Tomorrow things get hard" was not the kind of thing to say to someone just before "sweet dreams" She pulled her sweater out of the pack, rolled it up into a pillow, and handed it to Katie. She scooted her back up against Leron's soft, warm feathers.

Angelina heard Katie fluff the sweater pillow and curl up on the other side of Leron. She felt torn. On the one hand, she was beginning to like and care about Katie. On the other, she was disgusted by Katie's willingness to risk her friend's welfare. She shifted back and forth for a long time before finding comfort in the sound of Leron's breathing.

When she woke, which was frequent, Leron was awake and staring into the darkness. She slept fitfully, however, dreaming of whatever lay before her. Whose fire was that below them? What was causing the roaring sound they heard echoing off the canyon walls?

Heat That Gives You Chills

"LERON WASN'T KIDDING ABOUT THINGS getting harder," Angelina said to Katie as she shed as many clothes as was decent. Still, she was dripping with sweat.

The path was no longer the soft padded blanket of pine needles but rocks and roots that seemed to lie in wait, tripping one of them at every opportunity. Angelina had worn her knee boots with thick soles. She could feel the heat radiating from the ground, and these shoes protected her feet well. The wind stirred up ash until her nose ran black with soot. She wanted to stop, rest, or eat, but knowing they were being followed, she didn't dare.

She could see footprints in the dust every time she turned to look behind her. Several times she'd gone back down the trail to investigate, but the impressions of a foot—a bare foot—were blown away by the wind.

"Leron, look." Angelina pointed to one in the dust—this time, a bare foot had pressed deep into the blackened dust.

"Don't stop," Leron growled. His tone alarmed her.

Step after step, her mind raced with wild thoughts of who could be following her and why.

She knew Trek had realized she took the offering box. He'd have told the others. They'd have formed a posse by now to come to bring her back for punishment. She felt sick. She had to fix this and hope, no, pray, that they'd understand and someday forgive her.

She realized Leron was staring at her. "What?" Angelina blurted out. She followed his gaze to the box that peeked out of her pack.

"You told me to bring something valuable, so I did." She shoved past him and marched on up the trail as if she knew where she was going. One foot after the other, she walked. Periodically she turned around to check and be sure Katie and Leron were behind her. She worried that Katie's pace was going to hold them back because she was struggling, often tripping on the stones in the trail as she swatted at the flies buzzing incessantly around their face and ears biting every bit of exposed flesh they could find. Dark gray lizards lying deep in the dust darted for shelter under the nearest rock just before Angelina would have stepped on them.

"Leron, why don't we just fly up to the cave from here? This is miserable."

"The oil in my feathers attacks all the soot and ash in the air. As caked as my feathers are, I can only fly short distances before I have to stop and pick the thick paste off my wings. It should get better as we get up higher. For now, keep moving."

Suddenly, Katie screamed. Angelina stopped and turned to see what was going on. Katie yelled, "Snake," pointing at a pair of serpents slithering across the trail, rattling, hissing their annoyance at the intrusion. Angelina leaped sideways and was suddenly filled with dread. Magda had told her what to do for snake bites, but she wasn't sure she could remember.

Leron quickly grabbed the serpents in his talons' firm grip and dropped them over the cliff's edge. They all listened as minutes passed before the thud of their bodies was heard hitting the bottom of the canyon. Angelina shook her head as she watched Leron settle down to preen the soot from his feathers and spit the globs of gunk into the wind.

Katie's voice trembled as she said, "My father told me stories of men who'd died terrible deaths from spider bites they got in the mines. Snake bites have to be worse."

"Keep moving," Leron cautioned.

"Shut up, Katie." Angelina hushed as she scanned the dead tree branches above. They were thick with bats and the occasional vulture leered at every move. Exhausted emotionally and physically and wishing the sick feeling in her gut would let up, she searched for a place where they could spend the night.

Finally, they reached a spot on the trail wide enough to bed down for the night. She spread out her first aid supplies and searched for something that would help take the burn out of the scrapes and bruises she suffered when she slid out of the cave. Bloody, dirty feet splitting out of tattered shoes stepped into view. Angelina's gaze slowly moved from the feet, past the scraped knees to the hands with every nail broken, resting finally on Katie's fly-bitten face.

"I should have asked Magda about fly bites." Angelina's voice cracked as she grasped at any thought that would help convince her that they were going to get out of this alive.

As she tended to them, Angelina was relieved that most of Katie's sores had started to scab over, but a few on her elbows and one on her thigh still looked angry. Angelina wiped off the blood with her sleeve and coated them with some green goo that Magda had given her.

"Gag!" Angelina had never been the nursing type, and this task pressed her to her limit.

It smelled awful, but it made Katie's sores feel better. Angelina sat back on her heels when she caught sight of Leron studying something below them. She followed his line of sight. There were two fires now, one about a day behind them, the other perhaps another half day behind that. She rubbed her hands over her face, wanting to make all this disappear. She knew full well what this meant, though.

"Tomorrow, we have to move faster," she whispered. "We have to put more distance between them and us." She wondered if anything would work to overcome her anxiety. She also wondered if her false display of authority had fooled anyone into thinking she was brave.

"Sleep," she announced. Rest was essential. She watched Katie search for a place flat enough to lie down before realizing the stuff from her pack was still spread out all over the place. Gathering it up and tucking it into her pack left enough room for Katie and her to find a place to stretch out.

She felt uneasy as Leron moved up into one of the dead trees until she realized he intended to keep watch. Neither girl stretched out, though. Both managed to find a way to curl between a boulder and a couple of tree stumps. Each wrapped their arms around a tree for fear of rolling off the trail in their sleep.

Angelina awoke before sunrise and was ready to travel as soon as it was light enough to see the trail.

"Leron, how much farther is it?" she said.

Shocked to see him turn his head away from her as if he was avoiding the question, she was even more unnerved by the answer.

"The truth is that there's no good answer. Kidron will decide how long it will take you. And it's different for everyone who's ever had to make this journey. You saw the map. What do you think?"

"I don't remember, and it doesn't matter. Let's get moving."

She was worn out, but she got up, put on her pack, and headed up the trail. She wasn't giving up. Not yet, at least.

As she passed, she reached out to Katie, helping her to her feet. "Wait." Angelina looked at Katie's shoes. They were shredding, and blood had soaked through the left one. "You can't go on with your feet like that. You need to change into something else."

"I don't have anything else." Katie reacted to the alarm on Angelina's face. "I was running for my life," she shrieked. "I didn't stop to pack!"

Angelina stared at Katie but wasn't really seeing her. She was seeing the beautiful white boots folded in the bottom of her pack. She'd brought them just in case, but now it was clear that Katie needed them more than she ever would. Without a word, Angelina set down her pack and dug down to pull out her precious beaded white leather boots.

Resisting Katie's objections, she peeled the shreds of shoes from Katie's tender feet and tossed them over the cliff. Slowly she helped Katie pull the soft, white boots over her bruised and bleeding sores, only wincing once at the smears of blood that now streaked the upper cuffs. In the few times she'd gotten to wear them, Angelina never once imagined them being worn the way Katie was wearing them today.

By mid-afternoon, they were so tired that they could hardly move more than a few steps without a break for rest. But they were so near the top of the pass. They had to keep going to stay ahead of whoever was following them. From what she remembered of the legend, Angelina knew the hiding place of the diamonds had to be close. She could vaguely remember that the cave marked on the map was just over a pass. This had to be it.

Fatigue struggled to take over, and she, too, now stumbled more than she found firm footing.

"Leron, how did this place become such a dead or dying landscape? Everything is gray or brown and brittle. The fire that blackened the trees must have been horrific." He didn't answer her. She understood that she was better off not knowing.

The few animals she'd seen were small and scrawny. It was obvious there wasn't a thing to eat. She was looking at the barren skyline when the sound of Leron screeching her name startled her back into reality. But not in time to save her from tumbling into the vast mud pit that oozed across the trail.

Her feet hit the slime first, and she almost floated down into the mire. It swelled into every fold of her body, wrapping her in what first felt like a warm bath. Soon she grasped that what she fell into was more than just mud. It was a swamp that smelled of death and decay. Slime covered with crawling worms and leeches floated on the top. She had sunk up to her waist before she could scream, "Leron, help!"

By the time he was able to react, she had slid under the surface, getting one arm untangled from the weeds that had wrapped around her arms and legs and were pulling her downward.

Grateful to feel the swoop of his wings and his talons grab her arm, Angelina spit mud out of her mouth as she slid from the muck. Her skin was coated with green slime, making his grip on her slip. He dropped her.

"Sorry about that," he said as she landed with a thud.

"I can't do this! I can't keep this up!" she sobbed as she wiped huge chunks of the gunk off her arms and legs. Her boots were filled with muddy water and ruined. She pulled them off and poured the disgusting slime on the ground. "I give up."

"Let the mud dry," Katie said sternly. "We don't have any water for you to wash with anyway. It'll fall off when it's dry. Now get up, and let's go."

Angelina was shocked at the sudden burst of leadership from Katie. But she was too broken to argue. She got to her feet. Looking down at Katie, it hit her—the only shoes Angelina now had were the boots filled with muck. But that didn't alarm her as much as the sound of footsteps crunching the gravel on the trail behind them.

Boots and Hustle

RESPONDING TO KATIE'S DEMAND TO move, Angelina grabbed her pack. Whoever was behind them was close enough to hear her boots on the trail. But she was also worried that the muck she had fallen into was full of germs that had the power to kill.

She reached into her pack and rummaged for her first aid kit. "I have stuff for infection, but I'm supposed to make a tea out of it."

Leron and Katie looked at her in disbelief. Angelina toned down her panic, admitting, "I have no way to make tea." She looked at them and then at the pouch. "Well, if I was supposed to use a handful to make tea, I'd guess I could use a pinch and just suck on it. If I keel over dead, you'll know it didn't work."

Humor was replacing anxiety. She pinched a tiny bit of the herbal leaves between her fingers and stuck it in her mouth, hoping for enough spit to create the essential juices. Wiping her mouth on the back of her hand, she packed up her medicines. She saw that Leron and Katie had already hiked off without her. She tossed her pack over her shoulder and slogged off to catch up with them.

"Yuck, tastes like old socks." Angelina spit out what she hadn't been able to swallow. She hoped that before nightfall, they could camp on a thin ledge overhanging the canyon where they could see the camps of anyone still following them. The trail turned into a series of switchbacks. Angelina could see shadows and hear the faint sounds of voices drifting up the sides of the canyon walls. They were getting so close, but with Katie's sore and bruised feet, they couldn't move any faster.

As the three of them staggered up the trail, the distance between them got farther and farther apart until they all got separated. Angelina was overcome with panic. She couldn't see or hear Leron or Katie anywhere. Afraid to call out for fear of alerting their stalkers that she was alone, she had to find a place to hide soon. She couldn't let them, whoever they were, catch her before she got the diamonds. Once she had those, Trek would have to forgive her. The villagers would have to forgive her. They'd have to let her stay.

Her eyes scanned her surroundings frantically, and then, just a few feet from her, she saw him: a tall, handsome, and barefooted stranger.

She heard him call to her in hushed tones, "Come quick. They won't find you. You'll be safe. Quick."

She started to breathe rapidly. What should she do? If she stayed here, 'they' would find her. Angelina searched for Leron; he must have gone to scout the trail. He was too far away to hear her. Katie was too far behind to hear her. 'They' were too close for her to shout. This stranger was offering her safety.

Panicking over what to do, she pulled the pack off her back and, holding it tightly to her chest, she followed him into the shadows. She turned to look back down the trail. The last thing she saw was the terror on Katie's face. Again, his words echoed in her head. "Here, come here. Angelina, you can hide here." His face was kind, his voice reassuring. As her head began to spin, she saw him pull aside a hank of twisted vines. He gently guided her into a deep pocket in the side of the canyon wall and stood in front of her, concealing her presence. Paralyzed by her fear of capture, she held her breath. The heat of regret rose up her face when she realized that his body molded to the shape and texture of the stone on the walls.

What had she just done? The vines closed like a coarse, rotted curtain, and the entrance to her hiding place disappeared completely. In the distance, she heard Leron call her desperately as she realized she had also vanished into the side of the mountain.

Help or Hostage

REGRETTING HER DECISION TO FOLLOW this stranger, Angelina had become a prisoner in the silence of her hiding place. He had disappeared into the stone wall. She couldn't see through the veil of vines to know who was coming up the trail. She strained to hear any kind of sound that she could recognize but heard nothing for what seemed like an eternity. Her eyes darted back and forth as they scanned the darkness. Then she heard something.

It was Katie! "Please help me find Angelina. She disappeared."

"Calm down, tell me what happened." but who was the man she was talking to? He was asking about Angelina.

There was another woman's voice too. "We came to help."

Angelina realized it was Trek and Rabea. They were here. They'd come after her. Angelina didn't care if they were there to take her back for a trial or revenge.

"Rabea!" Angelina called out from the hiding place.

Her benefactor's form appeared from the stone, and he put his hand over her mouth. His eyes glowed red as he glared at her. In her ear, she heard him growl, "Hush. If you want to keep your friends safe." They were close enough now that she could hear them clearly. Rabea's tone was urgent, "Trek! Did you hear it? I can't tell where it had come from, but I'm sure it was Angelina's voice. Angelina?"

Next, it was Katie's voice. "She just disappeared. She was right in front of me, and then she was gone." Katie hadn't seen the stranger. Angelina bit her lip so hard it bled. She cringed as the stranger slowly reached out with his index finger and wiped her lip clean.

"Don't make a sound." The hiss echoed in her ears, and she knew she couldn't call out again, or something awful would happen. But her eyes never left his. He might have captured her body, but he wouldn't have her spirit.

All Angelina could do was listen while they searched for her. Again, she heard Rabea's frantic plea with Katie's agreement, "She has to be here. I heard her!" This time she heard Trek's voice, "I didn't hear anything. Are you sure it's not a trick?"

"I know what I heard. She was close, but there was no place where she could be. The trail is steep and narrow. If she were here, we'd be able to see her." Rabea's voice trailed off in confusion.

"It might just be one of the evil tricks they say the valley can play on people. We can't stay here. We need to find a place to bed down before dark," Trek said reluctantly. Angelina heard their voices fade, sure they had moved up and over the pass. Her heart sank as the dark stranger gently took Angelina's hand and led her down a short passage.

"Come, you'll find this trail much easier. Not so rocky and much cooler. You'll find the red and blue diamonds much faster, Angelina."

Angelina held back.

"Oh, don't look so surprised. I know all about you. There are no secrets in Kidron. Kidron always tells."

Angelina shivered at the sound of his low voice and struggled to stay in control of her very mixed emotions. Now she knew that this was Paimon. In her panic and hurry to get to the diamonds, she'd accepted help from the Devil himself. Now she had no choice but to follow him. At least until she could figure out how to get away from him. If she could get out in the open, Leron would find them, and hopefully, he could get to Katie, Trek, and Rabea to warn them.

How in the world was she going to do that? "God only knows," she whispered under her breath. She followed Paimon down a soft trail, free of rocks, rising gently, her hair blowing in the gentle, cool breeze. The sound of his overly sincere conversation made her skin crawl. Everything about this felt wrong. How could this trail be so beautiful when they were still in the Valley of Kidron—the Valley of Death.

"Isn't this so much better than the other trail? You stick with me, and your life will get much easier, Angelina. And stop worrying about your friends. I'll see that you are taken care of. Besides, they don't care about you. They'll never forgive you for stealing from them, especially when they find out you've given that collection box to me—and you will, you know." He turned to look at her. His eyes burned bright red. "As God is my witness, you will."

Angelina shivered with disgust. His tone and everything about him made her feel dirty. She reached up to the straps of her backpack and pulled it tightly against her back.

He smiled, no, sneered, "You don't even know what you've got there, do you? All in good time, all in good time. Here, let me help you. This is a big step." He held out his hand to guide her across a stream of fast-running water that glowed an eerie iridescent amber.

"I've got it." She was curt in her reply as she stepped over to the other side.

"Spunk! I like that!" His taunting laugh echoed off the walls of the canyon they'd entered.

Angelina realized that without help, she was going to have to figure out how to get away from this evil on her own. She was going to have to fend for herself.

Still, she whispered, "Leron, where are you?"

She watched Paimon's every move, studied how he walked, where he stopped, and why. She listened to every word he spoke, searching for clues to what he wanted, what he needed. She was discouraged when she realized he was keeping to trails sheltered by thick overgrowth or rocky outcrops. Leron would never be able to find her.

Unless. Unless he could sense her body heat. Once this occurred to her, she was determined to build up a sweat no matter how uncomfortable she'd be. She started complaining of being chilled and kept her coat on.

A day went by, then another, and during that time, she couldn't figure out how Paimon knew she had the collection box, but every time he asked for it, she told him, "You know I'll never give you this box. You'll have to take it."

She was confident that she could hold her ground no matter what he said or did. She took a bit of delight in seeing his frustration grow with each failed attempt. At least she had that.

"I can give you great riches, my dear, but I must have something from you to show your dedication and appreciation. That box is of no use to you now."

"I'll never give it to you. You'll have to take it," she said.

"But you brought that box to give to me. That's why you stole it. It is a gift for me as thanks for your safe passage."

"Never."

Finally, he'd tried flattery, lies, and bargaining, and all had failed. She watched with horror as he lost his temper and began to roar as if fueled by all the venom that ran through his veins.

"You're a fool! No one loves you! Not your father or your useless mother. Trek just wants your body. Rabea has no friends, so you're just a poor stand-in for the real thing. You think Magda cares for you? She just wants to find someone to take her job so she doesn't have to work. And Katie. She is the most pathetic of them all. So she got beaten. Big deal. She needs to get over it."

He had done it now. Angelina lunged at him. "You bastard. Don't you dare talk about Katie like that." Angelina was alarmed by her reaction, but he had finally crossed too many lines and this had to stop.

She spit on him, but he only laughed as the droplets sizzled and disappeared. He grabbed her wrists so tightly that he left bruise marks from his fingers when he pushed her away.

"I'm the only one who cares for you. I'm the one here helping you find the diamonds. You owe me! I'm the one who'll get you what you want!" He hissed and sneered, and his eyes flashed with rage. "Even that griffin has deserted you!"

The air around them grew hot, and the steam from his body rose high in the sky. Angelina stood firmly, staring at him, steeling her resolve not to respond but wary that her lack of response might enrage him even more. All she had to do was keep pressing his buttons, and he continued to get more and more angry. The angrier he became, the more steam flared from his body.

Angelina refused to meet his tone. Through clenched teeth, she declared, "Leron has not deserted me." This made Paimon roar with laughter that shook the walls of the canyon.

All day Angelina had prayed that Leron would be circling high above the peaks, hoping he saw the plume of steam. Steam wasn't unusual in Kidron, but surely she had caused Paimon to generate enough heat that it would rise with such force. Leron had to know it was a sign. He had to know it was her. He would find her.

Bargaining Over a Soul

A S THE DAYS PASSED, ANGELINA COULD hear Trek, Rabea, and Katie searching for her. Paimon had made sure she was aware of their every move.

"Do you hear your friends? They want to find you so they can get the diamonds. They will leave you behind once they have the jewels," he would tell her, obviously delighting in his cruelty.

She understood it was part of his plan to torture her, letting her know they were so close yet too far away to change her fate. She knew it was his intent to break her spirit, and she made sure it was her intent to never be broken. As they traveled, she calculated the distance she stayed behind him to leave just enough room for Leron to land when he found her. He would find her soon.

Early on the afternoon of the third day, the ground rumbled harshly. Small rocks began pelting Angelina from above. The rocks grew larger and larger, and within a few minutes, bodies came cascading down onto the trail between Angelina and Paimon.

"Trek!" Angelina exclaimed. She tripped over Katie and Rabea, who had also landed hard amongst the rubble. She reached out to hug them all. Katie had managed to roll herself away. Now she was crawling a few feet apart from them all.

Angelina was horrified as suddenly Trek was shoved hard in the back. It was as if an invisible force lifted him off his feet and plunged him to the side of the trail. Rabea was still on the ground under bits of rock and sand when

Angelina saw her yanked up by her left arm and pulled to her feet. Angelina recognized the finger mark bruises left by the tight grip on her friend's arm. Rabea's eyes were open wide and flaring with panic. She clutched her chest like she was being suffocated. Looking up, Angelina saw nothing but the bright red glow of Paimon's eyes. Terror filled her heart.

"Don't you move," Paimon hissed. Trek froze. "Katie, get back. You too, Angelina. If you move, I'll take her soul, and you'll never see your 'friend' again."

Before Angelina could measure her options, which were growing fewer by the minute, something hit her hard. She'd prayed for Leron to come to her rescue. She was grateful when Trek and Rabea arrived.

But she'd never asked God what He wanted.

Shame mixed with new unflinching courage, and she silently prayed. "God, tell me what to do. Now, please!" Angelina stood frozen in the moment. She had no idea what a response from God looked like. Was lightning going to strike? Would there be thunder, or would she feel the earth move under her feet? Nothing. She felt nothing. Nothing except she knew if she didn't do something and do it now, Rabea would be lost to her family and friends, doomed to live with the Devil forever.

Slowly she began to move towards Paimon, speaking in soft, gentle tones. "Paimon, she's not who you want. You want me and the box. Let her go. I'll give you the box. I'll stay here with you. You want me. I'll stay."

His eyes flashed at her. "How do I know you're telling the truth? Why should I care about a cracked and worn old box?"

Angelina's eyes flashed back at his. "Because I stole it for you. I stole it because I have to get the red and blue diamonds. My friend is being beaten because he can't repay a debt for an expensive gift I was too vain and greedy to refuse, and I have to make it right. You know this box is all I have to prove that I'm not just a common thief. But I am a thief. You've won that one. Let her go, take me and the box, and let them pass."

Angelina continued to creep closer and closer to him and Rabea. Rabea's face was filled with horror. Angelina had never seen anyone so frightened in her life. Not even her mother. Now Angelina knew that Paimon wasn't enticed by the box. She could tell by the way he stared at her that he was only interested because of its value to her. The fact that she was willing to give up the one thing that, if returned, might win back the favor of her friends and the others made his eyes glow even more brightly than when he was angry.

A wicked smile twisted across his lips as he ran his tongue across his teeth like he was about to eat something exceedingly delicious. She could see how getting her to stay with him pleased him immensely. She knew he had to think he'd won her. She felt Trek moving up behind her as he shifted towards Paimon and Rabea.

Angelina put her hands out, fingers outstretched, palms facing Trek. "Don't move, Trek. No one would be in danger if it weren't for my lust for those damned white boots. I wouldn't be trying to get the diamonds to help you pay those jerks beating you. I have to pay the price to make sure everyone stays safe."

Angelina watched as Paimon loosened his grip on Rabea just enough so she could breathe. Her hands were shaking and so soaked with sweat that her fingers slipped on the buckle of the belt binding the pack together. Angelina slid the backpack off her shoulders and let it drop to the ground, disgusted as Paimon all but drooled with anticipation. Once she handed him the box she knew she'd be his for eternity: another soul he would have power over, another one lost from God's grace.

Slowly, she reached in with both hands, removed the box, and gently placed it on the ground in front of Paimon's bare feet. He dropped his grip on Rabea, eyes glowing, teeth gleaming as his smile broadened.

"Rabea, go to Trek. Katie, don't move." Angelina motioned for them all to get against the wall of the canyon.

"You little fool!" Paimon's voice roared. "You're mine now and forever!" His tone turned to a growl, and he sipped the drool that ran off his teeth with every word. "And for what? These cowards who never loved you for one minute." He jabbed a crooked finger toward Trek. "He called you a liar and a thief." He spun on one heel and lunged his face into Rabea's, leaving her limp with fear. "She can't muster the courage to speak on your behalf. And you have given up everything for poor little victim Katie. Fool!"

His fiendish laugh rolled down the walls of the canyon. Rocks loosened by the echoes bounced off their heads and shoulders, leaving raw scrapes at every point of contact. Angelina held her breath, oddly thinking that this was what someone about to be executed must feel like. This could be a very good time, she thought. When was God going to show up?

She watched as Paimon reached for the box. Everyone gasped as it mysteriously slid out of reach. Angelina was stunned. Every time he reached for it, the box skittered again. Now she was just plain confused. What in the hell was going on? And why were her words only in her head and not coming out of her mouth?

And then it happened. A voice, not in her head but in her ear, said, "Evil cannot triumph over a selfless act. Your courage has been his defeat." She smiled. God had shown up. He was here and in her head. No lightning, no thunder, just a simple message from His heart to hers.

She laughed at Paimon as he trembled all over, consumed with anger. He reached again.

"You're the fool, Paimon."

Angelina was thrilled to hear Leron's voice drifting in on the wind. He glided to the trail and landed between her and Paimon.

"You!" Paimon howled.

"Leron, do you know what's going on?" Angelina needed to make sure she wasn't imagining things and was about to make a fool of herself.

"Angelina, he can never touch that box. When you willingly offered to give up everything important to you, to have your reputation blackened for all eternity, and to give up the one thing that could restore your relationship with those you love, you rendered the box totally unattainable."

Paimon lurched again, and again it slipped out of his reach. Angelina put her foot firmly on the top of the box. He bellowed in pain as she lifted her chin in a throaty laugh. They all watched as he sank to the ground, beating his fists into the dirt. His body was writhing and twisting until he transformed into the snake he had been ordained to be. Angelina never took her eyes off his.

"You will be mine," he hissed. "I will be your salvation."

Angelina looked down at her beautiful white boots, worn and dirty and on someone else's feet. She was aware of a warmth that washed over her entire body. She felt a peace and a strength that she'd never known before. She smiled a tiny little smile, not mocking but the smile that came from finally knowing the answer to something she'd struggled hard to figure out.

"You're wrong. I am a chosen one, and God loves me. That's all that matters. I will never be yours." She stepped forward, raised her foot, and brought it down hard, barely missing his withered body as she intended. "Never."

Paimon slithered off the trail and disappeared into the blackened earth.

Oddly, Angelina felt neither triumph nor joy in Paimon's defeat. She slowly leaned over, picked up the box, and handed it to Trek.

"I'm sorry," she whispered.

"No, I'm the one who's sorry." He looked down at his feet, not at her face. "I misjudged you. I had no right to accuse you without knowing the facts. You have the heart of the most courageous. I hope you can find it in that heart to forgive me."

Angelina put her hands on each side of his face, lifting his chin so she could see into his eyes. She kissed him gently on the lips.

After a moment, though, the glow began to wear off. They both stepped back quickly. She was hoping the others didn't see, but of course, they did. She laughed.

"It's about time, you two!" Rabea chided and pushed them back together. Angelina laughed again as she felt the warmth of Trek's arm wrap around her waist.

Leron broke the spell. "Children, I know this is important, but you really don't have the time for this right now. You really must hurry. Time is running out."

Angelina looked past Leron and saw Katie so pale her face was almost featureless.

"Wait. Katie, are you okay?"

Katie's stare was blank. Her voice was emotionally flat. "Well, shit. I've just tramped through The Valley of Death, lost a friend, found a friend, met the Devil, and now we have to go get some ridiculous red and blue diamonds. Yeah, I'm fine." She put her head down and muttered, "Come on, let's get this over with."

Angelina gave her a quick hug, followed by a playful shove. "Yeah, let's get some water out of here."

Diamonds, Angels, and
Books Filled with Giggles

NGELINA GRABBED HER PACK, CAREFULLY placing the box Trek handed her back inside, and, hand in hand, they headed for the top of the mountain. Katie and Rabea followed closely behind. Leron flew on ahead to scout the trail.

Trek stopped and stared at Katie. "Don't I know you? Wait, you were there when I bought the boots." They both looked down at her feet and began to laugh. Not sure she wanted to hear that story, Angelina took Trek's hand and hiked onward.

Angelina marveled at the change in the trees, which had grown greener. Grass now lined the trail as they rounded the final bend, and finally, Angelina could see the entrance to the cave. Drawn by a mysterious light glowing from inside, she reached up, grabbed a tree branch, and swinging herself up and overhead from branch to branch, she reached the top of the mountain far ahead of the others.

Angelina's eyes adjusted to the light, and what she saw made her forget to breathe. The cave was lit by a single crystal hanging from the ceiling. At her feet lay a treasure chest filled with jewels, pearls, gold, and silver—and red and blue diamonds. But what intrigued her were the stacks of hand-tooled leather books and the rows of tiny crystal bottles lining the wall opposite the treasure chest.

Leron appeared in the cave opening. Angelina was surprised but not really. They had come so far, and now, standing in the cave, she was overwhelmed by questions. Yet she understood that explanations would have to wait.

"Leron, look at all this. Someone's been stashing stuff here for what looks like years." She ran her fingers along the cover of the top book, leaving a trail in the dust. She blew the dust bunny off the end of her fingers and reached out with both hands to remove the book from the pile.

"What a gorgeous binding…." Gently she lifted the cover. The leather creaked, allowing the pages to open just enough that she could see inside. "It's blank." The disappointment in her voice echoed in the cave.

"Be patient. Listen." This was a new voice, one she hadn't heard before but one she knew well. It was the same lyrical voice she'd heard many nights when she was alone in the Enchanted Woods. Drifting up from the book came a tiny little laugh. As Angelina listened, it grew louder and more joyful, and Angelina smiled until she heard a faint little lilt at the end of the laughter. Suddenly, she snapped the cover shut and looked at Leron for an explanation.

"That's me! That's my laugh." She was very confused.

"Open it again," Leron coaxed.

Cautiously, she lifted the cover, and as her laughter filled the cave, she couldn't help but laugh.

"But how? Why?" she said. She searched Leron's eyes but didn't find any answers.

The glitter swirled and danced in the light until it settled into the form of an angel. Angelina was too stunned to respond until the angel turned to face her. The connection was electric. It was as if they had known each other all of Angelina's life. At the same time, her heart filled with the excitement of finally meeting someone she'd longed to know.

The angel's voice was so soft it almost shimmered in the air. "Angelina," she said. "Like every parent, God treasures every one of the important moments in your life, and He keeps them here." Little droplets of glittery light spread from her arms as she gestured around the room.

Trek and Rabea burst into the cave out of breath, soaking wet from dashing through the waterfall. Angelina looked back to see where Katie was.

She had obviously stopped under the falling water to rinse her hair and wash the grime off her face.

"Wow, I hate when you swing through the trees like that and get so far ahead. What'd you find?" Trek wiped his face on his sleeve to get the water and sweat out of his eyes. He stopped short when he saw the angel.

"What the?!" Rabea blurted out and covered her mouth when she realized she'd come so close to swearing in front of an angel.

Angelina laughed. "These are my fellow travelers."

They each bowed. Angelina figured they didn't know what one did when being introduced to an angel.

"I'm the angel that guards these treasures you have come in search of."

"Look!" Angelina handed Trek the book. She nodded for him to open it. The air was filled with a huskier giggle, unlike the laugh she'd heard before. Confused, she turned to look at the angel.

"His first laugh. You see, God has kept every single one."

As she and Angelina explained the find to Trek, Rabea, and Katie, they all began to explore the other books and bottles. Angelina stepped back to watch as they each found their own first tears, first songs, first 'I love you,' first kisses, first broken hearts—it was amazing. Still, everything that had ever meant anything in each of their lives was here.

Angelina watched them each fill with joy. She had a catch in her throat as she realized how much she loved these people. She found so much happiness in watching them explore.

The Angel continued, "And these, the ones you have come to take, are the most precious of all. The red and blue diamonds."

The angel stepped aside so Angelina could see the magnificent jewels lying among the pearls and other gems in an overflowing seashell. "The red diamonds were formed from the blood of Jesus when He was crucified, and the blue diamonds are the tears His mother Mary cried as she watched her son suffer and die."

Angelina looked at Trek, knowing that although no words were spoken, everything had just changed.

Blood, Tears and the
Darkness of the Abyss

ANGELINA FELT AN UNEASY TWIST in her gut. She turned to see Daiken—Daiken—pushing his way past Trek and Katie to get right up in front of the diamonds. He reeked of smoke and sweat and swamp slime.

"Daiken" Angelina exclaimed. "It was you – the other campfire."

"Yep, this is an interesting little party you're having here."

He leaned in to touch the diamonds, but Trek caught him by the wrist. Angelina watched the two stare at each other as an unspoken challenge.

"You seemed to have forgotten to invite me." Daiken shook his wrists loose from Trek's grip. "No hard feelings. It's just good to know that what was just diamonds before are really priceless relics." He chuckled. "I'll never have to work another day in my life."

To say that Angelina was not comfortable that Daiken stood so deep in the cave, his feet planted firmly, was an understatement. She was even more concerned when she realized he had a knife in one hand and a branch fashioned into a spear in the other.

"Right, missy. I've spent too many nights sleeping on the ground following you, but now it's all about to be worth it!"

He fingered a pouch he had tied to his belt. He dropped it on the ground. Kicking it towards Trek, Daiken jabbed the knife in Leron's direction, warning him to stay back. "Pretty boy, put the diamonds in the pouch, now!"

Trek picked up the pouch, but instead of moving toward the treasure chest, he slowly stepped toward Daiken. Angelina wanted to stop him, unarmed, but she was too far away to get between them. And Katie and Rabea were too deep in the cave to make a move that would mean anything.

"Hey, man, let's talk about this. There's plenty for everyone," Trek said to Daiken.

Angelina realized he was trying to get close. Somehow, she and Rabea needed to slip around each side of him so Daiken would be surrounded.

"Back off!" Daiken shouted. "I'm not kidding! Get those diamonds." Winking at Angelina, he smirked. "I wouldn't be here if it wasn't for you, missy. I'm not about to let any of you get in the way of my plans!"

Angelina needed to keep him talking. "What plans, Daiken? What are you going to do this all these jewels?" She watched Trek inch forward from the corner of her eyes, making Daiken back up a few steps toward the cave opening.

I'm going to see the world, sugar. Dance with pretty girls. No offense, Angelina, you kiss good, but your ears are a real turn-off. I want to hang out with the 'big boys, 'play poker, drink beer, and sleep all day if I want. I'm sick of life in the Woods and so bored with you. Now get me those diamonds! Move!"

Daiken lunged, swinging the knife. The tip sliced through Trek's shirt and caught the flesh just above his elbow. The blood began to run down his arm, making his hand almost useless.

Behind her, Angelina heard small snapping sounds. It was Katie breaking off bits of crystals from the cave walls.

"What are you doing?" was what she wanted to shout, but then she realized by tossing them at Daiken, Katie was forcing him to take his eyes off his hostages to search for the source of the sounds.

Angelina watched with trepidation as Daiken turned. Trek took his shot and swung at Daiken. Shifting his feet back and forth to be ready, Daiken got his feet tangled in the vines dripping off the cave walls into puddles on the floor. He stumbled. The knife clattered as it fell to the ground.

Angelina saw her chance and shoved Daiken. He struggled to keep his balance as he tossed the spear into the cave as if he thought he could strike one of them. Leron fell silently to the floor of the cave. Angelina screamed. "Katie, help Leron. Arrgghh!"

Angelina growled as she grabbed the knife. In a blinding madness, she followed Trek and Daiken. They were struggling down the trail kicking rocks and roots that tumbled with great crashing sounds down the side of the cliff. She could hear the blows as they landed, punching and kicking, each blow doing more damage than the last.

Trek tripped and fell. Angelina caught up to them and was now face to face, pointing the knife at Daiken. She leveled it at his chest. One by one, she tightened the grip of her fingers on the handle.

Rabea was shouting, "Stop! You, stop now!" but Angelina kept her eyes on his. He tossed his chin over his shoulder and taunted Rabea. "Or what?" His smirk made Angelina want to slap it right off his face. "You think you're going to hurt me with that knife? You don't have the guts."

He had finally infuriated Angelina more than she could contain. She lunged at him. But as he stepped back to avoid the blade, his foot slid off the edge of the trail. Angelina watched as he flailed his arms and legs, desperate to find anything to grab onto. In the slow motion she felt when her nightmares had her falling off a cliff, he silently disappeared over the edge and was gone from sight.

Shocked, they all froze. Daiken had just plunged into the depths of the darkness. Angelina knew she should feel something. Sadness, shock, anxiety. She felt nothing. The air was still, the silence deafening. Snapping back to the reality of now, Angelina dropped the knife, pushed Katie out of the way, and rushed to Leron.

Wrapping her arms around his neck, she searched for signs of life. Nothing. His eyes were closed, his breathing very, very shallow. His lion's tail wrapped around her leg and clung there. She buried her face in his feathers and wept.

Katie stepped forward and put her hand on Angelina's shoulder. Angelina dissolved into a puddle of sorrow.

The Gift

"LERON!" ANGELINA LOOKED UP, WILDLY searching the faces of her friends. "Somebody help! Do something. Somebody! He can't die." She nestled her face in his feathers. "Don't leave me. I can't lose you. Help my friend!"

Frantic, her mind raced. She had to think of something, anything, that she could do. She tightened her arms around Leron's neck and began to rock. Without conscious thought, she began to quietly hum. Her mother did that to ease her pain when she lay helpless after one of her father's beatings. It had worked for her. It had to help Leron. It had to ease his pain. Slowly, the words of her mother's song came back to her.

She moved closer to his ear, and through her tears, she softly sang her mother's song. She was vaguely aware that Trek had slowly pulled the spear from Leron's body. She moved her hands from his wound so Rabea could begin to treat it with the herbs she always carried in the pouch on her belt. Time stopped for Angelina as she felt Leron's tail slowly slide off her leg. When it no longer touched her, she screamed, "No!"

Trek reached out to hold her. She was sobbing into his shoulder when Rabea touched them both.

"Look," she whispered, pointing to Leron's body.

Angelina watched as his lion body faded away to be replaced by beautiful thick tail feathers. She stared at his form, trying to make sense of all that had happened. Was this what happened when a griffin died? Did it fade away into a single being?

The silence of the moment was broken by the sound of cursing and gravel scattering outside the cave. Angelina turned to see Daiken standing up, covered in blood, dirt, and brush. How had he survived the fall? He should be dead. He couldn't be alive. Then Angelina gasped. His feet were bare. Daiken and Paimon were now one. He had sold his soul to the Devil.

"Now, I am going to kill all of you."

He unbuttoned the breast pocket of his torn and tattered jacket and pulled out a small handgun.

"Get out. Move! Line up on the trail." He waved the gun at Trek, Rabea, and Katie. "Face me, you bitch" he barked at Angelina.

He herded them down the trail to a place where it was very narrow. He made them turn with their backs to the river. They were pinned between the cliff wall on one side and the straight drop to the river below.

Angelina made eye contact with Katie. The color was draining out of her face again. Angelina winked at her, hoping it would help Katie remain calm. Then she shifted to calculating the risk. If they survived the gunshots, they would plunge to a sure death on the rocks or drown in the river. There were no trees or brush to grab if they fell.

"Now, who shall I shoot first? You, pretty boy? You? Or you, the real misfit of the bunch?" He nudged Angelina's chest with the barrel of the gun. In a split second, between now and what would happen next, the air was filled with the sound of a great rush of wind coming from the cave, followed by the terrifying screech of an eagle. It was Leron.

Angelina shrieked, "Leron!"

Daiken turned just in time to see the great beast grab him with his fierce talons. He dropped the gun as he grabbed Leron's leg. Angelina and her friends turned and watched the silhouette of the eagle and his prey kicking violently and disappearing into the clouds. The walls of the canyon resounded with the sound of Daiken screaming. The sound of his terror slowly faded away until the valley was silent.

Slowly, Angelina turned around to Trek. She pulled up his blood-soaked shirt sleeve to examine the gash on his arm. He winced as Angelina gently touched the bruises on his face. "Now, we need to get you fixed up."

"We're going to need some water," Rabea said as she released the pouch from her belt. "Katie, can you find something that will carry water?"

Katie searched the cave for anything without any luck. Until she spotted a crystal bottle on the shelf that had her name on it. She carefully reached for it, taking great care not to disturb the other bottles. It was almost full all right; God had every one of her tears in it.

But they were her tears. That meant they belonged to her, to do with as she saw fit, right? Without another thought, she pulled out the teardrop-shaped stopper and poured every one of those tears on the ground. She stared at the puddle soaking up the importance of this moment. Then, she straightened her back. Flipping her hair back over her shoulder, she walked straight out of the cave to the waterfall. This bottle now had a more important job to do.

"I will have to figure out how to hold this poultice in place."

Angelina watched Katie hand the bottle to Rabea. Rabea was slowly pouring the water into her hand to wet the herbs when Angelina grabbed Rabea's wrist to stop her.

"Katie, what have you done? This is your tear bottle."

Rabea's head shot around to look at Katie. Katie just shrugged. "Sometimes you just have to get over it and move on." Not knowing what more there was to say, Angelina and Rabea just sat there.

"Hey, ladies. I'm bleeding here."

"Sorry," Rabea muttered. "Now I need something that will hold this poultice in place."

"Oh, I have string! Thanks to a friend, I have string!" Angelina dug into her pack for her survival gear. Once Trek was all patched up and ready for travel, the three friends put the cave back in order and did their best to repair the damage from the fight.

"I think it looks pretty good." There was a bit of a question in Angelina's voice.

"I don't think anyone passing by would know that something dramatic happened here. Hey, I'm ready to get out of this place." Rabea searched the faces of the others.

"Ready to head for home?" Rabea held out a hand so Trek could get up without using his injured arm.

Angelina hesitated. "You guys go ahead. I'll catch up."

Enthusiastically, Trek and Rabea took one last look at the cave, parted the veil of the waterfall, and started the long journey home.

Angelina went back into the cave, no longer afraid of what she might find there. She found Katie sitting with her arms wrapped around her legs and her head tucked between her knees. "Hey, kid. You okay?"

"You keep asking me that. Yes. No. I'm not sure."

"Talk to me." Angelina sat down next to Katie, facing the same way, so they didn't have to make eye contact if this got too intense.

"I don't know, Angelina. When you told that jerk that you'd stay with him if he'd let Rabea go, did you really mean it? You were really going to do it?"

"Katie, I think I really was. All that time I was with him, all I could think of was how all this was my fault. If I hadn't made the choices I'd made, no one would be in danger, and I was the only one who could make it right. It wasn't about just me anymore. It was about something bigger."

Angelina paused, letting Katie soak all this up. The silence lasted for what seemed like a very long time. Angelina was talking about herself but hoped Katie was hearing that it was about her too—and Angel.

Katie was the first to speak this time. "I know I should go back and tell what really happened to me, but I don't want this to go on anymore. I just want to forget that the beating ever happened and move on with my life."

Angelina watched her struggle, and finally, she said," Katie, today I learned that at some point, you have to use your voice. It can make a difference in someone else's life. Think about it. You have to do the right thing and use your voice for Angel. You're the only one who can keep Angel safe."

Angelina got up, leaving Katie alone in the cave with her thoughts, her tear bottle, and her book of precious memories. She hoped Katie knew what she had to do.

Katie stood in the darkness of the cave for a long time. The angel was gone. The crystal that had provided all the light for them until now had just turned off. Her heart was heavy. She had never felt this alone before. Not even in those first days living at the cottage.

"Please don't leave me alone," she whispered. "Please? I can't do this."

Afraid to be alone in the dark anymore, Katie hurried to catch up with the group.

Not too far down the trail, Katie watched Angelina's pace quicken. Leron was coming to meet them. With his "new" look, Katie almost didn't recognize him. In his dark mane and tawny coat, tail swishing arrogantly from side to side, he was now quite the handsome lion.

Katie caught up with them. She had resolved not to think about the beating anymore. She was going to stay in the moment with this bizarre experience. But she'd held her curiosity as long as she could. Hoping that the answer to her question wasn't obvious to everyone but her, she cleared her throat. When Angelina's eyes left Leron and turned to Katie, she took a breath. She quietly asked, "Angelina, did you do something magic to save Leron?"

"No, little one," Leron spoke in almost a whisper. "She sang."

"I let my heart go free, and as it swelled up in my chest, the song escaped." Seeing the confused look on Katie's face, Angelina continued, "It's a long story, Katie. I'll tell you more tonight." Katie watched Angelina look back at Trek and Rabea. "Maybe it was magic."

They all turned to continue their journey, all except Katie, who stood in the middle of the trail trying to connect the events she had just witnessed. The last thing she heard before they disappeared over the ridge was Angelina telling Leron, "It's been too long since you've felt the warm dust on all your feet at once or the grass between your toes. I think you should walk. I'll ride!"

She grabbed his mane in her left hand and swung her right leg over his back. He took off like a champion racehorse. Angelina shouted back over her shoulder, "We'll meet you at camp!" She and Leron disappeared in a cloud of dust.

Not wanting to get too far behind, Katie started down the trail, one measured step after another. When her right foot hit the ground, she repeated out loud, "I have to tell," Every time her left foot hit the ground, she said, "He will kill Angel."

This went on for miles. Tell. Kill. Tell. Kill. Tell.

Occasionally, her mantra was interrupted as she struggled to reconcile the last few days' events. Why was Angelina willing to sacrifice herself for Rabea? How did that kind of friendship happen?

"Tell. Don't Tell. Tell. Don't.'

When she caught up with the others, they were setting up camp for the night, building a fire, and sharing what little food they had left.

"You okay? Katie, you look really weird." Angelina patted the ground beside her.

Katie dropped down and folded her legs underneath her. "Angelina, how did you know you had to do something? I mean, how did you know you could save Trek from being beaten anymore? How did you know you could make that happen? And how did you know that Paimon wouldn't actually get your soul?"

"Well, it wasn't like a lightning bolt if that's what you were thinking. The guilt of causing it got worse than not knowing what to do. When I remembered the Legend of the Red and Blue Diamonds, things sort of fell into place as a way to help Trek." She shrugged her shoulders, staring at her food. "The Paimon thing was pure faith."

"I can't figure out who to tell about the beating. I'm afraid of what will happen next. What if they don't believe me, or he finds out and kills Angel before anyone can do anything?"

"That's where the faith comes in. Kind of like the path thing. You might have to wait for the Woods to show you the way. Want a sunflower seed? Rabea brought them."

Angelina reached out and handed Katie a seed the size of the palm of her hand. Katie's eyes widened as she took the seed, turning it over in her hand, trying to figure out how to crack the shell. Angelina showed her where the seam in the seed was yawning just enough to get her finger into pop the shell.

"I know. This place is definitely strange. What is even more strange is how quickly you get used to it."

For the next two days, Katie followed behind the rest of the group. She kept going over every scenario of who to tell what and how. Should she just say, "I was beaten"? Would she have to go into all the details? Even thinking about it made her feel sick with embarrassment, and she caught herself placing her hands in ways to cover the parts of her that were no longer private. When they came to the slimy mud pit, Leron offered to fly her over it to keep her feet out of the muck.

"I don't think it'll make any difference," she sighed as she looked down at the tattered remains of the white boots.

"We'll just hop over," Leron assured her.

Katie hesitated and finally found the courage to ask, "Leron, did Angelina tell you?"

"Yes."

"Dang her. Now I guess everyone knows." Katie stomped her foot. "That should have been private."

"No one knows except me, and she only told me because she is concerned about you and wanted some advice."

"What if I can't do it, Leron? What if I really am a coward?"

Katie kept her voice low, hoping they wouldn't draw attention to this conversation. But as they approached the others, they were interrupted by Trek, setting up camp for the night downwind from the slime pit. Katie watched the flames of the campfire lick at the shadows of the dead trees looming over them.

"Hey, Katie? Did you hear where Leron took Daiken?"

Katie realized she'd missed a bunch of conversations while she went down the trail alone. She turned and looked at Leron.

Leron answered quietly. "I took him deep into Kidron."

"Oh, Leron, that place was so awful. I know he's a terrible person but to leave him in the Valley of Death…." Katie's voice trailed off as she thought of all the horrors he would have to endure. She turned away to see if any sunflower seeds were left when she caught herself and spun back to the group. "Hey, which one of you has the diamonds? Can I see them?"

Trek jumped in on this one too. "Oh, I forgot to fill you in on that part. We don't have them."

Katie's head whipped around. "What? We came all this way, and you didn't take what you came for?"

"No, wait! We left them on purpose."

But before he could finish explaining, Angelina, staring into the depths of the canyon, interrupted. "Trek, what are they going to do to me?"

"To us, you mean. Don't forget, I took that money from my dad." He picked up a small twig and began to chew on it as he stared into the fire. "I don't know, Angelina. I don't know."

Katie was shocked when Angelina offered her plan. "Maybe I should just move on. I've been nothing but trouble since I came here."

"Absolutely not!" Rabea bolted upright. "You are not leaving!"

"Rabea, I may not have a choice. Trek is family. I'm nobody."

"Wait, all of you." As Leron stepped into the light of the fire, Katie prayed he'd have a better answer. "You forget that you will have a chance to be heard. You will tell your story. Then the good will be weighed against the bad, and they will decide."

Rabea nodded insistently., "He's right! You'll have to make them understand that you did it to help, not for your own gain. And you didn't hesitate to offer to take my place with Paimon. That's got to count for something."

"But they might still decide to banish us." Everyone knew Trek was right. The silence was almost overwhelming. "Look, let's just go to sleep. We can't do anything about it tonight." Trek lay down and rolled over, hiding his face from the others.

This entire conversation chilled Katie to the bone. They were talking about some borrowed money for a pair of boots. She was facing the shame of publically telling the world that she'd been beaten and the horror of possibly causing the death of her best friend. If Angelina and Trek could be banished for their sins, what would happen to her?

"Angelina, do you really think they will banish you?" she said

"Katie, all I know is that stolen things can do no good for those who steal them. Trek's decided to tell his dad the truth and ask him for a loan to pay off the gang. All this lying and sneaking around has caused so much trouble. I'm hoping I can help repay Gastor, too. You know, I've gotten pretty good at knitting. Magda bought a whole bag of this beautiful yarn. I thought I'd ask her if we could be partners. She supplies the yarn, I'll knit the things to sell, and we can split the profits. My part will go to re-pay Gastor."

Katie knew that Angelina wasn't trying to convince her this was a good plan. She was just telling her what they were going to do. She could tell Angelina owned this one, both the problem and the solution. Katie wondered which of God's memory books this moment of growing up would be recorded in.

"What do you think they will do to me?" Katie asked pensively, feeling the weight of ownership of her circumstances.

"God only knows, Katie, God only knows."

Voices, Many Voices

I T WAS ALMOST DARK WHEN the travelers reluctantly stepped into the village green. Angelina was concerned to find that, instead of the hustle of getting the evening meal ready, they found it completely deserted. There were lights on in a few of the huts, but no one was around anywhere.

"Where is everyone? They should all be here," Rabea said, coming out of Magda's hut. "Do you think they went out searching for us?"

"I don't know. This is really strange...."

Angelina watched Trek come out of his house, suggesting, "Spread out, everyone. Ring the bell at the school if you find anyone."

Angelina went towards the well, nodding to Trek, who was heading for the schoolhouse Rabea went to look in the Chapel. She watched the path to the schoolhouse fade as Trek approached the edge of the green. The path to the well was gone, too. The only path they had was the one to the chapel.

"This can't be good," Angelina told Katie. "I guess we're all going to the chapel."

Trek led the way, Rabea stepping into pace behind him. Angelina held back, not sure if she wanted to even try to ask for forgiveness.

"What's the matter, Angelina?" Katie whispered.

"I'm tired. Tired of trying to fit in, trying to do the right thing, and wondering if I'm ever going to be good enough to belong."

She knew Trek had heard her when he turned and saw her hanging back. He and Rabea reached out and took her hands.

"Come on. We'll do this together." But she wondered why Leron stepped quietly into the shadows.

The lights of the Chapel blazed in the dark night. Voices rose. Some were concerned, and some were angry.

"Katie, this has nothing to do with you. You need to leave now." Angelina saw the hesitation on Katie's face. "Get, now. You don't need to be sucked into this mess. You have one of your own to fix. Go!"

"But how, where? I have no idea how to get back to the farm." Katie's voice faltered while she fought back the tears of fear and sorrow.

"Just follow the path. The Woods will see to it that you get there. Trust me. Now go." Angelina turned her back on Katie and continued to speak to the others but not to her.

"Ah, guys, I'll just go get my stuff and ..."

"No, you don't! We are going to tell them what you did. Angelina, you fooled the devil and saved my soul! You're a hero, not a thief. They all need to know that. Now come on!" Rabea refused to let go of her hand.

As Trek opened the doors, the sounds of the voices flowed out into the night. The trio stood framed in the doorway, and the villagers fell silent. Everyone was frozen in the moment. Angelina took a deep breath, put her pack on the floor, and reached for the collection box. "Time to get this over with."

Katie looked down and saw that a path had appeared beneath her feet. The trees on either side had bowed away, revealing the sky filled with stars shedding enough light so she could see her way clearly. She began to walk but soon ran, pushed from behind by a clear and steady wind. Only once did she turn to look back—in time to see Angelina step into the light of the chapel and disappear behind the closing doors. The trees had bent inward, and the path behind her was gone.

Angelina slowly walked up the center aisle. She could hear the voices, starting as whispers and growing to angry shouts. They called her all the names she'd heard growing up and some new ones that stung like barbed darts. "Thief, liar, no good." tears seeped from the corners of her eyes.

"It's back. It's all here, every coin. I promise." She used her sleeve to wipe the dust off the top. "Just a little dust, that's all." Respectfully, she set the box in its place, just where she'd found it. "All good now." And she started to slowly back her way towards the doors and escape.

"Stop! You have a lot to answer for, girl. You owe us an explanation!" It was the same man who was so against her being in the village in the first place.

"Calm down, calm down." Gastor was making his way from the front of the chapel to Angelina. Trek and Rabea were closing in from the back. "Everybody, sit down!"

As everyone settled in their seats, Gastor led Trek, Rabea, and Angelina to the front, where they stood facing the congregation of their family and friends.

"Now, Angelina, explain yourself. Why did you steal the collection box?"

"Well, it started with the boots." She tried to smile, hoping that looking friendly would help, but her lips just twisted oddly. Tears were not far behind.

"I knew it! Vanity, thy name is Angelina!" someone shouted.

"No! It's not her fault. It's mine. I'm the one who stole the money," Trek shouted back. Angelina was watching Gastor's face hoping to see forgiveness. It looked more like Trek had just stabbed his father in the heart. The shame of destroying Gastor's trust and Trek's reputation made Angelina's shoulders sag with grief.

"I just wanted her to feel like she belonged. I wanted her to know what it feels like to have someone give you something just because. I just wanted her to know—" Trek was fighting back the tears too. Rabea reached out and held his hand so he could continue. "Angelina deserves to know that we love her, that we can be her family. That's all. That's what I wanted."

"You used the money I gave you for machine parts to buy the boots?" Gastor's voice was low. He spoke only to Trek, not the others.

"I'm sorry, Dad. I know it was wrong."

"But how did you get the machine parts? If you spent the money on the boots?"

"I borrowed it from a guy I knew. He's part of a street gang."

The entire village gasped, knowing precisely what this meant. Not making payments on time meant serious consequences.

"They beat me up every time we went to town."

Angelina could tell the shame of this was awful for Trek to admit. She stepped forward, hoping to shield Trek from the venom of the crowd. "Look, if I hadn't taken those boots he could've returned them and paid back the loan—none of this would have happened. It's my fault, not his!"

Now, everyone was muttering back and forth talking about who was at fault for what.

"Quiet!" Gastor shouted. The chapel was immediately still. "But why take the collection box?"

"Well, Leron said I'd have to have something of value to pay Paimon when we went to Kidron to get the red and blue diamonds, and I don't have anything and that's all I could think of and—." Angelina was interrupted by the gasps of almost everyone in the chapel muttering things like, "who is Leron? Who else has she taken up with?"

Angelina was concerned when Rabea spoke up. Maybe they'd all said enough. More might make all this worse.

"You should have seen her! She stood right up to Paimon! Told him to take her, not me! He was going to take my soul if she didn't give him the box, but she just stood right up to him and told him to take her. It was amazing!"

For the next two hours, Angelina, Trek, and Rabea fielded question after question, telling every detail of their travels into Kidron, encountering Paimon, battling Daikon, and all the wonders of the cave. Finally, Gastor asked everyone to return to their seats.

"We have a lot to consider. You have been through quite an ordeal and showed a great deal of courage. But our laws must be honored. We cannot have them broken, no matter how good you think the reason is. You three go back to the schoolhouse and wait while the elders meet to decide what to do. This is a sad day, no matter how it ends."

He hung his head refusing to make eye contact with Trek as he, Rabea, and Angelina left the chapel.

"Well, I'm going to go pack my stuff," Angelina said. "Thanks for trying, guys."

"Angelina, you don't know what's going to happen. Have some faith!"

"Rabea, faith doesn't work for people like me. Some of us are just what my father said—good for nothing. I'm not going to hang around and wait to be rejected again." And she started off through the woods without a path.

"Let her go," she heard Trek say quietly.

Angelina stumbled in the dark, now sorry she'd let Katie go so soon. She might have gone with Katie and gotten to hang out with human girls after all. But Katie's path was long gone, and Angelina knew she'd never find it. Not now. It was Katie's path—not hers.

The Power of a Strong Voice

ANGELINA MUMBLED THROUGH HER TEARS as she wove her way through the Woods, hoping to find the village green in the dark. She told the trees everything she wished she'd had the courage to say in the chapel. "I am good enough. I am worth it. I did make a mistake, but then I made it right. And I didn't steal the red and blue diamonds. I can make a good decision."

Leron stepped out of the shadows and roared a low rumbling sound that was almost inaudible.

"Geez! You scared the life out of me! Don't sneak up on me like that! What?" Angelina could see that he had something to say but was holding back. "Go ahead, have your say; everyone else has."

"I just never took you for a quitter. I thought you had more courage than this." His disappointment was clear.

"Look, I can't take a guilt trip from you, too. I did the best I could. I made mistakes, did what I thought was best to fix it, and screwed it up. End of story. Now I'm moving on. I can build another place. I'll be fine." She stomped to make her point.

The Woods sighed with sadness. Angelina brushed it off with a shiver. Leron stopped right in front of Angelina, blocking her path. She stared at him, and then glared at him, and then tried her best pout. He stood firm.

She turned on her heel and traced her steps back towards the Chapel, not at all surprised when a path appeared leading her straight to the tall double doors. She took a deep breath as she grabbed the handles with each hand. Then she flung open the doors and marched straight to the front. Shocked at her intrusion, no one said a word until she spoke.

"I have one last thing to say. I listen to you all talk about forgiveness, how God forgives you when you sin as long as you admit you did something wrong and ask. Well, I did something wrong. I thought if I had the prettiest boots you'd all envy me and like me. I was wrong. I thought if I got the diamonds and paid Trek's debt it would all be okay. I was wrong. But I didn't steal the diamonds—and I could have—and I brought back the collection box and I said I'm sorry." She wiped her nose on her sleeve and rubbed the tears off her face with the back of her hand. And with one deep snuffle, she said, "And I think God will forgive me because I tried really hard to do the right thing and I think you should forgive me, too."

She was ready to let the doors slam loudly behind her on the way out when she stopped. No one was moving.

Magda was the first to speak. "I think we have our decision. Angelina, go get Trek and Rabea and bring them back."

Everyone stayed in their seats and prayed. Angelina prayed, too.

Trek joined Angelina in front of the crowd holding her hand tightly. "It has been determined that Rabea has done nothing wrong so she can sit next to Magda," he whispered in Angelina's ear.

She saw that they, too, held hands. Gastor stood up, all eyes fixed on him, and he cleared his throat twice.

"You both know that you have done wrong and that the laws of our community do not tolerate stealing for whatever reason. You also know that the penalty is banishment."

Angelina's head dropped. She bit her lip to keep from crying, wondering how Trek had the courage to stare straight ahead, showing no emotion at all.

"But, Angelina, you are right about forgiveness. Knowing when to forgive is very important. It does not mean forgetting, though. You put our entire community in the path of great harm. We cannot forget that. Near as we can recall, no one told you that the map to the Enchanted Woods was carved into the collection box, so you didn't really know what you'd done."

Angelina's head shot up and she searched the faces focused on her. She started to speak but Gastor stopped her.

"We have decided you and Trek can stay but you'll be on probation for a long time. We will loan you the money to pay back the debt and you both will work for every family in this village until it is repaid. Trust is precious, and you will have to earn it."

Angelina threw her arms around Trek's neck. Then she turned to embrace Gastor who took her in his arms and held her like she imagined a father was supposed to hold his daughter. She soaked up his scent and the feel of his scratchy wool sweater. These were all things she never wanted to forget. Looking over his shoulder at the cross in the front of the Chapel she mouthed, "Thank you, God."

Seeing the Path Clearly as It Disappears

KATIE RAN UNTIL SHE COULDN'T breathe anymore. Her sides ached, her feet ached, but most of all her heart ached. She hadn't realized how much Angelina and Leron meant to her. Now, all alone at the edge of a starlit meadow, she longed for their company.

Looking down she realized that the path was slowly disappearing. She spun on her heels, hoping to catch sight of it before it was gone, and caught the toe of what was once a white boot on a tree root. She was hurled to the ground, landing with a thud, and twisting her knee in the process.

"Aggghh!" she wailed into the night.

For a brief moment she considered the option of staying in the Woods. Someone else would help Angel. It didn't have to be her. She rolled from being on her hands and knees to a seated position and leaned up against a large boulder. The guilt that gripped her belly told her that this wasn't a plan. It was pure selfishness. That was a feeling she couldn't live with for the rest of her life.

"I don't have time for this," Katie declared. "I have to get back to town. I have to find someone to help Angel."

She rubbed her knee with the palm of her hand. She knew she had to get better by morning. Absentmindedly she'd been digging at the ground with her finger until she'd peeled back a large sheet of moss revealing the earth below.

She patted her hand on the soft dirt, pleased to find it was warm. The night air was growing chilly.

"Hmm. Not a bad place to sleep."

She slid into the space, but this time she didn't press her back up against the rock or tuck her hands in between her knees. She lay on her back and looked up at the stars.

When the full moon rose in the sky, Katie heard the sounds of voices, whispers, giggles, and sighs. She could have sworn it was the trees. They seemed to bend down with the wind as if leaning in to protect her. In the wind, she heard faint voices singing what sounded like a lullaby.

She pulled the moss tightly up around her chin. She could have sworn she heard the wind whisper, "Sleep well." Above her was the sound of something shifting in the branches. The wings of the great bird spread widely as it silently took flight, crossing the moon and gliding into the darkness.

"Hey, Chuck," she said quietly, though she knew he was too far away to hear her.

The soft rays of the morning light warmed Katie's face. She finally awakened to the sound of violins, but she shook it off as lingering bits of a dream. She wanted to remember but it was like trying to grab smoke out of the air. She didn't have time for pondering dreams. She had to get back to Aspen Meadows and finally tell Miss Johnson everything she'd been keeping secret all these months.

She tossed the moss back out of the way, stood, and stepped on a mound of grass. Katie turned around in a full circle, wild-eyed with concern. Where was the path? It was here yesterday. All she found was grass and moss, and pebbles. It had to show up—there had to be a path.

Blinking hard, Katie realized it was there. It wasn't the clear, wide path she was used to and not facing the direction she had headed last night. Now it was heading off to the right of the trees, cutting right across the middle of the meadow.

"Okay, geez, this place is so strange."

Across the meadow Katie found large patches of wild raspberries. She made a pouch out of the hem of her shirt and filled it with the luscious plump berries. At the edge of the berry bushes was a bunch of four-foot-tall sunflowers.

She picked the sun-roasted seeds from the flower heads and plopped down on the ground to enjoy her breakfast. The joy of having such lovely food was darkened as her thought drifted to Aspen Meadows. What had happened to Char and her brothers? Was Brittany still under watch for her cutting? What would Kevin say to her when she saw him, and how could he ever forgive her for how she'd used him to steal from the kitchen?

"I couldn't have made a bigger mess of my life if I'd tried." She smacked her lips, trying to get the taste of guilt out of her mouth. "I'll just have to make it right." She stood, careful not to stress her twisted knee. She licked the raspberry juice off her fingers and waited for the path to show her the way out of the Woods. She needed to get home.

Late in the afternoon, the path came to an end right at the edge of her grandfather's field. She could see the house waiting for her. What she couldn't see was if there was a car in the front drive. Her muscles tightened all at once. The path was still there. She had time to turn and run back into the Enchanted Woods.

Turning Back, Now or Never

"GO!" A SMILE CREPT ACROSS Katie's face. She knew it was the trees coaxing her onward. Her only choice was to cross that field. When she stepped out from under the canopy of the aspens the path was gone. And she ran.

Once she got to the orchard, she had the cover of the tree trunks to shield her from view if he had brought Angel back to the farm. How evil could he be to bring her best friend to the very place where Katie had felt safe—safe from him? The only thing good about this realization was that it turned her fear to anger. She was going to get this jerk.

"Good, no cars." No lights.

Carefully creeping up the back porch steps, she gripped the doorknob. The kitchen door was still locked. Avoiding stepping on the gravel Katie stayed close to the house as she eased her way around to the front porch. Everything looked normal. She slid under the porch rail and knelt down to reach under the rug.

She froze when she realized the key wasn't there.

There was no air. She couldn't breathe. Then she saw it and her lungs collapsed in relief. He'd left the key in the lock. He must have forgotten it when he took off chasing her. That all seemed a lifetime ago now.

Katie couldn't trust that she was in the house alone. Slowly she crept into the kitchen, avoiding the boards in the floor that creaked. Carefully she opened the drawer by the sink. She slid the rolling pin out and wrapped her fingers tightly around the roller. Poised to defend herself, she moved slowly from room to room, making sure she was the only one on the first floor.

Getting up the stairs was harder. Almost all the steps creaked or groaned so she had to stay to the outside edges as she moved from one step to another. When she reached the hall landing, she stopped.

Something was wrong.

Her bedroom door was closed. She never closed that door, not even at night when she slept over and Grandpa's snoring kept everyone awake. Taking only very short breaths in and out, she moved to the door and stood listening.

Katie's eyes widened when she heard sounds from inside the room. Someone was in there. Someone was kicking and thrashing. Katie raised the rolling pin high above her head. There were more sounds coming from inside. Scuffling and the sound of moans. If he had Angel in there he was going to regret it. Katie took a deep breath and lunged at the door. As she burst into the room she cringed at the sound of the door smashing into the dressing table, breaking the mirror mounted on the back of the door. She ducked and covered her head to protect herself from the shower of broken glass flying in all directions. She dropped her arms from around her head and slowly raised her eyes, searching to see where he was in the room. Katie was shocked to see Angel tied to one of the posts of her bed.

"Where is he? Is he here?" Katie screamed at Angel who shook her head violently. Katie pulled the gag out of her mouth. "So, he's not here?"

"No, but he'll be back later tonight. He said he'd be back." Angel's voice trembled. "He had something to take care of first. Katie, help me, get me out of here."

Katie dropped the rolling pin on the bed and wiped the tears from Angel's cheeks. She threw open the drawers of the dressing table searching for anything to cut the ropes that bound Angel's hands and feet. Finally, she found a pair of large nail clippers buried under a tangled pile of curlers. Gnawing at the fibers of the rope, she was able to get it shredded enough that it broke when she yanked. Angel yelped as Angelina pulled the rope against the bloody rash on her wrists worn by her efforts to escape.

"Come on. We're getting out of here. Follow me." In the doorway she stopped. "Did he—hurt you—? Angel, did he do anything to you?"

"He threatened to. He told me he was going to do things to me, and when he was done, I'd be a woman. Katie, I'm really scared."

The thought of him doing to Angel what he'd done to her made her sick. Sick and insanely angry.

Katie grabbed her friend's hand and pulled hard. "Let's get out of here."

They crept out the kitchen door and hurried to the barn. Katie pulled the door back far enough to see that her bike was still there. She'd hated that old bike with the rider's bench on the back for many years. Now she was glad to have it.

"Get on."

With Angel on the back holding onto Katie's waist, Katie knew that both their lives depended on her now. She took off. The tires groaned to grip the gravel of the driveway. It was a struggle to keep the bike upright with the weight of both her and Angel.

When she reached the highway she turned onto the shoulder without stopping to look both ways. The drivers would have to fend for themselves and stay out of her way.

Help Turns Out Not to Be

DODGING CARS ON THE TWO-LANE highway, Katie rode into town where she could weave down alleys and side streets to cut the travel time from the farm to Aspen Meadows in about half.

"Hang on," she warned Angel as she blasted over the curb, across the grass median, and onto the main drive into Aspen Meadows. Kids were walking back and forth across the drive and the commons. Katie dodged around them, hoping she didn't knock anyone down. Then she saw Darrell. It must be the beginning of free time.

For the first time ever, Katie was glad to see him. "Angel, I want you to go with him. I'll come back and find you, but you'll be safe, I promise." She stopped the bike. Katie decided to play off the crush he had on her. "Darrell, come here."

He came running when he saw Katie like he'd just won the lotto. "Whoa, Katie. Where have you been? You're in a heap of trouble, girl. Who's this?" Darrell still spit when he talked, especially if he was excited.

"Darrell, focus. Don't stop for anyone. Take Angel to the infirmary. I'm trusting you to get her there. Got it? You screw this up, and I'll never let you forget it. Get it right. and I'll owe you."

She smiled to herself. He'd responded just the way she'd hoped.

"Sure. You can count on me. Come on, girl. I'll take care of you." He looked back over his shoulder as he led Angel towards the infirmary.

"I got this, Katie. You can count on me. I got this." Katie just took off without stopping to acknowledge him right now.

She rode up the drive and around the round-about island heading straight for Karen Johnson. She clipped a couple of kids with the bike as they came running to see what Darrell had been hollering about. Just about a block and she'd be there. And she almost made it.

Suddenly two security guards stepped into her path. They stood shoulder to shoulder, forming a wall. She laid the bike down on its side to avoid plowing into them. She hopped over the handlebars and crouched down in a bit of a wrestler's stance, plotting how to get around them.

"Hold up there, missy. Not so fast." One of the guards was reaching out for her when he darted a look to his buddy. "Hey, George, this is that runaway."

The second guard studied her face for a moment. Then his eyebrows shot up. "This is the one who ran off with the two boys."

"She stole some stuff, too, didn't she?" The first guard's voice was really stern, almost hostile. "Grab her, Bruce!"

Katie dodged Bruce's reach, but he was able to grab her. "I have to get to Miss Johnson. I have to talk to her now."

Katie twisted, trying to break his grip. He wrenched her arms behind her back. Then he wrapped his thick fingers around her wrists and yanked them up almost to her shoulder blades. The pain made her eyes fill with tears.

She pleaded, "Please, let me go. This is life and death."

"Not on your life, missy. You're headed to Juvenile Hall."

They marched her off toward the administrative offices, where she was sure she'd be met by the local police.

"You have to let me go!"

Katie leaned forward and made the guard drag her across the lawn. The second guard, who Katie now knew was Frank from the name tag hanging from his pocket, came up on her left side and took her arm.

"I got her, Tim. You get the door."

Katie took inventory of everything around her. There was a reception area, but no one at the desk to answer the phone ringing off the hook. Six upholstered chairs lined the walls. She was led down a short hall and into an office. All the offices seemed to have windows allowing the occupants to see the hallway. But there wasn't anyone in any of them. She was directed to a chair at the end of the desk. Her back was to the hall window. Officer Tim Dawson's name was on the name plate in the center of the desk. She sized him up. How much of a problem would he be when she found the moment to escape?

"Hey, Frank, can you get me the paperwork for Juvie? I'll start processing the release forms."

Tim Dawson glared at Katie with a look that told her she'd better not dare move. "Look, Officer Dawson, I have to go see Miss Johnson. Someone's life is in danger, and I have to tell her so she can stop it." Katie tilted her head to one side and did her best to look helpless.

"Not on your life. I've heard that story before. You're not going anywhere except to Juvenile Hall. Running away was a big mistake, missy, a big mistake."

Frank came in with the papers and dropped them on the desk in front of Officer Dawson. Katie heard him slip into the office across the hall. Tim Dawson switched his focus from Katie to the pile of paperwork he faced. Katie watched his look fade into frustration and disgust.

Scanning the office for anything she could use to get out of here, she spotted the trash can on the floor behind the desk. With him so focused on papers, Katie took a shot at her escape.

"Ah, I don't feel so good. I think I'm going to throw up."

Katie moaned, leaning over and clutching her stomach. She lifted her chin just enough to see that this had no impact on Office Dawson, so she gagged and made pre-vomit sounds followed by some wet guttural moans.

"Oh, I'm going to be sick. I need a can, quick. Agggghhh."

Katie was impressed with how realistic her act was becoming. "The can, quick the can."

More groaning and moaning until Officer Tim Dawson came around the desk with the can in hand. Katie calculated her swing carefully and hit the bottom of the can just as he leaned in to put it on the floor at her feet. She hit it hard enough for it to be propelled upward, the outer rim hitting him across the bridge of his nose. The sound of bone crunching, skin splitting, and a wail of pain filled the air.

He grabbed his nose with his left hand, and she ducked under his flailing right arm. She slid on the vinyl floor as she skidded around the door into the hall. Officer Frank was on his feet, trying to get around his desk and grab her as she slipped by, but he was too slow.

As she passed the upholstered chairs, she grabbed the arm of one and was surprised to find that they were all connected.

"Yes!" she declared as she pulled them across the space at the end of the reception desk.

The side wall formed a barrier between her and the men scrambling to catch her.

Office Frank tripped Office Dawson, and they flopped on the ground, trying to untangle their legs. This bought her just enough time to get out the front door.

Again, she caught an advantage because of all the hollering from the officers. Everyone outside on campus stopped to see what they were screaming about. No one noticed her racing to get to the counselor's office building. She rounded a cluster of bushes and almost ran Mr. Stanley over. He was hauling a wound-up wheel of hose. She stopped. She had just thought of a way he could help. She turned to face him.

"Katie!" he exclaimed. "Is that you?"

"Mr. Stanley, you've got to help me. Don't let them catch me. I have to see Miss Johnson."

Without missing a beat, he nodded. "I've got you covered. Go, girl."

She smiled and gave a gentle wave as she watched him toss that wheel of hose across the lawn. He pulled the loose end up, creating a jump rope. It caught the two officers just about the knees. She didn't have time to stop to look. She could tell from all the groaning and giggles that they had taken a spectacular spill. She took the steps two at a time and bounded up the steps to the office.

When What You Thought Was Turns Out Not to Be

INSIDE THE FRONT DOOR of the administration building, Katie bent over to try and breathe out the stitch that had developed in her left side. She took a few deep breaths and was on the move again, making her way to Karen Johnson's office.

The door was pulled closed, but it hadn't been latched, so it had drifted open and stood about 6 inches ajar. Katie stood at the door, listening to see who was in there and why, before she barged in.

"Well, well, Karen. It's been a long time. Seven years long, thanks to time off for good behavior." Through the opening of the door, Katie could see Miss Johnson stand up from her desk and back up to the windows behind her. The man's voice was low, almost a whisper.

"Jesse. What do you want? How did you find me?" Katie could tell from Miss Johnson's voice that she was frightened. She could see her fingers grip the back of her chair as she moved it between this man and herself.

"Oh, it wasn't easy. That's for sure. Took me almost six years in the prison library and a ton of laundry to earn the computer time, but here we are." He licked his lips. "You're prettier than I remember." He moved closer, but all Katie could see was the back of his jacket. It was so hard to hear. This all felt wrong. She wished she could get closer.

"Jesse, you need to leave. I'm going to have to call Security." Miss Johnson was trying to speak with authority, but Katie could tell she was scared of this guy.

"No. You will not call Security or anyone." He slammed his hands down on the desk. "We are going to finish what we started. I've dreamt of this every night for the last seven years, and I won't let you ruin it now. Get your coat."

Katie's eyes widened as her brain wracked to put what she thought she'd heard into context. She had listened to his voice in her ear for all these months: 'Don't you move. You little tramp.' The gravely sound of his voice reminded her of a howl she'd heard in Kidron. She knew that voice.

But this wasn't Paimon. This voice was the one she'd heard at her grandma's house. It was Him—the man who'd beaten her. Her eyes darted back and forth. Quick, think. Do something. But there was no time to think. She could hear him bragging and making cruel comments to Miss Johnson. Things he'd said to her. That did it. This was going to stop, and it was going to stop now. She hit the door hard and burst into the room.

The blast of her entrance startled him, and he turned, confusion overwhelming his face. His expression changed as he sneered at her. But Katie's rage was rising.

"Well, isn't this special. Two for the price of one." He moved towards Katie. Deliberately he pushed the door closed. "Karen, get over here." Karen moved slowly, though she seemed to be trying not to get too close to Katie.

"She was my first, Katie. We were just kids, but that didn't make it any less fun. Right, Karen? In fact, she was about your age, Katie. She didn't cooperate either. But I figured out ways to make her behave. Just like I did with you." He waved for them to get closer to each other. Cocking his head to one side, he said, "Angel, she's a bit different. All I had to do was tie her up, and she tamed right down. Now I have both of you in one place, and soon I'll have had my way with your little friend Angel, too. How lucky can a guy get?" His eyes glazed over as he slid into the disgusting depths of his fantasy.

Katie snapped. She grabbed the first thing she could get her hands on, which happened to be the air horn that Miss Johnson kept on her desk for Track and Field Day events. Startled back to the moment by Katie's lunge, Jesse came at her, grabbing a handful of her hair. She placed the bell of the horn against his left ear and pulled the trigger. The blast of sound dropped him to his knees. He clutched his head and bellowed in excruciating pain, pulling her down with him.

"Aagghh!"

Katie put the horn in his face and pulled the trigger again and again.

"Stop! stop!" he wailed, rolling back and forth with his knees pulled up to his chest, hands covering his ears.

"You didn't stop when I said stop." She pulled the trigger again. "Why should I stop for you?" She pulled the trigger again. "I won't stop until I'm sure you never hear another thing again," and she pulled the trigger again.

Miss Johnson put down the chair she'd grabbed to hit him with. She carefully reached out and took the air horn out of Katie's hand.

"You can stop now, Katie." Her voice quivered.

Katie dropped to the floor sobbing, not sure if she was crying out of fear or out of relief. But she had to laugh when Officers Tim and Frank burst in the door just missing being witness to the final bows.

"Nice of you guys to show up. You need to work out more, increase your response time."

Katie listened, snuffling back tears, while Miss Johnson filled Frank in on the details, and Office Tim Dawson gathered Jesse up from the floor. Lights from the ambulance and police cars came in the windows and bounced off the walls, casting red and blue waves across everyone's faces. Jesse was hauled off in hand cuffs.

"What are we going to do with her?" Office Frank asked Dawson.

"I'll take responsibility for her," Karen said as she put her hand on Katie's shoulder. "Come on, Katie. Let's get you back to your cottage." She put her hand on Katie's back to lead her out the door. "We could both use a good night's sleep. We'll talk tomorrow."

"No, we have to talk now. I have to tell you." Katie's mind had raced back to her mission, ignoring the events that had just taken place.

"Katie, I think I know your story. It's the same as mine." Karen reached out for Katie and wrapped her arms around the girl as they both continued to shake. "Jesse can't hurt anyone now. They've got him in jail and he's going to spend the rest of his life there after we're through with him."

Katie felt the dread of the unknown next steps flow over her again. She was pretty sure she didn't want to hear the details of Karen Johnson's experience with Jesse. Knowing hers was awful enough.

"Oh, shit. I forgot Angel. She's in the infirmary." Katie started for the door, grabbing Miss Johnson's arm as she went. "He was going to beat her, too, maybe kill her—he had her tied to my bed at my grandma's."

Katie regurgitated the whole story as she and Karen Johnson walked stride for stride across the campus.

Katie blasted past the receptionist at the infirmary. She pulled back the curtains around the beds until she found Angel sitting with her legs dangling over the side.

The girls hugged tightly. Katie whispered in Angel's ear, "It's okay. He's gone. They took him to jail. You're safe now."

"What happened?" Angel asked.

"I'll tell you all about it later. Are you okay?" Katie touched the bandages that wrapped each of Angel's wrists.

"Yeh, I'll be okay. I may sleep with the lights on for awhile, though." When Angel began to laugh, Katie was relieved. "Me, too."

"They called my parents. They're coming to get me. They should be here soon."

Katie fought off the feelings of jealousy. She wanted to go home.

Fair Isn't Always Right and I'm Sorry Isn't Always Enough

IT HAD ONLY BEEN A FEW HOURS but this afternoon felt like a lifetime. Katie stood on the front steps of the cottage waving goodbye to Angel as she drove off with her parents.

"It's not fair, she gets to go home, and you have to stay here. You're the hero."

Mel spoke firmly as she placed her hand on Katie's shoulder. Katie wasn't surprised at how fast word of the events of the last few hours had spread across the campus. She was surprised at her new status as a rock star, though.

"Nah, she needs her mom right now." Katie turned, spreading out her arms to embrace Mel, Chrissy, and Brittany. "I've got you guys."

Miss Brenda held open the door, and Katie led the group into the warm light of the living room.

"Brittany, I'm glad you're here."

Katie tousled Brittany's hair. Brittany reached up to smooth it all back into place when Katie grabbed her by the wrist.

"No way," Katie grinned at what she saw. "What is this?"

Brittany smiled back. "They let me get a tattoo to cover the scars when I went two months without cutting. It reminds me that I'm too good to hurt myself anymore. Do you like it? I picked a griffin 'cuz I think they're cool." Brittany grinned at Katie again.

"Yes they are, honey. Yes they are." Katie squeezed Brittany's hand but saw the bright look on her face fade as she dropped her chin. "What?"

"I got the idea from the one in your miniature village. We found it in the greenhouse when we all went looking for you. I took it. I'll put it back. Sorry."

"You keep it, sweetie. To remind you always." Katie moved past her to the sofa and sat deep into the corner so she could look at all of them. "Has anyone heard from Char? Did they all get to stay together when they went to foster care? Are they okay?" Her question was met with confused looks on all faces.

"Oh, you don't know," Chrissy piped up. "Their aunt came to get them. She adopted all of them. Even the two babies. She moved here from San Francisco, and they all live in a big house."

Katie's gaze jerked to Miss Brenda.

"Social Services knew they had an aunt but couldn't find her. It took a while to track her down. She'd married, divorced, and changed her name to their grandmother's maiden name. Yep, they are all together."

"But Darrell said…."

Everyone laughed.

"Katie, you know better than to believe Darrell. Come on, girls. Bedtime. I'm sure Katie's tired and there will be another big day tomorrow." She pressed her lips together and nodded at Katie. "You are going to have a long day of telling your story."

As they each unfolded legs that had been tucked underneath them or gathered shoes that were tossed and lay where they landed, there was a knock at the door. Miss Brenda nodded to Chrissy. "You can answer it."

Chrissy opened the door a crack to see who it was since it was close to bedtime now and visitors at this time of day usually meant something was wrong. She pulled it all the way back to reveal the young man standing at the threshold.

"It's Kevin," she announced looking from Miss Brenda to Katie.

"Hi, can I talk to Katie?" he asked, twisting his ball cap in his hands.

"Yes. It's okay, Katie," Miss Brenda said as she began herding the other girls towards the kitchen. "We'll leave you two to talk. Come on, girls." As she passed Katie she whispered in her ear, "He was very upset when you disappeared so be nice to him." Suddenly the living room was empty except for Katie, standing alone.

"Come on in." She gestured, almost flailing her arms. He'd dreaded this moment, and now that it was here it was very awkward. For both of them, obviously.

Kevin came in and stood in the middle of the floor, staring at Katie as if she should go first. When no one had said anything for quite some time, he spoke.

"I'm glad you're okay."

"Look, Kevin, I have to apologize to you."

"Yeah, I know you just used me to get the stuff you stole from the kitchen. I'm over it now. I just…"

Katie cleared her throat. "You're right, I did just use you at first but after a while… you're a super good kisser."

She blinked several times, hoping that blurting it out didn't seem too forward. She really wanted to say something to make him feel better.

"Geez, Katie. Go for the gut, will you? Look, I did really like you and I might like you again but what you did was really unfair and I'm not sure I'm over that part or if I'll ever be for that matter. I almost lost everything because of you. If it hadn't been for Mrs. K I'd have lost my job and never gotten a good reference for another. You almost took everything I had." He took a deep breath, shifting his weight from one foot to the other.

"I know, Kevin, and I'm sorry. Truly sorry. I'll do everything I can to make it up to you. Everything I can to earn back your respect." She skirted whining and managed to land on a sincere plea.

"Okay, well, I just wanted to be sure you were really all right. The gossip on campus is pretty rough so I had to see for myself." He reached out and patted her on the shoulder.

She really needed a hug. She really needed to know he was going to forgive her. But he didn't, and he wasn't going to—not yet.

"Thanks," she said.

"See ya around."

He pushed open the screen, and as it slammed and he stepped into the darkness, Katie felt a melancholy hollowness that she'd never felt before. She'd really screwed up a good thing.

"Shit." She closed the door and headed for bed.

Beyond the Fences Where the Paths Don't Go

"WHAT A GREAT DAY!" I've never seen the Flea Market that jammed with people! Of course, not that I've seen that many Flea Markets!"

Everyone laughed. Angelina's exhilaration was intoxicating, and the spirits of the entire group seemed to be lifted on the wings of her joy. She jumped in to help pull one of the wagons filled with the purchases they made from the profits. Like everyone, she was excited about getting something new. Clothes, books, and canned treats made up most of the bounty, and there was enough for everyone.

"It was a special day," Magda admitted. "I haven't sold that many baskets in one day since the holidays, and we sold out of the syrup before noon!"

Angelina reached out for Magda's hand, starting a chain reaction as the others joined in linking arms and lacing fingers, making their way back from the bustle and chaos of the city to the serenity of their Woods. The pathway, its ancient bricks hidden by the intentional overgrowth of moss and grasses, led them from one world to another.

Angelina loved this part of the trip. Reaching for her necklace, she felt her soul calm and her heart fill with peace. The charm, a large heart with a large keyhole cutout, had always represented something missing to her. Now, with her new family, it reminded her that she held the key to her happiness, and here there would always be more than enough love to fill her heart.

She ducked under the heavy vines draping from the magnolia branches and drank in the sweetness of the willows at the creek crossing. She loved the way the path evaporated behind them while its course ahead became more and more vibrant with each step. She looked forward to the place where the path divided, when they would choose to turn left and head over the hill to the village instead of choosing to turn right onto the path that led to her past.

Angelina was wrapped up in the happiness of this moment with this precious group and the journey home and counting the blessings. But her bliss was interrupted when Magda came to a stop and her hand dropped from Magda's gentle grasp. She was confused as to why Magda had pulled her hat down to cover her face and had stepped back while the others gathered around the two to see what it was that had brought the happy parade to a halt. Following Magda's gaze from under the brim of her hat, Angelina felt a hollowness set in as she realized she was looking at her parents. Engrossed in argument, they had not yet seen the travelers they were about to meet at the crossing.

She would know her father's bellow anywhere. "This is a pointless waste of time. We are not going to find her. Quit your sniveling, woman. Keep up!"

Nothing had changed. Her father was still a bully, and her mother was still afraid. And then she caught her mother's eye. Angelina watched pensively as the woman looked up. "Angelina! Oh my darling Angelina!"

But as her mother lunged forward to reach for her child, Angelina's father caught her arm with a bruising grip and held her back.

He stepped forward, squared his shoulders and, glaring at Angelina, shouted, "Well, finally. You have no idea what you've done to this family. Your selfish stunt was nothing but mean. Well, don't just stand there, get over here. It's time you came home. Move!"

Angelina felt Trek step up behind her and gently put his hand on her waist. No expression of concern, no worries that she was okay or being held against her will. Nothing but demanding that she do as she was being told.

"Angelina?" He stepped forward. Magda closed in from the side.

"It's okay, Trek. These are my parents."

She had focused her eyes firmly on her father's, daring him to make a move towards her. He didn't.

"Mom, you okay?" she asked quietly.

"Oh, I'm fine dear. But we've missed you so much and were so worried. Why didn't you come home? Where have you been? Who are these people? Please, dear, do as your father asks and come home now."

Her mother's pleading eyes said more to Angelina than the others would see. Angelina saw the terror behind the concern. Her father would beat her mother again. This time for sniffling. Because Angelina didn't immediately obey.

Angelina was bolstered by a new strength. After all, she'd met the Devil. Her father was close but not really that much of a match now.

"I don't think so, Mom. I belong here now. Dad doesn't have the right to hurt us, you know. You don't owe him anything, and neither do I. I paid my dues." She turned and with a sweeping gesture or embrace towards her traveling companions said, "These people are my family. They took me in when I was lost, they opened their homes and their hearts to me, and I belong with them. It's a choice, Mom, and I'm making it."

Angelina resisted the urge to step back as her father took one step forward. He stopped when Angelina's friends closed ranks around her. He was outnumbered.

"Look here, girl, we are your parents, your family. You belong with us. Get your things out of that wagon." His tone softened slightly. "Come on."

At that moment Angelina realized that she had never really looked at her father. She had always avoided eye contact, kept her head down and her eyes averted. Now, she studied his face. His nose was crooked, most likely from being broken more than once while fighting. His cheek bones were hard and chiseled, not like the handsome men she saw in the fashion magazines she used to hide, but cold and unfeeling. His mouth had no tenderness, no kindness. And his hair, thickly curled, had always been long, too long, hanging over his ears. He looked unkempt, like he didn't care how he looked, just how tough he sounded.

"It's okay, Mom. I'm fine here. I'm happy. I've found a place where I mean something, my place where I'm special." She added with pride, "I found my voice, Mom. I have my magic!" She took her mother's hand in hers. "I'm not leaving, but I love you." Tears of release dripped slowly from Angelina's long lashes onto her cheeks. Trek tightened his arm around her shoulders, and Magda reached out her hand to find Angelina's. They held on to one another tightly.

"Goodbye," Angelina said.

As Angelina turned and her new family began to make its way down the path towards home, she heard her father's outburst. Turning she saw him shove her mother aside and, waving his arms wildly, tossing his hair back out of his face and mouth, he shouted at Angelina.

And then she saw it, his right ear. She'd never really looked at his elfin ears before. Under all that hair it would have been almost impossible to see but there it was. He was missing a slice out of his ear. Just as Magda had described she had done to her sister's abusive boyfriend.

Shocked, she turned to face Magda, who was clutching a tiny little key charm on a long chain around her neck. She had always kept it hidden under her tunic but now her face told Angelina everything. Magda had been the only one who had ever had the courage to stand up to her father, and she had paid dearly for it. Now, as never before, Angelina knew she had the strength to do the same.

Reaching out she found her mother's hand and helped her to her feet. "Mom, you can make the choice, too. You can choose who you're with and how you are treated. You have a right to something better."

Tears began to seep out of the corner of her eyes and wash over her cheeks. She knew that she couldn't make her mother come. She knew it had to be her choice, so she dropped her mother's hand, turned her back on her past, and bravely faced her future.

Magda, Trek, and the others fell into step behind her. As they crested the hill almost out of earshot of where her bewildered parents stood, she heard her mother call her name, this time with defiance. Angelina smiled, wiping the tears away knowing that her mother had found her voice too.

Angelina turned to see her breathless mother running until she reached her daughter and the group. Her father never moved from the spot where he had stood his ground. She knew he'd lose sight of them as the path they took faded. He wouldn't be able to follow. He'd have no idea which way to go. He'd be lost.

She tightened her hold on her mother's hand as the tree spirits drifted out of the Woods like fog. Swarms of dragonflies filled the skies, making it dark and gray. Soon, Angelina knew there'd be no trace of her path. The one her father stood on had come to an end and his only choice was to turn and go back. But he would go alone. Suddenly, out of nowhere there came a great gust of wind, and the air was split by the screech of an eagle. Everyone and everything stopped, startled by the force. Angelina recognized that sound and chuckled. It was Leron.

He swooped down from the heavens and circled the travelers several times before making a spectacular dive through the clouds, descending so quickly on Angelina's father standing alone in the clearing that she would have missed it if she hadn't known what was coming. Angelina watched as Leron snatched her father up and into the heavens.

"Leron, where are you taking him?" she shouted over the gasps of the crowd.

"He's got some things to learn!" he shouted back. And he disappeared in the direction of Kidron.

Seeing the horrified look on her mother's face, Angelina reached around her neck, removed her necklace, and put it around her mother's neck. Then putting her arm around her, she said, "Don't worry, Mom, he won't be alone." "We just need to pray he listens." She winked at Magda just before they disappeared.

When the World Changes but Your Heart Does Not

FALL WAS IN THE AIR. It was cool and crisp and filled with the smell of kettle corn and roasted turkey legs. The trees were not quite sure what season it was. Their green leaves mixed with reds and golds. Katie wandered between the vendor booths of the flea market, stopping now and then to admire a bit of cloth or smell the sweetness of the latest crop of apples. She hoped their fruit would sell well today. It would be good to go home with some extra cash. The sounds of the hustle and bustle of so many people selling, buying, and bartering, mixed with the sound of the street musicians playing for coins, made her so very happy.

She was strolling to the end of the lane and turned towards the edge of the market when she saw her. That full head of curly chestnut hair was pulled back revealing the delicate curve of pointed ears.

"Angelina!" Katie called, hoping to be heard above the crowd. "Angelina." She saw Angelina pause to listen, so she called out again. "Angelina, over here."

Angelina turned slowly. "Oh my gosh. How are you?"

She and Katie flung their arms around each other and held on tightly. Katie was afraid this moment would dissolve if they didn't hang on.

"I'm fine. What about you? You look great. How is everyone?"

"They're all fine." Angelina pulled Katie down to sit on the street bench. She leaped straight into the crucial questions. "I never expected to see you again.

They let you go? You told them your story? They had to believe you."

Katie laughed at her friend's insistent interrogation. "Yes, yes, and yes. They believed me. I got probation for all the things I stole and for assaulting Jesse, that was his name. You know I could never say his name before. It made him too real. I just wanted him to go away."

"I understand. Wait—you assaulted him? You got to get even?" Angelina punched Katie in the arm with her fist.

"And then some. A bunch of us came together and testified. He's gone back to jail for the rest of his life. No parole. He'll never get out."

"I am so proud of you." Angelina gave Katie a fist bump in the shoulder. "What about your parents? Where are they?"

"Mom finished rehab and hasn't had a drink since. Dad completed his anger management course with flying colors and decided we should live at the farm. A simpler life, you know. No adventures, that's for sure." She smiled at Angelina. "We don't have much money but we're all happy and that's what counts. What about you? Did you go home to your parents?"

Katie watched Angelina's expression go from pleased for her to something more wistful or longing. That look was gone as quickly as it came. "No, Mom's with us in the Woods now. My dad's in Kidron." Angelina winced followed by a wink. "Leron, you know." This made both girls laugh. "But Magda is teaching me to be a healer so that's good. Trek is still the same, and we spend a lot of time together. Gastor has sort of adopted me, and I think he has a thing for Mom. We're all good. The Woods are still as crazy as ever. Never know what you're going to run into next."

Angelina sighed. The pause grew to an uncomfortable length. Katie wasn't sure what else there was to say either. Then, Angelina burst out with, "I'm so glad to see you."

Katie looked at every detail of Angelina. The sun bouncing off her hair, her delicate ears no longer hidden, her deceiving strong fingers and sharp, pointed nails. Her long slender legs and—there she stopped. Her head snapped as she looked Angelina in the eyes.

"The boots. I thought they were destroyed?"

Angelina laughed. "Oh, they were, believe me. But when the man who made them heard the story of our journey into Kidron he made me a new pair. For free this time." She twisted her feet from side to side to show off the gorgeous details. "The beading on these make the symbols for the 'Champion,'" Her grin filled her face.

Katie hugged her friend and gently kissed her on the top of her head.

"Katie?" a woman's voice called from somewhere in the crowd.

"Hey, that's my mom. I'd better get going." Katie put the strap of her bag over her shoulder. She paused to look at Angelina. "I'm so glad to see you. I've missed you."

"I've missed you, too." Now it was Angelina's turn to study every detail of her adventurous traveling companion. They rose to leave. Katie was painfully aware of how awkward the moment had become. "Well, good luck."

"You, too," Angelina all but whispered. And each turned to walk her separate way.

Katie's heart ached just a bit as she slowly walked away from what had been one of the most amazing times of her life. Hard and painful but so very rich. She wandered between several groups of people finally stopping at a nearby booth to finger the tapestry shawl draped over the edge of the table. All the terrifically colored threads woven around one another until they told a bountiful and enchanting tale.

"This was us," she murmured to herself.

"Excuse me, miss? I didn't hear you. Getting older, you know."

"Oh, sorry. I'll take this, please."

As Katie dug the money from her pocket, she turned her head just in time to see the back of Angelina's flowing locks disappear in the crowd. Turning back to the vendor she said in low, hushed tones, "Thank you. I think I'll wear it."

THE END

Acknowledgments

To my dear friend Janie Munson who was there when I found Angelina in the woods. She's met each of the characters as they emerged and was as shocked as I was when Angelina's first kiss didn't come from Trek but from Daiken. "Who's Daiken?" she shouted over the phone. At that time, I had no idea who he was, so we discovered him together.

To Nancy Rue, who coached me through the craft of writing. Our greatest challenge was weaving the dual paths of Katie and Angelina. Her encouragement and guidance were a beacon of light in a long tunnel.

To Loretta Oaks, who coaches with one very pointed tool—the question, why? The hardest thing in writing this book was to understand why. Digging deep into that answer led me to a depth of storytelling I had not known was there.

To Bruce Harris, who was a constant cheerleader, contributing all manner of used books as inspiration.

Special thanks to Lorie Aguilar, who was brave enough to share her story of being an abused child living at the Tennyson Center, a group home for abused and neglected children in Denver. As I listened to her tell how she found her voice and love of singing, I learned what it was like to be in the foster care system bouncing from one abusive home to another and back to the home that sent her to Tennyson in the first place.

And to six little girls who lived in one of the cottages at the Tennyson Center, whose creative storytelling was where this all began. Initially, I was creating a miniature treehouse to be used for fundraising, but I needed to know who lived in the treehouse and thought it would be fun to have the children tell me who lived in the treehouse. The counselor told me these girls didn't get along and I'd be lucky to get fifteen minutes of their attention. Forty-five minutes later, I had names and descriptions and ages of people who lived in the forest, and the girls were late for their next class! With a wave of the hand, they were gone.